Traitor Isle

Laurie Sanford

RIVER LEAF PRESS

Traitor Isle

Published by River Leaf Press

Cover Art by: Carpe Librum Book Design, carpelibrumbookdesign.com

For more information, visit:

www.lauriesanfordbooks.com

www.facebook.com/lauriesanfordbooks

To my Spin. Today I hold you in my heart. One day I'll hold you in my arms.

One

Summer warmth bathed Madeleine's skin as her tiny fingers wrapped around the crude fishing pole her father had constructed from a tree limb hanging outside their cottage. At five years old, she could hardly manage to keep a steady grip on the cumbersome object. Determined to make her father proud, she licked her lips and held her pole upright.

"Good, just like that." Pierre's pacifying voice touched her ear, his strong arms reaching on either side to even out her floundering hold. "Now cast it out in front of you, just like this." Her father's weathered hands guided hers, tossing the line and hook he'd devised into the pond's murky waters.

Madeleine giggled, tiny droplets of water splashing her arms and chin. Pierre's woodsy scent mingled with the wildflowers twisting among the weeds. Sunlight sliced through the clouds, throwing ripples of light over the pond and exposing a small group of fish wriggling beneath the surface. Even if she never caught a single one, she was in heaven.

After a few minutes, her arms felt twice as heavy. "Papa," she said, twisting toward the large man. "Why haven't we caught any yet?"

"Patience, my dear." Her father chuckled heartily. "You can't expect to lure a fish in only five minutes. Sometimes it takes hours."

Her conquering feeling sank low with his words. *"Hours?"* Already her untrained muscles shook, her hands begging her to drop the heavy contraption. "No wonder Mama doesn't like to come fishing with you."

At that, Pierre's laugh exploded, showering the girl in a familiar sensation of comfort. "And here she says you are just like me. I take it you won't become a fisherman, then."

"No, sir." Her fingers slipped from the makeshift pole, allowing her father to take over. "I'd much rather be a fighter, like you taught me." Nothing thrilled her like holding the miniature sword he'd fashioned for her high in the gleaming light, power coursing through her little hands.

Pierre ruffled her dark hair. "Don't let your mother hear you talk like that. She'll say my influence has tainted you."

Turning back, Madeleine studied his kind eyes and square jaw, his hair tethered at the nape of his neck. "What's wrong with that? Why can't I be a fighter, Papa?"

His brows climbed his forehead. "Oh, you certainly are a fighter. There's no doubt about that, and no one can ever take it out of you." His muscled arm tensed as his fishing line tautened. "But perhaps tell your mother you want to weave rugs for a living. For her sake."

Madeleine met his wide grin with a chortle. "All right, I will." Her little hands clasped behind her back as she considered the endless possibilities waiting beyond the realm of childhood. "What do you think I should be—that is if I'm not a fighter or a weaver?"

The fishing pole jerked to life, and Pierre expertly guided it out of the water, hauling a floundering trout at its end. Once he plopped it on the shore, he turned to her, dark eyes shimmering in the light reflecting off the pond. "I just want you to be happy, *chérie*. Do what makes you happy."

A bird's incessant chirping roused Madeleine from her sleep. Eyes drifting languidly open, she blinked a few times before the room came into focus. Above her, a canopy of blue and gold, beyond her, two bronze hawks and a room so lavish that it belonged in a palace. *I am happy, Papa. If only you could see how happy.* But not because of the finery to which she woke.

Rolling to her side, she regarded the man lying next to her, the man who had given her a new name and devoted the past six months of his life to their marriage. He looked so peaceful in the light pouring in from the window, his dark, curly hair untamed, a tiny puddle of drool collecting beneath his open mouth. Sometimes it felt like they had been married a lifetime, and yet as if they had wed only yesterday.

Gabriel snorted, startling himself. Squinting, he peeked across the bed at her, looking on in amusement. "Were you watching me sleep again?" He frowned, swiping the saliva from his mouth. "That's an unnerving habit, you know."

Throwing her head back, she enjoyed an unrestrained laugh. "I'm truly sorry. I'm still so used to rising with the sun. Besides, I can't help looking at you."

With a grunt, he waved her off. "Don't try laying your charm on me, Baroness. It won't work this time."

Madeleine leaned closer, propped on her elbows. "Are you quite sure about that, Baron?" she asked, teasing him with her batting lashes.

The corners of Gabriel's mouth tweaked up before he threw his arms around her and tugged her close. "You're lucky I'm madly in love with you," he said, rolling her to her back. His kisses crashed against her lips, full and captivating. Madeleine lost herself in her husband's affection, unhampered by a world that had once kept them apart.

"And I you." She laughed as his head nuzzled her neck, his bushy hair tickling her vulnerable skin. "Stop that now, you rogue!"

Uncontrollable giggles bubbled up from her stomach, his playful actions sending her entire body into convulsions.

A smile stretched across his handsome face as Gabriel leveled his adoring gaze on her again. "I like to hear you laugh." He sighed, twirling a strand of her raven hair around his fingertip. "Truly, I've never been happier than I am here with you, just the two of us. Not even close."

Her gaze entwined with his, promising an eternity of joyful mornings. "I didn't know this much happiness even existed." In all her years, with all the torment and rage that had surrounded her, she'd never imagined the safety and love that coursed through her as he pressed his palm to hers, lacing his fingers with her own. She'd never hoped to dream of a perfect ending, shared with the man she would give up her life for.

Unexpectedly, another man's face flashed through her mind. He had dark hair falling into equally dark eyes that searched her face. His mouth curled seductively, his strong jaw flexed and brow arching as he hovered over her. Madeleine flinched, the memory of his kisses flooding her, of his hands roaming her curves, his lips pressed to her throat. She saw herself clearly, unclothed with him beneath a tangle of sheets, returning his ardor. This man was not a stranger, but a lover.

"Madeleine?" a familiar voice yanked her back to the present. Gabriel lay near her, concern lacing his expression. "Madeleine, is everything all right?"

Sitting up, she swallowed, her throat like sandpaper. She attempted to smile, but only a grimace would emerge on her lips. "Of course, dear. I was just a little dizzy for a moment. But I'm better now."

Shoulders relaxing, Gabriel cupped her cheek. "Now that's not such a bad sign, is it?" Leaning down, he kissed her abdomen through her nightdress. Hadn't both their dreams converged there, hoping for a child to join their union?

But now, the thought of such hope merely conveyed worry. Madeleine arose alongside her husband, preparing to face the day. She could go about her routine, pretending it to be any ordinary day. Yet, no matter how hard she forced him back, she knew that face would not leave her. This new man, whomever he was, would not let her go. So, she took Gabriel's hand and kissed him, trying to forget that the man in her memories could change everything.

Two

"Cecile, get in here. I need you now." At the sight of her friend's face at her bedroom door, Madeleine seized Cecile's arm and yanked her inside.

"That's a fine good morning." Cecile pivoted back with hands on her trim hips. "Married half a year and already barking orders at me like Georgette, I see."

Madeleine poked her head into the hallway, catching a last glimpse of Gabriel sauntering happily around a corner. Breathing a nervous sigh, she snapped the door closed and leaned on it, shutting her eyes like she might keep the world out in so doing. "I'm sorry, I don't mean to command you. I just don't know where else to turn after the morning I've had."

Already, her friend's assuring hand was at her elbow. "I know, Maddy. I'm only jesting." Her fingers squeezed lightly. "What is it? You look paler than I've ever seen you."

When Madeleine at last forced her eyes open, blazing tears had erupted from within them. Could she really unburden her heart and admit the truth? That because of her past life, whatever it entailed, the perfect bliss she had found in Gabriel's companionship could be utterly obliterated?

"I—" The words burned in her throat. "I remembered something just now, as I lay in bed with my husband."

The passionate eyes staring back narrowed. "What did you see? I'll help you through this, no matter what it is."

Madeleine swallowed, that face still clear in her mind's eye, taunting her. "I saw another man. Not Gabriel. We—" Her cheeks heated. "We were in bed together. Naked. We seemed in love. We—" But the salacious memory stayed lodged on her tongue. How could she admit the unholy acts she had committed with another man?

A painful moment lingered in the air when only silence greeted her admission. Madeleine looked back at her friend to find an incredulous look on her face. "Cecile, are you laughing?"

Cecile clamped a hand over her open mouth, amusement sparking the eyes above it. "No, truly. I'm not laughing at you." Her bronze head shook ardently. When she lowered her hand, her look had grown serious. "What matter is it what you did before you met the baron? You're not with this man now. You're faithful to your husband."

"Of course I am." Arms chilly, Madeleine hugged herself through her nightdress and ambled to the window. The fields stretched endlessly beyond the château, dusted in snow and sprinkled with barren trees. When she finally spoke, her throat was raw, the truth almost too painful to face. "But I had imagined myself chaste. I thought Gabriel was the first man I had ever known in that way."

Cecile's footsteps tapped the floorboards behind her, a soft hand reaching out to cup her shoulder. "Oh Maddy, I'm sorry."

Hot tears swelled in Madeleine's eyes, her shoulders quivering. "I'm not the type of person to behave in such a manner." At least she hoped, from the burgeoning memories she used to construct her identity.

"You're not," she heard through the crystal fog of her tears. Yet the words refused to touch the place inside that had hollowed out, preparing for the bottom to drop from beneath her feet at any moment.

Madeleine toyed with the disheveled braid slung over her shoulder and turned to her friend. "That could only mean one thing, then. What if—" The very idea nauseated her. "Well, what if Gabriel isn't the only man I married? What if I have two husbands?" Panic surged in her chest, forcing her legs into motion. She paced, ringing her hands in front of her. "I knew I shouldn't have married him without all of my memories intact. I could have just ruined two lives with my impatience. Now I'll lose him and this other man, whoever he is, and I'll deserve it."

"Maddy, sit down." Before Madeleine could construct another sentence, Cecile had seized her by the wrists and propelled her onto the plush seat at her dressing table. "Your imagination is spiraling out of control, and it won't do you any good. Let's look at the facts for a moment, all right?"

Barely nodding, Madeleine exhaled through her nose. "Okay." Still, her heartbeat hammered through her veins like staccato notes on a piano.

"You have one memory of this man, hardly enough to assume that he is your husband," Cecile said, bent over Madeleine's fidgety form. "Don't you think Jean-Paul would have said something had you married someone else before Baron Clement? He's not like Auguste. He would have told you."

"That's true." From the short time she'd spent with her little brother since waking on Traitor Island, she trusted him with her life. "But what if Jean-Paul didn't know? Auguste and I lived in Italy for a time, and Jean-Paul stayed here."

Cecile's head shook once. "There's no use conjecturing until you can ask him yourself. He's coming to dinner tonight, is he not? You can approach the subject then."

"I suppose you're right. Still, I know my nerves will be on edge until then." Madeleine attempted a half-smile. "Thank you, Cecile—for trying to calm me down. I fear your work has been tenfold since Gabriel made you my personal maid."

A guttural laugh issued from Cecile's throat, her green eyes lit with humor. "You pulled me out of the depths of Georgette's realm of power downstairs. Spending my days with my best friend, gossiping and helping to dress her? I'll take that any day, thank you."

Madeleine joined in her snickering, glad Georgette's reign over them both had ended. "We do have our fun. Though I hope one day you'll leave me. Find the man who makes you happy and build an adventurous life with him."

Red hair blazing in the morning sunlight, Cecile threw her a poignant smile. "Let me know if you find the one who can put up with me." As if thrust by a lever, her finger popped up. "Oh, speaking of adventurous men." Reaching into her dress pocket, she produced a sealed piece of parchment. "I nearly forgot—this came for you by courier this morning."

Seizing the maid's offering, Madeleine pressed her thumb to the ornate seal before turning it over to examine the words etched on the front. "This is Christophe's writing."

"Addressed to the Baroness d'Avance," Cecile said with a clever smirk.

Energy surged through Madeleine's fingertips. What reason could Christophe have for writing her now, after she had wed another man? "I suppose we should read it." After extending it back to Cecile, she waited with curiosity while the woman broke the seal with one finger and unfolded the letter.

"Dear Baroness Clement"—the words still sounded so strange addressed to her—"I write to congratulate you on your recent nuptials. I realize it has been many months since the wedding, but a life at sea ensures I am perpetually behind on the world's happenings. While I cannot deny my disappointment at my defeat, I am certain the better man truly won. I wish you a lifetime of happiness with your baron. Please know that should any occasion arise that either of you need the services of my ship, I will be happy to oblige within my capabilities. We are currently trading off the coast of Spain, but we will stop in Rome for Carnevale. If you are in town, you should stop by the docks to say hello. I always appreciate seeing a friendly face. With my utmost humility and congratulations, Captain Christophe Roux."

A silent moment lingered in the bedroom, laced with only the warble of two competing wood thrushes in the tree outside her window. Madeleine lifted questioning eyes to Cecile, who merely chuckled. "Well, don't look at me," Cecile said. "I have half a mind to stuff this correspondence in my dress right now and run off to Rome myself to meet him."

Madeleine's cheeks bloomed with color. "I certainly can't go. The last time we spoke, he kissed me even after I told him I chose Gabriel over him." Just the memory of it sent her toes tapping with anxiety. "Let the past stay buried. It's better that way."

"You can't even be friends with the man? He acknowledged his loss in this letter." Cecile held the elegantly scrolled page up in the sunlight. "Surely he would respect your marriage vows."

"No." Madeleine sighed, wagging her head. "I have enough strange men occupying my mind for one day. Let's pretend this letter never came, shall we? Do me a favor and toss it in the fire once it's lit." For the first time, she noticed the utter chill spearing through her woolen nightdress.

"Forgive me." Cecile pressed a hand to her forehead as she jogged toward the fireplace sprinkled in last night's ash. "I meant to get a fire going right away." She reached atop the marble mantle and retrieved two pieces of flint before kneeling at the hearth.

Madeleine watched her diligently working the banked coals before she turned to the wardrobe. "It's my fault for distracting you."

My fault. The words sunk deeper than she'd meant them. The mysterious face who'd greeted her memories upon waking blazed in her imagination, reminding her that she had only just begun to face her many shortcomings. Tramping him beneath her bare feet, she marched on the wardrobe, determined not to let him take today from her.

T he friendly chatter filling the château's drawing room hardly touched Madeleine's ears. While Gabriel sat beside her on the floral settee recounting a humorous tale of their newly married life to Désirée and Jean-Paul, Madeleine sat with her stare frozen on the window. The air outside swirled with tiny flecks of snow, restlessly drifting about before settling on the freezing ground.

All day, her mind had stayed adrift despite her greatest efforts, trapped in the perpetual tug-of-war between worry and self-loathing. She had tried to resume her usual routine of practicing her reading and helping to run the barony, but she couldn't collect her thoughts enough to focus. Dinner had passed over them with her awareness barely present, and the rest of her world went on as normal without her.

The Château des Rêves fading from her senses, another drawing room in a far distant place commanded her imagination. She looked out the open window of this grand house among her emerging memories, and instead of snow, she saw the lights flickering off a canal winding through the center of the city. Ornate gondolas drifted past, the men piloting them dipping their oars rhythmically through the inky water.

A gentle wind laced with glorious warmth swept in from the street, ruffling the lace curtains. Madeleine sat in a velvet armchair trimmed in gold, as many of the lavish pieces about the room. The deep blues and damask prints adorning the space were accented by gilded sconces and a crystal chandelier showering prisms over the polished floor.

Turning a page in her book, Madeleine tapped her slippered foot on the leg of the settee beside her. The unpleasant scents of the canal streaming past the house were expertly masked with bouquets of gardenias and sweet peas. She had lost herself so completely in their captivating aroma and the pages of her story that she hardly remembered the man in the room until he cleared his throat.

Madeleine peered over the edge of her book to find him regarding her coldly from the corner of his eye, as if her mere presence offended him. "You're doing it again," he said, revolving his eyes back to the newspaper in his hand. "I never can concentrate when you tap your foot like that."

Even in their leisure time, he had a distinguished air. He sat with his back rigid against the settee, one foot perched on his knee. He'd shed his dinner jacket long ago, yet still his tight-fitting silk waistcoat and the ruffles beneath his chin bespoke the elegance of a gentleman. Glasses sat atop his straight nose, as they always did when he read in the evenings, his dark eyes stern with concentration. His smooth-shaven skin revealed masculine lines on either side of his twisted lips.

Ripping her stare away from the dangerously handsome man before her, Madeleine's gaze slid down her leg to her offending foot. "What, like this?" Driving her heel back, she rammed her toe as hard as she could into the base of the settee. The little piece of furniture jolted beneath him, disturbing the precisely arranged pillows.

The man didn't react as he kept skimming the page in front of him, yet the hint of a smile edged his mouth. A few moments ambled past them before he glanced her way, squinting to see the item in her hands. "What is it you're reading, anyway?"

"It's Robinson Crusoe," she said, still engrossed in the harrowing sea voyage.

"That's a children's book." He shook his head, smile widening.

Madeleine snapped the book shut, examining the gilded lettering on the cover. "Six months ago, I could barely read a word of your Italian translations. I'd say I'm doing just fine, thank you." Shooting to her feet, she angled toward the door to the hallway. "And if I'm being so bothersome, I might as well finish this in a place you can't hear my foot tapping."

As she marched a trail between the settee and tea table, a hand caught her wrist. "Now, now. I didn't mean it like that." The man deposited his newspaper beside him on the empty seat and seized her other wrist in his free hand. His warm fingers enveloped her pulsing wrists, tugging her closer.

Despite her irritation, Madeleine let him. Heat rushed up her neck and spilled into her face as his gaze roamed her exposed skin. "I've too long been away, I know." He took the book from her hand and tossed it over his newspaper. "What kind of a fool spends his evening pouring over the drivel of old men when there's a treasure like this under his roof?"

Before she could say a word, he had pulled her closer, eased her into his lap. Madeleine found herself seated atop him, her legs laying over the empty cushion. Her arms rested around his strong neck and shoulders as his wound about her torso. She could almost forget the dubious nature of their relationship with his sensual gaze capturing hers.

"I've missed you," he said, lifting her arm to leave a trail of kisses from her wrist to the inside of her elbow. He smiled against her skin. "Did you miss me?"

Madeleine's mouth quirked. "Only a little." She braced herself as his lips journeyed up her arm to the bare shoulder above her satin gown.

"Then I have not done my duty." His kisses climbed her throat, lingering there a moment before his lips found hers. Lost in the thrill of him, Madeleine sighed contentedly as he kissed her harder. Her fingers tangled in his hair, her heartbeat racing. His warm breath tickled her skin.

A sudden knock on the door wrenched them apart. With an exasperated grunt, the man sat up and glared at the offender. "Yes, what is it?"

The door creaked inward, revealing one of his advisors on the other side. Face pale, he averted his gaze anywhere but the couple on the settee. "Forgive me, sir. But they are here. I didn't suppose you'd want to make them wait."

Sighing, the man above her thrust his fingers through his hair. "No, you're right. I'll be down in a moment, Diego." With an apologetic flash of his eyes, he leaned down and kissed her, gently this time. "I'm sorry. This shouldn't take long."

The click of his polished shoes in the marble hallway had retreated before Madeleine pushed off the settee and glanced toward the closed door. A few voices chattered on the street, prompting her to the window. Madeleine peered down at the cobbled street along the canal to what appeared to be several drunks stumbling home after a night of imbibing. Still, she reached for the wooden shutters and secured them over the window.

The man had left his dinner jacket flung over the back of his chair. With a cautious glance around, Madeleine descended on it. Her fingers dove beneath the finely woven cashmere, hunting in his pockets until they produced a small slip of paper. Breath hastening, Madeleine unfurled the paper and skimmed its scrawled contents. The names of several other prominent Venetian diplomats stared back in fresh ink. Memorizing them, she tucked the paper into his jacket again, carefully replacing it. If only she could eavesdrop on their conversation, but his hirelings always stood guard outside his office—

"What is it that has utterly captured your mind today?" A voice yanked her out of the memory, hurling Madeleine back to the Château des Rêves. She blinked, finding her husband's inquisitive face looking her over.

Madeleine tried to laugh, the nervous sound of it falling flat. "Oh, it's nothing. Just remembering, is all." No use worrying him for something he couldn't fix anyway.

Brows tapering, Gabriel searched her face a quiet moment before the hint of a smile twitched his lips upward. "Well, whatever it is, I hope you feel comfortable enough sharing it with me when you're ready."

Inhaling a cathartic breath, Madeleine directed her attention to Désirée and Jean-Paul on the recamier, a lively discussion bouncing between them. "What do you make of those two, hmmm?" Désirée looked positively flushed as Jean-Paul chuckled madly at something she'd said.

Gabriel grinned. "I guess time will tell."

"What do you think about it, Maddy?" Désirée asked, her blue eyes bright in the cavorting light from the alabaster hearth. "Jean-Paul wants to travel to the Nordic countries. I say Asia would be fascinating. Where would you go if you could travel anywhere?"

Madeleine thought, gaze roaming the mahogany and gold-trimmed furnishings, landing on the wood-paneled wall. "Well, I—" Her mind sprinted, but not a single place emerged among her recollection, save for the dreadful island she'd woken to alone. With three expectant faces waiting, she finally blurted the one place fresh in her thoughts. "Rome, perhaps? I hear it's almost time for Carnevale."

A sharp breath sucked through Désirée's lips. "Rome for Carnevale. Truly, it's the most magnificent sight you've ever beheld." She touched the arm of the settee. "Gabriel, do you remember going there as children? I never wanted to leave. They had to drag me back home, kicking and screaming."

"Oh, I remember. We almost lost you in the crowds." His curls bobbed with his shaking head. "It was amusing, but there are simply too many people. I couldn't hear myself think."

Désirée waved him off with a swipe of her hand. "A few people never hurt anyone. It was good for you to get out of this house." Struck by the thought, she sat upright. "If Madeleine wants to go, you should take her to Carnevale this year. In fact, we should all go. I would love to relive my childhood adventures; see how it's changed."

Gabriel's nose wrinkled. "I'm not sure I'm ready to face it again in this lifetime. Besides, it would take weeks to get there and weeks to get back. I don't think the barony could spare us all that time."

"Georgette can hold down this fort just fine when she needs to. Just think how long you were gone when the Guardians took you. If we all leave now, we can be back before planting season." An urgent look had entered Désirée's eyes, a desperation Madeleine suspected involved the large man sitting beside her.

Sensing the woman's silent pleas, Madeleine reached for her husband's hand. "I wouldn't mind it. We haven't yet traveled in celebration of our marriage."

Sighing, Gabriel let his gaze wander her face. He would do anything for her, she knew. Even if it meant confronting his biggest fear. "Oh, all right. If you insist."

Désirée released a delighted yelp, clapping her hands. "Wonderful!" Cheeks blooming with color, she turned to Jean-Paul. "Oh, please say you'll come. We can all make a grand adventure of it."

Even as he tried to hide it, the blond man couldn't keep the enjoyment off his face. He tucked an errant strand of hair behind his ear and nodded. "I suppose I could. I'm still setting up shop here, and if my blacksmithing services aren't needed right away—"

"They won't be." Désirée looked like she might burst with excitement. "You're going to love it, I promise. The fireworks, the races, the dances. It's all spectacular."

"I don't know if I would be much fun at the dances," Jean-Paul said shyly. "I've never danced in my life."

"There's an easy solution for that." Désirée popped up from the recamier, extending her hand. "Come here; I'll teach you."

Madeleine exchanged a look with Gabriel as Désirée's lesson commenced, her color deepening within Jean-Paul's sturdy arms. The couple spent several moments trying new steps, a barrage of giggles between them, before an out-of-breath Désirée hailed Gabriel. "Will you help me show him this dance, brother? I know you remember it."

While Gabriel begrudgingly rose from the settee and acquiesced to his sister's wishes, Jean-Paul replaced him beside Madeleine. The two sat silently for several moments, watching Gabriel lead Désirée around the sitting room in a triangular pattern. Too elated to notice, Désirée toppled every footstool and plant her skirts came near.

At last, Madeleine whispered a prayer for courage and gently set her hand on Jean-Paul's wrist. Her gaze swam with his a quiet moment, pleading to know the truth without actually having to voice it. How much did she really want to know about herself, about the person she had left behind when she awoke on Traitor Isle?

Jean-Paul's bright eyes narrowed. "What is it?" he murmured, drawing closer.

Her gaze wandered down the dress of mint green crêpe sheathing her body, to the diamond bracelet winking on her wrist and the dainty slippers poking out beneath her skirt. The room about her buzzed with frustrating noise, the claret drapes and glittering finishes laughing at her from their lofty seats. This house, these clothes—she'd never deserve them. Every memory drove that fact deeper, strangling her.

Barely managing to lift her gaze back to him, Madeleine finally exhaled. "I saw a man today in my memories, someone I'd never remembered before." Her face heated, the burn of his lips against hers still fresh. "He seemed rich, very powerful. Possibly a diplomat. He was Italian, dark—"

"Cavaretta," Jean-Paul fairly spat the word.

Madeleine's heart pumped. "That sounds familiar. Do you know him?"

"I never met the man. I only know what little you told me when you came back from Italy." Jean-Paul's strong jaw tensed. "The two of you lived together in Venice for several years. Auguste worked for him. He introduced you."

Lived together. Relief flooded her, even as shame twisted around its roots. At least she hadn't bonded herself to the man in marriage. She could leave her outright sin in the face of God's law to struggle with another day.

She covered her flaming cheek with the cool of her palm. "Yes, I remembered that he was a romantic partner. But I—" Her mind hunted every detail she knew, the memory of her rooting around in the man's jacket befuddling her. "I was spying on him, too, wasn't I?"

Jean-Paul's gaze rose warily to the dancing siblings before meeting hers. His eyes glinted in the firelight, stony with solemnity. "Auguste needed funds to go sailing around the world looking for that treasure. He soon realized that Cavaretta had secret dealings that could make him rich, but he couldn't get far enough into the man's inner circle to touch them."

The truth stabbed her low in the gut. "So he used me to do it. Of course he did." Hadn't she learned last year that she was nothing but a pawn in Auguste's deviant games?

"Every piece of information you found, you took back to Auguste, who sold it to Cavaretta's rivals. It's why you quit acting, how you paid for Auguste's fruitless search for the nameless man."

Madeleine's vision hazed with tears, her eyes slipping shut. "So I seduced this man, then betrayed him. Every night, I shared a bed with him, knowing I was sabotaging him for money." The cruel truth of it suffocated her. How much more did she have to learn about herself before she went mad?

A large hand touched her elbow. "It's not like Cavaretta is a saint. He was involved in all sorts of illegal dealings."

Her eyes opened, gaze forlorn, body feeling as if it had weathered a storm at sea. "But still, that does not absolve me of my sin."

Désirée giggled again, pulling Madeleine from her train of self-deprecating thoughts. "You aren't even paying attention," Désirée said in a playful tone. One arm swept the air. "Come on, you two. Join us."

Long after Madeleine found herself in her husband's arms, bobbing around the drawing room to the hum of Désirée's voice, thoughts of Cavaretta consumed her. Gabriel smiled down at her, luring her back to safety, inviting her into his loving embrace. But deep down, she knew things would never be the same between them. She had betrayed him before she even knew him, and something inside told her the past would find her no matter how far she ran.

Three

T he Clement family coach trundled through the Italian wilds, winding along mountainous roads, hitting every bump and divot along the way. Madeleine readjusted yet again, attempting to get comfortable despite an aching back and rattling head. No wonder Gabriel had warned them against the excursion. After two weeks on the road, she wondered if she could handle the cramped space much longer. And they'd only just passed over French borders.

When she had traveled from Marseilles to Paris, at least she could stretch her legs in Christophe's luxurious carriage. Now, she found herself tucked next to her husband, folding her legs close to keep them from disturbing Désirée and Jean-Paul seated across the coach. Biting her lip, she worried over Cecile, enduring the journey on the tiny driver's seat with Serge. She'd warned Cecile of her probable discomfort, but the maid had insisted Madeleine take her to Rome on pain of death.

Tugging down the corduroy sleeves of her traveling jacket, Madeleine shifted her weary gaze to the window. The sweeping willows and snow-dusted spruces of home had given way to cypress and olive trees. Once freezing despite the cabin that enclosed them, the air now carried a pleasant breeze laced with orange blossoms.

A hand tickled her arm, and Madeleine twisted to find Gabriel regarding her with a half-grin. Returning it, she slipped her hand onto his warm palm and laced her fingers with his. His fine clothes smelled of cinnamon as she rested her head atop his sturdy shoulder. So much lay between them, so much she wanted to say, yet when she pictured disclosing her past, she only saw hurt in his eyes. Surely it was better to keep him in the dark, thinking his hands were the only ones to touch her, his heart the first to encounter hers.

The sight of their clasped hands in the jostling carriage evoked memories. Madeleine saw herself in a smaller rig, a firmer hand clamped around hers. She looked up into Auguste's earnest face, his wild eyes and flared nostrils.

"This has to go perfectly," he said, his concerned expression flitting over her hair and evening dress. "You look the part, but you must convince him with your words, your actions."

Madeleine wiggled in the crimson-colored taffeta he'd bestowed on her. It was so much tighter than her other dresses. The neckline left nothing of her form to the imagination. Her wrist, throat, and ears glittered with the diamond and pearl jewelry he'd convinced a jeweler friend to let him borrow, expecting a generous return of Auguste's profits.

"Quit fidgeting," Auguste ordered, slamming his palm onto the cushioned seat beside her. He glanced out the window at the impressive stone building they approached. "Now, listen. We don't have much time. Cavaretta is bound to recognize you. He's seen you on the stage. He remarked of your beauty the night we saw *Andromache*. Stick to your stage name, and make sure he sees you as soon as possible."

Nodding fervently, Madeleine hung on his every command. "So I should talk to him?"

"Do *not* seek him out. He'll come to you. Just be in his line of vision." Auguste gulped as the carriage slowed, his fingers nervously wringing. "You must act aloof, disinterested in him. It will only make him chase you. Cavaretta *hates* when people try to flatter him. He knows it's counterfeit. He has a dozen women following him around like dogs wherever he goes. He doesn't need another one making a fool of herself."

The carriage door opened, driving Auguste against his seat. Madeleine took the driver's offered hand, descending to the street. When her brother did not follow, she stuck her head back through the open door. "Aren't you coming?"

"I can't be seen with you," he said from the shadows. "I will come on my own when it's safe. Pretend you don't know me, and Madeleine, whatever you do—*don't* ruin this for me."

The door slammed shut and its stately horses yanked the carriage away, leaving Madeleine alone in the moonlit street. From within the bustling townhouse, warbling strains of violin music leaked from open windows glittering with candlelight. Voices mingled, laughing, singing, but here on the cobbled roadway, only the lap of the canal and the thump of boats hitting the docks surrounded her. Could she really do this? Could she pretend to be a completely different person for the sake of her brother's wild ambitions?

Sucking in a breath tinged with algae, Madeleine stood tall and advanced on the imposing house. A doorman welcomed her, opening the portal to a world of extravagance she'd once only dreamed of. A private courtyard opened at her feet, ivy clinging to the walls, candelabras shimmering from within a row of marble pillars. Everywhere she looked, guests mingled about, chatting above goblets of red wine. The women wore snug Empire gowns with feathered headpieces, the men equally posh in their ruffled cravats and high-cut tailcoats.

Thrusting aside the voice whispering that she'd never belong here, Madeleine crossed the stone floor and followed a staircase up to the main house. Surely the heart of the party rested within those walls, from which the tune of violin and harp floated whimsically down. Her palms began to sweat as she surveyed the swarm of people upstairs whirling about the expansive ballroom. Surely he was here, woven amid the richest of Venice's citizens.

Madeleine accepted a glass of wine from a passing waiter and forced herself into the crowd. Most people she encountered were pleasant, offering hollow conversation and flippant pleasantries. With her remedial understanding of the Italian language, she couldn't handle much else, anyway. When several pairs of eyes began trailing her around the ballroom, she gulped back her shame at her immodest attire and kept on. Only one man's opinion of her mattered.

Even with his back turned, Madeleine knew who he was when she spotted him amid a swarm of admirers beneath an archway. The wide shoulders and tall, imposing form spun fear in her middle, curiosity budding with it. The mostly female crowd that encircled him looked up at his face in wonder, their bejeweled bosoms swelling as he spoke, their lace-embellished fans flitting wildly like butterfly wings. Did his mere power attract them, his good looks? Or did he possess something more?

Before she could think on it further, another face invaded her vision. Madeleine blinked, her eyes focusing on the bushy brows and spectacles just an arm's length in front of her. *"Buonasera, signorina,"* he said, lips parting to reveal a gap in his front teeth. "Might I have the pleasure of this dance?" He extended a hand to her, his low bow accentuating his diminutive stature.

Peering down at the man's balding head, Madeleine did her best to manufacture a smile. *"Grazie, signore,"* but I regret I must decline," she said, slowly conjuring the right words in Italian. "I am not feeling well enough this evening."

The man laughed with a snort. "You will feel differently once you've had a whirl about the ballroom." He seized her arm as if to drag her there by force. "Dancing is the best medicine, after all."

"Really, signore, I must protest." Madeleine glanced at Cavaretta, who still had his back turned. She couldn't let this newcomer split her focus. "Your help is appreciated, but in no way necessary," she said to the little man now tugging her along as if she were a mule.

"You will see. I'm the greatest dancer in Venice. That's what all the courtesans say." His gold-bedecked chest swelled as he spun on his heel and forcefully tried to yank her toward the milling group of dancers.

Madeleine clenched her teeth, planting her slippered feet to the floor. She had dealt with enough men who didn't understand the word "no" in her life. "Signore, I said *no,*" she said, loud enough to attract a great many stares. She tried not to redden as she noticed Cavaretta turn from the corner of her eye.

Her pursuer turned back, glancing sheepishly at the partygoers who had halted their conversations to leer at him. "Signorina, I don't think you appreciate the honor of my offer." He moved close, tone lowering. "Don't you know who I am?"

Whipping her hand away, Madeleine took a sizable step backward. "I don't care who you are. When I say no, I mean it." She hadn't bothered to speak quieter for his sake, inciting snickers from the crowd around them.

Sensing a new presence at her side, Madeleine glanced up to find Cavaretta at her shoulder, his gaze flitting briefly over her before landing on her stubborn companion. "Spinoli, you know there are plenty of women primed to take you up on your offer. Why don't you accept this defeat with grace?"

The pompous man called Spinoli stretched himself as tall as he could, but still he only reached Madeleine's neckline. "There are those who don't appreciate elegance and superiority, I suppose."

One last disapproving scowl washed over her before he reeled about in search of a new victim.

Alone with Cavaretta, Madeleine nearly forgot to breathe. *He's the linchpin in our scheme,* Auguste's voice echoed in her mind. *He alone has the power to make our dreams a reality, or see that we never dream again.* Her brother had warned her how dangerous the man could be, and yet as he stood beside her, carefully watching her reaction, she couldn't quench the allure of playing with fire that coursed through her.

Remembering Auguste's command as they pulled up in the coach, she resisted the urge to blend in with his other admirers with flattery. Instead, she allowed her gaze only to lock briefly with the dark one staring back before she gave a slight nod of the head and turned away. An icy sensation trickled over her extremities as she forced her feet away from him. Auguste had prepared her for Cavaretta's handsome exterior, for the pull of his magnetizing presence, and still her heart thudded in her throat like a stampede of horse hooves.

"I don't even get a thank you?" a deep, masculine voice halted her trek away from him.

Madeleine pivoted back, praying for an even voice and steady hands. "What for?" She summoned disinterest upon her face. "I told him perfectly well on my own what I wanted. I didn't need help."

The slightest amusement edged his full lips. "Perhaps." His stern brows cinched, his eyes perusing her face. "Have we made acquaintance before? You look vaguely familiar."

She looked to the floor to keep from blushing under his scrutiny. "I doubt it. I don't know many people in this city." Despite her every instinct to engage the curious man in conversation, she pointed herself away. "Well, good evening. If you must, accept my thanks for your intervention."

25

With that, she thrust herself into the milling assembly, leaving Cavaretta with his mouth hinged open, primed to say more. Madeleine spent the next hour mingling with the party's opulent guests, plucking crostini and bruschetta from the hors d'oeuvres table, and admiring the stunning splendor of the house itself. Often, she felt a pair of eyes following her around the ballroom, her victory clear when she allowed herself a glimpse of him peering out from the center of his feminine patronage, his stare fixed only on her.

Winding a path beneath the chandeliers' crystal rays, Madeleine spied a door which opened to an empty balcony overlooking the canal. Just before she passed the threshold, she caught sight of Auguste watching her from among the guests, a slight nod indicating his approval. Amid the fear, despite the nagging ache that their deeds were immoral, her yearning for his acceptance won out. If successful, she might gain untold riches, but more importantly the brother she had sheltered in her heart for so many years.

For several moments, Madeleine basked in the quiet retreat from the chatter of guests beyond the closed double doors. Ancient stone buildings flanked the old, twisting streets in sophisticated beauty. The softly lapping canal far beneath her feet emptied into the sea, where a ribbon of white moonlight struck over the inky waves. Out here, away from the din of crystal and violins, she drank in the more serene sounds of the city—a mother crooning to her sleeping child, a few stray notes of a mandolin warbling a sad song to the night.

So engrossed was she in her surroundings, Madeleine had nearly forgotten her mission until a door creaked behind her. Her lips curled gently, the sound of his purposeful step on the stone balcony unmistakable. She set her palms on the cold marble rail and waited until he leaned on it beside her, silently watching her profile as she gazed out on the Adriatic.

"You're an actress," he said finally. "I saw you months ago on stage in Paris. I *knew* you looked familiar."

Madeleine swung her gaze slyly his way, fighting the urge to ask how he liked her performance. "How fantastic for you." Her gut recoiled at having to transform herself into this absolute shrew Auguste had conjured, and yet her response only seemed to goad her companion.

"The party is in there, you know." One thumb indicated the swirl of dancers beyond the glass. "It can't be much fun out here on your own."

"It's loud inside." Madeleine's gaze wandered to the shadowed street, the canal where gondolas drifted past, their oars dipping languidly through the water. "I like it here where it's quiet. *Was* quiet."

She held in her breath as his stare traveled her exposed arms, the curves of her shoulders and collarbone. "You came to a celebration like this for quiet?" Resting his elbows on the rail, he studied her face beneath the moonlight, so intensely Madeleine had to remind herself again not to squirm.

"Perhaps I thought I might meet one interesting person. Some-one I can talk to about more than how grand we all are for being here." She shrugged.

"I'm sorry we've disappointed you."

For the first time, Madeleine allowed the faintest of grins to dimple her cheek as she slipped her gaze into his. "That remains to be seen."

As if invited by the slight thaw in her icy shell, Cavaretta stepped closer, so his arm brushed her bare skin. "It's not safe to be out here, you know," he said with a clever grin. "Don't you know about the ghost of St. Cecilia?"

Madeleine's brow arched, her smile impossible to keep at bay against his charm. "Are you attempting to scare me with a tale of ghosts?"

"Oh, this isn't just any ghost." His eyes lit, one finger jabbing toward the tranquil street. "Every night, she comes out of that church over there and floats up the street, looking for someone to drag back with her into the underworld. She's done it every night since she's been trapped in that church. Townspeople have gone missing by the dozen. That's why you don't see anyone on the street anymore."

A laugh burst from Madeleine's mouth at his half-hearted attempt at folklore. "That's ridiculous. You should never repeat that story again."

A wide grin mirrored on the man's face, victory manifest in his handsome features. "Ah, but it made you smile. That's all I could ask." He looked thoughtful again, one hand reaching out to cover hers on the rail. "I know better than to ask after witnessing what happened to my friend in there, but I suppose I'm feeling lucky." His warm stare climbed up her arm to her eyes. "Would you dance with me?"

Despite every warning Auguste had blared at her, Madeleine let Stefano Cavaretta's bewitching power wash over her. Nodding softly, she followed as he led her across the wide balcony and pressed his palm into hers. His eyes never left hers as his other hand anchored at her waist. Those eyes burned through her, demanding to see beneath her exterior. Madeleine clutched his sturdy form and matched his languid pace as he guided them in the waltz.

The couple danced in silence for several agonizing moments, solemn stares entangled. Against every fiber of strength she possessed, Madeleine's heart bounded in her chest, sweat emerging beneath her swept-up hair. Fire blazed in the eyes above hers, a dangerous force that lured her to him as much as it twisted her gut with misgiving. She had come to play him, and yet somehow she knew he would swallow her whole if she didn't maintain her wits.

"You're not here on business," Cavaretta said, yanking her from her unbridled thoughts. "We haven't had a French theater troupe here in some time."

Madeleine's head shook gently. "No, I just wanted to see 'The Floating City' with my own eyes." It sounded weak. Suspicious. Madeleine kept her head up, her gut recoiling at the lie.

Cavaretta paused, his critical stare drilling through her. "Do you often travel alone to foreign cities? Such a practice could prove hazardous." His fingers compressed on her hip, a sign of protection or a threat, she couldn't decipher.

Injecting mischief into her gaze, Madeleine let it ascend his throat before she opened her painted mouth to speak. "Only when I'm feeling adventurous," she said with a shrug. "Life is too short to waste worrying about what might happen."

"Indeed." His head cocked, a quizzical look openly taking her in. "Forgive me for staring, I just—I can't figure you out. I don't know what you're thinking."

Surprised by his honesty, she tilted her mouth in a sly smile. "Is that such a bad thing?"

A chuckle escaped his full lips, his handsome features remaining serious. "When I saw you onstage in Paris, I thought you were stunning. But now, being this close to you, I—" He shook his head, his awestruck gaze wandering her skin beneath the moonlight. "I can't describe it. You are so much more than I thought." One gloved hand reached up, the backs of his fingers brushing her cheekbone.

Madeleine breathed out, forcing herself to avoid his trap. She stepped back, freeing herself of his touch. "Are you always so forward with women?" At his girded brows, she nodded toward the closed doors. "I saw your crowd of admirers, hanging on your every word, worshiping the very ground on which you step. I can't believe they remain so loyal without some inkling of hope."

A grin tickled his lips, his gaze diving to his polished shoes as if he were a schoolboy caught misbehaving. "Indeed, I fancied myself more charming before this night. You've flung me back to reality."

"I don't like games, signore." Her voice rang strong through the starlit air. "If you want something, just say it."

Her invitation prompted his head up, a million battling emotions flooding his face. A brief moment existed where he stood apart from her, chest pumping and hands working at his sides. With his building fervor, she worried perhaps he might hit her. Auguste had warned he was capable of worse. Then, before she could collect another thought, he had eliminated the distance between them.

Two strong arms came around her, lifting her to her tiptoes, crushing her form against his. Fingers wove with her hair, hot breath tingling her skin. His lips commanded hers, capturing them in wild abandon, thrilling her despite a mind screaming not to get swept away. Madeleine melted into the man's embrace, lost in his intoxicating presence, in the scents of vanilla and myrrh emanating from his fine clothes.

Then Auguste's voice catapulted through her mind, reminding her not to give too much away, to make him work. Madeleine enjoyed a last lingering taste of him before wedging her palms at his chest and thrusting herself backward.

Out of breath, she pressed a palm to her surging neckline. "I suppose I'm unaccustomed to the way of things here in Venice."

A look of pride skittered over his upturned lips, carrying not a hint of shame for his actions. "You wanted me to get straight to the point, did you not?"

"Yes, well—" Madeleine fluffed her disturbed hair. "You certainly did that. I think I'll take my leave now." Before he could advance on her again and upend whatever plans she still had to hold power over him.

"I'm sorry to have chased you off." But the look on his chiseled face said he had enjoyed unnerving her and would do it again the first chance he got. Madeleine turned away, only to have his voice freeze her. "Be ready by seven tomorrow night. I will take you out to dinner."

Revolving back, she lifted one brow. "That's terribly presumptuous of you, signore. You don't even know where I'm staying."

"I will."

Her head wagged, a smile creeping over her face at his. "I'll decide then whether I want to admit you."

"You will," he said, confidence beaming from every bit of his solid form.

Madeleine laughed, snatching two handfuls of skirts before scurrying through the ballroom and descending the stairs to the street. With his warm aroma still encircling her, his kiss still on her lips, she could almost forget it was all a farce. And how much easier to forget that she had traded her soul away for a brother's love.

Four

"Oh, how splendid!" Désirée gasped, springing from her seat and leaning her body out the open carriage window. "It's the most spectacular thing I've ever seen. Madeleine, you must have a look at this."

Madeleine lifted her head off Gabriel's shoulder before sharing a grin with him and moving the tasseled curtains aside. All along the congested street, a crowd of colorfully dressed Romans had convened. From elegant satin gowns and plumed feathers to homespun cloth, their costumes bespoke the mingling of a society normally kept apart. Their joyous roar shook the Clements' coach as it jostled along the cobbled street, tunneling into the thick of them.

"Look, Jean-Paul!" Désirée speared her finger toward a spectacle attracting a swarm of chortling citizens. "They're racing. Are they racing—children?" She turned her paled face back, one hand over her open mouth, then burst into giggles herself. "Forgive me, this is so bizarre."

Leaning over Madeleine's lap, Gabriel surveyed the carousing throng with a frown. "It's going to take us all night to reach our hotel at this rate. The coach can barely move." Just then, a pair of unseen hands rattled the cab, another carelessly smashing something on its side.

"Let's get going, then. I'm sure we can walk from here." Plopping onto her seat, Désirée reached into her bag and produced a wrapped bundle. "Here, I brought masks for all of us. It's never too early to join the festivities." Letting her cloth fall open, she revealed a stack of painted, glittering masks.

Gabriel swallowed as he glanced out the window again. "I suppose we don't have a choice, unless we just decide to forgo dinner tonight."

"Not a chance." Already securing a silvery, feathered mask over her eyes, Désirée laughed with a snort. "I've too long been eating whatever food we could conjure along the roadway. I'm going to enjoy some genuine Roman fare tonight."

After tying her purple sequined mask over her hair and helping Gabriel with his, Madeleine slipped a hand in his large ones. "It will be ok," she said, low enough so the others couldn't hear. "I won't leave your side."

Though concern sparked the bright eyes looking back at her from behind his mask, her husband nodded. "I love you." He planted a peck on her cheek, driving a burning ache down her throat. How long could she live at this man's side without revealing the darkness that shadowed her past?

The capering mass of Roman celebrants absorbed the group as they alighted from the carriage and mingled with the fray. Madeleine worked hard to keep up with Désirée and Jean-Paul, clinging tightly to Gabriel's hand behind her. Everywhere she looked, masked Romans shouted with glee—dancing, jostling, tossing confetti and sugared almonds into the air. The merry strands of a fiddle showered over them from an onlooking balcony, enticing the crowd to gambol about all the more.

Désirée appeared awestruck as she commandeered them through the joyous mess. First, she stopped at a row of women handing out oranges, accepting their offering with gleeful chatter. Then, they wandered up a wide stone street where the Roman citizens were, in fact, racing people. Madeleine caught sight of five old men desperately hobbling to beat each other and couldn't help but giggle.

When the group turned a street corner into a lively square adorned with a stone obelisk, Désirée yelped with delight. "Look, Jean-Paul. They're fighting." She practically hopped on the balls of her dainty feet, snatching his hand and dragging him toward a pair of muscular men poised to pounce upon one another at any moment.

The two men circled one another like a couple of caged animals, while the crowd whooped and jeered. One landed a firm punch to the other's jaw, sending him windmilling backward. Making a quick recovery, he ducked a second blow and charged at his opponent, lifting him off the ground and slamming him down.

"Oh, I can't look. It's too barbaric." Désirée shielded her face in her hands, wincing as the sound of another punch cracked through the air and left its recipient howling. Soon, her curiosity lured her back in, her bright eyes peeping over her fingertips for more.

Madeleine left her enthralled family behind, wandering through the square to a fencing match in full swing. The gleam of swords dancing in the moonlight pulled her closer, filling her with a sense of belonging. A fresh ache for her father blossomed within while watching the smooth elegance of the fighters' movements, sending her back to moments of proudly watching Pierre Bertrand instruct their neighbors on proper techniques.

Without warning, a fresh memory blasted through her, dashing her sweet recollections of her father. Despite the roar of the crowd, her eyes locked only on the dueling swords, clashing, scraping. She could feel the weight of a sword in her hand, feel her body performing the motions. Instead of a street packed with enlivened people, an empty, square-shaped room with windows on every side encircled her. The scent of sweat overwhelmed her. Rather than the fencers who had attracted her, she saw only *him*.

Holding firm to the hilt of her sword, Madeleine clenched her teeth and defended herself against Stefano Caveretta's repeated attacks. When one angle failed, he tried another. His blows came harder, more determined. Madeleine had to widen her stance and force unknown strength into her arm just to keep it from buckling beneath his crushing advances.

"You're going to die if you just keep on the defensive like that," he said between breaths. His sword glimmered in menacing grace as he jabbed at her again. "I *will* eventually wear you down. You have to seize your opportunity to strike me back."

Grunting in frustration, Madeleine fended off another slash of his sword and desperately looked for a gap in which to assault him. "You don't exactly make it easy," she hissed, breath barely escaping her weary lungs.

"You can't expect your opponent to play nice, either." Stefano came at her with several successive strikes, nearly driving the sword out of her trembling hand. "You have to move past the rudimentary lessons your father taught you and become a real fighter if you want to survive."

At the offense to her father's name, a fire lit in Madeleine's belly. After six months living with the man and learning his manipulative ways, he still managed to plant animosity within her when he so desired. Strange power burned down her arms, renewed strength surging through her body, lending her the stamina to keep fighting.

Delight blazed in his dark eyes as she growled through her gritted teeth and erupted toward him, driving him backward. The practice room with its marble floors and wide windows seemed to dissolve, Stefano Cavaretta her one obstacle and entire world. She would best him. She had to.

The pair wheeled about one another in a sophisticated caper of waiting and attacking. One moment, only her thundering pulse and the rush of blood filled her eardrums. The next, a mad flurry of swords thrashed the air in metallic clanging. Ignoring the perspiration rolling into her brows, Madeleine kept on, matching his every move with all the force and intelligence she could muster.

Stefano's dark hair, normally combed so neatly, flopped about as he darted this way and that. His brows drew in concentration, his strong jaw clenching with each lunge. An inkling of vulnerability shone through his stony facade when his mind was so engaged, a door he didn't often leave open, even for her.

Once their whirlwind romance had begun, Madeleine quickly learned hooking his interest that first night was only the beginning. Even after she had tearfully told him the playhouse in Paris needed her back and secured his invitation to live with him instead, he never let her too far into his affairs. What she did discover of his dealings, she had to sneak. Though he showed her genuine affection every day, he always left a piece of himself missing.

Madeleine braced herself for the blade swinging at her face, thwarting the hit with her sword and spinning around to gain a better vantage point. The better she got at fencing from their frequent melees, the less slack he gave her. He never employed practice weapons, claiming their weight didn't compare to real blades, and their design could never produce the urgency needed to really learn. One could only be prepared for a real match by knowing they could die in the preparation.

Chest heaving, Madeleine tightened her grip and lunged at his side. Stefano pivoted at the last moment, chuckling despite his own pitching torso. "You have to be quicker, Antoinette. I anticipated that move seconds before you performed it. Surprise me."

Flattening her lips into a determined line, she tried again at his middle, her blade narrowly missing as he swiped it away. "Quicker!" he shouted. "You won't manage to disable your opponent by being slow of mind. You must *think,* then *act.* "Without hesitation, he stormed at her, bashing his blade into hers until only the scrape of steel on steel rang in her ears.

Her stomach lurched and her arms felt like they might fall off, but Madeleine kept on. She had learned early on that Stefano was a man of physical conquests. If she wanted to get closer to him, two avenues lay before her. The obvious one joined them in a way that touched her, but he had still remained unattached until she found the second. Fighting sparked his true spirit—the rage, the excitement, the bloodlust. Something about it stirred him so that it impassioned her, too.

The familiar exhilaration grew inside as she ducked his blade and jabbed at his slim torso. This time, Stefano had to leap backward to avoid her, nearly losing his footing. He recovered quickly, striking back with a hard blow. Madeleine managed to unlock their swords and charged at him again, forcing him to work to defend himself. Their blades spun about one another in wild frenzy, worry lacing his tapered brows for the first time.

Fire raged in her belly, blazing up her body and down her arms. Her heartbeat thudded in her ears, the sight of him driving her onward. She wanted to beat him, yes, but something inside wanted to *hurt* him. Madeleine didn't stop to analyze the bizarre sensation as she leaned backward to dodge the pointed end aimed between her eyes.

He would show no mercy and neither would she. Gusting toward him, she threw several hits at him that he barely escaped. More fervor lit his dark eyes the harder she pushed. Striking back, he swept his blade at an angle, slicing through her dress and corset. Pain erupted at her ribcage, rippling through her. Madeleine hardly had time to notice blood pooling at her ribs before Stefano's sword plunged at her again. He wouldn't stop, not even after he'd injured her. Despite her pain, she propelled her blade up, wondering if her very life depended on it.

The match lasted only a few more maneuvers. Weak and dizzy with shock, Madeleine barely managed to defend against his attacks until he'd disarmed her, seizing her wrist and whirling her body against his. Stefano's blade pressed into her neck, his triumphant gaze wandering from her face down the length of her body. When it landed on the bloom of red spreading below her chest, a wicked, frightening light kindled in his eyes. Then, before she could think, his lips crashed into hers, his passion so furious she knew the fight alone hadn't produced his ardor.

Back in the Roman square, amid the shouts and dazzling lantern lights of Carnevale, Madeleine shivered. The dueling pair came back into focus, their familiar movements dropping a cold ache in her middle. Her hand instinctively shielded the spot that Stefano had slashed open, the patch of skin beneath her dress that now bubbled with scar tissue.

Her surroundings hazed with tears, the flaming lights stretching into crystals. How strongly she wanted to dismiss the unpleasant reminder of her past, and yet it descended painfully through her, finding no relief. Her relationship with Stefano had begun as a ruse, but she had grown to care for him. How could she not when she occupied his bed every night? The closer she drew to him for Auguste's sake, the more of her heart she'd sacrificed until she couldn't tell where the real person beneath her skin began and where her brother's puppet ended.

Shaking off her sour memories, Madeleine whirled to leave. The brash crowd pressing near her warned that she should find her family again before she lost them entirely. Eyes locked to the cobblestone pavement, she started when she ran straight into an imposing figure. "Forgive me." Her fingers clutched the person's arms for balance, the gaze beneath her glittering disguise fluttering up to a dark pair of eyes peering out from behind a golden mask.

Madeleine's breath hitched. The broad man above her had raven hair, a full mouth drawn into a solid line, and eyes that burrowed beneath her skin. Her fingertips reflexively tightened, her mind sprinting to catch up with reality. Surely she only saw Stefano because his presence haunted her thoughts. Yet the longer she looked into his unyielding stare, inhaled the distinguishable scents of vanilla and myrrh lingering on his clothes, the truth snared her in its ugly claws. A quaking fear shook her, even before she could quite comprehend why.

"Madeleine! Oh Madeleine, there you are!" The sweet chirp of Désirée's voice barely touched her ringing ears. Madeleine gazed silently up at the man as if in a trance. After the memory she had just recalled, she half expected him to draw his weapon and finish her on the spot.

"Madeleine, come along." Désirée's insistence snapped Madeleine into motion, her hands plummeting from the strong arms that had held her steady. "We're all dying of hunger and our hotel is only blocks from here."

With one last glance into the chiseled face beneath the mask, Madeleine turned and jogged up to the trio waiting for her a stone's throw away.

Even as Gabriel took her hand and led her away, she sensed those eyes eerily trailing her every step. Her husband's grip squeezed her, a sweet smile casting down from his tender face. Madeleine shifted closer to him, dodging the animated throng around them and trying to forget the man who had once commanded her entire existence. Perhaps if she held tightly enough to the one she truly loved, the past couldn't rise up to snatch her in its jaws.

The hotel Désirée had secured for them lay only a short walk from the square. A friendly, elegant-looking stone building sat along the busy street, with orange light glowing from the open windows and beds of oleanders adorning the balconies above. The first floor opened into an upscale tavern, teeming with stylishly dressed guests. Tables clothed in white linen assembled before a massive stone fireplace shedding warmth and capering light over the gathering. Piano music drifted from the corner, lending the room a sophisticated quality even against the boom of celebration outside.

"Thank God. I'm famished." Désirée already drifted toward a table like a parched wanderer in the desert at last finding an oasis.

Madeleine glanced out the windows, unable to shake the chill her encounter had volleyed through her. "I think I will freshen up first, if you all don't mind." She couldn't think about eating, not with her stomach roiling in fear.

"As long as I get to eat, I'm content," Désirée said, signaling a woman toting a pitcher with one graceful hand.

"Should I come with you?" Gabriel asked, one supportive hand on her elbow.

"No, that's quite all right." Madeleine shook her head, swallowing back the lump that had materialized in her gullet. "I'll just be a moment." Anything to get out of the crowd and into her own space. Anything to escape the pain of remembering.

A kindly man showed Madeleine to the room she would share with Gabriel. Even inside the lavish space, safe from the threat of whatever lurked beneath her feet, she couldn't tame her racing mind. If she hadn't deceived herself, if Stefano really was here and had seen her, her life could be flipped on its head. How could Gabriel want her, knowing she had freely given herself to a man before him, a man who still breathed and walked this earth?

She meant to pour herself some water from a porcelain chamber set stationed beside a gilded mirror, but her hands shook when she tried to lift the pitcher. Instead, she stumbled toward a set of double doors, behind which the festivities still roared. Lifting the latch, she swung the doors open and gazed out at the fantastic celebration below.

Everywhere she looked among the ancient stone buildings, people frolicked and sang, tossing confetti, laughing without restraint. A colorful swirl of joy and merriment paraded before her eyes, and yet she couldn't enjoy it. Not when she knew she didn't deserve to be here—didn't deserve the love of the man who had given her a new name and identity, opened his beautiful heart to her.

A sudden chill zipped up Madeleine's spine. Following her gut, she let her gaze tangle through the crowd until she spotted that black-clad figure again amongst them, his shimmering mask unmistakable. First, he looked through the tavern windows to where her family dined below. Then, with calculated severity, his intense stare climbed the building to where she stood. Madeleine recoiled into the shadows too late. He had to have seen her.

Slamming the doors closed, she collapsed against them with hands over her pounding heart. She couldn't catch her breath. She had only a few splintered memories of Stefano Caveretta, and yet somehow she knew his reappearance in her life would shatter the idyllic dream she'd built with Gabriel and alter her course forever.

Five

The city of Rome glittered beneath a full, white moon when Madeleine and her companions descended upon the streets. All day, they had explored the ancient metropolis, wandering around the Colosseum, the Pantheon and Palatine Hill. Madeleine had marveled at every building, every exquisite plaza, wondering if she'd seen it before. Each new site carried a sense of familiarity and unsettling visions of Stefano Cavaretta emerging at every turn. She half expected him to leap from the shadows at any moment, yet all her worry proved in vain.

Now, trailing her friends into the Piazza del Popolo, she couldn't help but shed her misgivings. The grand, elliptically-shaped plaza sparkled within a dazzling assembly of candelabras. Wavering light danced over the stone, painting it in ethereal beauty. From within the sea of milling dancers rose a stone obelisk and carved lions with water spurting from their mouths.

"Look at it," Désirée marveled, her gaze darting across the plaza. "Look at them."

Indeed, Madeleine had never beheld anything quite like it. The guests they had joined wore their most extravagant finery—colorful silk gowns embellished with frills and jewels, sequined masks, plumed headdresses. Each appeared to outshine the last, their adornments flashing in the candlelight as they swept gracefully over the stone floor, waltzing to the vigorous strands of cello and viola.

"They look like a bunch of fluffed-up poodles out for a morning constitutional," Cecile said with a giggle, inciting Madeleine to join her.

"Oh, stop." Désirée swiped at their friend with a bat of her hand. "Don't make me regret letting you come." Yet they all knew Désirée would never have left Cecile and Serge to sit at the hotel while they enjoyed themselves.

Cecile took in the splendid gathering from behind her pearl-studded mask. "You'll be happy to know that you won't have to deal with me for long. There are plenty of male specimens here to keep me occupied for hours." Before Désirée could protest, Cecile had already drifted into the midst of them, securing a dance with a muscular fellow within seconds.

"I just know she's going to do something to disgrace us," Désirée said before lifting her shoulders. "At least she's wearing a mask. Perhaps no one will know who she is."

Madeleine shared the smile creeping over Désirée's lips. "Nobody knows who any of us are, do they?"

"That's not exactly accurate," Gabriel said, touching her elbow. "This particular party has an exclusive guest list. We had to prove our status to secure a reservation."

Worry nipped at Madeleine's middle before she thrust it aside with great effort. "I rather liked the idea of anonymity. The masks are just a symbol, I suppose."

"They do have their uses." Her husband glanced nervously about himself, fingers working at his sides. "What do you say I get you something to drink?" he asked, his masked gaze hunting for the refreshment table.

Madeleine pressed a palm to her stomach, still roiling beneath cream-colored satin. "I'd like that, if it's not too much trouble."

LAURIE SANFORD

"I think I can manage," Gabriel said with a tilted grin. "I'll have Jean-Paul and Serge to protect me."

Once the three men had wandered off to retrieve sustenance, Désirée immediately descended on Madeleine like a bird snatching up prey in its talons. Concern lit the eyes peeking out from her silvery mask, her teeth biting her lower lip.

"Do you think Jean-Paul will want to dance with me?" She paced a few steps, the matching cape over her sky-blue satin gown fluttering behind her. "He hasn't shown any interest in me. He hardly says a word."

Suppressing the urge to chuckle, Madeleine watched her brother quietly follow Gabriel through the crowd. "Désirée, he never says much of anything. The more interest he has in you, the *less* he'll be inclined to speak."

Désirée's shoulders wilted. "Well, that isn't very encouraging, is it? Has he said anything to you? Left any indication that I'm not on a fool's errand to like him?"

"I regret that he hasn't." Madeleine reached out, stopping the frantic woman with a gentle touch. "Jean-Paul would be an absolute imbecile not to find you attractive. You just have to give him time. He'll come around."

Désirée sighed, nodding once. "I suppose you're right. Please don't judge me for behaving like a child."

Madeleine laughed outright. "You could always ask him to dance yourself, you know."

A visible shudder shook Désirée's slender form. "I'm not that desperate, thank you. What a notion."

Leaning close, Madeleine let a mischievous twinkle pass through her eyes. "If it's to be, it will be. Can you imagine—the two of us sister-in-laws twice over?"

Désirée tried to bite back the grin threatening to overtake her blushing face, but still it spread. "Don't aid me in conjuring such fantasies. I don't even know if he cares for me one bit." The pure

44

bliss of young love traced the lines of her face as she gazed at him across the lively party. No matter that she was a baron's daughter pining after a blacksmith. She'd never even considered his station, Madeleine guessed as she watched her with hopeful interest.

Before she could utter another word of encouragement, a shadow fell over them both. Madeleine glanced up at the looming figure, at once struck by the solemn face staring back. Icy chills skittered up her arms, her stomach plunging. He held out one gloved hand and bent low, a picture of elegance despite the turmoil his very presence erupted.

"Might I have the pleasure of this dance, signora?" The dark eyes beneath his mask lifted ominously to hers, fastening her in place.

Madeleine swallowed, her chest already pumping. She could try to run, but what would that do? Even if she escaped him, he could easily harm the family she'd left behind if he wanted to. She tried desperately to keep her hand steady as she placed it into his. "Of course." The words barely fled from her trembling lips.

Beside her, Désirée's brows furrowed as she tilted inward. "Madeleine, you don't have to dance with him if you don't want to." Concern lit her gaze, passing from Madeleine to their intruder.

"It's all right, Désirée." Madeleine could say no more before the man whisked her away, tugging her from any sense of security. Better for her to reunite with Stefano in private, far from the Clement family's cares.

The viola's whimsical song took on a grainy quality as it buzzed in Madeleine's ears. She could barely think, barely move, letting her former lover lift her arms into a waltzing pose as if a ragdoll cast into the shadows. Desperate for balance, Madeleine held tight to his sturdy form as they launched into a triangular pattern over the ancient Roman street.

Drawing in a quivering breath, she let her gaze lock with his. The coffee-colored stare shining back through his mask remained cold, mysterious. Even with half his face covered, the familiar divots around his mouth, his stern lips, his high cheekbones—twisted an unexpected sensation in her gut. She had loved him once. She had shared his bed. Though her broken memories told her to fear him, she couldn't deny the instincts reminding her of the bond they'd once shared.

"Nothing to say to me after all this time?" His voice rang strong, deep. It felt harder than the voice in her memories, and yet perhaps that was a result of whatever had transpired between them.

Madeleine's mind whirred with incomprehensible words, unable to capture the right thing to say. "You are the one who sought me out. You should say whatever is on your heart."

A mirthless smile dented his cheek, fire igniting in his eyes despite his placid facade. "You always did know how to turn things around," he said, voice dry. "Even after what you did, you insist I speak first. I don't know what else I expected."

Forcing her feet to keep up with the waltz, Madeleine searched his gaze. Her mind hunted for the truth amid what little she knew. What had she done? Sought a relationship with him out of clandestine motives, surely. But how had their union been shattered, when clearly her heart had yielded to his in spite of her wicked intentions? Scattered memories of him churned in her mind, and yet the deeper she dug beneath the surface, the more confusion arose.

"Do you think you can manipulate me into falling under your spell again?" he asked, calling her back to the present. "Do you think your beauty will entice me the way it did back on that balcony in Venice, when I never imagined the depths of depravity lurking beneath your skin?"

Her body quivered at his words. The hand on her hip clamped harder, bile spewing from his scowling face. The pain of his sword ripping her skin open surged anew, overwhelming her. Yet still she kept her head high, begging her every part not to wilt in fear of him.

"Of course not. The past is behind us. It's gone." Or buried until she discovered more of the wretched person she once was. "I have nothing to say that you don't already know. I betrayed you. I will not run from that."

Stefano regarded her angrily an agonizing moment before his grip loosened. "At least you admit that much." His head shook, candlelight glinting off his dark hair. "I should have known Auguste was a rat the moment I met him. A youth with that much ambition? He was bound to stab me in the back at the first opportunity."

"If it helps, he turned on me, too." Her own brother, her very flesh. The ache of it still clung to her.

His gaze tangled with hers a pensive second, the first glimmer of humanity sparking them. "It doesn't." He sighed. "I should have seen through *both* of you. Seen that what we had was nothing but a farce."

Stefano twirled her at that precise moment, spinning Madeleine's vision in a whir of light and disjointed music. When she landed back in his hands, a spark of vulnerability shone back in spite of his clenched jaw and firm mouth. She had hurt him—more than a proud man like him would ever admit.

"It wasn't always a farce," she said quietly. "Not to me."

He blinked, considering her a long moment. "How can that be true after the way you left me, deceitful as the day we met?"

Madeleine swallowed the emotion clouding her throat. How badly she wished she could remember what she did, why she did it, make sense of the conflicting emotions battling within her when she gazed into his face. "I'm sorry, Stefano."

The lips beneath his golden mask snarled. "'Sorry' doesn't begin to atone for what you did. You *owe* me."

At his cruel shift, the panic creeping over Madeleine for weeks blasted to the surface. She tried to pull away from him, but he held

47

her firm, the pace of their waltz never broken. "Please, Stefano. Let the past stay buried. I'm no longer the person I was in Venice."

"Indeed, you are Baroness d'Avance now," his voice rasped above her, "wife of Baron Gabriel Clement." His words stilled her, his curling lips sowing a seed of dread deep in her core. "You should know from all your *research* that I have as many eyes in Rome as I do in Venice."

Madeleine glanced through the crowd to find her husband looking on from beside an elaborate statue. She hadn't feared for his safety since Pascal had ripped through their lives. Now, the cold stare trailing hers to the place Gabriel stood said Stefano wouldn't show mercy. In fact, he would relish making her family suffer.

"What do you want?" she managed, breath quickening. Already, Gabriel wound his way toward them with urgency in his step. She halted their dance, attempting to wrench free of Stefano's constricting clutches.

His fingers dug at her skin the harder she pulled, the hand at her side keeping her flush against him. "You will make him do what I say," he said, hot breath showering her neck. "You will convince him to cement a deal with me or I will tell him exactly who you are. The things you did while you lived in my house." His evil gaze slid up her arm to her eyes, any shred of humanity in them gone. "I will ruin you both publicly and for my own amusement."

Her heartbeat bashed against his surging chest as they stood pressed to one another, the sins of her past affixing them forever. She knew it now as his malicious eyes held hers, as her flesh burned under his coiling fingertips. She would never escape him—not a man like Stefano Cavaretta. He would make her pay, one way or another.

"*Mi scusi, signore,*" Gabriel broke through their trance, addressing Stefano in broken Italian. "Unhand my wife at once."

With one last flash of his threatening glare, Stefano released her and stepped backward. "*Désolée*, Baron Clement," he responded in French, never looking away from her. "My apologies."

Gabriel took her hand gingerly, lifting her arm into the candlelight to reveal finger marks on her skin. "Are you all right?" he murmured, only to her. When she swiftly nodded, his fingers lovingly squeezed hers before he directed his flared nostrils and narrowed eyes at Stefano. "And who, may I ask, are you?"

The Italian stood tall, ballooning his chest proudly as if he hadn't just been caught injuring a woman. "Forgive me, Baron. We've corresponded so often, I feel like we truly know one another. I am Stefano Cavaretta."

"Ah, you're Cavaretta." Gabriel hooked a protective arm around Madeleine. "Well, in the future, I respectfully ask that you cease your requests on my barony and that you steer clear of my wife." With a gentle nudge, he began to lead her away.

A conceited chuckle lit the air behind them. "I think you will see things differently once we've had a chat in person."

Gabriel didn't bother to look back as he guided Madeleine through the rush of dancers. "I'm sure that I won't," he threw over his shoulder. "You should take your inquiries elsewhere. *Bon soir, monsieur.*"

Long after Gabriel had rescued her from the painful reminder of her past, Madeleine felt Stefano's eyes on her, his leering stare tracing her every footstep. She couldn't relax until they had safely returned to their hotel suite, and even then she sat at the edge of the bed, worry assaulting her every thought. Even if she succeeded in getting Stefano what he wanted, could he really leave her be after she'd tricked him so cruelly?

The mattress beneath her sank with Gabriel's weight. Madeleine turned to find him still dressed in waistcoat and trousers, reclined on his pillow and watching her in the flicker of candlelight. Loosening the final pin from her hair, she let her raven mane cascade over her shoulders. The freed strands tickled the neck above her satin nightdress. His stare never left her, a placid smile reaching his ocean eyes as she snuggled into the vacant spot next to him.

"Gabriel?" she asked, prompting his brows upward. She took a breath, wondering how to proceed. "Who was that man at the party? The one who danced with me?"

Irritation pinched his lips at the mention of Cavaretta. "He's a powerful diplomat who lives in Venice. A *criminal* is more precise a term."

The word pierced her gut. So he *did* know something of the man whose bed she'd once shared. "What makes you say that?" Her fingertip absently traced the elaborately stitched lines of the bedspread, trying to rip her focus off the quaking fear still shrouding her.

Gabriel sighed, sitting up and beginning to work the buttons of his waistcoat. "He has been writing to me for months now, requesting use of our land to haul cargo from Italy to Paris. Apparently everyone else on his route has agreed to his terms—a hefty sum in exchange for their cooperation."

An aching instinct told Madeleine exactly what Stefano's plan entailed, but she had to feign ignorance. "I don't understand," she said, inwardly mourning at this playacting with the one person she trusted above all others.

"No man who is running a legitimate operation needs to bribe land owners in order to transport goods." Gabriel opened his waistcoat and yanked it off his shoulders. "Whatever he's bringing to Paris is illegal, most likely dangerous. I don't want a hand in it."

Yet if he continued to deny Stefano, consequences would rain on his head. Madeleine bit her lip. "How much is he offering? Perhaps you should at least hear his plan before dismissing it outright."

Dumbstruck, Gabriel stopped unfastening the cuffs of his shirt long enough to look at her in wonder. "My dear, there is no amount of money that could convince me to aid in whatever malfeasance he's up to. You witnessed yourself the lengths he would go to threaten me. I won't put you in harm's way again."

Madeleine pressed her cheek to her downy pillow, watching in silence as Gabriel pulled his shirt over his head and donned his night clothes. How could she argue with such solid and compassionate logic? He believed Stefano's actions were directed at him, never dreaming that an even darker past than he already knew lurked behind his loving wife. Madeleine shuddered, the prospects of Stefano's revenge racing unbridled through her mind. She had to stop it, whatever he had in mind.

Surrendering to her husband's embrace, to the strong arms that enclosed her, the balmy kisses falling on her skin, Madeleine knew her answer. She would protect him, against an army of evildoers if she had to. She would keep this virtuous man from the pitfalls waiting in the dark to ensnare him, even if it meant selling her very soul to do it.

Six

Morning sparkled over the landscape of Rome in a brilliant splash of color. The tiny, kindling light on the horizon spread until it coated the heavens in purple hues. Wind swept over the hills, smashing into the stone houses and rattling the shutters. From her perch on her hotel balcony, Madeleine hugged her arms tighter around her satin robe and watched the night fade away through a mist of tears. She remembered now. Remembered why she had left, and why Stefano Cavaretta shook the depths of her soul every time the mere thought of him breached her memories.

Throughout the night's endless course, dreams had haunted her. She'd tossed about in bed, her mind a whirl of unpleasant visions with Stefano's shadowed figure lurking. At last, she'd woken in a shivering sweat, the memory of their parting so vivid in her mind, she'd thought for certain she lived it that very night.

She'd seen Venice, the elegant townhouse she shared with Stefano. In her dream, she sat at the sleek cherrywood piano nestled in his salon, her fingertips brushing the keys but never playing a note. Night had fallen over the city, the scents of salt and algae drifting through the open window, ominous shadows slanting across the posh furnishings.

A cold, nauseous sensation had sprouted within. She looked to the closed door. Stefano's voice drifted faintly from his study. Could she really tell him all that rested upon her heart? Auguste would hate her. Yet how could she maintain this act any longer—tricking the man she loved, selling his secrets at a profit?

Madeleine closed her eyes against the pounding in her head. She had expected something different when she agreed to seduce Stefano. Auguste had painted him as a vile man willing to step on anyone he could for his own gain. Surely, she had witnessed his dishonest practices while living within his walls, the untoward dealings he performed behind the veil. He knew how to work the people around him like chess pieces—employees, other officials, even those sworn to uphold the law. But did he deserve a woman pledging her love to him and stabbing him from behind at the next turn?

Her fingers gripped the piano's side, knuckles blanching. Each night she filled his bed, the heavier her burden weighed. She'd convinced herself she could tell him she loved him a thousand times and never feel it, unite her body with his and remain detached. But her guilt had matured until it suffocated her, the unexpected longing for him twisting amid her heartache like tangled vines.

Propelling herself off the piano bench, Madeleine marched toward the door. She would tell him. She *had* to tell him. If it came from her own mouth, he might still forgive her, begin a new, authentic relationship in spite of her sins. Her slippers clicked over the marble floors as she rushed down the hall to the landing, her plum-colored silk skirts rustling on the stairs.

Her skin flushed, her heart pumping with furious excitement as she lifted a fist to knock at the slightly open door to his study. Then, a voice froze her in mid-motion. He wasn't alone in there. The mingling of several masculine tenors touched her ears.

"You were the only person to have contact with Bianchi," Stefano said to an unseen person behind the door. "Who else could have apprised him of our plans?"

"I don't know, but it wasn't me. I swear it."

Madeleine carefully stepped to the side to get a better view. Through the narrow space by the doorjamb, she saw Stefano standing over a familiar employee, who appeared tied to a chair with ropes.

"That shipment from Barcelona was a secret," Stefano nearly shouted, teeth exposed. "The three of us were the only ones who even knew of its existence, yet somehow, another bidder materialized as if from nowhere and undercut us. You know how essential that cargo was to my plans, don't you?"

"Yes, yes, of course I do." The constrained man's voice had risen to panic.

"That's why you chose to betray me and aid my competition in obtaining the goods instead. You knew they would pay you handsomely."

"*No,* Stefano. I would never betray you."

The cold scrape of metal lit the air as Stefano withdrew a dagger from its sheath at his side. Chair legs thumped the floor as the man wiggled within his confines. Madeleine's hand fell limp at her side, her stomach churning. *She* had exposed his plans with Bianchi to Stefano's competition. She had read a correspondence between them and taken the information to Auguste.

"You had best come up with an explanation quickly," Stefano growled, knife glinting in the candlelight. Surely he was only threatening the innocent man he suspected of her crimes. He couldn't hurt a loyal subordinate, not for a crime he hadn't proved the man even committed.

"Please, Stefano. *Please!* It wasn't me." The man gulped against the blade now pressed at his throat as if an animal prepared for sacrifice. His eyes squeezed shut, tears rushing down his skin. "I didn't do it, Stefano. I didn't do it. Please, I—" But the blade cut through his pleading.

Madeleine silently gasped, her hand shielding her open mouth. The man slumped forward in the chair, blood pooling at his chest. Her whole body ached to watch Stefano nonchalantly accept a handkerchief from Diego and wipe his dagger before returning it to its sheath.

Stumbling backward, she caught herself against the wall before she exposed herself to the men in Stefano's study. Blood pulsed wildly through her veins as she moved as quietly as possible, tip-toeing her way to the bedroom she shared with him. She couldn't stay here another moment, sleeping next to a murderer, wondering when he would come for her. She had to get out, and quickly. After what she had just witnessed, surely her fear would reveal her the moment he touched her.

With hands like leaves trembling in the wind, she bustled about the candlelit bedroom, stuffing whatever valuables she could into a valise. Her clothes she would gladly leave behind. They could all be replaced. But she and Auguste would need her jewelry to secure passage away from the city tonight.

A sudden tap on the window made her jump. Madeleine swung wide eyes to the exposed pane, relief flooding her to see Auguste on the other side. She left her valise open on the rose-scented bedspread, her skirts dancing as she jogged to the window.

"We have to leave now," Auguste said before she could speak a word.

Madeleine poked her head out, stomach swaying to find her brother clinging to the flimsy trellis so high up on the wall. "What's happened?"

"You remember Costa, don't you?"

She nodded. "Of course. He partnered with Stefano last year when he needed to circumvent the embargo on tobacco. Stefano trusts him."

"Precisely." Auguste breathed, eyes wild. "He caught me passing information to one of my partners. It could have been by chance, but he heard everything. He's on his way here to expose us. He can't be far behind me."

Swallowing back her fright, Madeleine bobbed her head. "All right, I'm coming. Let me get my valise." She whirled in the opposing direction, only to freeze as footsteps approached the bedroom. Softly she moved backward, clicking the window closed behind her back.

Stefano appeared tired when he sauntered into the bedroom, ragged. He threw her a half-hearted smile, working at the cuffs of his linen shirt. His boots pounded the wooden floor, every step a stab to her gut, until he sank into a lounge chair by the bed. Staring off into the corner, he didn't seem to notice the valise beneath her pillow, wide open and sparkling with gems.

"Did you have an arduous day?" she barely managed the words, hoping her figure fully blocked Auguste's descent down the trellis.

"Hmmmm?" Stefano lifted a brow, still shrouded in his private musings. "It certainly was an interesting day." He frowned, inhaling through his nose. "Some tasks my business requires are not pleasant ones."

Madeleine's fingers clamped on the sill at her back, cold sweat forming on her skin. *Like killing a man, a man who did nothing wrong?* The sight of his poor victim, soaked in his own blood, still wrenched at her. Madeleine couldn't help wondering if she could have saved him from facing the penalty meant for her.

Stefano shook his head, slowly unfastening the buttons of his waistcoat. "I'd rather not think on it right now. Why don't you come sit with me?" His gaze fell over her longingly, seeking a distraction from his vile crimes, no doubt. When he held out his hand, Madeleine had no choice but to drag herself across the floor, feeling like a lamb being herded to the slaughter.

Her entire body cringed as she eased into his lap, feigning the smile she'd painted on her lips so many times before. Stefano's fingertips brushed the dark hair from her face, his admiring gaze tumbling over her features. Madeleine fought every instinct to harden as his lips gently pressed hers, forging a trail over her jaw and down her throat. Clinging to him, she tried to steady her rapid breathing and racing heart.

He paused, pulling back to watch the mad thump of her pulse in her neck. His narrowed gaze swept down her arms to her hands, confusion deepening their color. "Antoinette, are you quite well?" His concerned gaze lifted to hers. "You're trembling."

Stomach plummeting, she conjured a shaky smile. "I'm sure it's just a passing ailment. I haven't felt myself all day." Better he think her sick than terrified to be in his arms.

Reaching up, he pressed the back of his hand to her forehead. Even through his amber cologne, she caught the whiff of fresh blood. "You don't have a fever. Perhaps it's something you ate." She prayed he wouldn't see through her as he studied every plane of her face. "You should get to bed."

Before she could think to distract him, Stefano's gaze had curved to the bed they shared, her incriminating valise in plain view. He halted, staring at it a long moment as if trying to comprehend its meaning, before pinning an accusing look on her. "Were you packing to leave when I came in?"

Madeleine attempted to pull her hands from his, but his fingers held her firm. "I—" Her throat closed tightly, dry as desert sand. What could she possibly say to free herself? She remembered the body downstairs, icy chills peppering her skin to imagine her own being hauled away with it.

"You *what?*" Stefano's fingers pressed harder, digging to her bones. "You saw what happened, didn't you? You spied on my private affairs."

Hot tears sprinkled her cheeks, her wrists screaming in pain. "I didn't mean to. I was only coming to speak with you."

His suspicious stare darted between her eyes. "What I did has nothing to do with you, with *us.*"

"Stefano, please let me go." Panic surged in her chest. He would never let her leave, not after she'd watched him kill a man in cold blood.

Bewildered anger plagued his eyes, rage and deliberation warring there. "So you're leaving with every piece of jewelry I've ever given you?" His teeth gritted, breath cascading over her skin like fire. "You're so afraid of me now that you have to get away, but not before you take your payment for having to live with me these past two years?"

Madeleine stilled, surprised to see actual hurt teeming from the depths of his eyes. In her frenzy, she had nearly forgotten the bond they'd shared. Yes, he had revealed himself to be a criminal and murderer, but he'd never betrayed *her.* Perhaps she could still use this fact, employ the acting skills she'd worked so hard to acquire.

"Of course not. I lived here because I love you." Thrusting aside her fear, she gazed sincerely into his distrustful eyes. She didn't need to lie. "Stefano, I *love* you."

The hard line of his jaw reluctantly softened, the fingers clamped around her wrists giving slack. His own emotions bubbled to the surface in inky eyes that still shone with love for her, above the anger, above the suspicion. Madeleine knew in that moment that he still might forgive her, that if she could overlook his sins, their love didn't have to perish. Then carriage wheels jangling up the street plunged her back to reality, reminding her of Auguste waiting behind the house for her, replaying Stefano's image slicing an innocent man's throat. She had to take action before they both died at his hands.

Madeleine's heart mourned as she took one last long look into his eyes. His hands had slipped from hers; she had her chance.

Letting her palm glide to his forearm, she shook her head. "I can't stay here," she said, dropping her hand before he could react and snatching his dagger from its sheath.

Energy pulsed in her veins as Madeleine sprang from his lap, knife posed in front of her. The ominous weapon glittered beneath shifting candlelight, its pointed end all she could see over his incensed face. She couldn't think, couldn't form a proper plan. She would have to defend herself moment by moment.

Rising up on his palms, Stefano glared through slitted eyes, nostrils ballooning. "How dare you point that at me? I'm the one who taught you how to hold it." In one swift motion, he yanked another concealed dagger from his boot and jumped to his feet.

Madeleine stiffened. In all the time they'd lived beneath the same roof, she'd never noticed any hidden weapons. Perhaps her affection for him had blinded her. Now she stood face to face with the man she'd embraced a thousand times, every kiss tunneling genuine care for him deeper inside. She would have to fight him or die. The thought carried more sadness than fear.

Lifting her chin, she adjusted her hold on the dagger's hilt. "You taught me well. You know I have the potential to beat you." Indeed, endless hours spent in his practice room had ensured it. When he'd grown tired of swordplay, he'd taught her knife fighting. When that no longer interested him, they'd graduated to hand-to-hand combat. She had a multitude of bruises to show for it, but priceless training that he couldn't take back.

Rage visibly throbbed from every pore of his reddened skin. Stefano growled, positioning his knife beside his head, before charging at her full-force. Madeleine leaped to the side, his blade whooshing in her ear as it narrowly missed her face. Quickly recovering, she tried to jab him with an uppercut that tore the shirt beneath his unfastened waistcoat. When he returned her assault, their arms wound about each other's, both desperately trying to gain an advantage.

Breath rushed through her lungs, forming a staccato rhythm out her lips. She ducked each time his knife angled near her face, jumped back as it dove at her torso. The quick pace of knife fighting exhausted her in minutes, warm sweat slicking her skin and hair. They'd practiced this dance so many times before, and yet never like this. Never had their very lives depended on it.

Stefano swung at her in an arch, his blade nearly slicing her cheek. Almost losing her footing, Madeleine had to block his follow-up stab rather than avoid it. Pain wailed from her hand as his knife nicked her knuckles, the metallic clash of their blades reverberating through the air. Wrenching her wrist, she bent her dagger around his, thrusting upward. Stefano instinctively jerked his arm from danger, but in so doing left a gap for her attack. Trying not to think, Madeleine swiped hard at his torso, the action halting him.

Taking a step back, she watched in horror as Stefano's knife tumbled to the floor. He turned a confused expression on his chest, where a sickening stain of bright red had blossomed through his shirt. Everything within Madeleine begged her to help him as he dropped to his knees, his blood pooling on the wooden floorboards. He lifted his awestruck gaze to hers, his agony at her betrayal driving into her gut as if his blade had stabbed her, too.

Rushing footsteps on the stairs launched her into motion. Hand still gripping the dagger protectively, she snatched the open valise with the other and made for the window. She tossed the blade into her bag, swiping away at her tears as she climbed through the open pane and secured herself on the trellis.

Stefano's haunted gaze met hers through the window. She allowed herself one last glance of him, shirt soaked in the blood she'd spilled, his heart open on his paling face. "I'm sorry, Stefano. I'm so sorry."

Their bedroom door swung open, prompting her to scramble down the trellis and jump atop Auguste's horse behind him. The guilt of what she'd done clung to her as the horse's clopping hooves sprinted through the streets, transporting them over the bridge to their escape route. Throughout the next few arduous days, she'd often wondered whether he'd survived his wounds, questioned how she could go on after that night. When the news brought no word, she knew he would recover—and that he would keep their fateful dispute a secret to preserve his own reputation.

Now, standing atop her balcony, staring out at the glistening streets of Rome through her tears, she couldn't escape the past. Her hands pressed the cold stone railing, her body shivering at the memory of her own violence. She could have killed a man that night, a man she had loved and wanted to save from himself. Instead, she had become him, transformed into the worst version of herself.

Two arms came around her, the smell of a new man's musky cologne enveloping her. Madeleine closed her watery eyes, still drenched in past sorrows as his lips gently pressed her jaw. "You're up early," Gabriel murmured in her ear. "Did you have trouble sleeping?"

Her vision splashed with crystalized beams of light as she opened her eyes again to the city. "I just wanted to see Rome in the morning. When it's still peaceful and quiet." The confetti of last night's revelries remained strewn across the pavement, but nary a soul ventured out.

Gabriel smiled against her cheek, taking in the age-old homes and distant hills with her. "I'm glad we came. Thank you for dragging me out of my shell and into the real world." He cradled her through her nightdress, his strong forearms wound around her middle. "We should make a whole wedding tour of this. What do you say we see Florence after this, then the Alps on the way home?"

Revolving in his arms, she surveyed his face in the morning light—the messy mop of dark hair and sideburns, the subtle whiskers peppering his square jaw. "I would go anywhere with you." *I would do anything for you.*

His bright eyes gazed back with so much love, such trust. Her heart leaped in her throat to realize that it wasn't Stefano he needed protection from, but her. *Her* sinful scheming, *her* treacherous past. A man like Gabriel Clement didn't deserve a wife who kept buried secrets of torrid affairs, near murders, maybe a thousand other transgressions she couldn't yet recall.

Gabriel leaned close and kissed her forehead, the safety of his presence both calming her fears and propelling the guilt deeper. Laying her head against his sturdy shoulder, Madeleine tried to quiet the voice warning she must leave in order to save him. Yet still it persisted, the sinister walls of her past closing in, her evils no longer something she could outrun. So she clung to him, held onto today, wondering if they would see tomorrow together.

Seven

"**I**'m so excited. I can barely keep my heart from bouncing outside my chest." Désirée hopped to her tiptoes, trying to get a better view over the swollen crowd cramming the sidewalk.

Cecile leaned close and smirked. "She's going to be a chore to drag home once the festivities are over." She and Madeleine shared a chuckle, love for their friend alive in both flushed faces.

Anticipation winged about the huddled street, impossible to escape. Down the street, Madeleine could barely glimpse the Piazza del Popolo, where a throng of horses were being suited for the Berber horse race. Their slick coats glistened beneath the high sun, their necks adorned with garlands of roses and chrysanthemums.

Madeleine held onto Cecile as the crowd jostled and cheered, demanding the race to begin. High above the streets, opulent citizens dressed in jewels and fur watched from private balconies. Désirée hadn't been able to secure them such a luxury at the last minute, but Madeleine didn't care. The familiarity of the humble citizens brought comfort despite the crude smell and wild antics of those around her.

"I hope the men will find us," Désirée said, her worried gaze scanning the crowd. "I told Gabriel not to dawdle too long at the bathhouse. He just had to do something *historical.*"

"They'll come." Madeleine adjusted her yellow cashmere shawl higher on her shoulders. "I told them exactly where to find us. They can't be far behind now." Despite her words, a tingling sensation skittered up her arms.

Before she could even identify the feeling, a new face had emerged beside her. Madeleine glanced up to find Stefano at her arm, so close that gooseflesh dotted her exposed skin. He wasted not a sideways look at her, stern gaze fixed on the horses up the street.

"Any new developments in regard to our arrangement?" he asked, throat visibly swallowing above his knotted cravat. "Have you been able to manipulate your husband the way you so skillfully toyed with me?"

Madeleine angled toward him, wary of Désirée and Cecile noticing him. "I will never deceive him," she said in a low tone. "Just as he will never have a hand in your crimes."

Irritation flicked over his brow, though he kept his face even. "That's unfortunate. The baron doesn't strike me as the kind of man who deserves to have utter ruin brought upon him." He tugged at his gloves, as if preparing for the deed this very moment.

"He's a better man than you could ever comprehend." Madeleine's lips compressed, eyes flashing up at him. "Do whatever you like to me, but keep him out of it. He doesn't deserve to pay for what I did."

His dark gaze fell over her, studying her every feature, weighing her words. "I wish it were that simple. I would gladly deliver the consequences of your treachery upon you. But my ambitions hinge upon your husband's cooperation, not yours."

Heart fluttering, she scanned the crowd for Gabriel's face. "What is stopping you from just bringing what you need across our borders? How will he even know?"

"I could take that chance, but what if he gets wind of it? What if a farmer sees my wagons and reports my activity? The baron could get me in a lot of trouble, a problem I'd like to avoid. I rather like my life free of prison bars."

Madeleine huffed. "Are the law enforcement officials in Paris immune to your bribery?" She tried not to think about the content of his cargo—items meant for a sinister purpose, surely. Or drugs. "There has to be another way. I can't force Gabriel to do something he doesn't want to."

An unsettlingly pleasant smile tweaked his face as he watched the horses preparing to launch, the mass about them rippling with excitement. "You're a resourceful girl. I'm sure you'll think of something."

The race commenced with a trumpet's blare and the blast of a gun. Madeleine barely processed the horses springing from their confines in the plaza, thundering past the screaming crowd in a torrent of clopping hooves down the Via Lata. Their wild stampede only grazed her ears as she stared up at the bitter, wounded man above her.

"I know it doesn't mean anything now," she said, attracting his dark eyes to her, "but I truly am sorry for that night. I meant to deceive, yes. But I didn't want to hurt you. That was never my intention." The sight of him on his knees and swathed in blood still wrenched her insides.

Stefano locked his steady gaze on her face, penetrating her skin, searching the depths of her. The tiniest bit of emotion stirred behind his stony eyes, perhaps the remembrance that he'd loved her, too. That their relationship wasn't as hollow as they both liked to pretend. His clean-shaven jaw clenched, his breath ragged. Then, the icy shield slipped back over his face, his stare sweeping to the horses pummeling past them.

"That was a long time ago," he said, voice hard.

Swallowing back her emotion, Madeleine tried to concentrate on the last animals sprinting behind their comrades. She didn't expect Stefano to ever forgive her, but his silence stung worse than his cruelty. At least she could be angry at that. Silence forced her to evaluate her terrible role in their history, the despicable things she'd done for money.

"Signore Cavaretta," a new voice rang in her ear. Madeleine twisted around to find Gabriel behind her, dubious gaze raking her former lover. "Why is it every time I turn around now, you're standing too close to my wife?"

Stefano's banal laugh buzzed the air. "*Pardonnez-moi,* Baron. We were just catching up." His suggestive gaze perused her ashen face. "From last night, of course."

Gabriel stepped near, hauling Madeleine protectively to his side. "I hope you weren't trying to weasel your way into accessing our land for your own gain. My wife is not to be used as an arbitrator."

"Certainly not." A cool smile curled Stefano's lips, though danger flared in his eyes. "I was just leaving. In fact, I must depart Rome tomorrow night." Screwing his top hat over his styled hair, he backed away through the crowd. "There are many preparations and so little time left."

Long after he had turned and strutted down the street like a peacock, his words echoed through her mind. They were a warning, a time limit. If she didn't devise a plan before the sun fell over the seven hills, he would destroy her. Worse, he would hurt the kind, benevolent man that she loved.

Gabriel swept a thumb down her cheekbone, his eyes hunting hers. "He didn't hurt you, did he?" At the shake of her head, he sighed and drew her against his shoulder. The odor of sulfur from the bathhouse mingled with his cologne as she leaned into his velvety overcoat and closed her eyes. "I won't let anyone hurt you," he whispered into her ear.

Yet as the crowd milled and jostled around them, Madeleine knew the responsibility lay solidly on her shoulders. She alone could conjure the means to bind them together or watch them be torn apart. So she held tight to his comforting form and prayed for the resourcefulness and strength to outwit Stefano Cavaretta one more time.

M adeleine sighed as she adjusted her crimson silk skirts once more, her legs bobbing beneath. The carriage she rode in swayed to a stop, launching her heartbeat into a frenzied rhythm. She peered out the window at the endless sea, now a black well under a slice of moonlight. This had to be the best solution. *It had to be.* Yet still the sting of betrayal clung to her as she accepted Serge's hand and stepped down to the street.

"I'll only be a few moments," she said, avoiding his gaze. After lifting her velvet hood over her hair, she grabbed two handfuls of her gown and carefully traversed the darkened ground leading to the docks.

The air here felt light and cool, a welcome retreat from the heat of the day. The scents of oleander and lemon mingled over the lapping sea, whose tides beat against the shore and percussively knocked boats into the docks. Among the gathered assembly of masts lined up in the cloudless night sky, she spotted the one she sought. She would recognize the double mast and long bowsprit of that majestic vessel anywhere.

Heart in her throat, she thought briefly of asking Serge to join her. She could meet any member of Roux's ship upon her arrival, perhaps a number of them. Surely they wouldn't all prove as gentle and benevolent as their leader. Shaking her head, she kept on. She would have to risk it for the sake of her husband. Nobody else could hear what she had to tell Christophe.

As details of his ship emerged in the quiet night, Madeleine's blood warmed. The mighty brigantine appeared all but abandoned, except for a familiar figure seated on the deck keeping watch. He saw her instantly, standing to his broad, full height as she wandered down the gangplank and boarded the *Faucon*.

The man stood frozen in place, watching her approach. Despite her misgivings, Madeleine willed her feet to keep moving. When she stood a mere arm's length from him, her worries somehow dissolved. Hours beneath the sun had roughened and bronzed his skin. His hair appeared longer, its wild tawny strands loose about his muscular shoulders. He was bigger than she recalled, his sinewy arms flexing as he stepped toward her. But still he wore a relaxed smile, a spark igniting his eye as if he held a secret only she knew.

"Why, Baroness." The title sounded like a queen's on his lips. "I had hoped you would grace us with your presence."

A smile crept across her mouth without any effort. "How could I not, with us both so far from home?"

Stepping closer, his arms extended warmly. "May I?"

Madeleine nodded, her arms encircling him as he pulled her into his. The salty aroma of his weather-beaten clothes evoked so many memories, and yet, as she retreated from his embrace, an unfamiliar feeling surprised her. His touch didn't set her skin ablaze, didn't make her knees go weak. She was now simply a woman greeting an old friend.

Christophe's blue eyes perused her finely stitched cloak and beaded gown with approval. "Aristocracy suits you."

At his admiration, she clamped an uneasy hand over one elbow. "Are you all alone? Where is the rest of your crew?"

"I let them go off and have their fun." His eyes never left her. "I've had enough revelry for the week. It's my turn to guard the ship." He paused, voice lowering conspiratorially. "It's just the two of us."

Shifting from foot to foot, Madeleine glanced around for a distraction. Her gaze landed on the unfamiliar figurehead adorning the ship's bow. "Why have you replaced the falcon?"

Christophe's gaze flitted to the spot in question, where a mermaid with a fanciful tail and hair discreetly covering her bare chest proudly faced the world. "We hit a storm off the coast of Venezuela and ran aground. The ship managed to survive the assault, but our poor bird was destroyed. She's the *Sirene* now."

"The *Sirene*," Madeleine said, testing the name on her tongue. "I like it."

"So do I. A new name for a new age." Even with her stare averted, she could feel the weight of his gaze studying her. "But I gather talking about my ship was not why you paid me a visit tonight."

Madeleine ripped her wandering stare from the serene waters of the Tyrrhenian to his face. "What?" Could he really see so far into her, to know the turmoil plaguing her mind?

With a gentle smile, he covered the fingers she had fixed in midair with one giant hand. "You have not stopped fidgeting since you came aboard."

She sighed. "No, I suppose I haven't." Wary of his warming touch, she pried her traitorous hands from beneath his and fastened them behind her back. "The truth is, I came here to ask for a favor. A rather large favor that I have no business asking."

Christophe's crystal eyes searched hers a painful moment before he reeled away and strode a few steps to the bulwark. His hair lifted in the soft wind as he looked out at the empty sea. Finally, he turned and eased himself against the ship's side, a sense of calm having fallen over his face. "Don't you have a husband for that now?" he asked, his wounded gaze finding her in the dark. "Is he not able to provide your every desire?"

Her stomach soured at his words. If only she could share this with Gabriel. If only he knew the immense agony just remembering her former life planted within. But experience had taught her that knowledge was pain, a burden she refused to place on the shoulders of the man who'd never performed an indecent act in his life. This was her problem to rectify, not his.

"I'm afraid he can't help with this one," she said, swallowing the last bit of her pride before she continued. "My past is complicated, *too* complicated for a rich man like him to understand. I must shield him from this."

Christophe regarded her for several more moments before he crossed his sturdy arms over his chest and nodded. "Then of course I'll do it."

Confusion strangled the joy threatening to erupt within her. "But you don't even know what it is yet." Surely Christophe would question her wish for him to aid a criminal in whatever devious acts he performed behind closed doors.

His gaze steadied, drilling so far into hers she thought it might collapse her. Something in those moonlit eyes volleyed an icy chill over her skin. "I made my feelings for you clear that day in the library," he said, evoking memories of their stolen kisses, of his sheltering embrace. "You chose another man, and I respect that. But that doesn't change how I feel about you. I would do anything for you, Madeleine."

The air suddenly sucked from her lungs, Madeleine placed a hand over her corseted middle. How could he still remain faithful after she'd married another man? "Well, now I fear I'm taking advantage of your affections."

"Don't." Christophe's head shook, the surety in his stare quieting her. "I'm well aware that you are his. That the hopes I harbored for the two of us have perished." His jaw worked, emotion welling across his chiseled face. "But still I am your friend, a friend who admittedly loves you too much," he said with a laugh, "but still a friend. I will do whatever you ask, gladly."

Madeleine shared in his self-deprecating chuckle, tears filming her eyes. "Thank you, Christophe. You have always been there when I needed you. Your friendship is far more than I deserve." Her guilt at his admission gave way to hope—the possibility that perhaps the nightmare of Stefano Cavaretta could really be behind her by the time they left Rome.

"Now what is this you need?" He rose and gestured toward the staircase leading to his office at the stern. "We'll have this solved in no time, I promise."

Basking in the luring sensation of safety for the first time in weeks, Madeleine followed him below decks to the lonely office drifting atop the sea. "If only I knew where to begin."

Eight

Despite the open window welcoming distant chatter from the street, the air inside Stefano Cavaretta's Roman townhome was thick, strangling in its density. Waiting behind the closed door his close confidant Diego had disappeared behind, Madeleine pulled her cashmere gloves higher and set her quivering jaw. She couldn't appear weak—not today. Tingles raced over her skin, her nerves screaming to run as fast as she could in the other direction. But she would stand firm. She would look her fear in the face.

The door swung open, Diego materializing. "He's ready for you." Standing back, he allowed her to pass by him into an impressive office space decked floor to ceiling in lavish adornment. Madeleine's gaze meandered over the plush crimson rugs set atop rich walnut floors, the chandeliers and marble cornicing, the enormous windows overlooking the Pantheon, until they landed on *him*. The devil himself, seated behind a beautifully carved desk, fingers laced before him.

Madeleine forced her reluctant legs to move, her heels clicking on the slick floor and satin skirts rustling in the quiet space. When she stood but a meter from him, she settled her hands on a chair back, praying they wouldn't tremble and give her away.

Dark eyes narrow, Stefano let them plummet down her day dress an unbearable moment before they settled pejoratively on her face. "Well?" he asked, tone accusing. "Have you managed to fell the mighty oak from his lofty height of superior morality?"

She swallowed. "No. I told you I never would."

Stefano's head shook. "That's unfortunate for the both of you."

"There is another way." Madeleine lifted her chin at his questioning gaze, ballooning her chest into a confident stance that defied every emotion coursing through her.

He scrutinized her for a long string of seconds, the skin above his high collar and cravat reddening, the strong shoulders beneath his jacket working. At last, he signaled to the man still stationed behind Madeleine. "Leave us a moment."

Madeleine held her breath, surprised that he would converse alone with a woman who had once stabbed him in the gut. The reality that he could quite easily kill her if he so desired sparked fear in her corseted stomach. Perhaps she shouldn't have let Jean-Paul remain in the street outside. Her only redemption might be the pistol tucked covertly beneath her skirts.

"I'm listening." Stefano leaned back in his chair, challenging her with a raise of his thick brows.

Clearing her throat, Madeleine summoned the words she must have rehearsed a hundred times since meeting with Christophe the night before. "I have a friend who captains a ship that's docked here in Rome."

"A *friend?*" Roguish delight shimmered in his coffee-colored eyes.

"Yes, a *friend.*" Her arms knotted over her chest at the accusation. "A friend I trust with my life. He has agreed to transport your cargo to the mouth of the Seine, where he will transfer it to a riverboat captain he knows, who will carry it into Paris. He knows how to elude the authorities if need be. You won't be caught."

"All this in exchange for...?" Stefano held out his palms like scales.

Madeleine's fingers blanched on the chair back. "For leaving us alone, of course. For us never having to see your face again."

It sounded harsher than she meant it, and the curve of his lips betrayed his indifferent exterior a split second before they pursed into a wicked simper. "For *him*, Baroness. What does your captain friend stand to benefit from all this extra work and time he could use seeking his own endeavors?"

Familiar guilt sprouted low. Of course he could have used the time for himself, and still he chose to help her even as it would slow business Christophe relied on to survive. "Nothing," she managed. "He stands to gain nothing. He is a generous man who volunteered his services because he cares enough to help a friend in need."

Stefano's malicious grin widened, his gaze raking her in suspicion. "Yet another man you have wrapped around your little finger, I see. By *nothing*, do you mean he's enjoying the same benefits that you showed me when you wanted something?"

Fighting tears, Madeleine set her lips into a stern line. She remembered their relationship all too well now—every embrace, every touch. She had fallen in love despite herself, the intimate times they'd shared a sincere expression of her devotion. Yet how could she explain that now, after their vicious parting had nearly killed him?

"Do you agree to my terms?" she forced, ignoring his condemning question.

Annoyance rumpled his brow before he sighed and dropped his hands to the desk. "I suppose so, if once I meet this captain of yours, I deem him fit for the job." His gaze bore into hers, loaded with so much more than his words conveyed. "Then our business will be complete and you'll never have to see *my face* again."

The emotion behind his eyes shook her core in a way she hadn't expected. Madeleine compelled her head to nod, gaze flying to the window in self-preservation. "Good. His name is Christophe Roux, captain of the *Sirene*. He's expecting your visit." With the final word barely choked from her aching throat, Madeleine whirled away and set off toward the door.

Before her shoes could hit the plush rug beyond the set of chairs at his desk, Stefano's voice halted her. "Christophe Roux, Gabriel Clement, me. How many more will get caught in the wake of your treachery before you've had enough of your games?"

Madeleine's breath came hard, her chest throbbing. She could only stand frozen as his chair legs scraped the wooden floor and the thump of his ominous footsteps neared. How badly she wanted to defend herself, to deny his every accusation. Yet as her trembling hands balled into fists at her side, the truth speared into her like a fisherman's hook. She was every bit as evil as he claimed, and so much more. She deserved whatever consequences awaited.

The vanilla scent of his silk clothes reached her nostrils before his presence loomed at her back. Madeleine made no move to avoid him, knowing he could knock her to the ground or thrust an unforeseen knife through her side with hardly any effort. Something deep inside wished that he would. At least penance might be paid for the endless list of sins piling at her feet.

"I'm not accustomed to thinking myself naive," he said, balmy breath sweeping the nape of her neck. "I've often questioned how I let you sleep beside me night after night for two years and never suspected a thing. How I could have been so tragically blinded to your schemes when usually I can sniff out a rat a town away." His fingers clamped on her ribcage. "But you're no ordinary rat, now, are you?"

Body stiffening, Madeleine forced herself to remain fixed in place despite her every instinct to recoil. She would fight. She would not run. Yet she knew if she moved against him, he would kill her and have an easy reason to justify it.

His fingers tightened, his touch growing simultaneously more intimate and commanding. Madeleine's jaw clenched, her stomach roiling at his audacity, her disgust somersaulting with her fear. "Take your hands off of me," she hissed through clenched teeth, cursing the quiver in her voice.

With his pompous face visible at her ear, Stefano let his amused gaze wander her openly, rising from the surging swell of her bodice to the blanched skin of her neck. His hold only constricted, his body pressing her back, his licentious gaze roaming her face before settling on her eyes. Malice lurked beneath their depths, his mouth curving mockingly. "Don't feign innocence with me now. Don't pretend you haven't been touched by a thousand different men in a thousand different ways."

The allegation sunk low in her gut, her stomach knotting. Of course she had let *him* touch her, more times than she cared to recall. But beyond that, she knew nothing. She remembered only Gabriel and the man now toying ruthlessly with her emotions. Whatever wicked lie he was about to conjure, she must remain firm against. She couldn't let him trick or intimidate her.

"What are you insinuating?" she finally dared to ask, eyes locked squarely with his.

A haunting chuckle escaped his throat, her skin creeping beneath drops of his spittle. "You really think I don't know after all this time?" He clicked his tongue, head shaking. "Honestly, I thought we knew each other more—*intimately* than that."

Her frustration swelled at his haughty brow and unnamed accusations. "Whatever it is you have to say, I wish you would just say it." Enough of his games. With her plans complete, she wanted nothing more than to race back to the safety of Gabriel's arms and forget this man forever.

Stefano leaned even closer, his chin resting upon her shoulder as if holding her like a lover would. "The truth hurt me more than

I expected it would. The manner in which you playacted your chastity truly fooled me."

He sighed, hands shifting to her middle, his embrace turning bizarrely affectionate. "You were so beautiful—this unattainable goddess I just had to possess. I threw aside any misgivings I might have otherwise had, especially when my advisors told me they could find no pertinent history for an Antoinette LaRivière. No family, no place of origin. I ignored their every suggestion and claimed you for my own because I wanted you *so badly.*"

The heat of his skin on hers launched electric shivers down her arms. She just wanted to be free of him, and yet the more tenderly he touched her, the more memories flooded her mind. She had loved him once, given herself so freely because she had worshiped his every move. It almost felt natural when his hand found hers at her hip, fingers lacing gently, even as it sent her heartbeat pounding with terror.

Stefano's lips grazed her ear as he turned to whisper into it. "Once upon a time, I imagined a life for the two of us. I thought you might be my forever home." Her eyes slipped shut as he held her tighter against him, memories of that sentiment fresh in her heart. "But that was before I knew you were seducing me in order to steal from me. Before I knew you were nothing but a *street harlot* who had clawed her way into my life from a filthy brothel in Paris."

At his final growled word, Madeleine's every hope plummeted. She made not a move, only let the horror of his accusation sink through every part of her like the slow descent of the sun. That couldn't be true. It couldn't. No brothel lay in her memory, no men besides Stefano and Gabriel. She had gone from her parents' home to the baker's shop, to the theater and Stefano's townhouse in Venice to the Château des Rêves—hadn't she?

"I was an actress when you met me," she said, eyes still shutting out the world. "You knew I was an actress. Some might say differently, but actress and harlot are *not* the same profession." Please, God, let that be what he meant.

"Yes, you were a very good actress, indeed." Stefano's hold tautened, digging into her ribs, his fingers crushing her hand. "But you failed to mention that before you graced audiences on the stage, you had a different lot gathered outside your door every night, waiting for a more sensational kind of performance. I never would have let you into my home had I known the gutter you climbed out of."

Madeleine's eyes popped open, her vision blurred in hot tears. The window's light crystallized as she swung her gaze from the blinding array into his narrowed brows and snarling lips. She hardly felt his vise-like grip compressing. The fury in his eyes said everything.

"No." All at once feeling as if locked in a cage, she struggled. "No, you're a liar." Frantically she wrenched her body free, whirling to face him. Her chest heaved beneath her disheveled bodice, tears threatening to wrack her body. "You would say anything to hurt me now. I never set foot in a brothel. I was *an actress!*" Her desperate words became a shout, her finger posed like a weapon.

Stefano stood with arms positioned outward on either side, the veins in his fists popping. "Why must you refuse to dispense with this useless charade after all you've put me through? I know who you are. I could run to the baron this very moment and destroy your entire life if I wanted to."

Gabriel. Oh, Gabriel. What would a claim like this do to him, real or fabricated? Madeleine pushed a hand over her flushed cheek, the possibilities running rampant. She had to protect him from the sting of this, no matter the cost. "You will stay away from my husband. We agreed."

Nose flaring and lips clenched, Stefano advanced on her, stopping only a hair's breadth away. "An accord with a strumpet like you means nothing to me. I will never seek your husband out again because I will not allow your defiled presence to dirty my doorstep again." A red hue had mounted from his chest to his seething face. "Now get out before you give me reason to kill you."

Madeleine blinked, the weight of their strained relationship pummeling her. How had love so easily transformed to hate, violence overturned affection? Even now, she saw twisted excitement blazing his body at their confrontation. He could easily reach out and take her to him, kiss her, hurt her, possess her, kill her. It was all the same to him, all a coiled mess within his perverted mind. Thank God she had escaped with her life the first time.

With one last look into his searing eyes, Madeleine spun and raced from his office. Her footsteps on the marble floors carried her down the stairs two at a time. She had to get out, had to feel the air on her skin once more, to cleanse herself of Stefano's lingering touch. His words replayed over and again in her mind as she burst from his front door into the street. *I would never have let you in my home had I known the gutter you climbed out of.* They crawled over her like spiders, burrowing into her darkest places.

Jean-Paul emerged from the shadowed alley, concern lacing his wrinkled brow. Two strong hands reached out to cover her arms. "What is it, Maddy? Did he hurt you?" His fingers contracted, the gleam of rage pouring into his usually placid visage. Madeleine knew if she waited a moment longer to answer him, he might charge up the stairs and cause a bigger problem.

"No," she said shakily. "No, he didn't hurt me." Tugging herself free, she moved away from the stone building Stefano occupied in Rome and stumbled into the plaza beyond. People milled about everywhere—throwing coins in the imposing fountain, excitedly shuffling into the Pantheon. Madeleine ignored them all, her head aching as she plunked down on the fountain's edge.

Her mind awhirl, she hardly noticed when Jean-Paul approached her cautiously, his colossal form casting a long shadow over her. His brows worked, his expression soft as he watched her. He looked so much like Mama when he worried—her kind, benevolent heart peering out from his sky-blue eyes. Madeleine's heart cried out to her memory, longing to feel the security of her mother's arms about her one more time.

"What is it?" Jean-Paul asked again. "What happened up there?"

Madeleine's shameful gaze dove to her boots. How could she even attempt to broach this subject with her brother? Her cheeks flamed just to imagine it. Yet as she listened to laughter echo off the walls of the buildings surrounding the piazza, she knew she must if she ever wanted to harbor joy in her heart again. She must know.

"Did I—" Her insides twisted, her fingertips scrunching her satin skirts. "Did I ever tell you where I went when the war separated us?"

"Of course. You lived with a baker's family in Butte-Chaumont."

She swallowed, daring herself to venture onward. "And after that? Before I discovered the theater where Auguste found me. Where did I go when the baker died and his family could no longer keep me?"

Silence met her question, driving fear to her bones. An agonizing moment lingered with only the splash of the fountain and chatter of Roman citizens buzzing in her ears. Then Jean-Paul shifted on his feet. "It doesn't matter now. That part of your life is over."

Madeleine lifted her gaze to find sorrowful eyes staring back. *"Please,* Jean-Paul. I need to know." Her heartbeat thumped wildly at the pain plaguing his face. "Cavaretta said that I worked in a brothel. That I was a—" The word refused to dislodge from her tongue, tears springing up to imagine the horrifying picture he had painted.

Jean-Paul's lips pressed together, his powerful arms flexing as he crossed them over his broad chest. After a long breath, he finally nodded. "Yes, he is right. You told me once when we were alone, but you never spoke of it again. You were only fifteen or sixteen. You couldn't find another way to survive on the street, so you—" His unfinished thought shattered her, its implication flogging her with guilt, disgrace.

Whirling away, she let the fountain's spray pepper her heated skin. The grotesque masks and dolphin faces carved into the stone clouded as her salty tears plumped and bled down her cheeks. She knew the truth of it now—all of it. The shadows lurking in her mind had begun to trundle away, making room for the worst of her memories to surface. No wonder she had buried them the deepest.

"It isn't your fault," she vaguely heard her brother say as he dropped to the fountain beside her. "You had to survive by any means that you could. We all had to. You did what you had to and you got out when you could. You shouldn't have to shoulder the guilt of it now, after all this time."

But somehow, even after the days of her life had run their course, she knew she would. Madeleine closed her eyes against the world, her unbearable memories flowing. She had been only fifteen when the baker's wife had tearfully clomped down the stairs, terrified gaze drifting over her seven children before landing on young Madeleine. "Papa has died," she'd said, launching the pack into a fit of exclamations and tears. "The fever has taken him."

Madeleine had clung to the baker's youngest, a five-year-old girl with hair the color of straw. Heartache overtook her—to lose the only father she'd known for ten years, to remember the one she'd lost when she'd been as little as the one in her arms. Their losses mingled until she couldn't tell where the pain for her father ended and the baker's began.

"I don't know what we'll do," the baker's wife said. "I lack the skills to keep this business afloat. Perhaps my sister can take us in. Some of us, at least." Her forlorn gaze coasted to Madeleine again, and the girl recognized a reality she'd learned long ago. If she wanted to live, she would have to find a way on her own.

She had never faulted the grieving widow for turning her out that day. With seven mouths to feed and no husband to help her, Madeleine doubted the woman would be able to keep her own children in one household. Still, the ache of their separation fused to her as she wandered the lonely streets, looking for any kind of work she could. She would miss the little brothers and sisters she'd had at the bakery. She would never forget her surrogate Mama and Papa.

The days dragged and the nights proved cruel in the heart of Paris's meanest streets. No work could be had, she heard over and again, especially no work for a young girl with no practical skills but baking. Body exhausted and stomach growling, she turned to begging as a last hope to stay alive. What little she earned put a pathetic amount of bread in her belly, her water gleaned from puddles of rain, her bed an alcove in the street with nothing but stone to cushion her.

Madeleine had already fought off several men in the street when she first wandered up to the red lantern swinging in the fog. She hadn't a clue what it meant beyond shelter, food, a bed. The madame had welcomed her as no one else did, bathing her and wrapping her in beautiful clothes. By the time she understood what was expected of her, she couldn't return to her dismal existence on the streets. She would starve, be raped, murdered. Better to give herself freely here, in exchange for a life, however miserable it was.

Opening her eyes to the fountain's obelisk and cold water spraying against the wind, Madeleine saw every night, every face, every man who had carried away a piece of her in exchange for a cheap thrill. They would haunt her until the last breath she drew. She could no longer hide behind a ruptured memory. She knew it all now, her every wicked deed and befoulment. Gabriel Clement deserved a wife of virtue—not a peasant, a harlot, a potential murderer. With an aching heart, she realized the best she could do for him now was to disappear from his life forever.

Nine

Madeleine gazed at the rocky Italian coastline, her dreams crumbling into oblivion as the ship beneath her feet pulled her farther from shore. A shroud of fog trundled over the ancient stone city, rolling from the hilltops to the houses below. She shivered, drawing her shawl over her head. In the early morning light, the normally crystal-blue waters of the Tyrrhenian Sea appeared dull and swamp-like. Or perhaps her mourning heart only knew how to paint them in dismal colors.

A group of seagulls blasted through the murky sky, squawking as they whirled and dipped about the misted air. Madeleine secretly wished to be one of them—free to sail through the breeze without concern for the world below, free to love whomever they chose. Her gaze drifted back to the hilly terrain, knowing he slept peacefully among them, never suspecting that his wife now coasted over the endless sea, intending to leave him forever.

The very idea shook her core. Madeleine steeled herself once more, memories of their last night together torturing her. They had enjoyed the festivities as any other evening, dining on Rome's finest cuisine and laughing as the city's extravagant revelers paraded past them. He'd held her close under the boom and sizzle of fireworks, the smoky air filling her senses as she leaned into him and wished her past away. But it wouldn't leave her, no matter what she did. It would always be there lurking, venomously waiting for her to trip and stumble into its net.

She and Gabriel had danced until their legs ached with wonderful pain. Hands intertwined, they'd ascended the stairs to their room at midnight, still flushed with the night's excitement. Their fancy hotel room seemed bigger now than on their arrival, a home they'd filled with memories and expressions of love.

When Madeleine went to open the balcony door, Gabriel pulled her back to him, her torso colliding with his solid chest. Pure adoration and pride beamed from his eyes as his gaze rained over her, taking in her every feature from forehead to chin. Leaning in, his lips captured hers, his kisses tender yet passionate. A contented sigh escaped him. "Oh, Madeleine," he murmured against her lips. "Madeleine, how I love you."

The words choked her, and yet her arms wound about his body, gripping him as never before. She realized with harrowing sadness that their time together was dwindling, stolen moments like these slipping into the void. If nothing else, she could give him tonight—an untouched moment of happiness, frozen in time, a symbol of the love they'd shared.

Gabriel's fingers dipped to her chin, leveling her gaze with his. His dark eyebrows dented. "Are those tears in your eyes?" His thumb brushed a warm streak away. "Why are you crying?"

Madeleine shook her head, attempting to quell the emotions spilling from her. "I'm only crying because I'm happy. You've made me *so happy*, Gabriel." Her heart wrenched to see the slow smile spread over his face, her sentiments mirrored in his loving eyes.

"Just wait until we get home," he said, tracing a finger down her cheekbone. "We'll make a family, fill the château with children." Excitement lit his face as he drew near. "Children with their mother's mind, her beauty, her heart." His kisses fell with his words, one to her head, one to her cheek, and the last to her collarbone.

Taking his wooly head in her hands, Madeleine forced a smile despite the pain his words inflicted. "Let's not think beyond today. We only have a short time left in Rome. Let's live in the moment, cherish tonight as if it's our last." She couldn't tell him there would be no children, no future, no tomorrows for them. He would try to make her stay, and her staying would only break him.

Grin tilting playfully, Gabriel dipped one arm beneath her legs, the other still fastened at her back. "Whatever you wish, Baroness." In one smooth motion, he lifted her off her feet. Madeleine giggled, her feet kicking in midair as he carried her across the room with roguish delight and deposited her on the silk bedspread. Her newly blossomed memories threatened to impose on their happy union, but she shut them out, shoved them back for another day. Tonight, she would bask in the safety of her husband's embrace, forgetting it was their last.

Hours later, the candle on their table had nearly melted, its flame sputtering in a pool of hot wax. Madeleine sat beside it, tears falling as she dipped her pen into her inkwell and scrawled the words that sickened her to write. She realized with deepening guilt that he wouldn't be able to read them. A stranger would have to decipher her Italian writing, a stranger to deliver her gut-crushing news. Yet she saw no other option. Cecile would beg her to stay if she asked her to write it. Désirée would insist upon it.

The scent of oleanders from the trellis outside drifted to her nose as Madeleine sealed the letter and rose on shaky legs. Gabriel slept in the shifting candlelight, muttering softly, content in his ignorance of her sins. Creeping up on her tiptoes, Madeleine set the letter on her empty pillow and took him in one last time. Her heart bled to know she'd never look on that face again, never feel his embrace or hear the laugh that echoed in her soul. Whirling away, she smashed down her weakness and grabbed the valise she'd packed when he went to sleep. *This is for the best,* she reminded herself again, slipping from the room before the dawning sun could illumine her escape.

Now, its brilliant light breached the distant hills, casting a ribbon of blue and yellow across the sky. Madeleine held tight to the bulwark of Roux's ship, watching the heavens explode in color, thin shreds of clouds swirling and stretching in the glorious array. Salty wind brushed her face, soothing the heat that remembering evoked. She hardly heard the shouted orders and stomp of hurried crewmembers around her. One face blazed in her mind; one pair of eyes tortured her. What would her betrayal do to the man she loved?

The slow, confident stride of another man filled her ears. Madeleine didn't need to tear her gaze from the fading coastline to know who had approached. The scent of him, all sea and spice, floated on the breeze. Silently he watched her for several moments, his blue eyes hunting her profile as if afraid to voice the unspoken questions between them. After all, Madeleine hadn't said much when she'd boarded his ship and unexpectedly besought his rescue.

"Thank you for taking me with you," she said, gaze fixed on the distance. "I don't know what I would have done had you turned me away." Climbed aboard another ship, captained by a man she couldn't trust? The very idea made her shiver.

"I told you I would do anything for you." Christophe let the thought linger in the briny air. "Did he hurt you?" he asked finally, his muscular forearms tensing as he gripped the *Sirene's* edge.

The notion would have made her laugh if she didn't feel like crying so. "No, Gabriel would never hurt me." Certainly not like she'd hurt him. "The truth is, he is far too good for someone like me. I have to go before I—" The words caught in her throat. "Before I destroy his life forever." Even if it meant denying every fiber of her being that pleaded with her to swim back to shore and beg his forgiveness.

"I have a difficult time imagining that's true," the captain said, his brawny hand coming to rest gently on her shoulder. "But Madeleine, you must know you are safe here. Whatever you need, I'll have it for you. Just say the word and I'll find a way."

Turning, Madeleine peered past the edge of her shawl at the concerned face staring back. "Thank you, Christophe. I am truly grateful." What a treasure knowing she still had his friendship after discarding the others on the Italian sands. Her stomach ached to imagine Désirée's horror, Cecile's disappointment at her actions.

"We'll dock in the Caribbean in a few weeks." Christophe glanced across the sea, squinting out the rays of rising sunlight. "Then it's on to North America from Florida northward."

A smile edged her lips at the possibilities. "Perhaps I could make a new life there. Settle in Boston or New York." Establish a home in a foreign place where she could leave her shadowed past behind.

Christophe said nothing, only gazed at her a quiet moment, the longing in his eyes saying he wanted her to stay with him, even if his mouth respectfully abstained. At last, he swallowed. "Yes, I think you will find many cities there to your liking. America is a place for new beginnings."

"Then it just may be the place for me." She had only pictured the thriving cities and wooded mountains of America from tales that trickled back. The prospect of seeing it herself injected a tiny shred of thrill to her sorrow.

Remembering the solemn events which had led her to Roux's ship, Madeleine pressed a hand to her middle. "I trust your dealings with Cavaretta went well?"

Christophe nodded, a glimmer of misgiving in his eyes. "His cargo is safe in our holds. Once I've made my last trade in St. John's, I will turn the ship eastward and leave it for him in France."

Despite the conflict on his face, Madeleine felt her tautened muscles release. At least Gabriel would be safe in the hardest moment of his life. At least Stefano's evil wouldn't continue to poison him.

Without thought, she reached out, covering one of his large hands in both of hers. "Thank you, Christophe. I can never repay you for this, for all that you've done, really." She shook her head, a dismal laugh on her lips. "I regret that I am nothing but a burden to you, marooned on deserted islands, threatened by Italian diplomats. It's rather a weary story."

Turning fully to face her, Christophe covered her fingers in his free hand, his warmth surging to the bone. "You could never be a burden to me. *Never.*" His jaw tensed, his eyes telling her that if she let him, he would protect her always.

His touch awoke memories of his declarations in the château's library, of their stolen kiss at the Black Lion. Something within her screamed to pull her hand away, while another urged her into his arms. In her hour of mourning, she needed the comfort of a friend. With a pang of regret, she realized that he might be the only one she had left.

"I don't know what you must be feeling right now," he said, bringing her back to him. "But you can talk to me. I'll always listen." His fingers curled gently around hers, his pulse thumping along her knuckles.

"Thank you, Christophe," she barely squeezed from her throat. The image of Gabriel's haunted face tortured her mind, riddling her with self-loathing. "Right now, I—I can't seem to find the words."

Seeming to understand, he softly pried his hands away. "When you're ready, I'll be here." He studied her a moment longer, tucking a loose strand of his hair behind his ear. Then, as silently as he'd come, he dissolved into his throng of crewmembers milling about the deck.

Madeleine shivered once more, her painful reality setting in as she noticed several interested pairs of eyes on her. She was a woman alone in the world again, with no home or man to protect her. The impulse to rush back to her husband rocked her, even as she willed it away. Gabriel didn't deserve such torment. He would be so much happier with Caroline, or any woman of virtue. Cursed be the day she'd ever set foot in his home and ripped his heart open.

Inhaling the dewy sea air, Madeleine spun on her heel and ambled toward Christophe's cabin. She couldn't stand here all day, gawking at a man she'd once cherished feelings for, a man who would sweep her into his arms the moment she asked him to. The succor of his touch, his reassuring words might prove too tempting for a lonely heart craving solace.

He'd left a hot meal for her on the table in his cabin. Madeleine's stomach churned with hunger, but one bite of the sweet biscotti turned it nauseous. Instead, she sat back in her chair and drank the milky coffee he must have purchased in Rome. Its earthy warmth seeped through her as her gaze wandered Christophe's tiny wardrobe, his bookshelf, his bed—all tidy and neatly made up despite no one seeing them but him. A sad smile crimped her mouth. It all looked so different from the haphazard whirlwind that followed Gabriel wherever he went.

Gabriel. Just the thought of him made her body ache. He must have known by now. He must have raced to the docks and looked into an empty sea laughing back at him for trusting someone like her. If only she could simultaneously leave and bring him comfort. He would realize one day the favor she'd done him, when the truth finally made its way back to his doors. She had never been fit to call herself his wife, to mother the children he so desperately wanted.

Madeleine squeezed her eyes shut, the grief overwhelming. She must learn to go on without him, to rebuild from the ashes her life had become. In time, she prayed he would find a good woman and accept her into his life. And she would do penance for a life of evil deeds, alone. No man would again face what she'd put him through. She would allow no one else to love her.

The hours crept by, the slosh of waves and chortle of rowdy men her only companions. When fatigue at last overtook her, Madeleine stumbled to her room beyond Christophe's and collapsed onto the bed. The captain had purchased a new washbowl, one of ornamented porcelain. The freshly changed sheets smelled of lavender sprigs, an exquisite new quilt blanketing the top. *He's made it a palace for me,* she realized with stinging remorse. He must have acquired such beautiful items when he asked her to come back to him.

Too tired to ponder it, Madeleine drifted between thoughts of Gabriel and hazy visions of sleep. Darkness took hold at last, filling her mind with agonizing dreams—of Gabriel, of Auguste, of that brothel along a filthy street in Paris and the seedy clientele who had frequented her room. Madeleine tossed upon her bed, fighting the memories that stabbed her weary mind, until sometime in the afternoon, her door clicked softly open.

Keenly aware of the intrusion, she kept her eyes closed, every muscle in her body preparing for attack. Nearly a hundred men sailed aboard this vessel. It was only a matter of time until one of them tried to have his way with her. Gabriel's warnings stampeded through her as the footsteps neared, shuffling across the wooden floor. Madeleine imagined what she might do as the figure leaned over her, deciding to pull him down and deliver a kick to his groin before her fists pummeled the life out of him.

Then, the scent of Moroccan spices stilled her. Madeleine recognized the cadence of his breath, the gentle touch of his fingertips as they swept back her hair. A blanket settled over her, two soft lips dropping a light kiss on her forehead before he turned and left. Opening one eye, she caught a glimpse of Christophe's retreating form before the door obstructed her view.

Madeleine burrowed her body deeper beneath the plush blanket and slid back into a more peaceful sleep. For the first time since leaving the port of Rome, she felt loved and safe.

Ten

Madeleine stood at the mirror in her little cabin, depressed by the hollow eyes staring back. When last she'd boarded the *Faucon*, a sad shard of a dingy mirror had been plastered to the wall. Now, her image appeared from within a silver frame of roses and leaves, the mirror attached to a chestnut vanity strategically fit near the door. Sighing, she turned back to her dress laying across the bed. Certainly Christophe had wanted a wife, and she'd ravaged his plans by marrying Gabriel instead.

Lifting her crêpe gown off the bed, she held it above her head and pulled it over her body. Over her skin still crawling with Stefano's unwanted touch, over the scar he'd inflicted those years ago. She had only brought two of her most practical dresses, planning to alternate while she washed the other. The thought of taking more than she needed from Gabriel had sickened her.

Emerging from her cabin into Roux's, she took a moment to absorb the quiet space. Over the last few days, he'd risen before the sun but never woken her. Some type of food always waited on his table for her, a second portion of the breakfast he'd enjoyed while she slept. Today, she spied dried fruit and wheat cereal with a glass of milk beside it. It looked cold by now, but it would provide the sustenance she needed. Her first day or two aboard ship, she'd barely eaten. Now, her stomach roared in protest.

After she'd eaten and wiped out the tin bowl and cup from breakfast, Madeleine stood lonely once more at the foot of Christophe's bed. It hardly appeared slept in. Orderly rows of leatherbound books weighted his shelves, secured by straps for when the weather tossed the ship around. She had fruitlessly tried to read them, wishing against hope that she would acquire her own language, but now the effort exhausted her. She needed to get out, do something different, push Gabriel far from her mind or she'd go utterly mad.

The stairs leading to the deck groaned beneath her shoes as Madeleine ascended them. Muffled shouts flew over the assembly of men, trickling down to her. She heard Christophe's voice issuing commands, chuckling against the baying wind. The smell of the salty sea encompassed her as she stepped into the shadowed alcove at the top of the stairs.

Just beyond her, two sailors conversed, heads bent together and speaking low as if sharing a secret. The taller and younger of the two wagged his unwashed head. "She certainly is a thing to look at," he said, tone lustful. "She could make a man's time on board this ship a lot more enjoyable."

The shorter, fatter man's head bobbed. "Aye, but the quarter-master says the captain gave strict commands to steer clear of her. He has a fancy for her. Same thing last time she came aboard. Threatened to throw us off if we so much as talked to her out of turn."

Madeleine's disgust converted to pride as she watched the first man stretch to his full height, responding to the challenge. "He can't see everything on this ship at once."

"You'd best rein yourself in," the older man said, poking his comrade's chest. "You haven't been on this ship long. You should see what the captain did to the last man who crossed him. You wouldn't survive it."

Reveling in the fear sparking her would-be paramour's eyes, Madeleine surfaced from her hiding spot. Indeed, she'd watched Christophe shoot Alec Brassard when he refused to let her go. The captain wouldn't hesitate to protect her if the need arose. Sidling past them, she threw silent daggers at both as she passed.

"Madame. Ma-madame," they stuttered back, rounded eyes blinking.

She ripped her gaze away, strutting regally toward the commotion of actual working sailors. She realized with biting self-hatred that she'd dealt with their kind a thousand times before. Some men would never look at her as anything more than a prize to be conquered, making those like Gabriel and Christophe all the more revered in her eyes.

At present, the captain worked among a group of men propelling sails up the masts. Shirtless, his hard-earned muscles gleamed in the morning sun as he stood ready at the spoke of a circular capstan. On his command, he along with several sailors thrust the capstan into motion, spinning it with the might of their working bodies. Ropes shifted above her head, a pulley conveying a giant square sail up the mast and into place beneath one of the broad yards sitting horizontally across it. Christophe and another man yanked at the ropes now, until the sail spread and billowed against the wind.

Out of breath, Christophe stood back a moment, swiping an arm over his perspiring brow. His impressive arms still clenched and released, his back and shoulder muscles moving as he stretched. Squinting out the sun, he caught her standing there, one corner of his mouth lifting slyly.

With a few more instructions to his men, Christophe leaped to the platform above and took the wheel from one of his subordinates. He stood tall behind it, clothed in nothing but a pair of trousers and a black cord around his neck with a whale tooth attached. When he cast her a clever grin, Madeleine prudently looked toward the gleaming sea. It was indecent enough for a married woman to look at a man dressed like that, especially one who harbored emotions and hopes for her.

"Does he always sail around like that?" she asked Monsieur Simon, Christophe's first mate who stood nearby coiling a rope around his shoulder. "Dressed like he's about to dive into the ocean for a swim?"

The man glanced up at his self-assured captain, a knowing look piercing his amused gaze as it landed back on her. "No, Baroness, he does not."

Madeleine stole a peek at the wheel to find Christophe still beaming mischievously down at her. Her face reddened. Had he behaved so overtly her first time aboard ship, she just might have stayed with him. Now, with one betrayed husband and a past so dark she had to run from it, she knew she must dodge whatever advances he threw her way.

"Do you remember the things I taught you when we sailed from Traitor Isle?" he called down to her, compelling her gaze back to him.

"Some of it." She flattened one hand above her brows to block the beating sun. "You position the sails against the wind in order to catch it and use its energy to propel the ship." Over their heads, the majestic white sails bent and billowed in the swirling air.

A smile stretched his lips. "Very good. We could reach ten knots with wind like this, if we do it the right way." He lifted one brow, a playful light in his eye ever-present. "Are you ready to prove your worth, sailor? I can't have slackers just looking for a free ride."

Despite herself, Madeleine felt a grin tickling her lips. "If I had sleeves, I would roll them up. Just give me the chore, Captain." What a welcome relief—actual work to occupy her wandering mind, even if Christophe was just giving her the most medial of assignments.

"What do we do after we put a sail in its proper place?" he asked.

Madeleine thought a moment, refreshing her suppressed visions of hoisting sails alongside a man she'd found frighteningly irresistible. Had her attention been fixed on him or the task at hand? "We tie it off," she said finally, "so it stays in place."

"Good." Christophe speared one finger toward the lowest sail on the mast, the yard suspending it drooping to one side. "That sail needs to be tightened. Do you think you could loose that rope over there and pull it taut?"

Assuming a walk more confident than her actual feelings, Madeleine strutted to the rope in question and set her hand over it. "This one?"

"Aye, the very one. Untie it carefully, pull it back until the yard is straight again, then tie it back down."

Biting her lip, Madeleine worked at the intricate knots Roux's sailors had fastened to the belaying pins. She keenly recalled him sitting up nights with her by candlelight, teaching her every one and the names for each. Still, her unpracticed fingers fumbled as she tugged this way and that, her efforts hardly producing an effect on the stubborn rope. When she'd nearly given up hope, one solid yank undid the final knot, the rope unraveling so swiftly, it escaped her hands.

"Madeleine!" Christophe's urgent voice cried her name. "Madeleine, duck!"

Before she had time to think, Madeleine obeyed his voice, hitting the deck as the yard whipped down from its roost on the mast. It narrowly missed her head, swinging wide and flying back again.

"You must grab the rope and pull!" Christophe shouted over the pound of his running footsteps. "Quick, Madeleine. Before it damages the mast."

Springing up, Madeleine jumped to catch the floundering rope, trying to ignore the huge column of wood barreling at her once more. With teeth gritted, she used every bit of strength she possessed to haul the rope backward until the yard halted its path to her head and slowly rose back to its proper spot.

"Good. Good," Christophe's voice cooed in her ear. Two muscular arms came around her, his expert hands guiding hers. "Just like that. Steady, now. We don't want it to snap under the pressure." His racing heartbeat thudded against her back, the earthy scent of his sweating skin reaching her nose. "Good. Now let's tie it off."

Letting the rope slip from her hands into his, Madeleine watched as the captain worked utter magic over it, twisting and threading until it bore an intricate knot secure enough to withstand such weight. His hands rested on her forearms a laden moment as they both inhaled the sea air and let their breathing slow.

When Christophe's eyes found hers, Madeleine didn't look away. The arms around her sprouted a sensation of warmth and safety, even as a warning voice said it was wrong to take comfort in his affections. "I suppose I should stick with the swabbies and only mop the decks from now on," she said with a smile.

He laughed, a hearty sound that rumbled through her. "It's only one setback. We'll get you sailing in no time." When his eyes grew serious once again, they trailed over every aspect of her face. "Just please don't scare me like that again," he whispered, fear and yearning mingling in his vulnerable gaze.

Madeleine shook her head, letting herself relax within his hold, letting her gaze swim with his. Hadn't she wanted this so badly from the first moment they'd met? Hadn't she made up her mind to run away with him when he'd come to the château? Now, those remembered emotions encased her, a heady warmth trickling from her head to the ends of her toes. She could fall into his love now, leave behind her bitter past and spend her days forgetting.

Then Gabriel's face emerged in her mind as it always did, his wounded gaze blighting her, the fact that she'd left him wracking her body with shame. Madeleine tore her eyes from Christophe's, scanning the open ocean. She had to make a life for herself apart from both of them, far away from the life she'd ruined here.

The ocean tossed gaily in the whipping wind, white waves dancing over its surface. Soon, Madeleine saw grayish bodies bubbling beneath. A snout poked through and then another, rising and plunging as they chased each other across the water.

"Look!" She pointed in their direction. Glad to break free of Christophe's hold, Madeleine jogged to the ship's edge and leaned over the bulwark. A mere stone's throw from the *Sirene*, a pod of dolphins splashed playfully in the water, leaping into the air and diving beneath the waves. She watched them for several moments, awestruck at the lovely sight.

Christophe joined her at the side, keeping a polite distance this time. "We see them all year long through these waters, but especially this time of year." He laughed as a mischievous dolphin sprayed ocean water their way. "Sometimes they try to let us in on the fun with a race."

"How marvelous." Madeleine couldn't keep the grin off her face, the sight of their slippery bodies frolicking about the sea delighting her. "They are simply spectacular."

"Aye," Christophe said, gaze pivoting to her. "A life at sea truly is spectacular."

Madeleine didn't need to look at him to know what he meant. *She* would adore a life on the open ocean, each day chock full of new discoveries. But he failed to mention the sunburn, the endless days without company or land to roam, the odorous and pernicious men, the rats and the scurvy. A life at sea had seemed so romantic on her first voyage. She had blinded herself to the reality of what a lifetime meant.

Hours later, after the day's work had finished and the supper dishes been washed, Madeleine sat within a chair at Christophe's table, watching the lantern light flicker off the walls of his small cabin. *Strange,* she thought, pulling a woven blanket around the shoulders of her nightdress. Christophe employed a giant office at the stern, one wall covered in beautiful windows, yet slept in these crowded quarters. Perhaps not so strange when she remembered that his work reigned supreme in his life. He barely touched his own cabin.

Footsteps plunked down the stairs and echoed over the corridor outside before the door swung open and revealed his face. He looked worn from the day's duties, his walk slow and laden. A linen shirt now hung from his shoulders, though his hand dove beneath it to massage his neck muscles. He groaned as he sank into a chair beside her, bending to remove his heavy boots.

"This job only grows more difficult as I age," he said, untying his laces. "Maybe I should quit and become a bookkeeper. Save my back from further ruin."

A chuckle flew from her lips at the idea. "You would never be content as a bookkeeper. You would sneak aboard the first ship that docked in the harbor." Indeed, she had to respect a man who poured so much of himself into the trade he loved.

"You're probably right." Christophe set his boots beside the chair and relaxed into it. "I am chained to this godforsaken life as long as I live. That's why I have this to ease my troubles at the end of a long day." Reaching beneath the table, he produced a hefty bottle from a crate nailed to the floor. After sloshing brown liquid into two pewter cups, he handed one to her.

The strong odor of ale tickled her nose before Madeleine brought the cup to her lips and sipped his offering. Immediately, a biting sensation overpowered her tongue, the warming liquor burning a path down her throat. Madeleine scrunched her nose, setting her cup on the table with a swipe to her protesting lips.

Christophe's loose hair tossed with his jovial laugh. "Not for you, is it? I can't say it's as sophisticated as the wines you're no doubt used to drinking, but it gets us through the rough days."

"That's utterly disgusting." Her shoulders shook as she joined him in a good laugh. Tears sprouted in her eyes, from the laughter alone or the hopelessness she felt, she couldn't be sure. "Oh, I wouldn't mind forgetting, but not with that."

Pulling her knees against her chest, Madeleine stared into the blazing lantern a quiet moment, the laughter dying around them. She could feel Christophe's eyes perusing her every feature, peering into the soul she tried so desperately to keep hidden. A part of her wanted to secret it away, while another wished to lift it from her shoulders and bare it.

"What is it you want to forget?" Christophe asked gently, prompting her hesitant gaze into his. "Don't go this alone. If you can't share it with a friend, then who?"

Madeleine inhaled the cabin's musty air through her nose. What would he think of her if she told him everything? A painful reminder that she'd abandoned all of her other earthly friends pinched at her gut. If she lost him, she surrendered the one last ally she had.

"I fear you won't look at me the same if I do," she said at last, gaze searching his in the lantern light. "There are aspects of my life that even I have trouble coming to terms with."

A sad smile curved Christophe's lips. "I have enough demons of my own, enough misdeeds to fill this entire vessel. I have no room to judge another person's path or attempt to determine their motives."

She shook her head, unable to fathom a benevolent man like Christophe having sins as dark as hers. "You know I left my husband, forsook my marriage vows. That's reason enough to cast me aside."

"I assume you had good reason." He paused a quiet beat. "Perhaps he didn't hurt you, but words can sting as badly as the hand. He couldn't forgive you for whatever it is you've done."

Warm tears welled beneath her lashes, her head wagging once more. "He doesn't even know what I did. I left before he could find out." Her stomach clenched to imagine his wounded eyes when word reached him. "I'm sure he'll discover it one day. Someone will be brave enough to tell him, and I can only pray by then his love for me will have faded." Her hands clenched into fists. "I hope he hates me for leaving. I hope he rues the day he married me."

Christophe's chair creaked as his body angled forward. "You don't think he will accept you after he finds out?"

Madeleine's lips trembled. "It would break his heart. It would destroy him."

A comforting hand covered her blanket-clad knee. "It will not destroy me, I promise you."

One look into those ocean-like eyes shimmering in the cavorting lamplight was all Madeleine needed to judge his sincerity. The fingers on her knee gently squeezed, urging her onward. Inwardly throwing off the cloak of security she'd fastened snug around herself, Madeleine chose to fall into the unknown.

"Even if I told you I once stabbed a man?" she asked, testing the waters.

Christophe remained unmoved, one side of his mouth ticking up. "Haven't we all?" he teased. "The scoundrel probably deserved it."

"What if I told you that I wormed my way into Gabriel's life? That when we met, all I wanted from him was his family's wealth?"

Brows lifting, Christophe released a quiet breath. "I would not have predicted that. You don't strike me as a money chaser. It's obvious that you love him now, no matter your motives in the beginning."

So much, it gnawed at her until she thought she would waste away. "He knows that part, actually," she said, the soft light blurring with her tears. "But what if I—" She drew in a quivering breath. "What if I said I once worked in a brothel, *not* as a maid? What would you think of me then?"

The cabin retreated to silence a prolonged moment, only the lap of water against the ship's hull filling it. Christophe stared into the hand he had pressed to her before lifting his gaze to her eyes. No judgment resided there, only the desire of a kind man to help his hurting friend.

"So that's it," he said. "That's what has made you believe that you aren't good enough for the baron, the catalyst that drove you aboard my ship."

She nodded, salty tears beginning to streak her face. "It's all of it, but I—I can't bear the thought of Gabriel finding out he's not the first man to know me. That there have been God only knows how many before him. He deserves a chaste wife, someone free of a past who will love only him. I can't give him that."

"Madeleine. Oh, Madeleine." Sinking to his knees, Christophe reached to cup her face, his fingers brushing away her tears. "Perhaps he *should* have all those things, but what about you? What do *you* deserve from life?"

His words produced a sob in her throat. "Nothing. I deserve nothing after what I've done."

"It isn't true. Madeleine, look at me." His fingertips rounded her chin, directing her face toward him. "Your past is beyond you. Now you have only today. Despite what you believe, you deserve someone who loves you for who you are, who doesn't count past wrongs. You deserve to be happy."

His declarations sounded so wonderful, and yet they rang with horrid dissonance in her ears. "No," she murmured through blinding tears. "I deserve to pay for what I did. For selling my body on the streets. For marrying him without telling him the truth. I deserve to die." The depths of her feelings at last tumbled from her quivering lips, engulfing Madeleine in unbearable grief. Her legs gave way, plunging her to the floor with a painful blow to her knees. Sobs wracked her body, every emotion she'd kept locked inside to protect herself spilling out.

Two powerful arms came around her, pulling her to his chest. Madeleine clung to him, allowing her body to crash against his in mad waves of heartache. Christophe refused to release his sturdy hold until her last tear had fallen, until her body sagged against his in exhaustion. Then, pacifying fingers stroked her hair, his warmth and security tunneling through her hopelessness, conveying the first inkling of peace she'd felt in a very long time.

Eleven

A light wind tossed the *Sirene* over the frothing sea, driving her westward beneath the cloudy sky. Even when the sun set on the distant horizon and the moon cast her rays across the ocean's face, a smaller crew emerged from their berth below decks, ready to commandeer the ship through the dead of night. Their occasional shouts and chatter hardly reached Madeleine's ears as she lounged on the forecastle deck, propped on one elbow.

Across a checkered blanket, Christophe lay the same way, a lantern near their heads spitting light over their game of Liar's Dice. The captain's eyes squinted as he peeked below his cup and promptly slammed it back over the top of his dice. "One five," he said, a clever grin pinching his lips.

Madeleine's brows narrowed. "Two fives."

"Three fives."

Her pulse quickened slightly beneath the loose strands of her hair. Should she risk a lie, knowing she only had two fives under her cup, or should she call his bluff? His eyes twinkled back at her in the lantern light, playfully saying she would not glean the answer from his face. "Four fives," she said, assuming her most confident voice.

Christophe's grin stretched wide. "Liar."

Feigning shock, Madeleine's mouth dropped open in a gasp. Reluctantly she lifted her cup, revealing the pathetic display beneath. "How do you always know when I'm lying?" she asked with a giggle of delight.

"I'm just a better liar than you are." His deep chuckle floated on the breeze as he pulled back his cup to show no fives at all.

"You're just too good at reading me, I think."

Madeleine let her arm fall limp and rolled to her back on the hard deck. An odd sense of peace had swept over her, the days bringing unexpected healing. Her heart still ached, still longed for the husband she had left in the ancient streets of Rome, but now she glimpsed hope on the dim horizon. She would one day rebuild whatever broken pieces of life she had left and move on.

"How do you go for such long stretches of time without sight of land or people?" she asked. She'd last spied civilization days ago through the Strait of Gibraltar, the trundling sea their only companion since.

"That is the hardest part of my job," Christophe said. "Though with it comes meeting new and interesting people from all over the world, some who change your life."

Turning her head, Madeleine caught him pondering every line of her face and knew he meant her. "I think I'd like it both ways," she said with a sigh. "To put down roots but fly off whenever I felt like it and explore whatever corner of the world fascinated me most at the time."

Christophe hooked one brow. "So the life of an aristocrat. Forgive me, but didn't you already trade in that life for this?"

Madeleine swiped at his arm for teasing her. "Don't be mean!" Leaning back on her shoulders, she joined him in a merry laugh that sunk low into her soul. How wonderful it felt to laugh again, to poke fun at herself, to share conversation with a true friend. She needed him as much as she needed his boat to sail away.

"But truly," she said once their laughter had settled, "how does one even become a sailor? Was it something you had always wanted or did it happen upon you?"

With a deep sigh, Christophe laid back on the deck beside her. "It came from necessity, actually. As a youth, I was a footsoldier in the army. My commander was the sort of man who tried to break his troops into mindless slaves. He would starve us, nearly kill us doing runs in the pouring rain or sweltering sun. I had to run away or die."

Her head shook sadly. "Could you have gone home or would they have found you if you did?"

Christophe stared into the glittering stars overhead as the waves sloshed against the hull. "I had no home to go to," he said, voice strained. "Like so many others, I was a war orphan."

Heart heavy, Madeleine rolled to her side and studied his profile in the white light of the moon. No wonder he was private about his past. He had still never mentioned the woman who once had owned the clothes he gave her. He never mentioned where he came from. Now, the truth made so much sense, sparking cruel memories in her mind.

"I didn't realize that was a past we shared," she said gently.

His gaze reached hers before his body pivoted her way. A silent moment lingered between them, the horrors of their childhoods alive in the dense air, unspoken experience binding them together. "I'm sorry." He needed to utter no other words to tell her he understood, deep in his soul, in a way he never should have had to.

Drinking in a breath of brackish air, Christophe dropped his gaze in thought. "I could have climbed aboard any ship to escape, but I chose this one. I liked the bird." He cast her a slanted smile. "When Captain Chapelle found me, he had every right to throw me over, but instead he took me in. He taught me his trade, raised me into the man I am today. Sometimes he was as harsh as that army commander, but he equipped me with the skills I needed to thrive in this life."

Madeleine smiled at the happy recollection. "And he left you this ship when he died."

Something indiscernible passed over Christophe's face, his strong jaw working. "Yes, it fell to me," he said quietly. "I couldn't have known as a boy that the ship I chose would become my home, but I never wish to live anywhere else. I am utterly in love with her."

His surety moved Madeleine's soul. As the wind whipped over her unbridled hair and the ship rose on the churning waves, she hoped she would one day belong somewhere so much, love something so fiercely. The château had once felt like that place, but how blinded she'd let herself become. She had never belonged in that home, that life. She could never have made herself into the wife that Gabriel needed at his side.

"What about you?" she heard Christophe ask. "Where will you go from here?"

The possibilities paraded before her mind's eye, so many unexplored places laying somewhere in the dark night, waiting to be explored. She could make her home in any of them, become anyone she wanted to be. The opportunity to start fresh brought with it an incredible sense of freedom.

Madeleine shrugged. "The only real skill I have other than cleaning is baking. Perhaps I'll find a quaint village in New England and open up shop. Delight the locals with sophisticated French treats."

Christophe grinned at the picture she painted. "You would never find me far from it whenever my ship found occasion to visit." He blinked, his eyes shadowing and a thoughtful look replacing his smile. "It's a tough world out there for a woman alone. You should find a husband to protect you."

A disbelieving laugh burst from her lips. "You've never seen me in battle, Captain. I'm perfectly capable of handling myself." The gruesome picture of Stefano on his knees passed through her mind, the memory of his spilled blood still pummeling her with guilt.

The captain's frown deepened. "I'm serious, Madeleine. People will lie to you, try to cheat you in business. The sight of a woman alone without a family will rouse suspicion, the kind that can turn deadly. I don't have to tell you that men will try to hurt you." His gaze darted to a sailor perched on the rigging, adjusting a sail. "You have no idea how hard it has been just trying to keep this lot away from your door."

Skin flushing, she fiddled with the wool blanket beneath them. "Well, I'm grateful for your concern and your assistance, but I'm quite practiced at being alone. I'll be fine. Besides—" A hard lump rose in her throat. "I'm already married. I can't marry again, for protection or otherwise. It's unlawful and an abomination in the eyes of God." A sinister voice inside whispered that God already considered her an abomination.

Christophe's mouth opened as if to speak, then he paused. "Have you considered divorce?" he asked gently. "It's legal under Napoleon's Code. You could be free to marry again if you obtained one."

The very thought sickened her. Madeleine's chin began to tremble as she envisioned not only leaving Gabriel, but having him served with papers that cut off any tie they had ever shared. "I would have to accuse him of adultery. No, I could never do that to him. I could ruin his entire life."

"I'm sure there are ways to go about it discreetly." Christophe was silent a moment, watching the emotions that must have warred on her face. "You realize that just as you can never marry until you obtain a divorce, he won't be able to either."

Her breath hissed. "I hadn't thought of that."

At her searching gaze, Christophe looked back with compassion. "You want him to move on from you, do you not? How is he ever to do that while legally bound to another?"

She nodded shakily. "You're right. I can't have him waiting for me. He should be with someone who can fulfill him. He should be happy." Her stomach lurched at the prospect, her skin peppering with gooseflesh. "I will have to begin the process when we land. Though the idea makes me anxious all over."

A warm hand reached out to cover her arm, Christophe's body closer than she remembered. "He isn't the only one who deserves happiness." His thumb softly stroked above her elbow. "You needn't be alone, Madeleine. You should be loved."

His touch blended her anxiety with warmth. Despite every instinct to punish herself, a part of her wanted to let him hold her, let him soothe away the raw ache that running away had planted inside. How alluring it was to feel his reassuring hand, to know a man like him cared about her well-being. Madeleine peered into his dazzling eyes and felt her resolve wearing thin.

"No." Her head wagged. "God granted me life and I've done nothing but fill it with crimes against his name. Who could ever love me now?"

A soft smile touched his lips. His giant hand swept up her arm, his fingertips curling to stroke her hair from her cheekbone, tracing her skin until they had settled at her chin. "Well," he said, inching toward her, "there's me. I do."

As his body neared, warming tingles raced over her limbs. Madeleine caught the scent of his sun-worn clothes—salty air and sandalwood mingling in her senses. "Christophe," she murmured, his face so close it grew hazy on the moonlit deck. His looming form clothed her in heat, launching her heartbeat into a hammering rhythm. Half of her wanted to pull him close, the other screaming at her to scramble away before she gave another piece of herself to a man.

His lips pressed hers—gentle, sweet, the promise of a million more if she let him. Madeleine closed her eyes, picturing herself staying with him, being his wife, escaping to the security of his love for the rest of her existence. Then reality bit back at her, the remembrance of another man haunting her every part.

Pushing him up with one hand to his chest, Madeleine whipped her face away. Her breath came hard, confusion circling her head. "I—I can't. It's too soon. I'm—still married." Brows cinching, she looked back at the face hovering above hers. "Why would you kiss me now, when I'm still in mourning for my husband?"

Jaw clenching, Christophe sat up with one hand propped behind him. "I'm sorry. I thought I could bring you comfort."

A fire kindled in her belly. Madeleine rose to a sitting position, wrapping her arms protectively around her legs. "You wished to comfort me by bringing confusion into the most difficult moment of my adulthood?"

Christophe's narrowed gaze snapped back. "I *love* you, Madeleine. Do you know how hard it is to restrain myself when everything in me wants to erase your unhappiness, to show you how much I care?"

Madeleine blinked. Her head hung, the weight of it crushing her. Why had she brought him into her pain, knowing he harbored such feelings for her?

"I don't care about who you were," he said. "All the things that you think make you unworthy are nothing to me. I've lived through every one." His breath wheezed with each passionate word. "I've loved you since that first day on the beach, when you could barely look at me, you were so unsure of yourself."

The memory burned bright in her mind, Christophe in his captain's attire, strutting boldly over the sand. "That's impossible. You didn't even know me. You didn't even know my name."

"Oh, I knew you." His fervent whisper invited her gaze to latch with his. "I didn't know who you were, but I saw in you a kindred spirit from that first moment. I knew you had sadness and joy and war in you like me. I knew we would understand each other."

Inhaling the whistling wind, Madeleine could do nothing but hunt his vulnerable gaze. Perhaps they were two halves of one soul, a pair of friends who could relate to each other like none other. But her heart still yearned for the man who wore half his meal on his clothes when he wasn't paying attention, who studied more oft than he slept. If only she had been the good woman he needed.

"You saw what you wanted to." Just like Gabriel, just like Stefano. Before Christophe could protest, Madeleine jumped to her feet. "You paint such an idealistic portrait of the two of us. You talk of love and marriage, but you know the truth. You're never going to set down roots. You're never going to leave this ship. You chose the life you wanted long ago and nothing is going to change that. Not even love."

"Madeleine." Christophe knelt, then planted his feet to stand.

Turning, she swept up the lantern they'd left on the deck before whirling back to the imposing man now standing in front of her. "I need you to understand something, Christophe." Her stare pierced his, her chin lifting to meet him full in the face. "I did not leave Gabriel behind to run off with you. I chose *him*. I love *him*. You can't just pick up my broken pieces and attempt to mend them with your affections. I don't want you to."

Before he could offer another word, Madeleine spun on her heel and tramped over the moonlit deck. "Madeleine, wait." But she kept on, her lantern bobbing and casting an orange light around her rushing boots. Without thought, she turned a corner and sprinted down a set of stairs she didn't recognize. Surely the labyrinth of hallways beneath the deck would lead her to her cabin. She couldn't spend another moment staring into that tortured face, knowing he would keep on pursuing her despite her every effort.

At the bottom, Madeleine stumbled into a wide corridor. To her left stood a door that led in the stern's direction. With an exasperated huff, she found it locked. Reeling to her right, she wandered into a darkened room she had never seen before. Details emerged one at a time within the spindly strands of her lantern. It had to be a storage cabin of some sort, with barrels and crates lining the walls.

The floorboards creaked under her boots as Madeleine explored it, desperate to forget her encounter with Christophe, to get the scent of him off her clothes. His kiss still burned on her lips, the sensation gutting her. She'd ridden her hand of the ring Gabriel had placed there when she left it with him in Rome, but the fact of her marriage remained. She had let another man kiss her. The list of her transgressions piled high, suffocating her.

Steadying herself against the brigantine's rocking motion, Madeleine again distracted her mind with the mundane room. Alongside the crates of goods, nautical supplies were crammed in one corner. Extra anchors and boards rested beneath a tangle of ropes, a collection of saws lined up nearby. She sighed, ready to find her way back to her bed. Hopefully, Christophe had retreated from her path by now. The thought of meeting him again so soon twisted her with dread.

Spinning away, Madeleine came face to face with a sight that froze her. She lifted her lantern higher, casting its golden rays over the wooden talons, the feathered chest, the hooked beak and beady eyes staring back. "The falcon." Gazing at the figurehead, her brows narrowed. Hadn't Christophe said the rocks had destroyed it in South America?

Shifting her lantern to the left, she found a new sculpture, carved into an ornate depiction of the sun. Beyond it stood a unicorn, then an angel, followed by a stunning likeness of Zeus. Sidestepping, she found an entire row of beautiful figureheads, all fastened to the wall with a pole affixed to each one.

The hand holding her lantern trembled. Whatever use Christophe and his crew had for these rotating figureheads, it couldn't be honest. For the first time since knowing the captain, she felt deceived, and afraid.

Twelve

The groan of the *Sirene's* hull as it rode the whirling waves and crashed down upon them woke Madeleine from a fitful sleep. At first, she could not tell if it was day or night in her windowless cabin. Then, the scurry of footsteps and jaunty voices above deck told her the day crew had commenced their labor.

Madeleine dressed quickly in the dark space, contemplating her next move. Worry still gnawed deep into her bones, but hope had seeped in among it. After all, she'd known Christophe a good while. There had to be an explanation for the half-dozen figureheads crowding the ship's storage room.

Pulling on her blue floral-printed day dress, Madeleine adjusted the high lacy collar and moved to don her stockings. Next came her boots, her fingers nimbly buttoning and lacing, reaccustoming themselves to dressing on their own.

Tossing her satin skirts over her knees, Madeleine felt confident that Christophe would share whatever use he had for the figureheads with her. The silver-handled brush slid smoothly through her hair. Madeleine chose to weave it into a simple braid and pin it to the crown of her head. Regarding her shadowed face once more in the mirror, she bit her lip. She owed the thwarted captain an apology for how she'd treated him the night before, yet dread filled her at the prospect. The sound of him moving around in his cabin caused her to inhale deeply and determine her feet to move. She would face him head-on despite her misgivings.

A successive strand of bumps and shuffles halted Madeleine as she neared the door. Leaning her ear to the wood, she made out what sounded like books being rearranged, solid objects scraping one another. A distant voice told her not to pry even as she quietly fell to her knees. An overwhelming premonition had seized her.

Careful not to unlatch the door, Madeleine leaned into it and closed one eye. Through the keyhole, she saw the murky interior of Christophe's cabin resting in the soft light of early morning. The man was stationed near his bed, facing two shelves nailed high on the wall. The small collection of books he kept there had been moved aside, sitting in a stack beside a bookend shaped like an elephant head. Reaching up, Christophe dipped his hand into a darkened space cut into the wall and produced a small wooden box.

Madeleine's brow furrowed, her breath rising against the door-frame. She watched with spellbound interest as Christophe lifted the box's lid and peeked inside. He spent several seconds analyzing the contents before snapping it shut and returning it, seemingly satisfied. After a meticulous rearrangement of his books, he turned and walked around the bed. The breath arrested in her throat as he paused at her door, hand extended as if he might come in, before he changed his mind and left the cabin, his heavy boots rumbling the floorboards.

Sagging against the door, Madeleine placed a hand over her hammering heart. Her mind raced with ideas, each seeming more fruitless than the last. She should find out what Christophe had hidden in that box before she spoke with him. Surely she needed to know. *You can't,* another voice tugged at her. *He's given you so much and you want to betray his trust now? You're as ungrateful as you are selfish.* But what if the mysterious figureheads had something to do with his box? What if her safety depended on what lay inside that hidden alcove?

Making up her mind, she waited until the last of the captain's footsteps faded on the stairs. Then, with electricity pumping through her veins, she rose and crept into Christophe's cabin. In the quiet light of morning, she could almost forget her growing distrust for him. He'd left another breakfast for her on the table, complete with sliced bread and orange wedges. Madeleine ignored the guilty sting in her gut as she glided across the cabin and looked up at the secretive shelf.

Frowning, she glanced around before deciding to use a chair to gain a better view. Four legs screeched along the uneven floor as Madeleine dragged it to her desired spot. Seizing her skirts, she delicately climbed up and began pulling aside the books there as Christophe had done. The box in question was made of stained cherrywood, its glossy face sleek beneath Madeleine's fingertips as she drew it from its home. Intricate carvings of songbirds and rosebuds gave her pause. This could be a cherished, private piece of Christophe's world that would hurt him to invade.

Forging ahead, she positioned her thumbs beneath the lid. Memories be cursed. She had to know why the man kept so many secrets if she were ever to trust him. Slowly, the lid creaked open beneath her fingertips, the thin light revealing several small items Madeleine didn't recognize—a ring, a pair of cufflinks, a fob watch, a piece of rolled-up parchment. Her breath hitched, one object standing out among the others. Fingers shaky, Madeleine reached in and retrieved a beautiful brass key adorned with a rose and a cross. *Her* key, stolen so ruthlessly away last year.

Her mind sprinted to catch up as Madeleine revolved it in her hand, examining its every detail. There was no mistake. Gabriel had given her this key late at night in the château's kitchen, vowing it would help her when the time came. She'd found it under her dress when she'd woken on Traitor Isle. A thief had ripped it off her neck on the streets of town, a man trapping her before she could chase her assailant. A blond man with muscles she couldn't hope to confront.

The gut beneath her gown scrunched, nausea seizing her. Could Christophe really have stolen her key? Why would he? How? Questions flew at her one after the other, cavorting about her head and landing nowhere. He had deceived her—that much was clear. If danger waited for her, she would have to find a way off this ship, have to playact until she could escape.

A sudden noise erupted outside Christophe's door, an unseen object hitting the wood and shaking it. Madeleine dropped the key into the box, her hand flying to her neck and heart beating faster than she knew it could. Then a bird squawked, the flit of its feathers trailing behind as it alighted from the door. Madeleine released a strained breath, closing the box and settling Christophe's possessions back over it. She couldn't risk him finding her here, snooping through his things. Out here, she had nowhere to flee but the unforgiving waters of the Atlantic.

Once satisfied that she'd returned every item and piece of furnishing in the captain's room to its precise spot, Madeleine climbed the stairs to the deck with a rod of iron through her back. She must act naturally with him, confident. He couldn't catch a whiff of her doubt in him, or the consequences could prove deadly. With swelling sadness, she realized she had no idea what the man she'd considered her friend was truly capable of.

The wind swept over the deck as Madeleine stepped out of the shadows, whipping pieces of her braided hair and fluttering the giant sails above her. Everywhere she looked, men went about their work, ascending the rigging or tugging on ropes. Ahead, she spotted Christophe with his back turned, wrapped in conversation with one of his head crewmembers. The man nodded to the captain when he saw her, stirring the storm within her.

Christophe turned as she approached, his subordinate respect-fully retreating. He had dressed in his blue double-breasted jack-et and breeches, gold buttons shimmering in the mounting sun. Casting her a sad smile, he extended an ornamented teacup and saucer her way. "Good morning. I made you some—" He faltered, gaze briefly plummeting below her face, before regaining himself. "I made some tea. I thought you might enjoy it. Honey and clove."

Forcing a genial smile, Madeleine accepted his gift, cursing the quivering fingers rattling the cup and saucer against each other. "Thank you, Christophe. That's very kind of you." Lifting the violet-painted cup, she wondered briefly if she should trust what he gave her to ingest, before she sipped the calming brew. If he sought to kill her, he would have done it long ago.

The captain regarded her closely for a terrifying moment before turning to the open sea and leaning his elbows on the bulwark. He appeared lost in a flurry of thoughts, his eyes narrowed and jaw working. Madeleine felt torn between comforting and escaping him, wondering where she stood and why he would steal from her.

"About last night—"

"Don't." His single word silenced her. He didn't bother to look her way, only knit his fingers in front of him. "You made yourself very clear. I'll not kiss you again, I promise."

The raw hurt in his voice didn't elude her. "Thank you," she whispered, wishing he would say more, or at least look at her. In spite of what she'd found this morning, she still abhorred her words the night before.

A time too long stretched between them, only the gull's cry and the ocean's roar filling the awkward silence. Christophe sighed heavily. "Why don't you just ask me what's on your mind?"

Madeleine set her teacup down, frowning. "What do you mean?"

His expression a blend of irritation and haunted sadness, he straightened and stalked toward her. When he stepped close, his shadow covered her. "I always dust my most important possessions in a bit of gunpowder," he said, reaching for her hand and gently lifting her fingers between them. "It's impossible to see in the dim light of the ship, but it's quite clear in the sunlight." His pointed gaze directed hers to the fingers he gripped, where gray dust littered their tips.

A quiet gasp passed through her lips, her trembling beginning anew. Christophe still held her hand, disillusion crowding his eyes. "You have some on your neck, too. I saw it the moment you approached me." Letting her fingers slip from his, he blinked several times and turned aside.

"I—" Her mind whizzed, grappling for an explanation, searching for something she could say that would fix this. But nothing could. He knew she had rummaged through his private collection, and she knew he had Gabriel's key. Both of their secrets lay bare.

"Why were you looking through my things?" he asked quietly, mouth converting to a thin line.

Defensive rage boiled up inside her. He had so much more to account for than she did. "Why do you have my key?" Lifting her chin, she forced herself to stand her ground.

Anger flashed across his face as Christophe locked his blue eyes with hers. His nostrils ballooned, his emotions changing quicker than the tides. "Brigitte gave it to me after she took it from you." He laughed mirthlessly. "I sincerely hope she was a better maid than she was a spy."

Madeleine blinked, her memory flying to the mousy little brunette always lurking about the château's kitchen. She'd felt sorry when Georgette tortured the poor girl with her endless tasks. She'd never expected deceit in her. "You hired Brigitte to watch me?"

"You, the baron, anyone who could give me any information." He sighed, raking a hand through his abundant hair. "It turns out, all the good she could do was to help me acquire that key off your neck."

The day it was stolen flashed through her mind, the struggle with her attacker and chase through the village streets. Two arms had detained her, the powerful arms of a man who worked for his living. Madeleine let her astonished gaze wander Christophe's physique, recognizing the unyielding but gentle touch of the man who had locked her in a storage shed.

Disbelieving, Madeleine strode toward the ship's side and set her saucer atop the bulwark. Her hands gripped the wood there, spreading wide and supporting her against the *Sirene's* reeling motions. "You're a treasure hunter," she realized, the pieces of their friendship clicking together. Of course he had shown up on Traitor Isle just when she needed him. Of course he had taken her aboard his ship with nary a question asked. He had wanted something from her. He had *always* wanted something from her.

"You knew who I was when you found me on that island, didn't you?" she asked, fear and anger doing a tug-of-war within.

"I didn't know who you were, but I knew you had something to do with the treasure. Nobody would have left you there if you didn't. For decades, that island has been nothing but a dumping ground for traitors who vow to earn their way back aboard ship by finding the Moon King's gold."

Madeleine pushed off her hands, spinning to face him. "So you gave me a bed and clothes, you fed me and befriended me, all so you could get closer to your precious treasure?" Her lips snarled, the wound of betrayal opened wide. "Those clothes never belonged to a woman you loved, did they?" What a romantic tale she'd imagined for the woman who had once donned the beautiful gowns he'd given her.

"I never said there was a woman." He stood firm against her approach. "Plundering has its rewards, the least of which being spare chests full of feminine attire for the occasion that it might be needed."

"Plunder." Madeleine's mouth hinged open, the word bitter on her tongue. Even upon imagining that Christophe had orchestrated all of this for his own advantage, she'd never taken him for a thief. Now her own hunt for Henri Clement's treasure played over again in her mind, the truth rattling down her nerves and shaking her core. "You're the pirate who is chasing my brother around."

Christophe rolled his eyes. "*Was* chasing your brother. That man will drink himself to death before he ever finds any treasure."

Ignoring his hurtful remark, she stepped closer. "You killed François Martine." The nameless man, the one whose ancestors had reportedly buried the treasure on Traitor Isle. The afflicted eyes of his father still burned in her memory, rage consuming her to know she stood before his son's killer.

"You weren't there," Christophe said quietly. "You don't know the mental state he was in." His eyes implored her, touching the soul she fortified against him. "I only went to talk, but the man was deranged. He lunged at me with a knife and I had no choice but to defend myself."

Madeleine shook her head, unsure what to believe. "You wrote that letter to Auguste that nearly got me killed. You used me." That hurt above all else—the fact that the friend she'd trusted saw her as nothing more than a pawn in his game.

"I fell in love with you." Christophe stood over her, so close that his breath touched her skin. So much passion swathed his face, yet how could she judge his sincerity?

"What do you know of love?" she asked through her salty tears. "You steal and murder for your living."

"And you bring men to bed for yours!" His nostrils widened, his jaw clamping. His shouted declaration hadn't avoided the closest crewmembers, drawing their curious stares. Madeleine shrank within herself at his words, familiar self-hatred taking hold.

Christophe blinked, taking a step backward. "I'm sorry. That's not what I—" One hand wrenched the back of his neck. "Listen, Madeleine. We're the same, you and I. You may put on the clothes of a superior class, and I may pretend to be this grand, important ship captain. But we're really nothing but orphans, castaways from peasant farms. We have to fight for everything we have."

Her lips pinched together. "I never hurt anyone to get it."

"Oh, but didn't you?"

His words drifted through her, landing hard in her belly. Madeleine's hair whipped across her face at the howling winds, forcing her to close her eyes. Christophe's cinnamon odor mingled with the pungent sea, a combination she'd once found so charming. Now, disillusionment possessed her. She hated to admit he was right. Gabriel, Désirée, Cecile, Jean-Paul—how many others had she trampled on in the very same quest? She had even stabbed a man in a similar fashion to the crime she condemned him for now.

"I *love* you," he repeated against the baying wind. "I don't want to be enemies in this; I want to be partners. I want to find the treasure together."

Madeleine opened her eyes to his, hunting their ocean-like depths. Perhaps they were the same, but oh how senseless these riches seemed to her now. "Leave me in the Caribbean when we dock," she said, throat dry. "I don't want any more of this. I don't want Henri's treasure."

His silence, the harrowed look in his gaze, spoke for him.

"We're not going to the Caribbean, are we?" Madeleine asked. At Christophe's sullen headshake, her spirits plummeted. *No,* not to the place of her isolation, to the moment her memories began in a baffling world of beating sun and sand. *"Why?"* It sounded more like a cry than a question.

"You know more than anyone about this treasure."

"I don't." Her dark head shook vehemently. "You think because Gabriel married me, he would have shared his family's secrets, but he knows nothing."

"You do." Surety clothed Christophe's narrowed eyes. "You've seen the map, I know you have. Why else would you have conjured that ridiculous fraud you gave your brother, but to throw me off its course? See, there?" His finger trained on her face. "I can see it in your eyes. You've seen it."

Madeleine glared back, rising on her toes. "I won't go back there. I'll sooner jump off this ship than help you ever again."

His head shook, compassion stirring his gaze. "Madeleine, please don't do this. I don't want to be your enemy."

But before she could think, she'd seized the cutlass at his side and yanked it from its sheath. Madeleine leaped backward, posing the weapon in front of her. "You stay away from me! You let me off this ship at the closest dock, I don't care where it is."

Her outburst had attracted the immediate action of the *Sirene's* crew. A dozen men surrounded her, swords and pistols drawn. Madeleine swallowed, head awhirl. No matter her skills, she could never hope to defeat this many in combat. Christophe stood in place like a statue, pity and yearning battling on his face.

"Madeleine, please." His boots thumped the deck as he strode toward her extended sword until it nearly touched his chest. "I don't want to treat you as a prisoner."

She pridefully lifted her chin, her skirt fluttering in the breeze. "Pretend what you may, but that's precisely what I am. I have no wish to be aboard your ship, Captain Roux. If you want me to stay on it, you will have to lock me away."

Christophe stared mournfully into her eyes a torturous moment before signaling his men with a nod. Three men descended on Madeleine, ripping the sword from her hands and binding them behind her back. "Don't hurt her," the captain barked over the melee. "I'll have your head if I find a single scratch on her. Take her below decks to the holding cell."

With one last look at the man who had transformed from virtuous sea captain to vicious pirate in a single day, Madeleine felt herself dragged away. The men's fingers dug into her arms, their chortles echoing off the stairwells of the ship, their rope biting into her wrists. How long had they waited for this chance, she wondered as their body odor enveloped her senses, their leering gazes slipping down her. Rough hands marched her down the stairs and through a corridor, tossing her into a barren cell with bars that shook as the door slammed shut. The sailor who had expressed his plans for her days before smirked at her through the bars before joining his comrades.

Slumping against the wall, Madeleine let her feet slide from beneath her until she landed on the floor with a thud. How quickly she'd found her path from guest to captive on a ship commanded by a man who professed to love her. With a sickening ache, she wondered how fickle his love would prove, and just how far his protection would extend to a traitor like her.

Thirteen

All night long, the winds spat Roux's ship over the churning waves, the vessel's sturdy planking groaning beneath the pressure. Madeleine lay on the hard floor of her cell in a fetal position. On her first ride from Traitor Island, she only recalled smooth seas. Now, the roiling inferno coined the Atlantic laughed at her as it played with the *Sirene*, nauseating her until she could barely stand it. The sea was hell.

From the shouts and dashing footsteps above her head, Madeleine guessed the morning sun had dawned. She pushed herself off the gnarled floorboards, a stinging pain racing down her spine. Hunger stirred amongst her seasickness, but she once again ignored the plate brought for dinner the night before and sat against the wall. The waves lapped behind her head, the only light in this place a thin sliver beneath the door. The thought of dwelling in this dismal darkness for weeks to come plunged her into despair.

Boots pummeled the stairwell outside, followed by the slow creak of the door. Madeleine squinted, her eyes protesting to the intrusive sunlight. The muscular silhouette outlined there left no mystery as to his identity. Christophe ambled forward and closed the door, the lantern in one hand casting a gleaming circle around his feet. At first, Madeleine pondered why he would waste the natural light, then concluded he couldn't have his crew hearing whatever it was he wanted to say.

The floorboards bounced with his powerful gait. The captain stopped in front of the bars, setting his lantern on the floor and producing a silver key from his jacket. Metal scraped metal, the lock springing as he twisted his key, the cell door squealing on its hinges. He didn't bother to close it behind him, his boots scuffing the floor as he wandered into her confined space.

Madeleine shot him a look of contempt, unable to miss the pain plaguing his bright eyes. He glanced from the untouched plate of last night's offerings to the tin with a biscuit and a pear in his hand. "You should eat if you want to keep your strength up," he said. "We have a daunting task ahead."

"Strengthen myself so I can help you?" Her jaw hardened. "I think not."

Sighing, Christophe eased himself to the floor, then set the tin beside her. "I sincerely wish you would reconsider. It's not my intention to starve you."

She glared at the offensive meal. "No, just to imprison me."

Christophe inched backward, leaning himself against the bars across from her. "That is your choice. If I had my say, you would be sleeping in the most comfortable bed aboard ship—with me."

Cheeks reddening, she glanced away from him at the open cell door. "You know, I could easily get out that door. I'm fairly certain I could outrun you."

"Into the welcoming arms of my crew?" Christophe clicked his tongue. "We both know that's suicide, Madeleine. Even if you did make it past them, the only place you have to go is over the side. We're a great distance from any land."

"It's suicide to stay here, too," she said, voice hollow. "All night long, I wondered which of your crew was going to defy your orders and sneak down here to have their way with me." The idea sickened her while conjuring so many memories she desperately wished she could bury again.

"Not with their captain sitting against the door." Christophe's words snapped her head up. He cocked his head, pleading with his eyes. "Come back to your cabin, Madeleine. I can't stand to see you down here alone."

Madeleine swallowed, wary of being lured in by his obvious sincerity. "Alone is how I belong. I no longer know or trust anyone above decks."

Setting his head against the bars, Christophe inhaled through his nose. "I suppose that's fair. I should have told you so many things before you found them out on your own." He drew his knees up, setting his open palms on his breeches. "But now all I can do to remedy that is to be honest. Ask me anything, Madeleine, and I'll tell you."

One of her brows quirked, misgiving rising at his offer. "How do I know you aren't lying to me again? Why should I believe anything you say?"

A soft chuckle flew from his lips. "What do I have to lose now? You know I love you. You know the worst about me. What could I possibly say to make my position with you any worse?" His eyes slipped shut momentarily. "I can't let what we said yesterday be our last conversation. Hear the rest of my story and then judge me, if you choose."

Madeleine's natural urge to console her hurting friend battled with her newfound knowledge of the man who had emerged from him the morning before. She wanted to believe him, but how could she trust someone who would lie to her all this time for the sake of money?

"I looked into the eyes of François Martine's father," she said finally, her fingers knitting together and squeezing at the disturbing memory. "I swore to him that no harm would befall his son."

Remorse seeped over Christophe's face. "I would never have killed him had I been presented the choice. I went to him only to discuss his knowledge of the treasure's location. He lunged at me before I could even open my mouth. He left me no option but to kill or be killed."

The picture he painted evoked her memories anew—of grappling with Stefano in the dead of night, of watching the look of horror engulf his face as her knife pierced his skin. Didn't she know the panic of having no choice but to hurt someone to preserve one's own life? How might she feel if Stefano had perished that day, if fate had turned her into a murderer?

"He worked with a pirate before you," she said, her conversation with François's father still fresh in her mind. "The one I asked you about at the Black Lion. A man he called J.C."

Christophe nodded. "I regret that I lied to you that night. J.C. is the man who commanded this ship before me—Jacques Chapelle. He found François and brokered a deal to split the treasure."

"But he lied to François. He planned to kill him and take the money for himself."

"Oui, Captain Chapelle was that sort of a man. He had singular focus when he wanted something. He didn't care who he hurt to get it."

Madeleine blinked, the words all too familiar. Hadn't Christophe led her down a path of betrayal to position himself closer to Clement's treasure? Hadn't he killed in pursuit of it?

Appearing to sense her thoughts, Christophe wagged his head. "It isn't the same. I don't flog my men for sport. I don't kill people or leave them on islands just because they've spoken a single word against me."

"What about Alec Brassard?" she asked, remembering her gaunt companion on Traitor Isle. "You shot him because he was going to tell me information about you that you didn't want me to know."

Christophe's lips clenched. "Alec Brassard was left there for dead by Jacques Chapelle, just like every other set of bones you saw scattered on that beach. Yes, I shot him, but he would have lived had he just followed the commands I gave him."

A sharp breath hissed through her teeth. "You mean he—" How could she not have questioned where he went, why she hadn't seen him again aboard the Faucon? Had Christophe truly enamored her so much, he'd rendered her blind?

"He was ordered to stay below decks. I had my surgeon tending his wound, which had barely torn his flesh." Christophe took a slow breath. "But he was crazed, as you might well remember. He attacked my surgeon and the group of crewmembers helping him. One of them shot him dead before he could injure anyone else."

Madeleine clamped a hand over her open mouth, tears springing to her eyes as Christophe's forlorn gaze met hers. "They threw him overboard during the night," he said. "You never suspected what was going on around you. You had an idyllic view of this ship and I didn't want to ruin it."

Sinking back, she let the weight of his revelation settle over her. How much had gone on that she'd simply closed her eyes to? Murder, thievery, greed. She'd seen only a handsome ship captain bravely navigating his vessel through the glittering seas. Perhaps she'd chosen not to see the underbelly of his work, not to blacken her utopian view of Christophe Roux.

"I sailed with Alec Brassard," Christophe said. "He was a good and steady sailor before Chapelle put him on that island." His head shook sadly. "Chapelle couldn't find the treasure himself, so he devised Traitor Island as a place to dump whomever he felt like, telling them they could earn their way back on his ship if they found it. Say what you like about me, but I have never and would never leave a man out there to die."

Recovering from her shock, Madeleine lowered both hands to her lap. Perhaps Christophe spoke the truth, but it didn't change the fact that he'd chosen to shoot Alec. His bullet had contributed to the man's death. But would the lunatic have killed her if Christophe hadn't intervened?

Mind awhirl, she felt her brows gather. "How did Jacques Chapelle know so much about the Moon King's riches? How did he know where to look for it?"

Christophe reached into his jacket and produced the rolled-up piece of parchment she'd found in his secret box the day before. "Perhaps this might shed some light on the matter."

Accepting the paper with a hint of uncertainty, Madeleine unfurled it and fruitlessly poured over the words scrawled across the page. The writing appeared older in style, fanciful letters elegantly whisking over the parchment. It occurred to her that she'd seen it before, the familiar bold signature at the bottom making her heartbeat flutter. "Is this—"

"Oui, Henri Clement's letter to his family."

The ancient relic rested in her very hands, and yet she refused to believe it. "How did you acquire this?" A thought crossed her mind, her brow lifting with a sarcastic flair. "Did you steal it like you stole my key?"

Despite her accusation, a barely perceptible smile edged his lips. "No, I didn't steal it. Josephine Clement did."

"Josephine—" The name died on her tongue, the voice of her husband weaving tales of the treasure alive in her mind. "Gabriel's aunt? The one convinced of the treasure's existence?"

"The very same." Christophe's boots scraped along the floor as he stretched his legs out in front of him. "A long time ago, before I even knew Chapelle, he seduced a much older Josephine Clement. He convinced the poor old woman that he was in love with her and that they would find the treasure together. She went so far as to forge her own letter and replace Henri Clement's with hers."

Madeleine found her mouth curling upward, remembering how she'd found the fake. What a rascally old woman Josephine had turned out to be. "I suppose he left her behind when he got what he wanted."

"He wooed her for a while, hoping a map would follow the letter. But it never did." The captain stared at his crossed ankles. "Chapelle ran off to find his treasure and Josephine was relegated to the life of a demented old fool, rambling to anyone who would listen about a fortune they thought didn't exist."

"And Henri became nothing but an embarrassing thorn in his family's legacy."

Christophe nodded toward the page in her hand. "You should read the letter. It's rather enlightening on that front."

Throat dry, Madeleine held the paper out to him. "I can't read the French language. I never learned." She was through pretending in order to save face with him.

The captain's mouth widened, understanding dawning in his eyes. Nodding, he took the page from Madeleine and held it near his face. "My dearest family, I decided to cease delay of this letter, as my ailments have increased of late. I am well in my mind, but every day my body grows weaker. I must leave my final instructions before I take my journey to the life beyond this mortal world.

"You have walked beside me as many have besmirched my character, called me a thief and a liar, and attempted to drag our ancient family asunder. For that, I thank you. It is only proper for me now to leave my greatest gift with you, and trust that you will employ it correctly for all the generations after me. I have this faith."

Christophe cleared his throat, adjusting his back on the bars. "Below, you will find coordinates to a place special to me since childhood. I have left a key that will help you to acquire what lies there, but please do not store them together. You know too well how greed can motivate a man to violence. Finally, I've devised a map in my beloved home. Its secret lies in Colbert's library.

"Some of the stories you've heard are true. Some have been concocted to destroy me. The truth is often more complicated than we might imagine. There is a treasure. There are riches beyond compare. But I charge you—do not blindly go in search of it, thinking you will own the world in so doing. I have built this home and estate to provide for your every need or desire. However, I anticipate dark times ahead. I sense a day on the horizon when calamity will befall our beloved nation. When the need arises, when the monarchy wavers, then you may find what I have worked a lifetime to hide. Not a moment before.

"Now I bid you farewell. Though there may be the firmament between us, I pray my spirit will remain with you always, and that my life's work finds fulfillment in the generations to follow. Faithfully, Henri Clement."

Christophe's final words echoed in the tiny space, the spirit of a man who'd walked the earth hundreds of years before indeed alive again. Madeleine contemplated his final words, watching the flicker of lamplight over the barren walls, the tongues of flame barely audible over the sloshing waves. He had wanted a legacy—nothing more. Surely the power-hungry villain described to her had been born of slander.

"No wonder his family didn't pursue the treasure right away," she said, still processing Henri's letter. "If they knew him and loved him, they would have respected his wishes and told their children to do the same."

Christophe nodded. "Every clue he left behind remained together until Captain Chapelle got wind of the treasure. His family never betrayed him."

Bizarre fury rose within for a man she'd never even met. "And Chapelle ruined a woman's life; he killed hundreds in pursuit of his obsession. For what? He never even found it and died without consequences."

"He paid the price." Madeleine's gaze latched with Christophe's at his unexpected words. He set the letter beside him and crossed his brawny arms over his chest. "We'd all had enough of his *disci-*

pline, as he called it. We knew the lot of us would end up dead on that island if we didn't take action."

Grief swam in his solemn gaze, the weight of remembering strong in his eyes. "I led a mutiny. We gave him a choice—go to the island he'd marooned so many others or walk the plank. He knew the slow and anguishing death that awaited him on those shores. He jumped into the Atlantic and sank below its waves, the hatred and the madness never absent from his heart." Christophe swallowed. "Once he was gone, the crew voted me as their new captain, and I vowed never to lead my men as he had, treating them as pawns in a game of chess."

Madeleine's skin shivered as if someone had doused her with a cold bucket of water. She wanted to condemn him for what he'd done, for behaving so cruelly and cavalierly with another human life. Yet after hearing Chapelle's horrific crimes, she understood. "He was a coward."

Christophe nodded sadly. "Aye, he was. And he died a coward's death." His chest rose in a deep sigh. "Still, I can't help but acknowledge that I wouldn't be the man I am today without him. He taught me how to sail, how to assume a different identity based on geography, how to masquerade as a legitimate merchant ship when the need arises." A wistful glimmer passed through his eyes. "He taught me about the matchless fortune that has fueled my every moment since those stories first crossed my young ears."

A fortune that had ripped families apart, stolen countless men's lives. Madeleine wondered just how far it would plunge him as its magic danced over his longing expression. "Now you have the letter and the key," she said, attracting his gaze.

"There is only one element left to acquire." Christophe's gaze searched hers, his emotions shifting from hope to yearning to fear and back again. Then, resolution set in. "You've seen the map," he said—a statement, not a question.

Madeleine looked back, unblinking. "I have."

Despite himself, his breath picked up speed. "You know where the treasure is on that island."

Her jaw set determinedly. "I do." At his growing excitement, she forced rigidity into her mind and voice. "And I will never help you find it. I've seen the destruction that awaits those who devote their lives in search of this monster, and I'll not have a hand in it."

Christophe fell silent. His mouth opened as if he wanted to retort her claim, then his lips clamped into a thin line. She saw the war in his eyes—the struggle to do good despite his nefarious profession, his hunger for the Moon King's bounty begging to overtake his affections for her. He was caught on the brink of a precipice, and he wouldn't survive without sacrifice.

"There is more you should know," he said finally, an ominous note in his deep voice.

Closing her eyes, Madeleine let her head roll back against the ship's wall. "Please, don't tell me any more." Her body ached. Her mind reeled beneath the enormity he'd already laid at her feet. Alec Brassard, Jacques Chapelle, a hundred other dead bodies lying on the shores of Traitor Island.

"It's important, Madeleine."

Grimacing, she bit her lip. "Tell me in a fortnight when we've landed on Traitor Island. My mind is weary with knowledge." How happy her ignorance had been.

Silence drifted over them a moment before his voice finally breached it. "Land is not so far away from us. We dock on the island in only two days' time."

Madeleine's eyes flew open, squinting through the murky light until they found him. "That's impossible. It took us weeks to sail from Traitor Isle to Marseilles before."

Christophe heaved a heavy sigh, his eyes speaking before his mouth dared to open. "It actually takes just over a week from the European continent. I may have had my crew sail the ship in circles before we reached Marseilles." At her incredulous look, his shoulder lifted. "You can't blame me for wanting to spend more time with you."

She huffed, knotting her arms across her torso. "You wanted information out of me. You would never have wasted the resources otherwise." Now it made so much sense why he had wanted to flee Marseilles as quickly as he could, why he had relentlessly scanned the cityscape.

"Perhaps I wanted both in equal parts. Perhaps I still do." Christophe reeled his legs in, looping his arms around his shins. "In any case, we'll be there soon. I think you might change your mind if you just hear what I have to say."

Madeleine wagged her head, her chin pointed upward. "I've made my decision and it is not subject to change. Now you have an important one to make, Captain Roux."

At the man's lifted brows, she took a breath and steadied her gaze. "When we get to Traitor Isle, you can torture the information out of me, as I'm sure a great many of your crew would willingly assist you with." She paused, noting the way his neck stiffened at her words. "Or you can love me, as you claim to, and let go of your lifelong dream."

Fourteen

A chill hung in the air as the mighty *Sirene* blasted through the waters of the Atlantic toward the tiny strip of land where all of their fates lay. Madeleine stood at the ship's helm, watching the misty island take form in the distance. Unexpected excitement churned within her, an unquenched thirst for adventure, even as a foreboding voice urged not to indulge in the treasure's lure.

"We're nearly there," Christophe said near her shoulder, driving her reservations deeper. The scents of clove and orange blossom lifted off his best suit as he stood next to her and leaned his palms on the bulwark.

Madeleine let her gaze spill over his navy jacket, the mop of blond hair he'd gathered and tied with a ribbon behind his neck. He looked so sophisticated in that guise, so powerful and strong, yet noble. No wonder she'd fallen so easily prey to his schemes.

"You'll have me run free?" she asked, glancing down at her bare arms, prickling with gooseflesh in the morning dew. "I thought you would want to keep me chained."

Christophe turned sad eyes to her. "We must work together on this mission if we want to succeed. No, I will not enslave you. You are my friend, not a prisoner."

Hardening herself against his words, Madeleine drew her shawl tighter around her soiled gown. "I will not help you. I told you as much. The last thing I wish is to see you succeed in finding this treasure and destroying yourself on the journey."

His gaze hunted her face, as if he might somehow pull secret knowledge from the depths of her. Madeleine only scowled back, determined to thwart his every effort. She would not fall victim to his charms again, not knowing what she did now, having learned his every ambition and sin.

Tenderness enveloped his face a placid moment, the wind whipping stray strands of his hair out of his perfect queue. As he watched her in silence an uncomfortable amount of time, Madeleine wondered how hard he'd considered her challenge below decks. If he truly loved her and chose her over his decades-long quest for the Moon King's treasure, might she compel herself to return his affections? Surely only a deceitful woman would spurn him after he'd surrendered everything for her. Yet something dark within her echoed the truth that he would never love anything or anyone as he loved the thrill of the chase.

"I still have every confidence that you will one day see things my way," he said, unspoken worry skittering over his brow. "I meant what I said here, the day you found out who I am. We both may come from nothing, but we could have everything. We could move anywhere in the world you want. We could build whatever home suits you. We could be so happy, Madeleine."

The boat lurched, forcing Madeleine to steady herself with one hand. She stared through the morning mist at him, envisioning that warm portrait of family and peace he had contrived. It filled her with hope, longing—for a husband who loved her in spite of her sullied past, a home to call her own. How enticing and agonizing a picture it was to imagine such beauty absent of the one whom she'd already pledged her life to.

Inhaling the salty air, she pivoted toward the island emerging from the fog. Details she'd forgotten materialized one by one—the enormous rocks jutting out from one side, the crooked palm trees with their spidery fronds shivering in the breeze. She could almost feel the warm, white sand beneath her toes the closer they sailed, the sensation nauseating her. When last she'd walked upon that sand, she'd had a gun pressed to her head, hunger gnawing below her ribs.

A glimmer near the cove caught Madeleine's attention. Screwing up her eyes, she leaned in until the vague outline of a ship took shape. A sharp gasp hissed through her lips. "Christophe, look." Her fingertip speared toward the planked wood and white sails beating in the wind. "There's already a ship here. Someone else must be looking for the treasure." Could it be Auguste? A rival pirate? The possibilities stampeded through her, quickening her already anxious heart.

To her surprise, the captain didn't move to follow her pointed finger. He merely sighed, brushing a hand over his weary face. Madeleine frowned, noting the lines of exhaustion that had taken residence under his eyes, the regret buried deep beneath the surface. He was hiding something; that much was clear. Something he knew could rip whatever bond they shared asunder.

"What is it?" Her voice shook, fear budding in her middle. "Whose ship is that?"

Christophe angled his head, grief swamping his face. "I tried to warn you. I didn't want you to find out like this."

Blood thundering through her veins, Madeleine snatched the golden spyglass in his hand and held it up to her eye. "Madeleine," his weak protest implored her. Wrenching away from him, she trained the glass on the tall ship anchored near shore. Whatever he wanted to hide, he couldn't. Not this time.

The cold premonition within her converted to utter fear. Through the narrow shaft of Christophe's spyglass, she saw first the Italian flag beating against the mast, then the familiar maroon and gold crest she'd come to abhor, its bold roses and vines taunting her. Below the square sails still unfurled against the wind, a swarm of men dashed across the glittering ship's decks, snatching up supplies and readying rowboats to disembark. At last her glass found him, standing proudly at the ship's bow, watching their approach with immense pleasure written on his smarmy face—Stefano Cavaretta, her avowed enemy.

Breath tight in her chest, Madeleine stumbled backward. Christophe lurched to catch his spyglass before it could slip through her slackened fingers. Meeting his gaze, she stared at him a painful moment, comprehending that the whole of their relationship was a lie. From those first few weeks aboard the Faucon to the late-night talks in which she'd borne her soul, she could never trust him.

"Madeleine, listen to me."

Her hand flew up, cracking across his face before he could say another word. Several deckhands rushed forward, but Christophe held them back with a signaling hand. His jaw tightened, but he moved not a muscle to confront her attack.

"You claim to love me, and yet you've invited him here?" The words poured from her aching lungs, a shouted, agonized cry. "You've brought me to the one man who wants to see me suffer above all else?"

Christophe reached for her. "Madeleine, please."

"No." Pushing him back, she whirled away and fixed her tearful gaze on the island that could only bring her death now. She felt it in her bones—the slow trickle of rot that would eat away at her until she had nothing left.

The ship cut through the sea, coasting toward Traitor Isle until it slowed near Stefano's vessel. From across the shimmering waters, he smirked at her as the *Sirene* drew close, looking nothing but satisfied in his ruffled shirt and brass-buttoned waistcoat. Madeleine cursed herself for not anticipating this result. She should have known Stefano would never let her go so easily. His enormous pride would never allow for it.

Madeleine drank in the tepid air as best she could, her breath rising at a rapid pace. All around her, men dashed to and fro, tossing anchors, tying off ropes, lowering the massive sails. Alone she stood frozen in space, staring back at the man she had once called her lover. A wicked smile captured his lips, his dark eyes taking her in as if he owned her. Perhaps he did. Perhaps she would never be free of his imprisoning claws.

She had expected a rough escort off the *Sirene*, much like Christophe's sailors had seized her and forced her below decks. When a gentle hand nudged her elbow, she looked into the captain's torn expression. With a nod, he summoned her to walk with him, and she reluctantly obeyed. Even after his gut-wrenching betrayal, she knew she stood her best chance of safety close by his side.

Feet aching, she climbed down the rope ladder and into the rowboat below. Leering eyes burned into her skull from a similar boat bearing Stefano's seal, but she snapped her face away. She wouldn't let him see her fear and disappointment. She would use her time to plan—an impossible means of escape, redemption, anything to ensure her unlikely survival.

The island welcomed her, birds cawing and branches twisting in the breeze as she stepped onto the familiar sand. Its fruity, untamed odor enveloped her, bringing unexpected comfort. She had survived this place once. Her gaze skimmed the jagged shoreline, where the ocean rushed in swells against the white sand. Yes, she knew the island and it knew her. She would use this to her advantage.

A sinking sensation grabbed hold again as Stefano's rowboat touched the shore. He stepped out of it, his high boots splashing through the shallows toward her. His chest expanded, malicious delight alive in every detail of his face. He would make her pay for hurting him, make her suffer for every sin she'd committed against him.

Knowing she must play her role to perfection, Madeleine planted her boots in the sand and stood tall. Stefano strode across the beach with intent, hardly casting a glance the captain's way. Christophe's fingers pressed her skin again, protectively curling around her forearm.

"So good of you both to join us on this beautiful island," Stefano said, his eyes silently noting the intimate touch between them. "I trust you had a pleasant trip here."

"It was adequate," Christophe said, tone dry. Madeleine kept her lips latched in spite of her fear. The familiar scent of Stefano's vanilla cologne launched tingles through her.

His haughty gaze descended her, mockery turning his lips up. "I've seen you look better, Antoinette."

Madeleine self-consciously lifted a hand to her hair, the dirty strands barely clinging to the braids she had woven days before. "You know my name is Madeleine."

"Yes, and what name did you give this fellow?" Stefano asked, his derisive gaze shooting to the captain.

Christophe stepped forward. "Enough with your games, Cavaretta. You're aware of our agreement. This is a business transaction—nothing more."

Stefano's mirthless chuckle lit the air with tension. "Business, yes. But every business transaction has a personal motive buried beneath it." One brow cocked accusingly. "Wouldn't you agree, Captain Roux?"

Avoiding Stefano's bait, Christophe turned his sights on the two ships now conveying boatloads of crewmembers to shore. "We will keep our camps separate to avoid confrontation. What do you say to setting up in the jungle? I think my men would sleep better on the beach. They are seamen, after all."

Cavaretta held up two hands. "That's fine with me, as long as your plan isn't to take the treasure and abandon us in the middle of the night."

The fingers on Madeleine's forearm constricted. "We will hold up our end of the bargain, I can assure you," Christophe said, irritation lacing his voice.

"As will we." Stefano glanced at his men, who carried chests over the beach in pairs. "Then we will move the supplies to my ship to make room for the treasure on yours, as agreed." The words sounded affable enough, yet an unspoken strain rebounded between the two men.

When Stefano turned back, his dark eyes bore straight into Madeleine. "A great deal depends on you, my dear. I'm told you carry the secret of where we might locate this fabled fortune."

Madeleine swallowed, attempting to comport herself with the same amount of confidence she displayed to Christophe. "As I've informed the captain here, I have nothing to say on that matter."

Fire erupted behind his gaze, his body shifting menacingly toward her. "You what?"

Christophe yanked her backward, pressing her protectively to his side. "She is stubborn. I'm sure you know that too well." He sighed as she ripped herself free of his touch. "She will give us the secret, I promise you."

With a smile that made her skin crawl, Stefano traced one finger along the hilt of his dagger. "I have ways to ensure that, you know. I'm certain my methods would prove quicker." Madeleine stiffened, the memory of him thrusting his subordinate through with a knife turning her blood to ice.

"That will not be necessary," Christophe's voice growled in her ear. "You agreed to very specific terms, and you will uphold them or you will face the wrath of my men, who are quite practiced in the art of war."

Fury moved over his face, but Stefano gave back nothing but a glare. His narrowed gaze slipped down her, settling places meant to unnerve them both. "I suppose that's your call." His nose wrinkled. "Forgive me, dear, but you could really use a bath. I could smell you before we had even landed ashore."

Fists clenched and nostrils flaring, Madeleine matched his unyielding stare. He meant to unsettle her, demean her, discount her very existence. As if she could feel any worse about the woman he had revealed her to be.

"I'll see to that." Before she could confront Cavaretta herself, Christophe had seized her again and steered her away. "Come along, Madeleine." Even as the captain dragged her along the shore, her eyes locked with Stefano's as long as they could, a clear challenge bounding between them.

"Monsieur Simon," Christophe hailed his quartermaster, "would you see that someone brings Baroness Clement's clothes and possessions to shore right away?" The man nodded and hastened toward a rowboat ready to return to the *Sirene*.

Madeleine huffed, ripping her arm out of his hold. "I am *not* bathing for you or anyone else."

"He's right, you know." Christophe winced. "You've been locked in that cell for days without any means of getting clean. I should have brought you a basin."

Fingering the soft satin of her gown, Madeleine reddened against her will. The fine clothes had once smelled of sweet perfume, but now even she couldn't ignore the dank blend of sweat and odors from the ship's underbelly clinging to her. "I don't care what I smell or look like. I am not here to impress anyone."

Christophe couldn't keep the grin from creeping across his lips. "No, but you are still a lady. It's my responsibility to treat you like one."

In mere minutes, a rowboat returned loaded with sailors and Madeleine's valise. Monsieur Simon snatched the bag from among them, carrying it across the beach and depositing it into Christophe's waiting hands. The captain cast Madeleine an expectant look, prompting her to sigh and start off toward the forest. She saw no use in arguing a point that would get her nowhere. Besides, it would be good to feel clean again.

Gingerly stepping over Alec Brassard's barrier of scattered bones, Madeleine journeyed into the lush jungle with Christophe close behind. How much easier the feat had been without the burden of company. Madeleine focused, carefully avoiding fallen branches and tangled vines intent on tripping her. The quiet floor of whispering ferns opened to them in minutes, skirted by the rushing waterfall beyond. Glancing at Christophe, Madeleine couldn't miss the expression of wonder that had captured his face. He loved this place as much as she hated it.

The fresh, clean waters of the river bubbled past their feet as they reached the bank. Madeleine gazed up at the white wall of water plummeting from the rocks high above them, knowing Henri Clement's secrets lay just beyond their luminous veil. How had nobody looked here before in all their years of searching for it? The idea seemed impossible.

Turning to her companion, Madeleine noticed him pulling her one clean dress from the leather bag he had perched on a rock. He shook out its ivory crêpe layers, smoothing it beneath his hand and laying it neatly over a blanket of ferns. Catching her looking, he straightened and gestured toward the river. "Well, are you going to get in or am I going to have to throw you in?"

Madeleine peered back toward the beach they could no longer see, a hand self-consciously shielding her bosom. "I can't just bathe out in the open like this. What if one of your sailors is lurking in the woods?"

"If one of my sailors is lurking in the woods, I'll gut them through and they know it," Christophe said, hand squeezing on the hilt of his sword. "I promise you'll be safe."

When he did nothing but stare at her, Madeleine volleyed him a perturbed frown. "Am I obliged to let you just stand there and watch? Busy yourself elsewhere, if you don't mind."

Christophe's mouth lifted into an amused grin, but he spun on his heel and pointed his boots away from her. "I shall remain on guard as long as you need. And I promise not to peek."

Despite his vow, Madeleine eyed him warily as she undid the ties of her dress and drew it over her head. Here amongst the dense foliage, the air bit at her naked skin. Madeleine shivered as she grabbed the bar of soap he had set beside her valise and ventured into the chilly river.

Icy waves rose from her bare feet to her knees, then her waist and finally her neck. Soon, she felt nothing but free within their turbulent depths, the once freezing water losing its bite. Madeleine lathered her bare skin with the soap she'd brought from Rome, its lemon scent both comforting and ripping her apart with memories. Shoving them down, she closed her eyes and let the water cleanse her skin, hoping it might reach her soul.

When at last she felt like she'd sufficiently scrubbed the *Sirene's* odor off her body, Madeleine looked to the shore to find that Christophe had laid a towel over her valise. He faithfully remained stationed beyond the bank with his back turned, appearing to scan the jungle's edge for any eavesdroppers. As stealthily as she could, Madeleine tiptoed up behind him and snatched the towel from the rock, wrapping it around her trembling core. She reached for the dress he'd lain over the ferns, but her fingers fell short.

Biting her lip, Madeleine leaned over the rock and stretched until she thought her arm might break off. "Christophe?" she asked, cursing herself for needing him.

"Hmmm?" The man stood straighter, keeping his back to her.

She sighed sharply. "Could you—well, could you hand me my dress, please?" Humiliation reigned over her just to voice her request. After all he'd done, she didn't want to owe him a thing.

The captain glanced at the gown beside him. "Certainly." Bending to retrieve it, he turned seemingly without thought to hand it her way. Christophe stopped short, frozen by the sight of her dripping with river water and garbed in nothing but a towel. He looked awestruck, the way she imagined he must have appeared upon seeing the ocean for the very first time. Regaining his senses, he leaned closer and transferred the gown to her hand.

Madeleine took it from him, his warm fingers brushing hers. Her gaze latched with his a moment, shame swamping her despite the adoring light beaming back at her. "Thank you," she hardly managed, grateful when he simply nodded and turned away again. Madeleine gulped back the lump in her throat and dressed as hastily as possible. Ironically, she wanted nothing more than to get back with the crew she feared so much.

"You can look now," she said, plopping down on a rock to fold up her dirtied dress and sandwich it back into her bag.

Christophe turned, his face a pinkened hue as he let his gaze drift over her. Madeleine doubted she'd ever seen him blush before. He cleared his throat, but a mournful light still escaped the blue eyes fastened to her. Thrusting his hands into his pockets, he looked to his boots and said nothing.

"Things could have been different between us, you know." Madeleine stood, bending to gather her belongings and place them in her bag. "If you had only been honest with me, I might have stayed with you on that ship. I *wanted* to stay with you."

Swinging his gaze to her, Christophe worked back whatever emotions attempted to crowd his face. "You would never have been content to spend your days with a pirate. No good woman would."

Madeleine shrugged. "I'm nothing but a penniless harlot, remember?" His words had stung that day aboard ship, but now they only fueled her desire to escape this place. "Your mistake was in missing the fact that something's changed in me since those days.

Now I'd rather give up my life than to see someone like Stefano Cavaretta gain even more power to kill and destroy."

Christophe swallowed, his arms clenching beneath his rolled-up sleeves. "I wish you would reconsider. I don't want to see any harm brought your way." He paused, blinking several times. "I'm afraid I might sacrifice my own life to prevent it."

The two stood staring at one another in silence for a prolonged moment, the birds winging from tree to tree above their heads echoing across the forest in strident caws. How divergent a life they might have led together in a different world, under different circumstances, but now the truth blared so brightly, Madeleine couldn't ignore it.

Seizing the handles of her bag in one hand and her boots in the other, she reeled toward the beach and began walking barefoot through the ferns. "Then you'd best prepare yourself, Christophe Roux, because we both might die on this island fighting for our ideals."

Fifteen

The first day back on Traitor Island passed in a whirlwind of activity. Madeleine kept to herself, watching from beneath a patch of palm fronds as men from both ships journeyed back and forth across the beach, lugging supplies and setting up camp. As instructed, all of the extra food and provisions were moved to Cavaretta's ship. A base area took shape just outside the forest, the hammering of nails filling the air as tall poles went up and canvases for tents were staked to the earth.

With an escort, Madeleine managed to go back to the river and wash out her dirty dress. She tried to remain inconspicuous, her gaze darting to the plunging waterfall every so often, but she saw nothing beyond the spewing wall of water. Even with her back turned, she could feel her companion's licentious stare moving down her working body. Madeleine steeled herself, knowing she would have to get used to such treatment with no ship to hide on and twice the men around her as before.

Indeed, her presence on the beach could not be missed. Madeleine meticulously rearranged her skirts over her knees, the dress she'd rinsed in the river flapping in the tree branches behind her. Some of Cavaretta's men leered at her more than worked, her company new to them. With a shudder, Madeleine wondered if

Stefano had explained her role here, or if they thought she was a strumpet meant for their amusement.

Not until the sun began to sink on the western horizon and her belly cried out for sustenance did Madeleine realize the men had worked through lunch. She fixed her gaze on the dusky sky, watching the blue melt into a dazzling haze of pink and purple, sparkling over the moving waters. If only she could sit here and enjoy such beauty without worry of what may come.

When she finally made her way over to Christophe's completed camp, the aroma of boiling stew greeted her. In the center of camp, a fire raged in a circular pit, an iron pot suspended over it from a bail. Everywhere she looked, men dotted the ground, feasting with feral appetites from tin bowls. Madeleine realized with some relief that at least one aspect of this trip would prove easier than the last. She wouldn't have to swim or forage for food.

From his spot on a large rock near the fire, Christophe lifted a bowl to her. "Come, have something to eat. You've barely eaten all day."

Madeleine sighed, wanting to resist, but instead complying with the rumble in her middle. She plopped down beside him, accepting the soup with gratitude. A bouquet of black beans, garlic, and thyme met her nose before she lifted her spoon and let the warm stew fill her aching stomach. The concoction certainly didn't live up to Georgette's standards, yet it always amazed her what Christophe's cook could do with limited supplies.

"It's good, Hugo," she told the slightly paunchy man tending the fire.

Hugo glanced up, casting her a shy grin before he threw some more branches on the fire and stoked it with a stick. Sparks flew from the top of the licking flames, scattering the air in glowing embers.

Not until that moment did Madeleine notice Stefano's men scattered among Christophe's. Hugo must have been charged with feeding them all tonight, an enormous task for one man to perform. Despite her desire to comply in no way with their combined venture, Madeleine decided to help him in the morning. At least she could do some good with the time she had.

Christophe shifted beside her, his muscular arm brushing hers. "It's been a long day," he said, gaze fixed on her sandy bare feet. "When you're ready to rest, I've constructed a tent there, beneath those trees." His fingers indicated a small beige tent sitting near the jungle's border.

"Thank you." She had been idle all day, but still the trauma of the last hours blanketed her in fatigue. The idea of her own bed, a quiet space to be alone, had a priceless allure to it.

Somewhere down the beach, a pirate struck up a jaunty tune. Several more followed behind until the sandy shore buzzed with the song of a weary traveler and his bonny lass. Madeleine found herself laughing, watching their lively faces in the firelight, delighting to see two older sailors begin dancing and twirling around one another.

Christophe leaned close to her. "See, pirating isn't all bad," he said through the tendrils of hair at her ear.

Madeleine flashed him a tender smile despite her lingering anger. With the lash of waves against the shore and the campfire's smoky scent, she could almost forget her heartache at his betrayal. Yet too many questions remained unanswered. Too many doubts plagued her mind as she allowed herself to look fully into his chiseled face. The bond of friendship between them had shattered when she saw Cavaretta's ship among the island's shallows, and something deep within doubted it would ever mend.

A cold shadow fell over them both. Madeleine looked up to find Stefano standing between them and the fire, a knowing smirk on his full lips. "Care if I join you? That is—if I'm not interrupting a moment."

Madeleine's cheeks heated as Christophe jumped to his feet and swept his hand toward the spot he'd vacated. "Please, be my guest. I have business that needs attending to, anyway." Before he turned to leave, he pinned a warning look on their intruder. "I won't be far. Don't forget our arrangement."

Quaking anxiety rose within Madeleine as Stefano settled beside her on the rock. He said nothing for a painfully long time, as if daring her to show fear. Madeleine finished the last of her soup, trying to keep her fingers steady as she planted her bowl in the sand. What she wouldn't give to know what this furtive agreement was and how she fit into their plans.

"You two seem terribly friendly." Stefano's dark eyes shone in the firelight as they revolved to the captain's form retreating into a group of his men. "I suppose you've forgotten all about the husband you abandoned in Rome. You never had much need of him anyway, did you?"

His words strangled the very life out of her, but Madeleine squeezed her hands upon one another and set her jaw defiantly. "Christophe has been a good friend for a long while now and nothing more—not that it's your business to know."

He released a hollow laugh. *"Friend."* The word drifted over the snapping fire, taking on a shameful air. "Perhaps you've grown smarter in your dealings with men. You no longer have to bed them to get what you want, just promise you will."

Madeleine's eyes narrowed. "I never told him any such thing. In fact, I've said nothing but the opposite."

Stefano turned to her, wicked delight swarming his face as it neared hers. "My dear, you said that very thing the moment you boarded his ship. The moment you fled your husband with him." His gaze descended her face. "You may fool yourself into believing that man is your friend, but he wants nothing more than all the others who have lined up outside your bedroom door. He's just willing to pay a lot more to get it."

Shame flooding her skin in warm hues, Madeleine pointed her body away from his. "A man like you could never understand a friendship between a man and a woman." Especially one as complicated as the friendship she shared with Christophe Roux.

"Perhaps not, but I do know a thing or two about the way a man looks at a woman." His breath swept her neck as he angled close again. "He isn't preparing to trade stories of Sunday mass with you when all of this is over."

Sitting straighter, Madeleine wrapped her arms around her shoulders and let her gaze fall on Christophe. He had his back turned, speaking with Monsieur Simon and a select few of his crewmembers. She'd long feared exploiting his love for her, but had she misread his advances? Could a man lie so much simply to fulfill his lust?

She gulped back her misgivings, choosing to believe him. "You are confusing Christophe with yourself. That is precisely how *you* looked at me when first we met."

Stefano chuckled. "What a night that was. I'll never forget that cherry red dress and the way you looked in it." His gaze roamed her pinkened arm from wrist to shoulder before he shook his head. "But no, I only desired you that night. I had no ulterior motive to darken my intentions."

Her gut constricted. "You're saying that Christophe does?"

"The treasure, of course. I don't need to tell you the lengths he'll travel to find it. The man has dedicated his entire life to hunting it. He'll not let simple matters like you or me get in the way if he can help it."

A familiar fear blossomed within, branching out to her arms and fingers. Hadn't she considered the very same scenario—her pitted against the treasure, Christophe forced to decide between their values? Surely she would lose that contest every time.

"I believe he will not choose the treasure over my life," she heard herself say, desperate to convince herself.

Stefano somberly shook his head. "Open your eyes, my love. He already has." When Madeleine's eyes found their way into his, he peered so far into her, she thought he might see her soul. "Why do you think I'm here? *He* brought me here. *He* promised to share the treasure's wealth with me and my men."

Her forehead scrunched. "Why would he do that? What does he gain from your presence here?"

A sly smile tilted his mouth. "Well—you, of course." At Madeleine's questioning look, Stefano exhaled. "I told you my men found nothing when they investigated your past. I didn't know a thing about your *questionable* profession until the night your honorable Captain Roux found his way to my Roman town-house."

Madeleine's chest ached. "Found his way to you?" How could that be? Christophe had agreed to wait for Stefano's men at the docks.

Stefano nodded. "The night before you came to my study to arrange our meeting. Captain Roux already had a plan in mind. He asked me to name a price in exchange for convincing you to board his ship. I told him I would accept nothing less than to see this fabled treasure with my own eyes and to take a portion of it home with me."

"Convince me to board?" Madeleine wagged her head, setting her hands on her knees. "You didn't tell me to leave with him. I left on my own."

"Oh, but did you?" Stefano's face angled, his malicious expression almost melting to pity. "You left because of what I told you about your past, a past I knew nothing about until he delivered the information to my doorstep. He assured me you would leave with him if I disclosed everything." His brows rose. "I didn't understand it, of course. How could revealing a history you already knew drive such drastic actions? Yet here you are. He was right, after all."

Her head awhirl, Madeleine barely heard the jumble of Stefano's words. Her body trembled. She rose on unsteady knees and fixed her dogged stare upon Christophe's back. All this time, he had professed love for her, said he was her friend. Now, the truth emptied her of any last clinging affections. He had used her, played on her memory loss and heart-wrenching guilt over a past littered with sin. Pondering how he must have acquired such information freckled her skin in gooseflesh.

Christophe turned, his brows quirking at her angered expression. She wanted to charge him. She wanted to seize a pistol off one of his men, as she knew she easily could, and shoot him clean through. Yet certain death stood at the end of that route. Instead, she quelled her hammering rage and marched across the beach toward her tent. At least she could think there. At least she wouldn't have to stare at his duplicitous face and force herself not to pummel it with her fists.

Tossing back the canvas flap door, Madeleine ducked into the small space and landed on her knees. Her eyes took several moments to adjust in the dim light. A single pole erected in the tent's center held the canvas just high enough for one to stand in that spot alone. Under her knees lay a bedroll covered in a patchwork quilt and the feather-stuffed pillow from her bed aboard the ship. Madeleine's stomach reeled as her gaze drifted over her leather valise to another bedroll stationed beside hers. Of course he planned to sleep here. Stefano had warned her, hadn't he?

Mere seconds passed before boots pounded the sand outside and the tent flap flew back again. Christophe stood for several moments just staring inside, his form an imposing silhouette against the blue-black sky. Madeleine glared up at him, unable to make out his face, but seething with venom for the man who would trick her in so cruel a fashion.

"What did he say to you?" Christophe bent and stepped inside the tent, allowing the flap to fall back into place behind him.

"Only what I presume is the truth, what I should have seen all along." She inhaled shakily through her nose. "It all makes so much sense now. I've been a fool to trust you."

Christophe fell to his knees as if shot in battle. His face coming within an arm's length of hers, Madeleine could see the worry and the hurt mingling over his brow. He still had an uncanny ability to draw her in, a trait she cursed herself for falling prey to so long. His eyes searched hers in the darkness, pleading with her to forget all that Stefano had told her.

"How did you find out about my memory loss?" she asked, voice demanding. He owed her answers.

He breathed, but did not break his solemn eye contact. "Brigitte overheard you talking to your friend Cecile about it."

"And the brothel? What of that? Brigitte couldn't have told you. I didn't know until you delivered the news to Stefano."

His brow wrinkled, a wounded expression capturing his face. "Once I discovered who your brother was, it didn't take long for your real name to follow, then the truth of your past to come out. There are plenty of people in Paris willing to spill their secrets for a few spare coins."

Madeleine's stomach knotted. She knew that too well. Hadn't she assumed the stage name Antoinette LaRivère for that very reason?

"So you just sat there and listened to me pour my heart out to you that night aboard ship?" Tears stung behind her eyes, threatening to emerge. "You listened to what you already knew and never said a word to me?"

His palm turned up in the air. "What was I to possibly say or do in that moment?"

"You could have told me the truth." Madeleine drew her knees to her chest and hugged them, unnerved at his proximity. "Instead, you used your knowledge of my past against me. You manipulated me into leaving my husband and running away with you." Her head shook sadly. "Did you go through all that trouble to woo me or simply to have your treasure?" Either choice made her stomach sour.

Christophe stared into her eyes a quiet moment, conflicting emotions shifting over his face. Then, his broad shoulders lifted. "Both, I suppose. I wanted you and the treasure."

A bitter laugh hissed through her lips. "And now you'll have neither. I would hate you if I didn't pity you so."

Tenderness converting to steel, he clenched his jaw and shot unseen fire back. "Don't forget, you came to me. You brought me into this arrangement with Cavaretta. I never planned to seek you out in Rome."

"I asked you for a favor. You twisted my request to your own advantage."

"You put my entire crew in danger!" Christophe nearly shouted, fury storming his flushed features as he leaned close. "Did you even stop to consider what this *upstanding* man would want covertly transported to Paris? Weapons. Explosives. Gunpowder. He couldn't have Napoleon's agents getting wind that he's arming the enemy." His nostrils ballooned. "Here you are, always decrying the evils of war, yet bringing it to my very doorstep."

Madeleine gasped, feeling as if punched in her gut. "I—I didn't know." Her fingers coiled around her knees, her mind racing to catch up. Every man in her life had used her for their own gain. "I should have left when Stefano first threatened me. At least Gabriel might have escaped him, and I wouldn't have contributed to his madness." Her husband's instincts had proven correct this time. If only his inclinations toward her hadn't steered him off course.

"Yes, your beloved husband," Christophe said in a caustic tone. "The man can do no wrong in your eyes, can he?"

She bristled at his jealousy. "He would never even think to do something as evil as you have to me. He's a good man, an honorable man."

Christophe's face softened, an unseen burden drawing his lips down. "Yes, and I am not. I am broken and weak and selfish." Unexpected tears blossomed in his eyes, his lashes beating them away. "Now you know all of me, Madeleine. You *see* all of me. I'm weary of hiding behind a mask. I am a criminal, a traitor to my country, a filthy pirate with nothing to my name but a ship. You may hate me, but at least you know who I am now."

Madeleine looked away, unable to meet the pain teeming from his eyes. Half of her cried out to comfort the hurting person he'd laid at her feet, but the other half still filled her with rage. She could never trust him again.

"There is no need for mincing words anymore," he said. "I am a pirate captain, which means my men can throw me over at any time and elect a new leader. Then I lose my beloved ship and just like that, I could be stranded on an island like this one, as if I'd never commanded anyone."

Curious, Madeleine's gaze rushed back into his. Stony solemnity had replaced his pain.

"You have a serious choice to make," Christophe said. "Withholding what you know about the treasure's whereabouts could kill us both. If you don't tell us, both Cavaretta's men and my own crew will grow impatient. They will cast me aside unless I force you to produce what we want by any means necessary." His head shook, raw emotion swathing his face. "That's something I will not do—ever."

Her gut recoiled in pure terror. Madeleine knew he spoke the truth. He had nothing to hide now. Perhaps she could sacrifice herself to thwart their plans, but to endanger the life of another human being? Nothing was worth that decision.

"I'll let you think about it." Christophe gave her one last solemn look before turning to leave.

"I'll not allow you to sleep in the same tent."

The man pivoted back, the muscles in his neck tightening. "You must."

Despite the battle raging in her, Madeleine stuck up her chin. "I'd sooner sleep on a raft anchored to shore."

Eyes narrowing, Christophe came so close, she could smell the saltwater and foreign spices lifting off his shirt. "Part of my agreement with Cavaretta states that I can protect you at all times. He has no authority over you." His finger speared toward the sound of his carousing men. "Now, do you know what will happen the minute I leave you alone in this place? There are hundreds of men just waiting for a chance at you."

Madeleine swallowed, drowning her fear at his words. "I *will not* share a tent with you," she declared through her gritted teeth.

His fist pounded the ground and launched sand around them. Christophe released a grunt before he rose to his knees. "Fine." He snatched his bedroll. "Then I'll sleep *outside* of the tent to protect your precious dignity." Irritation swarming his every clenched muscle, he yanked his bed outside and threw it in the sand. Bending low, he poked his head back in the tent. "I'm going back for a drink. Think about what I've said."

In the wake of his departure, Madeleine's pulse thundered. He had presented her with an impossible choice—help a man like Stefano Cavaretta and a group of pernicious pirates to claim unimaginable wealth, or pronounce their own deaths. Heart racing, an alternate plan took shape. She might never have this chance again. He might never leave her alone. Scrambling to her feet, Madeleine peeked out of the tent. All of the men still laughed and danced around the fire, unconcerned with her presence. Christophe stood among them, chugging ale straight from a bottle.

With a breath of courage that tunneled through her body, Madeleine crawled out of the tent and scampered into the woods. Soon, a cover of foliage engulfed her, a welcome friend and a mysterious enemy. Thrusting her fears aside, she ran until her burning legs gave way beneath her.

Sixteen

The night felt like it stretched on forever, an endless parade of lonely hours spent running, hiding, barely breathing the feverish air blasting through her lungs. With no light to guide her, Madeleine forged a rough course around the river and imposing waterfall, climbing the rocky terrain to higher ground. So much of this island she'd never explored for fear of Alec Brassard. Now, the desperate need for shelter screamed at her as she scraped her knees scaling rocks and pushed through thick patches of fronds.

Madeleine had run for the better part of an hour before voices rose from the beach she'd fled. Ice poured through her veins as she clamored onward, searching in the muddled dark for any place she might disguise her presence. She thought briefly of heading to the cliffs as she had before, but surely someone from one of the ships would spot her there. No, she needed the cover of trees to hide her.

Whistles and shouts echoed in her ears. Crouched behind a flowering bush, Madeleine spied several streams of lantern light casting yellow rays over the dense foliage. How could she hope to prevail against a hundred men, all sniffing the wind for her like savage dogs? If Christophe's crew found her, they might spare her for fear of their captain's retribution, but what of Stefano's? What would he do to her once Christophe no longer stood between them?

Shaking herself of the terrifying notion, Madeleine kept to the ground and stealthily crawled through the brush. Her face and hands were soon plastered with mud, the clean dress she'd donned that morning hanging off her like a soiled rag. The sailors' voices grew closer every second, their garbled commands sharpening into distinct words.

"Look over there, behind those rocks," one of them shouted. "I'll have a look at these bushes."

A cold ache plummeted through Madeleine's body. Footsteps approached, twigs snapping beneath the heavy trod of boots. Madeleine pressed her cheek into the malleable earth and flattened her body into it, wishing she could fuse herself with the ground. The man stood so close, his raspy breathing hissed through the air. Madeleine squeezed her eyes shut, the rapid thud of her heart drowning out all else.

Soon, the footsteps retreated and her breathing began to slow. Waiting until the sound of her pursuers diminished, Madeleine pushed off the ground and slunk silently through the under-growth. Glad she'd left her shoes on the beach, she let her bare feet pad quietly through the mud as she darted from tree to tree, using their trunks to conceal her.

Her efforts conveyed memories of childhood, of hopping be-hind trees in the forest to escape the Jacobins' clutches. How brave a task she'd performed as a five-year-old child, preserving her life against the odds. She reminded herself of this truth as she slipped through the palm trees and viny rock walls, intent on staying alive through another impossible feat.

Madeleine's lungs ached and her sides howled in pain when she reached the other side of the island. A sliver of moonlight struck over the waves, the sight barely visible among the canvas of trees separating her from the beach. The placid waves lapping the shore defied the turmoil racing through her body. She could almost sink down on this peaceful shore and stare at the blackened ocean, forgetting the peril that lay around every corner. Then, two more voices froze her.

"She can't have gotten far. This island isn't all that big," one of them said, no more than a stone's throw from her.

Gingerly stepping over a fallen log, Madeleine sandwiched herself within a thicket of palms and waited, praying they wouldn't hear the rapid breath she tried desperately to keep at bay.

"Think of all the places to hide," his companion said. "She could be anywhere. She could hide out here forever if she likes."

The first man laughed, launching a skitter down her spine. "She can't hide forever without food or water. She'll have to come out eventually." Their lantern threw an orb of light around their silhouetted bodies, nearly catching Madeleine's skirt in its rays.

The men wandered closer, their lantern light illuminating two sailors she recognized from the *Sirene*. Their gazes wandered the vegetation surrounding her, lips wet with anticipation beneath scruffy beards. Madeleine pressed her hands to the rough trunk of the palm tree before her, trying to remain steady on legs that begged to waver.

"I'll tell you one thing," the larger of the two men said. "I've done enough staring at that woman for the past week. If I find her, I'm keeping her."

His friend clucked his tongue. "Captain Roux will have your head."

"Do you think I give a hang about Captain Roux?" The man's dark eyes shone with wicked intensity as he scanned the forest. "Half the ship's already done with his theatrics, making us cart her around without giving us a taste of her. If I bring her back to share after I've had my fill, *I'll* be the new captain of the *Sirene*. Then we can forget about this nonexistent treasure and do some *real* pirating again."

Madeleine tried not to breathe, her chest rising in hurried waves at his callous remarks. Christophe's command over his ship had always seemed like an impenetrable fortress, absolute against whomever might threaten it. Now the truth he had revealed to her that night burrowed deep inside, strangling her. His crew could throw him over at a moment's notice, his protection gone, he along with it. She shuddered to imagine what might happen to her at the mercy of his untamed crew.

Early morning light began to crest the eastern horizon, slowly spilling over the verdant mass of land protruding from the sea. The pair of men had sauntered past her to explore another bunch of trees, but they could easily reach her in a few quick strides. Glancing at the leafy sky, Madeleine knew she only had minutes before the waking sun revealed her hiding place. Already, the milky blue light of dawn had converted to pinkish beams streaming through the trees.

With a thundering pulse and sweat emerging from her hairline, she took one soundless step and then another. In one electrifying moment, she stood in full view of Christophe's men with nothing to conceal her should they turn in her direction. Madeleine sucked in an uneven breath, tiptoeing around the trees and easing her feet into the foliage. Her gaze never left the scrounging pair as she inched backward, her toes cautiously brushing the leaves with each step.

Her vision of the two sailors faded the farther away she moved. The forest enveloped her, the trees taking her in like a loving mother. Madeleine could barely see the men through the quivering branches when her foot missed its mark and snapped down on a wayward twig. A loud pop echoed through the undergrowth, a scattering of birds squawking and winging skyward. Both men jumped to attention, searching the expanse of trees for her.

"Where are you?" the one who had threatened her safety taunted, his malicious laugh flitting from leaf to leaf. Already he charged in her direction, eager to hunt her like a wild deer.

With no choice but to run, Madeleine snatched up her skirt and whirled in the opposing direction. Nothing but a lush stretch of beach lay beyond the trees in front of her. Turning to the left, she ignored the jagged branches jabbing into her skin and shoved her way through the dense cover of trees. Whooping and breathless laughter tainted the air behind her, their footfalls closing in. Panic spread from her middle out her trembling arms and legs as she comprehended her reality. No amount of running could ever save her. Eventually, she would reach a dead-end and fall victim to their whims.

Refusing to succumb to such fate, Madeleine burst from the tree line into a clearing flanked by an enormous rock wall covered in tangled vines. Grabbing hold, she thought she might scale the monster before her, but the tender shoots broke off before she could even place a foot to the wall. Frustrated, she raced along its side, her fingers brushing the cold, uneven surface. She couldn't climb it and she couldn't get around it fast enough. Either she must duck back into the trees or fight with no weapons to aid her.

The boots trailing after her stomped into a nearby thicket, crunching branches beneath them. Gritting her teeth, Madeleine kept on running with no foliage to hide her. This wall had to end somewhere. Yet the harder she ran, the more hope dwindled within. They had nearly cut through the trees. Their hastened breath and excited grunts preceded them. She pivoted back to find their position, her foot hooking a twisted branch and launching her forward.

Her world a blurry haze of green and sunlight, Madeleine flew toward the rock wall with her palms extended. She expected to meet its solid face with a painful thud, but instead, one of her arms glided straight through the hanging vines and into a chasm beyond. Gasping, she felt around the hollow space, lifting the veil of ivy to inspect it. There, the mouth of a cave yawned from within the mammoth rock. Planting both hands at its entrance, Madeleine groaned as she hauled herself up into it. Her burning muscles shook, but she managed to collapse on the cave floor and drag her feet through the twisted vines before her pursuers emerged into the clearing.

"Where'd she go?" one of them asked, so out of breath he could hardly manage it.

The other one swore, stomping into the clearing with the grace of an elephant. "I heard her close by. She couldn't have gotten far." His voice ricocheted off the rock wall, coming so close to her hideout, she was sure he would notice the disturbed ivy.

"She must be hiding in the trees around here. Come on, we'll find her."

Her body plastered to the cave's cold, grimy floor, Madeleine moved not a muscle until long after the two men's voices had been swallowed by the forest. They had poked in vain around the area she'd disappeared for some time, finally growing weary and deciding she must have outrun them. In the quiet of the abandoned wilds, her heartbeat slowed and her frenzied breath evened out. Nothing but the rushing wind and titter of birds overhead found its way into her little cocoon.

Pushing off the cave floor, Madeleine unfurled her body until she stood. Her head nearly touching the roof, her fingers stretched on either side of her until they brushed the sides. With arms extended, she ambled deeper into the cave until it opened wider in every direction. She had to feel along one wall to find a circular area in the back where the rocks converged. The dank odor filled her with a strange sensation of peace. It meant she was cut off, protected against the herd of men desperate to exploit her.

Terrified of venturing out, Madeleine spent the night in her little cavern. Her back ached and her shoulders cursed her, but the cave's sturdy walls kept her somewhat warm against the chilling night winds. By morning, her dry tongue and grumbling stomach reminded her that she couldn't stay hidden forever. She hadn't had a drop of water since dinner the night before. Even the salty ocean water beating against the shore enticed her.

The day passed slowly, with nowhere to retreat but her thoughts. Sometime in the afternoon, Madeleine heard a search party make a half-hearted attempt at finding her among the trees again, but they never made it near her shelter. She leaned against one uneven wall, staring into the darkness, the pangs of hunger transporting her to a place she kept buried in her mind's recesses.

Like magic, she was that little girl again, raw with grief over her parents' deaths, scrounging the streets for any scrap of food that might fill her pleading stomach. She saw herself—tiny, broken, sitting before a fire in a back alley of Paris, surrounded by other homeless children. The flames did little to bring her warmth. Wrapping her arms tight around her tattered dress, she ignored the growling monster in her middle and bit her lip to fend off the tears.

All around her, poverty thrived. Some children stretched their filthy bodies over the street, so malnourished they could barely lift their heads. Others played games to distract themselves. Madeleine gazed through the crackling flames at a trio of lads who begged from every passing adult, charging onward despite often receiving venomous words or the back of a hand across their faces.

"They're fools," a little voice said beside her.

Madeleine swiveled her head to find a blonde girl about her age, clothed in torn threads and a blue handkerchief tied over her dirty hair. She smiled despite her sad eyes, dimples emerging from her dirt-caked face.

"Those three would have better luck stealing from a horse's trough, the way they lunge at people." She laughed as one of the boys performed a jig, trying to capture a passerby's attention.

"At least they are trying." Madeleine perched her chin on her raised knees, languidly watching the boy's performance. She had begged for weeks after finding her way to Paris, yet so few people were willing or even able to open their bags for a starving child.

A shrewd look pierced the little girl's eyes. "How long has it been since you ate anything?" she asked.

Madeleine shrugged, the very effort of trying to remember making her head spin. "Three days, I suppose."

"Three days?" The other child scoffed. "I saw you in the street yesterday when the nuns brought scraps of leftover bread. You took one, I saw it."

"Yes, well..." Madeleine's gaze rolled to a little boy she'd befriended, his emaciated body curled into a fetal position before the fire. "He hadn't eaten in a week. He couldn't even walk when we heard the nuns were coming."

The girl nodded, understanding dawning on her face. She stared solemnly at Madeleine's dying friend a sorrowful moment before she snatched her hand and rocketed to her feet. "Come on."

Confused, Madeleine stumbled to a stand beside her. "Where are we going?" She teetered on her feet, dizzy with hunger.

"I'm going to show you how to *really* survive in this place," the girl said. "You can't sit around waiting for scraps off someone else's table. You'll die in the street like a dog if you do that."

Her words sounded callous, but they were uttered with such respect that Madeleine followed the girl already scampering down the twisted alley. "I'm Camille," the little blonde threw over her shoulder. "What's your name?"

Despite her weakened state, a smile slipped over Madeleine's lips. She liked this new friend—full of life and energy amid a war-torn city chock full of despair. "Madeleine," she said, trailing the dancing footsteps in front of her. The jovial girl led her through a maze of streets, all covered in beggars and women hanging their laundry from balconies above. When they finally stopped in a quiet alley before a door with no ornamentation, Madeleine thought perhaps she'd gotten lost.

Camille held up one hand, her diminutive fist hammering a specific, cheerful rhythm. In moments, footsteps answered her knock, the door squealing open on its hinges. A round face with cherry pink cheeks peeked around the edge, his handlebar mustache lifting with his wide smile. "Why, *chérie,* I wondered when you'd come pecking at my door today," he said, pulling the door open to reveal a slightly rotund body covered in a white smock. "And I see you've brought a sister along."

"Not a sister, only a friend in need."

The stranger's gaze took Madeleine in, his sparkling eyes splashing a deep sense of warmth over her. "And this friend enjoys brioche, I suppose?" His plump hand swept the air, revealing a treasury of baked goods lined up behind a glass partition in the space beyond him. Madeleine's stomach twisted at the sight of iced pastries, fruity tarts, strudels, and bread so pillowy, she could almost taste it dissolving on her tongue. The yeasty aroma nearly lured her inside the little bakery like a fish caught on a wire.

"Anything will do, monsieur," Camille's voice rang through her delirious thoughts. "She hasn't eaten in days."

Clucking his tongue, the baker shook his head. "Now that simply won't do." He held up a finger. With a spin of his chubby form and a few quick steps over the checked floor, he returned with a panful of baked delights with steam rising from their centers. "Have your pick, child, before my wife finds out and brains me."

Disbelieving, Madeleine's gaze brushed the perfect assortment of rounded buns before her hand suspended over them indecisively. Their heat kissed her palm and fingers, driving a thrilling warmth through her. At last, she selected the heartiest pastry she saw, scooping it into her grasp and lifting it like one might examine the crown jewels. "*Merci, monsieur.*"

The man produced a buoyant laugh. "It is my pleasure, mademoiselle." When Madeleine moved to stuff the warm bread into her pocket, he crumpled his lips. "Now, you would deny me the pleasure of watching you enjoy my creations? Fill your belly, little one. We only have today."

At Madeleine's sheepish look, Camille sighed. "She's going to take it to her friend, monsieur. He is dying and she has been feeding him to keep him alive."

Compassion moved over his brow. The baker hunkered down before her, his blue eyes locking with hers on her level. "That is a very noble deed for one so young." His head cocked. "I admire your courage, but still, you must eat. You will not survive if you put others before yourself every time."

Madeleine self-consciously clasped one arm over her body. Her father's words sprang to mind, the heart-wrenching vision of him standing over the dinner table on a night so distant, quoting the gospels. "Man does not live by bread alone, monsieur."

A slow smile spread over the baker's lips, something deep within silently connecting with the child before him. "We have a biblical scholar, I see." Reaching for his pan, he seized another bun and presented it to her. "If I give you another, will you eat it or will you give it away?"

She studied the steaming brioche, torn between her natural urge to rescue and the hunger gnawing at her middle. More than one child she'd befriended on the street existed on the brink of death.

Sighing, the baker plopped the bun into her hands and produced another. "Promise me you'll eat this one. I can't afford to feed the whole city of Paris, though I wish with all my heart that I could."

Burrowing the second bun into her empty pocket and accepting the third, she nodded. The pastry warmed her skin as she brought it to her mouth and took the first, glorious bite. Its creator stood back with satisfaction, watching her devour the first bit of food she'd eaten in days.

"There, now," he said, plopping three more buns into Camille's waiting hands. "Take that back to your Mama and Papa. Has the little one been born yet?"

"Just last week," Camille said. She expertly juggled the brioche and a fresh loaf of bread he placed in her grasp. Her woolen jacket bulged by the time she had it all stored away.

The baker looked back at Madeleine, the last of her bun disappearing between her lips. "You come back when you're especially hungry, you hear me?"

She nodded, overcome by the generous man with the boundless heart. Madeleine would return countless times for a warm loaf of bread or a sweet pastry to indulge. When her friend eventually passed heaven's gate, to the baker she ran. He was the only adult she knew who could provide the solace and trust she needed to keep going. Despite his wife's protests, he opened his door to her, gathered her in among his natural children. They had been bonded since that first day on the street, their selfless spirits at home with each other.

As the golden sun over Traitor Isle melted into the horizon, Madeleine longed for the cottage of her childhood, for the security of the baker's home, for any place but this. Her stomach groaned, her tongue like sandpaper. She laid her head on the rocks, wishing she possessed the power to wing herself away. But cold reality closed in all around her. She would have to venture out soon if she wanted to live.

The morning met her with a pounding headache and eyes fairly glued shut with dryness. Madeleine rose up on trembling arms, determined to make her way to the river. No other option remained. If she stayed alone in her cave, dehydration would take her. How could she ever hope to prevail against Christophe and Stefano's men without an ounce of fight left in her?

Her worn body ached as she eased it out of the cave's mouth, careful not to make too much noise. Madeleine crept through the

170

abundance of trees, the leaves and fronds sweeping her skin and stinging the spots she'd injured in her flight. Her footfalls barely sounded amid the rustle of branches and strident caw of birds swooping through the cloudless sky.

Madeleine's pulse quickened the closer she got to the sound of rushing water. Down an embankment she climbed, glancing in every direction for any signs of the men. They must have all been at camp this early hour, for only the cascading water and shivering trees surrounded her.

With anticipation blasting through her, Madeleine knelt on the riverbank and dipped her hands into the cool water. Her spirit sang as she splashed it over her face and into her mouth. Unconcerned that it might make her sick if not boiled, she pushed her face into the rippling water, lapping it like a dog. Madeleine laughed, the water like tonic to her body and soul, the river dissolving her dizzying thirst. She could have lived here for the rest of her life, imbibing the nectar of nature's bounty.

Then, a branch to her right snapped. Madeleine froze, a queasy sensation grabbing hold as a figure emerged from the woods beside her. She turned to find one of Stefano's men looking down at her, a conquering look in his eye. His lips curled, and she knew at once she would have to escape him or die trying.

Seventeen

Madeleine's gaze climbed the intruder before she forced her-self to rise on wobbly legs. Much like his fellow sailors, he wore tan buckskin trousers and a loose tunic that opened at a vee below her throat. His waist was girded with a leather belt, a sword and pistol glinting from either side of him. She tried not to study them too closely as she stood tall before him, feigning confidence despite the anxiety drumming every fiber of her body.

A wry smile twisted his lips, his dark, shoulder-length hair shaking with his head. The man knotted bulging arms across his tree-like chest, promising Madeleine that he could subdue her by barely lifting his little finger. Could he outrun her, too? She was fast, but the long legs shifting among the ferns made her hesitant to try escaping him.

"You're a terribly long way from camp," he said in Italian, his haughty gaze flicking in the direction of Stefano's tents.

She lifted her chin. "I'm not going back. Stefano cannot force me to reveal where the treasure lies."

His forehead scrunched slightly. Had Stefano and Christophe not told their men about her knowledge? It made sense, consider-ing what Christophe had said about their loyalties. Inwardly, she cursed herself for such a flippant slip of the tongue. Now they might all turn on her, bypassing whatever orders their leaders had imposed on them.

"I don't believe Signore Cavaretta cares much about the treasure," the man said, humor lighting his intense gaze. "He is obsessed with finding you. They both are—he and that yellow-haired captain he can't stop quarreling with."

Hands balling into fists, she stood firm while the man wandered toward her, dark gaze slipping down her muddied dress. Even with Stefano's training, she doubted she could match him for strength alone. Endless days spent aboard ship had defined his muscles and probably produced a skilled fighter. Holding her ground, she tried not to tremble when he circled her, his self-assured gaze openly scouring her.

"I don't understand him." The man scratched his shaven chin. "How could he want to destroy such beauty? Who would want to kill a creature like you?"

A bizarre mixture of relief and misgiving tangled within her. Was he trying to bait her? "I am walking evidence of what happens to anyone who crosses him."

His thick eyebrows rose. "A lesson to take with me, no doubt." Yet still, a spark of rebellion lingered in the gaze roaming her neck and face. She could seize this advantage if she played her cards correctly. Hadn't she made a living at acting, and before that, seducing men?

Quieting the ache just thinking of it evoked, Madeleine narrowed her eyes and looked back at him the way he examined her. How many men had passed through her chamber door in that year she'd dwelt in the brothel? How many men had she convinced she wanted them, dangled on their every word, lifted to the center of her universe if only for an evening? Surely she could sway this one to her side, or at least attempt to.

"So are you going to take me back and let him kill me?" she asked, a teasing lilt in her voice.

"That would be the sensible thing to do." After circling her once more, he stopped in front of her, one brow hooking roguishly. "Do you happen to have a better offer? I really would hate to see someone like you meet the end of the sword. It doesn't seem natural."

"I might." Madeleine compelled her lips into a simper. "Stefano doesn't know where the gold is. Neither does Captain Roux. I am the only person on this island who has any clue where to look. You might be the second if I decide to share what I know with you."

A grin tickled his lips at her suggestive eyes. "If I take you back to camp, I am quite certain we might find out what you know, anyway. I can't haul away such treasure on my own, after all."

Madeleine angled her head, letting her gaze slip down his muscular neck to his open collar. "Yes, but would you rather be the only one with that knowledge, or have everyone know?" Her gaze darkened as it moseyed back to his. "Would you rather I sleep in Stefano's tent or yours?"

Swallowing, he stepped toward her, covering her in his earthy scent. One hand rose and then stopped, suspended in midair near her shoulder. No doubt, much like Christophe's crew, Cavaretta's men had been ordered not to touch her. The power and wealth of a statesman like Stefano might well usurp whatever urge channeled through him.

Madeleine moved closer, her torso lightly brushing his. Though her enticing gaze remained locked with his, her fingers explored the air at his side. How far would she have to reach to seize one of his weapons? Could she perform the task quickly enough before he grabbed her? Blood thundering through her, she could barely breathe this close to the stranger who could overpower her in every way.

Chest surging, he gripped one of her forearms. Madeleine stilled, aware she was doomed if he caught her trying to steal his weapon. The man's dark eyes searched her face, indecision warring on his strong features. His pulse thumped along her skin, quickening her own. Her very life hinged on this moment, on the ability of a man to chase or thwart his desires.

"I've heard talk you are a temptress, that you can steal a man's soul with one glance of your eyes." His fingers tensed on her arm possessively. "Some even say you are a witch. They think you put the captain under a spell."

She smirked at the hilarity of the statement. "What do you think? Have I cast a spell on you?"

Desire hooded his eyes, his jaw tensing. "No." The man took one solid breath. "No, I see clearly what I want." Before she could react, he yanked her to him, slamming his mouth against hers. Agonizingly aware that yet another man besides Gabriel kissed her, at first she stiffened like a startled possum. Then, as his arms encircled her, as his lips moved over hers, she forced herself to melt against him. This was simply another part to play.

Fighting the inclination to push him away, Madeleine placed her hands at his sides. His arms were still tightly wound around her, making any chance of fleeing him impossible. Perhaps if she showed affection, he might too. Slowly, she let her hands glide up his back, as if she enjoyed this moment, as if she liked being drowned in the stench of whiskey and body odor. Her heart thudded as his hands released her, skimming up her back and into her hair.

Now or never. Gathering her courage, Madeleine dropped her hand and tugged at the first weapon she could reach. The man's sword scraped loudly against its sheath as she drew it out, taking several sizable steps backward. She lifted the pointed end toward his astonished face, out of breath and wiping him from her lips with the back of her hand.

"You stay back!" she said, noting the way his hands curled. "You stay away from me."

Recovering, the man gave her a pitying grin. "Signora, what do you think you're going to do with that?" His head cocked, as if he spoke to a young child pointing a toy at him.

"I assure you, I can do plenty." Madeleine gritted her teeth, adjusting her grip on the gleaming sword. It had been some time since she'd had the need to even hold a weapon, let alone use one.

The man laughed, but he made no move to attack her. Instead, he crossed his brawny arms over his chest again and looked her over in his usual conceited manner. Did he really still think he could so easily conquer her, that she'd crumble beneath his touch?

Madeleine gulped back her fear, raising the sword higher. "I meant what I said about the treasure. I need an ally." Someone she could trust, ideally, but she had no room to be choosy. "I will tell you where it is—as long as you can grant me freedom from this place, safe passage away. I won't ask for anything else."

True contemplation dented his brow. Well aware he could simply lie to her and drag her back to his leader with the information, Madeleine nervously awaited his reply. Her efforts felt like a useless endeavor, a sure way to get herself killed. Yet what could she do in this moment? A woman alone couldn't hope to fend off the lot of them. She couldn't even stay hidden for more than a day.

The man shook his head. "As you well know, Cavaretta is a dangerous enemy to make." His dark eyes scanned the trembling tree branches over her head. "I cannot risk my life for the sake of yours, treasure or no."

Her stomach knotted. "When he finds out you kissed me, he'll kill you anyway." She met his questioning stare with fire in her eyes. The very idea of getting a man killed over one moment of weakness sickened her, but perhaps he wouldn't challenge her bluff.

"Then we're both as good as dead, anyway," he said, shrugging. The man took two steps forward, his boots trampling the grassy bank. Madeleine retreated to a spot where the plummeting waterfall sprinkled her arm with dew. Despite the pain surging through her upheld arm, she kept her weapon posed.

He held her gaze for a silent moment, the passing river's ripple unable to muffle the unspoken truth between them. The two of them were nothing but servants to Stefano, puppets in his game of life and death. Neither could truly ever break free, whether for fear of his retribution or the relentless power he held over those closest to him.

"He came here for you," he said finally, head wagging. "He's never going to let you go. He has one mission in mind—not only to kill you, but to make your very existence a hellish pit of misery until the day he decides to be rid of you. Not even this captain of yours can save you from what he has planned."

Nostrils burning, she dragged in the tepid air. He was telling the truth. She could see reality painted over the bold lines of his face—that Stefano would never stop, never release her, never let her live any type of life that would bring her joy. He could have easily murdered her that day in his office, but the hunt would have ended before it began. No, he would relish every moment he got to dangle her over the fire, her petitions fueling his maniacal pleasure.

No doubt remained within her. She knew her next move before her arm dropped beside her and fire blazed through her legs. "Then I shall save myself." With one last flash of her gaze, Madeleine spun and raced through the underbrush, hopping over rocks and ducking low branches.

Behind her, the man's pistol clicked. "I'll shoot you," he warned.

Bile singed Madeleine's throat to imagine him standing there with his gun cocked and aimed at her fleeing body, but still she kept on. He couldn't shoot her—not unless he wanted to face Stefano's rage at stealing his most precious game. The man swore, then blasted a high-pitched whistle with his fingers, summoning his comrades from camp. As his boots pounded the earth after her,

Madeleine realized she'd soon have not one, but dozens of men chasing her through the woods.

Using her pursuer's sword to slash away the untamed growth in her path, Madeleine wound her way through the trees. Desperate to reach her hiding spot but also to throw them off her scent, she fashioned a path that circumvented the way she'd come. The unfamiliar trees crowded in from every side, a baffling maze in her unfed state. Madeleine had still only refreshed herself with a few handfuls of water. How could she hope to outrun the group of strong, nourished men sprinting after her?

As she burst from the woods and leaped across the sandy beach beyond, unexpected memories flooded her. In her mind's eye, her father stood proudly at the helm of their humble home church, his loving smile showering over the parishioners gathered in secret beneath their roof. "Do not fear, little flock," he said, his kind gaze moving over her. "For it is your father's pleasure to give you his kingdom."

I don't want to fear, Papa. Yet the raised shouts and cheers amassing in the woods behind her buried nothing but the deepest of dread within. "He loves you, Madeleine," she heard him say as his giant hand swept her raven head. "He will do amazing things in your life if only you trust in him." How deep his words had touched her soul that day, burrowing into the believing heart of a child. But now, tainted by a world of evil, she could hardly hear that promise of long ago through the angry drumming in her ears.

How can I call on him, Papa? How? After all she'd done to disgrace his name, surely the God her father served would spit her out of his mouth and condemn her to the eternal fires of Hell. Yet still his urging persisted, the warmth of her father's love reaching into the depths of a heart she'd thought had frozen over long ago. Words she couldn't even articulate cried out to the sky, begging the God above for solace, for some type of reprieve from the evil flooding toward her.

Snaking her way back into the woods, Madeleine charged through the bushes, determined to forge ahead. The huge rock wall containing her secret cave rose out of the trees, so close she could reach it with a few more strides of her aching legs. Her sides screamed in pain, her arid throat begging her to quit. She would not. She *could* not.

Madeleine aimed her head down and charged toward the cave, one goal firm in her weary mind. Several voices from the nearby beach tempted her to look back, but she had to keep on if she had any hope of survival. Rounding one last tree, she didn't see the figure standing behind it until she'd rammed into it. Madeleine shuddered, aware first of a man's torso, then the arms that had unwittingly taken her in. Fear gusted through her as her gaze ascended his chest and met his face.

Gasping, she blinked several times before her mind would believe who stood before her. Mouth agape, she could only stare into the concerned eyes of her husband.

Eighteen

"Gabriel." The word barely pressed from her aching lungs before she jumped into his arms, anchoring her head at his chest. Madeleine looked up, her eyes searching the ones turned down on her, the solemn jaw now sprinkled with a week's worth of untrimmed whiskers. His very presence was like sustenance to her starving soul, yet it shook her with ferocious dread. If Stefano's men caught her, they had no reason to let him live.

The boom of men's voices volleyed through the leaves, so near that it sprang her into action. Seizing Gabriel's hand, she yanked him toward her shelter. "Quick, we don't have much time." He didn't protest as she scurried the last few meters of her journey, dragging him along with her fleeing form.

When they reached the cave, Madeleine hoisted herself with a grunt and turned to help him up. Gabriel took her outstretched hand, climbing its rocky face and entering into the narrow space behind her. Madeleine had only seconds to rearrange the vines they'd passed through before shouts reverberated off the wall.

"She had to have gone this way. Come on." A pack of thundering boots rambled past them, intent on the thicker brush growing farther down the rock's edge. Chest still pitching fervently, Madeleine leaned against the cave wall and waited until their voices drifted away, still victorious despite losing her trail yet again.

The quietness of the cave rattled her nerves. Madeleine glanced back to find Gabriel watching her intently, his light eyes sober and jaw working. How must he feel to see her again, the woman who had promised her life to him, then vanished with hardly an explanation? Her soul mourned for what they could have been together, what they could have done in this world. If only she hadn't sinned so wretchedly against him before they even met.

Gabriel's brows girded as his concerned gaze slipped down her weary body. "You look like you haven't eaten in days." Slinging a knapsack off his back, he brought it to his lap and dipped his hand inside. "Here." He handed her a metal canteen, cold beneath her touch.

After unscrewing the cap and bringing the spout to her lips, Madeleine nearly cried at the fresh water wetting her parched tongue. How had she never tasted how good it was before? She hadn't the strength to worry in that moment if he had enough for himself or if he'd brought more. The cool liquid trickled down her throat and sunk into her, reviving a body nearly lost to the lack of it.

So engrossed was she in fulfilling her needs, Madeleine hardly noticed the small chunk of hardtack he held out to her. "Thank you," she said, her hand brushing his as she took it into her trembling grasp. Unconcerned with formalities, she tore through its solid shell with her teeth. The flavor of baked flour and salt burst in her mouth, stirring a belly that had long ago given up on its next meal.

Gabriel watched her eat in silence, shifting emotions moving over his face. At last, he scooted back and leaned his head against the opposing wall, his gaze never leaving her. Was it anger or mere hurt that fueled the glum stare he trained on her?

When her stomach could take no more, Madeleine set the hard-tack on her lap, scattering crumbs over her filthy dress. She looked through the dim light at Gabriel, her mind still scrambling to catch up with what she saw. "How are you here? How did you find me?"

He studied her a few more quiet seconds before he looked down at his knees. "When you left, I went looking for you. Cecile told me that Roux was in Rome. I thought perhaps you'd left with him, but his ship had already set sail before I reached the docks."

Her heart cried out at the sad vulnerability teeming from his eyes. What must have that moment been like, standing lonely on the Italian shore, staring out after the wife who'd abandoned him? Inwardly, she chided herself yet again for letting him into her life only to punish him with such cruelty.

"Anyway, there was talk on the docks that morning," he said, fingers fiddling with one another. "They said Cavaretta's ship had launched in the dead of night. I sensed something was wrong when I heard that."

Of course he had. Why hadn't she seen the conjunction of two wicked schemers earlier? "So you hired a ship to follow me?"

"I recognized someone on the docks who could bring me here."

Madeleine's brow wrinkled. "Who?"

Taking a breath, he swung his gaze upward to latch with hers. "Auguste."

A cold, nauseous sensation uncoiled in her middle. "Auguste? Auguste has a ship? How could he afford such a thing? He has debts up to his eyebrows."

"*Had* debts up to his eyebrows." At her incredulous stare, Gabriel sighed. "When he left the château, I might have given him some money."

She started at the information, panic prickling her skin. "Why would you do that after he tried to kill you? Surely he would only use funds like that against us to get to the treasure. It's all he cares about anymore."

Gabriel's solemn stare blazed back, calm yet firm. "I gave him the money on the condition that he left you alone. That he never bothered or tried to harm you again."

Breath sucked from her, she ran her hands over her face. "And now he's purchased a ship so he can scour this island, looking for what will only destroy him." She shook her head mournfully. "You can't trust him, Gabriel. He isn't that little boy I left in the woods anymore. He will trounce anything in his path to getting that treasure."

His shoulders lifted. "I know this is difficult to believe right now, but I think he's changed. After what happened between us all, he hit the bottom. He hates himself for how he treated you. He wants to make amends."

Something deep inside her ached to believe it, yet how many years had she wasted, trying against all logic to truly gain the love of her brother? "How am I ever supposed to accept anything he says at face value? He tried to take the most precious part of my life away from me."

Gaze softening, Gabriel studied her for a long moment. Wind whipped through the trees, rustling the vines hanging over the mouth of the cave. The ocean roared and crashed against the shore, throwing its briny scent into their little cocoon. For an instant, Gabriel looked like he might reach out and touch her. Then his hands fell limply at his sides, cold reality slipping over his face.

"Auguste is the one who warned me about Roux," he said, bringing Madeleine's head off the cave wall. "He purchased his ship in Marseilles, eager to discover the island's location and race out here with the map Désirée drew. Roux found him first."

Madeleine sat up, intent on listening as Gabriel crossed his legs in front of him and leaned his elbows on his knees. "Roux got him drunk, of course," he said, "which wasn't a difficult feat to handle. Auguste told him all sorts of things he knew about the treasure, about us. He woke up from his drunken stupor with the forged map and any notes he'd made about the treasure gone."

She huffed through her nose. "Of course he did. The two of them are a perfect match—they care for nothing but their own greed." Shoulders relaxing, she swallowed. "You tried to warn me about Roux. I'm sorry I didn't listen to you sooner."

The hurt in Gabriel's eyes pierced her straight through. He blinked, then shook his dark head. "Well, now we know for certain. Auguste says that he's been trailing Roux ever since. He assembled a crew and tracked Roux to Rome and Carnevale."

"So he could follow him to the treasure's location, just as he's doing now."

"So he could protect you," Gabriel said, surprising her. "He found out Captain Roux had written to you, that he had hopes for you to meet him in Rome." A shadow passed through his eyes with the words. Did he suppose she'd planned to leave with Christophe all that time?

"Auguste always did know how to spy on people. He's made a career out of it." She avoided his wounded gaze, the unanswered questions crying out through his eyes. "So you boarded his ship and followed me here, hoping to rescue me from my own stupidity?" How shameful a notion it was now, to have someone risk their lives for her after she'd utterly betrayed him.

"We all did." He grinned at her silent question, the first hint of mirth she'd seen since their meeting. "Jean-Paul and Cecile, even Désirée are all waiting on the decks of Auguste's ship, eager to bring you home."

Her throat nearly closed in on itself. "All of you? You all came for me, even after—" She couldn't speak it, not while staring into the benevolent eyes of the one she'd hurt the most.

He nodded gently. "They love you." So much more than his simple words poured from his fervent stare. She saw in him the depths of a broken man, all of his love and trust in her lying shattered at her feet.

Distracting herself, she glanced through the twisted vines. "Désirée is aboard ship?" she asked, a chuckle escaping her throat.

"Indeed, she is. She is appalled daily by the uncouth behavior of Auguste's crew, but she's surviving."

A smile touched Madeleine's lips. "No doubt Cecile has made a few *friends* in her time at sea."

The knowing look her husband shot back answered her question without words. They both chuckled, scattering the gloom of their meeting, reminding her of days long past when nothing but joy filled their union. *If only.*

Her gaze wandered over him—the fine attire now sullied with dirt, the shaggy hair and unshaven face. Even besmirched with moss and mud, he still looked like a gentleman in his high-collared shirt and linen trousers, his knee-high leather boots caked in wet sand. One could probably remove every bit of refinery from home and he would still emanate the presence of a dignified man.

A shy smile curved her lips as she leaned forward and reached out, softly tugging at a vine tangled in his hair. Gabriel's bright gaze followed her hand from his head to the space she held out her open palm with the plant atop it. A boyish grin captured his face, drowning the hurt screaming out through his gaze. Every fiber of her being begged her to fall into his arms, to let him love her again. Oh, but how could she without destroying the very person she adored?

Madeleine closed the vine in her fist, dropping her gaze from his. "Christophe and Stefano have a combined crew of over a hundred men," she said. "They know I possess the knowledge to help them find the treasure. They will not rest until they've found me—and now you." The very idea of a single hair on his head being harmed launched frightening tingles down her arms.

"We saw them when we approached the shore," Gabriel said. "Auguste ordered his crew to turn the ship around, just beyond the reach of their spyglasses. I rowed in under the cover of night. I have a boat waiting on the shore to take us back as soon as night falls and we can safely cross the jungle."

The first inkling of hope she'd dared let in sprang up inside. Madeleine searched his face, wondering how he could still save her after all she'd done to him. "Thank you." The words barely squeezed from her throat before silence enveloped them once more. Words could never express what she felt in this moment—the longing and the gratitude, the utter shame.

Gabriel watched her in silence, the warble of birds and swaying tree branches coasting into the cave. At last, he set his jaw, swallowing back whatever hesitation plagued him. "We might not be alone like this again in a while. The girls will certainly smother you in their concern the moment we reach Auguste's ship. We might not get the chance to—" His eyelids fluttered before he took a determined breath. "I want to know why you left like you did. The letter—it said I had no fault in it, but how can that be? I must have done something to hurt you."

The sincerity in his eyes wracked her with guilt. Madeleine shook her head swiftly. "You never hurt me. You were nothing but the perfect husband to me every day of our marriage. Please don't think I left because of you—not for a moment."

His shoulders visibly relaxed, though the question remained on his face. "You chose him, then. You wanted to be with Christophe Roux." His fingers coiled around his knees.

"No, Gabriel. I never wanted anyone but you." Her throat prickled, pain rising up at the hurt dwelling on his features. "I know it must have looked like I ran away to become romantically entangled with Christophe, but it's not the case. His ship was simply a means of escape for me. I considered him a friend and nothing more, even when he made it plain to me that he desired a more intimate relationship."

Fire lit Gabriel's face, his nostrils fuming and skin red before his anger melted back into hollow sadness. "Then, *why?*" His question sunk low, permeating the recesses of a soul she'd cautioned not to feel. He must have wondered it every day since the morning he woke up to an empty pillow and a hastily scrawled note instead of her.

"Jean-Paul didn't tell you?" At the shake of his head, she inhaled an agonizing breath. How could she bear herself in front of this man, this flawless being who could never even fathom the depths of depravity she'd crawled from to reach him? He spent every day, desperate to cure the disease that had taken his mother, battling the evils of men who wanted to rip their nation asunder, helping people. How could she tell him he'd strapped himself with a harlot from the street who had spent her youth doing nothing but entertaining seedy clientele and chasing money? He deserved so much better than her.

"I—I'm sorry." She shook her head, the words falling flat on her tongue. "I wish I could explain right now, but I can't. You deserve to know everything, and I can't manage a sentence of it." Hot tears burst from behind her eyes, and Madeleine bit them back. "Please, let us wait until we're safely back aboard ship. Not while the threat of being captured and killed still looms over us."

Her husband opened his mouth as if to speak, then clamped it shut. A swarm of emotions clouded his face before he leaped to his feet and strode into the cave's yawning darkness. His boots would pace the stony floor for hours, his restless energy never ceasing until night settled gently over the island. Madeleine could only listen, pressing her face to the cold granite, praying he'd obtain the strength to let go of her for good.

When the sun plunged past the horizon, the golden air giving way to dusty purple and finally a shroud of black, Madeleine and

Gabriel prepared themselves to head for the beach. Gabriel stuffed the few items he'd taken from his bag back into its canvas shell and retied his knee-high boots. Though he'd brought a lantern with him, he kept it fastened to his bag. They'd agreed to use the cover of night to their advantage. Any light or sound they might make could draw undesired attention their way.

Sweeping aside the cave's viny cover, Gabriel waited for Madeleine to crawl out of its mouth before he alighted behind her. The rocky surface jabbed at her bare feet, the wind whipping through her thin layers of silk. Ignoring the bumps gathering on her bare arms, Madeleine used the rock's uneven face to guide her through the dim moonlight trickling through the trees.

Once they reached the forest, touch became her primary sense. Madeleine blindly swept her arms through the dense foliage, swiping back leaves and fronds. Her feet cried out every time she took a misstep into a thorny bush or dead limb protruding from the ground. More than once she tripped, Gabriel's sturdy arms the only thing that kept her from tumbling to the ground.

At last, the moon shone its brilliant white light at the edge of the trees, casting a path to the ocean. Madeleine followed the water's salty aroma, the sound of its nocturnal waves beating against the shore. With the sand finally under her feet to relieve her throbbing skin, she looked out across the turbulent water. Only a sliver was visible beneath the moon's glow, stretching from the lonely beach to the edge of eternity.

Turning back to her companion, Madeleine noticed him basking in the island's beauty along with her. He turned in a circle, his gaze skimming the palm trees bending over the sand, the white waves smashing the beach with mighty force. It occurred to her that he might never have seen such wild beauty before. For all the wealth he possessed, he hardly ever stepped foot from the château. Yet somehow, he'd conquered his fears in order to save her from her own perilous actions. The thought lodged an unexpected lump in her throat.

When he had his fill of the lush beauty surrounding them, Gabriel squinted at the thick brush lining the trees. He took a few steps forward, leaning in. "I left the boat tethered to a tree and under a bush somewhere around here. The beach looks different than it did this morning. I could have sworn these trees were farther back from shore then."

"The tides rise significantly at night." Madeleine joined him near a cherry tree, peering through the hair flying free in the wind. "Did the tree have any significant markings?"

Gabriel's mouth contorted, his brows narrowed. "It did, actually. It formed an "x" with another tree, and it had fronds that dipped lower than the others." His hands went to his slim hips as he scanned the tree line again. "There," he said, pointing farther down the coast. "It's over there near that rocky spot."

Excitedly trailing her husband over the wet sand, Madeleine imagined the ship waiting for her somewhere in the distance. Just one boat ride away waited safety, food, the chance to forget that Christophe Roux and Stefano Cavaretta ever existed. Squelching her fear over seeing Auguste again, she focused on the good. At least Gabriel wouldn't fall prey to this godforsaken island.

Swept up in her musings, Madeleine nearly collided with her husband as he stopped short before they'd reached the trees. Following his gaze, she noticed the water now surging up to the palms he'd described, the bushes below them soaked. Gabriel carefully meandered into the remaining muddy space, bending low and throwing the bushes aside. After a few moments of searching, he stood up, empty-handed.

Even in the dim moonlight, Madeleine saw the horror on his face when he turned back. "It isn't here," he said, face paling.

Panic twisted her gut. "What do you mean, it isn't there?"

His broad shoulders lifted, his hands splaying on either side of him. "I don't know. This is the spot I left it. I thought I'd secured it to this tree, but the tides were so much lower when I left it."

Madeleine frowned. Could one of the men have found it in their quest for her? If so, they would know someone else had found their way to the island, and Auguste's entire ship could be compromised. She looked back to her husband, only to see him staring off into the ocean, his normally statuesque form wilted. Shifting her gaze past him, she saw what occupied his attention.

There, tossing among the blustery waves, his rowboat drifted farther from shore every second. It had lost its oars, the boat alone coasting out to sea. They'd never reach it now, not at this hour with the undertow so furious.

"Will Auguste come get us?" she asked, knowing the absurdity of her question even before Gabriel pivoted back to her with a sober expression. Auguste couldn't navigate his ship this close without endangering the lives of everyone aboard his vessel.

"I told them not to send help unless they could see we were clearly in danger."

Gabriel and Madeleine stared at one another in silence, the ocean surging and retreating at their feet. The icy water chilled her bare toes, but it couldn't produce the shiver that rippled through her body at her awakening knowledge. They were two people alone against a hundred men, and no one could rescue them but themselves.

Nineteen

Madeleine tiptoed through the brush, careful not to make too much noise. Her bare feet shifted from muddy soil to twisted branches and back again, daintily navigating the island's untamed foliage. Gabriel had offered his boots to her that morning, but she'd grown accustomed to running wild without anything on her feet.

A brackish wind blew over the verdant space, rustling the trees and prolific flowering shrubs around them. Madeleine inhaled the scents of tropical fruit and nectar, her stomach full for the first time in days. With enough food to last them halfway through the week, they'd both enjoyed a modest breakfast of bread and pecorino Romano.

Glancing through the quivering fronds, Madeleine took in her husband's form, stealthily creeping among the vegetation beside her. His watchful gaze darted this way and that, alert to the unseen dangers lying in wait. The poor man had never trained for battle a day in his life, but she knew he'd defend her with everything he had if the need arose.

After their unsuccessful venture on the beach, they'd dragged themselves dismally back to the cave. Nobody had spoken for what seemed like days, each retreating into their own thoughts within the cavern's chilly darkness. Madeleine knew he wanted to ask about her leaving again. It had plagued his eyes ever since he first dared to voice it. Yet out of respect or self-preservation—she didn't know which—he kept his lips shut.

When the urge to sleep crept over her, Madeleine crawled deeper into the cave and stretched herself over the hard floor. Even with her arms bundled tight around herself, the chilly air speared through her thin dress and pricked her arms. She'd barely slept the night before, shivering beneath the gusts of wind tunneling through the cave. Tonight, she expected no different.

Moments after she bedded down, Gabriel's footsteps scuffed the rocky earth. His masculine scent quickened her heartbeat as the sound of him easing his body to the floor stirred beside her. "May I?" he asked, one tentative hand on her upper arm.

Madeleine nodded, then realized he couldn't see her in the blackness. "Yes." The single word invited him to lay beside her and wrap an arm protectively around her. Whether simply to warm her or to show his abiding love, his presence soaked into her like the shelter of a home after hiking a snowy mountain.

Melting into his embrace, Madeleine let her breath fall in sync with his, drowning herself in the steady rhythm of his heart beating against her back. She closed her eyes, content with the brush of his stubble on the nape of her neck, the way his arm gently cradled her. How fiercely she'd missed this when she'd ripped herself from his life. How hard it would be to let it go again.

"We can't hide out here forever," he said, fracturing the stillness. "They'll eventually find us, or we'll run out of food."

Either prospect planted a dreadful ache within. "What else can we do? We can't hope to face Christophe and Stefano's combined forces." Her mouth twisted in contemplation. "Perhaps we can wait them out. They're bound to give up eventually. We can live off of fruit and fish until they do."

Gabriel released a low chuckle that tickled her neck. "You certainly are the adventurer, aren't you?" He sighed. "I wish we could, but they'll find us. This island isn't big enough to hide us indefinitely. They'll scour the entire thing before they turn their ships around and waste the resources it took to come here. I doubt Roux would even go then."

Frowning, she knew he was right. Both men had waited so long to reach her, for clandestine motive or otherwise. They wouldn't let her go without leaving every stone unturned. Her survival might well depend on which one found her first. Gabriel's might stand in jeopardy either way.

"So we only have one card left to play, then," she said. "We are the only two with any knowledge as to the treasure's whereabouts."

She felt him nod against her. "If we find it, we'll at least have leverage. Perhaps we can negotiate a way off this island in exchange for the money. I don't trust either of those deviants, but it might be our only option."

Madeleine let silence enfold them as she thought on his words. Christophe had so long been obsessed with finding the Moon King's treasure, perhaps he would find a way to protect them in order to claim it. It revolted her to imagine relying on the traitor again, but she would do anything to save her husband's life.

Within the stormy fog of her thoughts, Madeleine at last drifted off to sleep, secure in the arms of the one she loved. When morning dawned and streams of sunlight filtered through the vines, she found herself still tucked in his embrace. How alluringly wonderful it felt to imagine she could stay here, warm against his chest, that she could love him without bounds. Then memories of all the men before him flooded in, affirming the fact that she must run before she dismantled his entire life.

Now, the jungle beset them on every side. They'd set off from the security of the cave, knowing their only hope lay beyond the waterfall plunging through the island's center. As its booming presence grew closer with every step, Madeleine's pulse picked up speed. There were bound to be scouts along the river. They knew she needed water to survive and she had no other way to get it.

Staying as close as possible to the enormous rocks flanking the fall's splattering sides, the couple snuck to the river's edge. Gabriel glanced in all directions before he bent low to refill the two canteens he'd brought with him and slung them over his back again. The cold water stung Madeleine's feet as she stepped into the rushing waves, taking the hand Gabriel offered her.

The water rose higher, first dousing the hem of her gown, then making the silk float around her as she descended deeper. Gripping Gabriel's hand, she navigated the hard, slippery rocks beneath her feet, nearly toppling several times in the tempestuous currents. The couple wandered deeper, until the river covered their bodies to the neck. The rumbling waterfall plummeted into the gulf just meters before them.

"We'll have to swim from here," Madeleine shouted over the thunderous roar.

Gabriel nodded, squinting through the splashing water. He let go of her hand and ventured toward the falls, his arms propelling him onward.

Following suit, Madeleine clenched her teeth against the cold and swept her arms through the water. Her feet kicked behind her like frog legs, driving her over the rushing river and under the falls. The cascading water hammered over her head and shoulders as she ducked beneath it, holding her breath until she'd emerged on the other side.

Head surfacing from the icy waters, Madeleine gasped one giant breath. Her arms and legs paddled around her as her eyes adjusted to the dim light. Over their heads yawned a serene grotto, its ceiling so high, she couldn't make out the top. Madeleine treaded water until her bare feet touched on rock again, its pointed edges creating an uneven floor for her to stand.

All of the waterfall's sound was pushed out to the river, creating a quiet space within its hidden compartment. Gabriel sloshed through the water, climbing onto a bordering ledge. He turned and held out a hand to her, chest pumping either from exhaustion or excitement, or perhaps both. Madeleine reached up, letting him grasp her hand and haul her from the bone-numbing pool.

Shivering, she took handfuls of her dress and squeezed water from her skirts. Her hair was plastered to the sides of her face, the thin fabric of her gown clinging to her tremulous form. She looked through the dark space and saw Gabriel appeared much the same—like a drowned rat just pulled from the sewer.

Her heartbeat pounded in her ears as Madeleine surveyed the small space. Jagged walls of black rock flanked their every side, save for the falling water at their backs. Sunlight spilled through the thundering curtain, glistening off its droplets and painting the walls in ethereal reflections. As far as her gaze could wander, she saw nothing but rock.

"How did Henri even find this place?" she asked, quelling her disappointment while standing in awe of its beauty. "How did he know about this island in the middle of the sea? How could an aristocrat like him have explored a piece of land so remote?"

Gabriel shook his head, his face tilted upward as he took it all in. "I don't know. In all my years of studying him and the things he did for the barony, I never heard mention of this place. You would think he would have tucked it into a letter or a story somewhere. Clearly, he knew the island intimately."

Feet scuffing the rocky ledge, Madeleine approached the wall and stretched out her arms in front of her. The hard, craggy surface of the wall stood firm beneath her caressing fingers. She sidestepped once and then again, feeling her way along the wall for some type of unseen passage or hidden clue. Beside her, Gabriel did the same, fanning out wide in the opposing direction.

The wall and its adjacent ledge extended another few meters, but soon Madeleine hit the spot where it ended. She spread her arms out on either side, feeling the space high above her head and bending low to explore the area at her feet. After several fruitless minutes of groping the rocks and finding nothing, she sighed.

"Have you found anything?" Madeleine called across the cavern.

Materializing from the darkness, Gabriel wagged his head. "Not a thing. There's nothing but a bunch of pebbles this way. I thought perhaps Henri had located a concealed cave like the one you found."

Shoulders falling, Madeleine looked around the quiet space once more. "There has to be something. If Henri went to the trouble of designating a secret room and painting the treasure's location on its ceiling, surely he left something here—a clue, another map, a relic, *anything* that might explain why he brought us here."

Her husband's mirthless chuckle echoed off the walls. "If there's one thing I've learned about Henri, it's that he liked to make a spectacle. Think of all the dead-ends we've reached, only to find a hidden element behind the obvious that pushed us forward. He was a master of deception, and I think he had fun with it."

Madeleine gazed out the shimmering cascade rushing past them, inhaling the earthy scents it carried that mingled with sweet perfume. "I'm weary of playing his games, especially when my very life depends on winning them." If they failed to find Henri's treasure, surely no safety net remained for them. Stefano would find and kill them both.

When Gabriel said nothing, Madeleine shifted her gaze back to him. He studied her quietly in the pool's crystal reflections, his thick brows drawn contemplatively. "What are we supposed to do now?" she asked, wishing beyond reason that her husband in all of his intelligence could devise a plan that eluded her.

Gabriel leaned back against the wall, planting his hands in his drenched pockets. "We keep looking." He shrugged. "What else can we do? If we never find the treasure, then at least we'll die with the knowledge that we fought until the very end—together."

The prospect chilled her. He said it with such surety, such calm, that she could almost convince herself he spoke of something other than their demise. Would he really sacrifice so much for her? Or like Christophe, would he find a way to employ her as a bargaining tool?

"I'm sorry I led you here," she said finally, throat aching. "You shouldn't have to die for me. You shouldn't have to make that decision."

Reflected light from the pool at their feet danced in his bright eyes. He studied her intently, completely, the depth of love in his gaze channeling through her frozen places. "There is no decision," he said, voice husky. "You are my wife. I go where you go. I never let you walk alone."

Biting back her tears, Madeleine stared into his devoted face, into the flared nostrils and clenched jaw. He would join her through fire—she knew that now. But at what price? He'd thrust aside his every fear and plunged into the unknown so he could chase her to an island that could only bring him harm. What a waste of a good man's life, to throw it away on the depraved soul withering away in her shell of a body.

"We shouldn't neglect the pool," Gabriel said at last, pushing off the rock wall. "Henri might have hidden something beneath the water."

Madeleine nodded, still swallowing back her tears as she dipped into the river behind him and flooded herself again in the frigid waters. Welcoming the numbing effect it had on her tingling skin, she dove beneath the surface and felt along every crevice hiding in the pool's recesses. When neither of them found anything of note, they swam beneath the falls again, their heads popping up in the rampant river.

The sun was high overhead now, dribbling through the trees in honey-tinted rays. Madeleine basked in it showering her skin, its warmth contrasting with the cold pulsing through her extremities. Easing her head back, she floated on her back for a cathartic moment, watching the white water plunge from the rocks above and splatter over the river's dancing face.

Letting the river carry her downstream, Madeleine dragged in the fresh mingling of coconut palms and wildflowers drifting through the air. She could almost forget in a place like this, with the treetops swaying above her and the water caressing her broken form—forget that certain death lurked behind the trees. Raising her head, she looked across the water's rippling surface at Gabriel, who treaded water an arm's length away.

Madeleine couldn't help the grin that slipped over her lips at the sight of him, his normally curly hair masking his face. He tried to push it back with his hand, but the mess impossibly clung to his eyes. A giggle burst from her lips as she watched him shove a handful of hair to the top of his head, leaving a messy mound over his forehead.

Lifting one brow, he peered back at her with a frown. "Are you laughing at me?" he asked, a playful lilt in his feigned growl.

Shaking her head, Madeleine tried to match the serious look he gave her, but yet another chuckle erupted from within. "I'm sorry, truly." She covered her mouth in her hands, kicking her legs to keep her afloat.

"I'll have you know, this hair is the source of much admiration in polite society," he said, lifting his chin in imitation of a pompous vaunter. "It's sparked many a conversation at the dinner table. Everyone is curious how I keep it properly fluffed."

Madeleine broke into a fit of laughter, a snort issuing from her nose. "Oh, indeed." She caught her breath, her arms struggling to keep the river from sweeping her away. "How have the birds and fish told you they like it? Have you already made admirers out of the lizards?"

He glared in return, a spirited glint in his light eyes. "As a matter of fact, they have." Without warning, his arm blasted through the water, tossing a freezing wave over Madeleine's head. Stunned, she gasped the air before another assault splashed her face.

Energy surged through Madeleine's core as she swam toward him, blocking his attacks with one hand. When she'd nearly reached him, she found her footing on the rocky riverbed and scooped armfuls of water toward his face. Laughing, Gabriel returned fire, dousing her yet again. The pair bombarded each other mercilessly, the waterfall's roar drowning out their laughter, until Madeleine's arms burned and her sides ached with laughter.

Chest surging, she gulped a long breath and let her body sag against the rocks. The delighted look hadn't fled Gabriel's face as he caught his breath, laughter still escaping his throat intermittently. He still stood so close to her, one hand steadying himself on the rocks behind her head, their legs brushing in the moving water.

Breath slowing, Madeleine peered back at him. Golden reflections moved over his face, his chin so low it dipped into the water. His eyes glimmered as they roved her face, examining every curve until they locked with her steady gaze. Despite the cold spearing through her, warmth descended. It felt like coming home to look into those eyes and remember the shared moments between them. If she listened to her instincts, she would have pulled him close and kissed him, ended the sting of their separation. But she couldn't. Not after what she'd done.

Just then, two male voices breached the tranquil scene. Gabriel slammed himself against her, pressing her to the rock. One finger touched his lips to indicate silence as his wary gaze lifted to the sound just above their heads. Boots scuffed the rocky soil, their chatter growing more distinct above the waterfall's roar.

"I still don't see why we have to scour this place looking for her," one man said. "She's bound to come out when she's hungry enough."

"You heard the captain," his partner replied. "Said she'd sooner starve than help us find the money. Two men in every corner of this place—that's the only way we'll find her."

"Seems to me she's over near that eastern shore. Lost her trail twice in those trees. I'd bet anything she found a place to hide."

"Hiding or no, we'll find her before the week is up. Captain's organizing the search parties as we speak. He'll find her, all right."

Their voices faded as they tramped down the river, leaving Madeleine with a sense of dread. Her eyes flashed into Gabriel's face, so near his breath warmed her cheek. His jaw clenched, every protective instinct he had emanating from his worried expression. As his gaze hooked with hers, she saw her heart's fear mirrored in his eyes. They had to form a plan, or nothing but destruction lay in their future.

Twenty

The scorching afternoon sun had nearly melted to evening when Madeleine and Gabriel crawled back into the cave they had jokingly dubbed their home. It couldn't shelter them much longer—that she knew. Once Christophe scattered his scouts over the island, they were bound to discover the secret hideaway. Then she and Gabriel would have nothing left to do but beg for their lives.

Henri Clement's voice taunted her as it so often had since she'd become acquainted with his wily ways. The words in his letter played over and again in her mind as she watched Gabriel pull his tinderbox and lantern from the pack he'd brought with him. Why would he leave such clear instructions for his offspring if nothing lay in the spot he'd indicated? Surely, he wasn't enough of a trickster to set up one huge, elaborate joke.

Shaking her head, Madeleine turned her sights on the soaking dress cleaving to her body. After their adventure at the river, she and Gabriel had foraged for a lunch of berries and coconut, intent on returning to the site marked on Henri's map. The river had risen with the afternoon tides, splashing over the ledge they'd stood on before. They once again searched every nook they could find in the secret space, but yielded nothing. If only Henri hadn't chosen a spot so dark, where a lantern was impossible to bring.

Body weary and shivering in the chilly cave, Madeleine debated removing her clothing. It was the sensible thing to do, what with river water still dripping from her hem, but how might Gabriel react? When last they'd shared such an intimate moment, they were in dizzying love with each other, swept up in passionate embraces. Now, the idea of peeling away her clothes in his presence felt awkward and strange.

Madeleine's teeth knocked together, reminding her she needed warmth despite her misgivings. With a few strikes of his tinderbox, Gabriel's lantern hissed to life, shedding yellow rays over the cave's walls. It would never be enough, not with cold seeping to her bones and numbing her toes. Madeleine scanned the expanse of cave behind her, surprised to find a pile of twigs and dry brush gathered on the floor near the back. Someone must have employed this cave before them.

Taking Gabriel's tinderbox, Madeleine knelt before the twigs and swept her wet hair over one shoulder. Striking the piece of steel against the flint, she worked until sparks ignited, falling into the kindling. With her face near, she gently blew until a flame erupted in the box. Carefully, she grasped the tinderbox in one hand, touching it to the dried-out vines neatly bunched on the floor.

Looking on, Gabriel's brows gathered. "Aren't you afraid they'll find us if we have a fire? The smoke will certainly give us away."

Madeleine shook her head, gently coaxing the small flame with a twig. "I won't build it high enough for the smoke to leave the cave. Just enough to warm my hands and feet before they fall off."

In mere moments, the flame had consumed the brush, licking the air as it ate through the firewood. Satisfied, Madeleine returned Gabriel's tinderbox and snatched the crumpled blanket from the floor. He was busy hunting through his pack. Now was as good a time as any to remove her dress.

Careful not to get the blanket too wet, Madeleine wrapped it around herself and began tugging the cap sleeve shoulders down. She struggled to wiggle out and simultaneously keep the blanket high, but she refused to let it slip—especially when Gabriel stopped his searching halfway through her endeavor to stare up at her. Yanking the sodden fabric down, she worked until it had rolled completely off her torso and fell around her feet.

Her husband's gaze glued to her as Madeleine crouched low and laid her dress out to dry by the fire. What must he think of her—behaving so boldly and thoughtlessly in his presence? Her actions had to remind him of the times they'd shared. If she'd seen any other road to take, she would have.

Avoiding his gaze, Madeleine turned from her soppy dress and plunked down before the fire. Immediately, the warmth she'd created began to sink through her frozen limbs. She kept the blanket tight around her shoulders as her feet emerged, her bare toes wiggling in glorious splendor. The scent of ash curled into the air, pacifying her startled nerves.

Madeleine relaxed as she looked across the small fire and saw Gabriel pulling off his own shirt. He appeared thinner than she remembered. Beneath the lean muscles of his chest, his stomach slightly dipped. Had he been eating at all since she'd left? He'd been known to forgo a meal or two at the château, especially when something troubled him.

"It's a good idea," he said, unfurling his shirt with a flick of the wrist and laying it beside Madeleine's gown. He made no move to take off his trousers, a fact which relieved her. Enough awkward tension drifted about the cave already.

Taking a seat opposite her before the fire, Gabriel reached again into his pack and produced a new hardtack biscuit. He'd only brought three, and they'd finished the first that morning. After breaking off a piece, he reached over the blazing branches and handed it to her.

Grateful for sustenance, Madeleine accepted his offering in silence. She watched him take a bite and crunch it, that look of contemplation never fleeing his face, before she brought her own food to her lips. Her tongue rejoiced with the home-baked flavor bursting over it, even if it did have a stale tinge. She didn't care that it was dry and difficult to chew. At least she wouldn't starve today.

"How long do you think we can survive on what I brought with me?" Gabriel asked, drawing her attention from her thoughts.

She frowned, thinking on his question. Sometimes she forgot that he'd never experienced want before, never had to feel the pangs of hunger as she had. "A week, maybe." She sighed dismally. "Christophe's men will catch us before that time, anyway."

Gabriel nodded before retreating into silence once more. A terrible burden crushed his normally vibrant expression. His forehead wrinkled and mouth curved down as if he were attempting to solve the greatest of mysteries. Every bit of light and joy had evaporated from his eyes, now tortured as they flitted about the cave, searching for an answer that simply wasn't there. Madeleine bit into her bread again, accepting that nothing remained for them but falling on Christophe's mercy. For her, he might grant it.

Wind rushed over the cave, rustling the vines and carrying the sweet odor of hibiscus. In the distance, the swell of ocean waves almost lulled her into believing their promise of serenity. When she looked back over the fire, she noticed Gabriel watching her, the reverie in his eyes replaced with yearning. A chill skittered up her spine, and Madeleine replaced the blanket that had slipped off one bare shoulder.

"I know you said you didn't want to talk about it," Gabriel said, his look intensifying, "but if these are our last moments together, I can't stand for it to be like this."

Madeleine glanced away from his pleading expression. It tugged too strongly on her heart. "Like what?" she asked, as if she didn't feel the weight of their frigidity as much as he did.

"Distant. Taciturn." He shifted, tucking his legs beneath him in order to kneel before her. "Every time I look into your eyes, I see heartache and brokenness, and I want to know why. I want to help."

Her head shook, her gaze fixed to the darkened wall beyond the fire's glow. "You can't help, just as I can't change what's done. It's useless to try."

Gabriel issued a frustrated grunt. "How can you believe that? How can you throw away everything we had for whatever it is that afflicts you?" He rose up on his knees. "We shared six months of marital bliss together—six perfect months of spending nearly every waking moment together, learning about each other, loving each other. Then, one morning in Rome, I woke up to find a note that explained nothing, and you floating across the sea with a former beau. How am I expected not to have questions?"

A surge of tears stung behind her eyes, but Madeleine forced them back. Of course he wanted to know why she'd fled. She owed him an explanation. But the truth would rip everything she loved about him away. It would destroy the innocence that spending a lifetime sheltered within the barony had built.

"You aren't," she said at last, watery gaze still fastened to the wall. "But please believe me when I tell you that I'm only protecting you with my silence. Time will reveal the truth, I'm sure, but right now your heart is too entangled with mine to hear it without getting hurt. Only when your heart lets go of mine will you be able to know the truth without devastating consequences."

"Madeleine, my heart will *never* let go of yours."

At his solemn declaration, her gaze swept to his face. He knelt before the fire, hand over his heart, imploring her with every fiber of his soul. "Please, tell me," he said, his passion stirring her. "Please let me in." The firelight capered in his eyes, spilling the contents of his haunted soul for her to pick up and either mend or crumble.

Madeleine swallowed, wagging her head once more. "I can't, Gabriel. I'm sorry. I *must* shield you, even from myself."

"What if I don't *want* to be protected?" He slammed his fist against the cave's solid floor.

The question startled her, wrinkling the skin between her brows. "What?" Of course he needed her protection.

Gabriel breathed in the smoky air for a few moments, his heated face softening. "Madeleine, you are a *good* person. Your heart *bleeds* for those around you."

As she opened her mouth to protest, his hand rose, halting her. "When the Guardians took me," he said with one hand still firmly over his heart, "you wouldn't rest until you knew I was safe. When Pascal threatened your life, you didn't give a second thought to yourself or your own happiness. You set that all aside to ensure that Désirée and I survived." His head angled, the depth of his emotion sweeping across the cave and into her. "That night we met in the old church and I told you I wanted to marry you—your very first concern was how Caroline would feel."

Madeleine's skin flushed as she tucked the arms beneath her blanket securely around her body. She still wondered about Caroline sometimes, hoping she'd found happiness.

"You are brave, and loyal, and wonderful," he said. "These qualities are among the many that caused me to fall in love with you." He shook his head, sadness emptying into his eyes. "But Madeleine, you take too much of a burden on your own shoulders. You take yours and everyone else's."

Her head wagged in defiance. "That's not what I'm doing." Hadn't she invented this burden herself, the day her weakness whispered into her ear that life in a brothel would at least bring her comfort?

"You blame yourself for *everything.*" He sank down on his legs, staring into the crackling fire before speaking. "When you thought your brothers were dead, you took the responsibility of it on your shoulders. You charged yourself, a child of five at the time who could barely save her own life, with the guilt of their demise."

The urge to defend her reasoning heated her blood. "I should have done more for them. We could have been a family all those years if only I'd devised a better solution."

The fire she'd constructed on the cave floor had weakened to diminutive flames licking the wood, but still it highlighted the pity in his eyes. "Listen to yourself." His voice chilled her. "You saved your brothers' lives. You couldn't have stopped those men from coming after them, just as you couldn't have prevented Père Andres from being shot or kept Caroline from hurting. You *can't* save everyone, all the time. You're only one human being."

Tears budding in her eyes, Madeleine averted her gaze to the floor, where the firelight's shadows frolicked in soft waves. She could barely feel its heat anymore, only the chill that their angry exchange of words planted deep inside of her. The fire snapped, piercing the rush of evening tides along the beach beyond their cave. Madeleine savored its woodsy aroma, letting it drift through her lowest, most aching parts. He could never understand the life she'd endured, not even after he'd followed her to the world's edge in the attempt.

"You could have come to me," Gabriel said, voice tender. "When Pascal threatened to harm you, if you'd only told me, we could have devised a solution together. So much heartache could have been avoided if you'd have only let me in."

When she didn't answer, he came closer, walking around the fire's edge on his knees. "Don't you see? I don't need you to rescue me. I don't *want* you to rescue me." He stopped before her, palms facing up in supplication. "I want to be your partner, the one you come to with your problems. I want to face the storms of life together. Let me be the one to rescue *you* sometimes. *Please, Madeleine.*"

Her gaze climbed to him, his vulnerable sincerity nearly driving her into his arms. Shifting protectively, she pulled the woolen blanket tighter against her skin. How could she explain all that had transpired before she met him, the things she'd done to survive? He would never look at her the same. He would utterly scorn her, and if he didn't, he should.

"You don't understand," she said, trying miserably to control her quivering voice. "You can't. We grew up in such different worlds. I became a woman in the impoverished streets of Paris, not the gilded walls of a château."

Gabriel reached out, taking the hand she'd left poking out from her blanket. "Tell me about it."

Blinking back her salty tears, Madeleine looked down at the strong hand cradling hers. "I thought remembering would bring me peace, but it has only brought agony. Each new memory drives me further down. Apart from those early days in the little cottage with my parents, my life was black—meant to stay in darkness, meant to stay buried forever."

He squeezed her hand. "I know about Cavaretta." The statement flung her gaze to his. "Cecile told me. I confess, it bothered me at first, but"—he blinked, emotion crowding his face—"I've come to terms with it. I've accepted the fact that I'm not the first man you loved. I just want to be the last."

Her stomach knotted, his innocence crippling her. "If Stefano were the worst of my sins, I never would have left you in Rome."

Gabriel hunted her eyes, lips pursing as if deciding. At last, he swallowed and set his jaw determinedly. "I don't care," came his resolute reply. "I don't care about Caveratta. I don't care about Roux. Only you. *You* are the one my heart longs for. Blast the men of your past."

His devotion quickened her tears, but it would never be enough. If she allowed him to try to keep her afloat through all of this, she'd sink him, surely. She would break the defenseless heart peering out through his fervent eyes. He *must* be free of her. Despite every voice screaming against her, she must make him understand.

"Gabriel—"

His free hand cupped her cheek. "I don't care if you had five lovers. I don't care if you had ten—"

"Hundreds." The single whispered word stilled him. Gabriel looked back into her eyes, a stunned expression grabbing hold. "There were hundreds," she said again through her fiery tears. "When I was sixteen years old, I was a prostitute in one of the poorest neighborhoods of Paris. I made my living serving the seediest clientele you can imagine, pouring myself out night after night, emptying myself of any glimmer of the person I was before."

Her heart mourned at the utter anguish swimming in his eyes. His hand went limp, falling from her face to the fire warmed floor. Madeleine trembled inside, wishing she could go back—if not to the time she'd stumbled into that brothel, at least to the time before she'd met him, to keep him from the agony she saw in him now.

"I only wanted to keep you from it," she said, her vision a crystallized blur as Gabriel raked a hand through his abundant hair, his gaze darting about the cave's darkened corners. "You must free yourself of me. Pretend I never existed. It has to be this way." She could barely voice the last of her words, emotion choking her.

Gabriel's gaze swung to hers. His chest swelled, the battle clear along every surface of his agitated body. His jaw flinched, his neck muscles tight, as he opened his mouth to speak. Yet no words came. He could only look at her, disappointment mingling with his shock, the sting of betrayal alive in his ballooning nostrils and clamped lips.

At last, he unfurled himself and ducked on his way out of the cave. The sound of his boots scuffing the floor lingered in her ears long after he'd departed. Heart shattered, Madeleine collapsed to the floor, staring into the dying fire as tears swamped her eyes. At least he understood now. At least he knew why he must let her go. But oh, the ache that swelled anew within her.

Madeleine wept against the cold stone floor, her sobs unhindered as the wind and waves swirled outside her cocoon. How safe she'd once felt here. Now these walls were a prison, binding them together against their wills. This island, as beautiful as the sand and sea were when glistening beneath the sun, had proven nothing but the trap Jacques Chapelle had devised it to be. It surrounded her, taunting her, a thousand voices laughing at the foolish love she still harbored for her husband.

Squeezing her eyes shut, Madeleine cried into her open hands for hours, prayers she couldn't even articulate groaning from deep in her soul. If God really cared the way her father had so often told her, would he still turn an ear to her pain? Or would her words even reach heaven's door after the depth of her sin?

Hopeless, she cried until she had no tears left, her body weak from struggling for so very long.

Twenty One

Despite the expectation that it would die at any time, the flame Madeleine had sparked still quivered among the twigs for hours. She lay with her back pressed to the stony cave floor, blanket snug around her naked body, staring vacantly at the ghostly shadows shifting over the ceiling. A rumble in her stomach gnawed at her, but she ignored her persistent hunger pangs, letting her warm tears roll out from her weary eyes and pepper the floor beneath her.

How fruitless it all seemed now—life and the pursuit of happiness. For a short, glorious time, she'd fancied herself among the luckiest of humans to bask in unhindered joy with the one she loved. How quickly and ruthlessly such bliss could be ripped from beneath a person, leaving nothing but an empty, aching void.

Her thoughts drifted to the little cottage she'd been reared in, to the perfect peace she remembered from her childhood. Despite their lack of means, her family had been bound together in love. They needed nothing but each other, their worlds wrapped up in one another, in God and the satisfying work of reaping the land. But how long did that peace last for her mother and father? How close had God stood when her neighbors tied a noose around her father's neck?

From the age of five, she'd known nothing but war and poverty. Hate had ensnared her in its claws, stripping her innocence and immersing her in the world's harshest realities. She'd learned to numb her conscience, to quiet her father's gentle voice in her head, urging her to do good in spite of the dangers lurking near. The rich might do good if they so wished. She had only to survive.

Madeleine rolled to her side, her back sore from its uneven bed. Lifting her knees, she curled into a fetal position and stared listlessly at the crackling fire. Defying her best efforts, Pierre Bertrand's face kept surfacing in her mind, his dark, knowing eyes stirring her soul. *I'm not strong like you, Papa. I can't keep on with an army at my back.* Her father had preached until his dying day, standing firm in his faith even as they dragged him to his execution. If only she had such fortitude, such assurance in the unseen forces around them.

She realized with dwindling hope that she might very well be living her last days, estranged from the person who mattered more to her than life. Christophe's search parties would undoubtedly find them. Even if she disclosed what the map said, they would think her a liar when they explored the cove behind the waterfall and found it empty. What a cruel joke Henri Clement had played on them all.

Christophe might try to save her, but the combined strength of his crew and Stefano's men would overpower any effort he could make. A sliver of hope rested in her brother's vessel, anchored far off the eastern shore, but even that presented little chance of helping them. If Auguste did unwisely decide to rescue them, the number of his crew could never match the amount camped on the beach and the forest beyond. Then, Cecile and Désirée's lives might be lost along with them.

Pressing her face to her flattened hand on the floor, Madeleine sunk into defeat. Perhaps she should have acted her way through her confrontation with Gabriel. She could have told him she left because of Stefano and at least relished their last moments together. What did it matter now, with the threat of death so imminent? Why hadn't she just lied and took him up in her arms, comforting away his grief? Now he wandered the island alone, aware of his wife's every painful transgression, wrestling with the truth she wished so desperately to bury.

The vines at the mouth of the cave rustled, but Madeleine supposed the wind had scattered them. When the jangle of boots climbing the wall outside reached her, she stiffened. What if one of Stefano or Christophe's men had found her? Lifting her bleary gaze to the bend in the cave, she didn't relax until Gabriel's face appeared around it. His skin was pink and hair thrown askew by the night wind. He looked tired, as if he'd spent these endless hours in constant motion.

A sense of assurance shrouded him as he walked across the quiet cave, his eyes locked on her withered form. He stopped short before the sputtering fire, close enough that she could see speckles of ocean water on his windblown clothes. He took all of her in, deeply, as if pouring over a work of art that moved him.

Heart in her throat, Madeleine pushed off the ground to a sitting position. Just the sight of him rammed tears to her eyes once more, her unworthiness crushing her. How had she been allowed to love this man—this perfect specimen of humanity who had never performed an evil deed in his life? How could God have allowed him to suffer at her hands?

Gabriel knelt before her, nothing but the most tender love for her beaming from his eyes as his hand found her cheek. She shook her head, the urge to fight sprouting from her basal instincts. "No. Please don't do this." *Don't choose to love me and sacrifice yourself.*

His fingertips swept her cheekbone, his thumb finding the cleft in her chin. He pulled a long, soulful breath through his nose, resolution capturing each of his placid features. "I chose you in the walls of that crumbling church the night we took our vows before God. I choose you now."

"You can't," she whispered shakily. "Don't you see? I'm so very far beneath you. My humble birth aside, you can't be married to someone with as dark a past as mine." Why couldn't he just see reason?

The corners of his mouth lifted, even as deep thoughts knit his brow. "You are not so far beneath me. I can still look into your eyes. I can still hold you." One arm hooked around her, drawing her close.

"No," she said, two hands on his chest pushing him back. "Someone will recognize me. They'll start rumors about us—whisperings that could rip your entire world apart."

Gabriel chuckled softly, the firelight capering in his eyes. "Madeleine, if you worked in the poorest parts of Paris, no one I associate with will recognize you, especially after six years." His gaze wandered her face lovingly. "If they do, I will gladly relinquish whatever they try to take from me as long as you're at my side."

Her vision misted with uncontrollable tears, fiery streaks running unchecked down her face. Gabriel anchored her head at his chest, letting her cry against him, letting her every emotion spill out like a broken dam. "I saw your face," she hardly managed, sobs wracking her body. "You hated me the moment you found out. You only convinced yourself otherwise in the meantime."

Holding her tighter, Gabriel stroked her hair. "No, my dear one. I hated myself." He sighed, his chest swelling and falling beneath her head. "The day we married, I promised to be a rock you could lean against through the deepest of your valleys. I vowed to love you no matter what came our way, and I meant it."

The tips of his fingers massaged her scalp, the study thud of his heart pacifying her. "I failed you the day you set sail off the Italian coast," he said. "You thought you couldn't come to me. You believed me to be so weak that I would crumble at hearing of your past."

Madeleine sniffed. "It isn't your fault. I made that decision for us both."

"Oh, but it is." Gabriel's open palm meandered over her hair and blanketed shoulder. "I shut myself in that château for so long that I dreaded to venture into the world beyond it. I let my fears dictate my life and yours. How could you imagine that I'd follow after you, attempt to rescue you, when all I've ever done before is run from what scared me? You had every right to think of me as a coward."

Her hands gripped his arm. "I could never think that."

A laugh bubbled in his chest. "You would have been justified if you did." Taking her head in his hands, he raised her up to look at him. "I had a long talk with God on the beach tonight. I saw my shortcomings, everything I could have done differently to show you that I will fight for you as you have fought for me."

Pure devotion radiated from his face in the fire's red-orange glow. "I love you, Madeleine—always. For everything you were before me and everything you will be." His hand found hers in the dim light, their palms warm together and fingers lacing with natural ease. "Say you'll let me walk beside you and not behind. Let me be your shelter when you need one, and you can still be mine."

A sad smile touched her lips. All this time, she'd focused on how deeply she'd failed him those many years ago. She hadn't paused for a moment to consider he might wish to protect her as she had so fervently done for him. She found herself nodding, even as the weight of the past weeks crashed over her in waves, her tears converting to sobs once more.

Gabriel placed one hand at her back and the other below her legs, gathering her into his lap. His strong arms wound tightly around her, his woodsy scent filling her every sense. The tears came unbidden, her bitterness and self-loathing, every moment of condemnation pouring forth. Safe in her husband's loving embrace, she released them into the shadowed night, the hope of restoration supplanting every place she left vacant by letting go.

Sometime in the night, Madeleine awoke. Her eyes were weighted from so much weeping and her body weary, but somehow her heart felt unchained. Peering through the cave's stillness, she squinted at the last glowing embers of the fire she'd started. Gabriel stirred beside her beneath the blanket, his hand tethered to her waist. How peaceful he looked, asleep with one arm tucked beneath his head and his unruly hair falling over his forehead.

Madeleine gazed at him a long time, appreciating the man she'd married like never before. He was so much stronger than she had ever imagined. News that would have sent most men scampering off to the hills met him with dignity and bravery. If only she'd seen herself through his eyes sooner. If only she'd given herself the chance.

Gingerly lifting his hand off her bare stomach, Madeleine eased herself from his embrace and crawled past the dying fire. The cave's uneven floor jabbed at her knees, but she crept on until she reached the veiled mouth. A trickle of moonlight barely dripped through the vines, scattering over the floor in moving crystal rays.

Sweeping them aside, she tossed her legs out the rocky entrance. A light breeze pricked her naked skin, but she climbed out of the cave anyway and landed on the solid earth below. Her dress probably hadn't fully dried yet anyway. With her loose hair whipping behind her, she wandered carefully through the forest, using the moon's white light to guide her.

The beach resting beyond the cave's wall sat in tranquil beauty as she approached. The forest held nothing but the quiet sweep of wind in the trees, but here the waves billowed and crashed by their own rules, dumping the salty sea over the sand without inhibition. Madeleine gazed into the canopy of winking stars overhead, her feet treading a path in the cold, pliable sand.

Eternity stretched before her—the endless sky telling of its journey over the vast earth, the sea writhing in motion to the moon's pull. Madeleine's dark hair flew on the wind, loose strands whipping into her face. She made not a move to sweep them back, but instead stretched her arms out on either side and let the gusts blow over her. Closing her eyes, she stood there like a bronze statue, letting herself finally feel what she'd refused to for so very long.

She had been a peasant, a prostitute, an actress, an unscrupulous treasure seeker. For the first time, the flow of her life had no interruption, no hidden memories clouding her understanding. For the first time, she accepted all of herself—the mistakes she'd made and the unwise roads she'd traveled. They were each a part of her now, but finally she grasped that they did not need to shape her future.

Her eyes fluttering open, she honed in on one particular star gleaming brighter than the others. Papa had always spoken to her of God's love—his strong, caring leadership a living example of the deity he revered. Madeleine had never truly understood it until now—the depth of love and mercy that passed earthly understanding. Now she could feel it everywhere, all around her, coursing through her. An unfathomable spirit shrouding her in unmerited grace.

Ignoring their icy chill, Madeleine stepped a foot in the rumbling waves, and then another. She kept on until her body was surrounded in the cleansing Atlantic waters, her head dipping below the surface and emerging with cold, salty trails running down her face. Her bare arms and legs worked steadily to keep her afloat in the tempestuous tide, but no fear overtook her. At long last, peace blanketed her soul as she gazed into the boundless sky.

The ocean tossed around her, moving through her, cleansing her. Her life had passed through the bitterest of storms, and now the waters of the deep renewed her, giving her baptism into her future life. Madeleine could only stare into the diamond-studded sky, gratitude filling her. No matter what she encountered tomorrow, she had been given the strength to face it. For the first time since the pieces of her memory had finally clicked together, she had hope. She would never walk alone again.

Twenty Two

The first rays of morning brought endless prospects, a renewed sense of purpose, hope in the face of certain defeat. As the dawning sun gradually spilled over the treetops, its presence should have ushered in panic. After all, it carried the reminder that Christophe and his men were close behind, ready to hunt them like a pack of wild dogs. Instead, it met two welcoming souls, entwined together in love despite the forces of life that had sought to separate them.

Madeleine and Gabriel stood on the beach beneath a shelter of palm trees, watching the morning sky flood with pinks and sparkling yellows, the bleakness of night melting away. He held her from behind, his arms wrapped around her torso, his heartbeat thumping at her back. Madeleine leaned into him, savoring his warmth as they enjoyed the splendor of the waking sun together.

When she'd crawled back into the cave in the wee hours of night, exhausted but invigorated, he'd woken to her nuzzling beside him. He'd frowned at her wet hair, a smile quickly replacing the expression as he gazed into her eyes and stroked her soft face. They were at home in each other again, the way it should be, the way God had designed their union.

The night had joined them together as man and wife again, fear and self-loathing dissolving into trust as they met in perfect harmony. Madeleine had always cherished this time with her husband, but never like this. Not with the reality of her past spread open before them, their passions awakened in the knowledge that although carnal sin had once gripped her life, this act would only bind her tighter to Gabriel for the rest of their days.

In the hours before dawn, a plan had formed as they lay discussing all that had happened since she'd fled Rome. She told him about Christophe's romantic advances, about Jacques Chapelle and the Moon King's letter. Gabriel listened with girded brows, the parts of her story doubtlessly moving around in his mind to determine their next move. By dawn, they'd arrived at a solution that could very well work. After a breakfast of dry bread and cheese, they set out for the beach, ready to meet the day's challenges head-on.

Madeleine smiled, Gabriel's hair tickling her neck as it fluttered in the morning breeze. It seemed unreal that they could be standing together in a marital embrace on this island—this mysterious place that she'd thought could only bring greed and death. His constant love for her had proven otherwise. He'd taken her hand and lifted her from her mire of self-destruction, granting her new life. They would face this island's demons together, and they would prove victorious.

Turning in his arms, she looked up into his eyes, a shimmering blue in the dawning light. Gabriel leaned close to kiss her forehead, a vow of protection against all they must face. His large hand moved down the side of her face as his forehead came to rest on hers. If these were truly their last moments, at least she had this perfect memory. At least they were bound together in love for the rest of eternity.

"Do you think it will work?" she asked, voice tentative.

His broad shoulders rose. "I don't know. I hope so." His thumb brushed her cheekbone. "Either way, I'm going to fight for the woman I love with everything I have."

With Gabriel's assurance coursing through her, she sighed contentedly. "We'll have to get going soon," she reminded herself. "Christophe is bound to send search parties out soon, and the longer we stay here, the more danger we're risking."

Lifting his head, he skimmed the shore with a worried expression. "You're right, I just—" His gaze darted back to her, taking her in as if for the last time. "I just want to hold onto you a moment longer. I want to relish this moment."

Her fingers tensed on his bicep. "I know." After what they had planned, they might never hold each other like this again.

Gabriel's brow creased. "Are you sure you don't want to switch roles in this plan of ours? If Cavaretta hurts you—" He let the thought coast in the air between them, unspoken but unmistakable.

"No." She shook her head. "It won't work any other way. If you do what I'm planning to, his men will kill you before we have any chance of distracting them. It will all be for naught and I'll lose you." Her stomach soured at the thought. "I can't let that happen."

Swallowing, he nodded. "All right. I suppose I'll just have to trust that God will keep you safe." The back of his hand swept lovingly over her cheek. "You are strong and you are mighty, but never forget how much you mean to this man who holds you now. If you have the chance to save yourself, *do it.* Even if it means leaving me behind. I would rather die with the knowledge that you're safe than to put you in jeopardy."

To promise such a thing ran contrary to everything within her, but she found herself nodding. She would allow her husband to protect her, to sacrifice himself for her if he must. But she would move heaven and earth to save him if she could. Hadn't he done the same for her when he hopped aboard a ship and followed her here? Their destinies were bound together. With poignant sadness, she realized that they would likely live or die as one.

The island seemed to forge a path for her as she reluctantly left her husband and journeyed through it. The tall grasses parted in the wind; the billowing treetops pointed her toward the island's heart. She would go forth in courage, despite the heartbeat hammering against her ribcage and every instinct begging her to turn back. If she had any hope of saving Gabriel, she knew there was no other way. She must face the lions of her past and emerge triumphant or at least die trying.

The soft earth squished beneath her bare feet, fallen leaves scattering before her. Madeleine wound a solo path through the forest and along the river, glancing back at the towering falls as she passed. The mystery of Henri's map had yet to reveal itself, and she almost didn't care. Perhaps the glorious rush of clean waters was a treasure to Henri in itself. It sparkled like nothing else she'd ever seen in the golden rays of morning sun.

Turning aside from the river's flinging spray, she pointed herself back the way she'd first come. Before long, the din of men's voices echoed through the trees. She heard them chatting amongst themselves as they partook of a meager breakfast around their campfires. It took every bit of courage she had not to duck and run as the sight of their bobbing heads rose into view. She would prove courageous. She would not flee.

Forcing a rod of iron through her spine, Madeleine stepped around a thicket of trees and into a clearing, in full view of the first men skirting the edge of camp. At first, they did not seem to notice her. Then, as she strode regally through the dirt, one head swiveled toward her, then another. Madeleine kept her back straight and head lifted as Stefano's men jumped into action, standing to attention and seizing the hilts of their swords.

Without the trees to hamper her vision, Madeleine could see the whole camp. Canvas tents dotted the entire clearing, surrounding a much larger tent that no doubt housed their leader. Three firepits were scattered among them, each with its own fire and group of sailors gathered around it. By now, every eye had pinned on her, some wrathful and others curious, none absent of the fear working for Stefano must have planted deep within them.

Madeleine kept walking toward the center of camp, willing legs wanting to buckle to keep moving. Before she could reach Stefano's tent, two brawny men had grabbed her by the arms, eager to pretend they'd captured her themselves. Steel shrieked in the morning mist as every man with a weapon withdrew it from its scabbard and aimed it at her. Her face remained calm as someone rushed up to Stefano's tent and whispered through the flap.

Blood surged through Madeleine's body, her heart pounding in her eardrums as the tent flap flew back and Stefano's face appeared from behind it. His cold stare raked over her in one terrifying sweep, starting with her bare feet and ascending slowly to her face. He hated her dirty, tattered appearance, no doubt. Yet as his glinting gaze settled into hers, a malicious expression of triumph lifted his lips. Good. Better he think she'd come crawling back on her hands and knees than to imagine she might have a plan to ensnare him.

With a jerk of his head, Stefano ordered his men to bring her inside the tent. The pair obeyed, their iron grips clamping hard around her upper arms as they dragged her toward the enclosure. Stefano swept back the flap for them to pass through, his hawk-like leer never leaving her.

"Over there, in the chair," he said, indicating a single wooden chair tucked under a small table.

The chair noisily scraped the dirt as they hauled it across the ground and tossed her into it. Madeleine couldn't help but marvel at the artistry of the piece itself. It had carvings of fruit and vines surrounding the back and around the seat, as if he'd plucked it from the midst of a palace. Only Stefano would employ such extravagance while camped on a deserted island in the Atlantic's midst.

Her gaze wandered his temporary dwelling as he found a rope and began looping it around her hands behind her back. The tent was tall enough to walk through at any point and about five times larger than the one she was meant to share with Christophe. A large bed lined one canvas wall, an actual mattress, silk sheets, and pillows resting atop a raised platform. Besides the table and the chair she sat on, he had several brass-studded chests along one wall, no doubt for clothes and weapons and whatever sort of supplies a twisted maniac like him might need.

The ropes dug tight into her wrists as Stefano yanked them with a grunt. Madeleine had to bite her lip to avoid crying out. Instead, she tracked his cat-like movements as he stalked to the table and retrieved a glass decanter she hadn't noticed before. The two who'd deposited her here vanished beneath the tent flap, leaving her alone with their leader, now sloshing red liquor into a glass with a long stem.

Stefano swished the drink around in his glass, a smirk curving his lips. "Wine?" he asked, tilting the glass toward her so the fermented odor touched her nose.

"No. Thank you." Madeleine lifted her chin, aware he was toying with her. She'd seen him play these ridiculous games with many a guest who had passed through their doors in Venice.

Shrugging, he brought the refreshment gingerly to his lips before taking a slow swallow. His gaze met hers over the glass's edge, full of delight as he lowered the glass and set it back on the table. "That's delicious. You really should try some."

Rolling her eyes, she exhaled. "I really didn't come here to share a glass of wine with you."

"Oh, yes?" One thick brow arched roguishly. "And what did you come here to do with me?"

Madeleine fastened her lips, his insinuations already digging below her skin. He would try to disarm her, debase her, make her feel like nothing so he could manipulate her in whatever way he fancied. She had only to stall him until Gabriel could complete the task at hand. Reminding herself of this fact, she took a breath through her flared nostrils.

"I came here to talk," she said. "To negotiate an agreement between the two of us."

Stefano paced the ground in front of her, an amused look sizing her up. "From your appearance, I can only gather that you don't have much to negotiate with. You're weak, hungry, thirsty. You're dying. Why should I help you? What can you give me?"

Madeleine perused his lithe figure from his finely sewn tweed waistcoat and white silk shirt to the imported trousers and polished boots that betrayed not for an instant the wild landscape surrounding him. He had jewels on his fingers, silver buttons on his waistcoat. One concern above all others motivated his every waking moment—wealth, *power*.

"I can give you riches beyond compare," she said, noting the way his shoulders unconsciously perked. "I know where the Moon King's treasure lies, and if you seize it before Captain Roux, you'll be richer than you ever dreamed, far richer than you are already. You could own Venice and everything around it for days."

Stefano considered her offer, two fingers brushing his chin. "How do you suppose I remove it from here without him noticing? I can't very well whisk it magically away."

"Using me, of course. Christophe won't let me go, no matter how much he wants to. If you tell him you've captured me, he's bound to behave foolishly to get me back. He would even sacrifice the treasure itself if he thought my life was in danger."

Stefano's brows gathered. "What about his crew? I doubt they're so willing to throw away such riches for the sake of their captain's ill-fated obsession with you."

Madeleine feigned a casual laugh. "Those men worship the very ground he walks upon. If he conjures a lie good enough to convince them, they'll blindly follow him. I've spent weeks on board that ship. I know the buffoons those men are."

A sly grin slipped over Stefano's face as he spun toward her. "And why would you bring such a proposition to my door rather than Roux's, when he so clearly wants to protect you?" His shrewd glare bore through her. "Why would you risk yourself by coming to me instead of him?"

Compelling a clear, strong voice despite the urge to shrink before him, Madeleine looked him square in the eye. "Because you are the only one on this island with enough wit to truly save me. If I went to Christophe, surely you'd find a way to outplay him."

Something wicked twinkled in his eye, a secret satisfaction enveloping him before he slowly fell to his knees on the ground beside her. Tingles raced over Madeleine's skin the closer he came. His dark gaze moseyed along her every curve, his chest pressing her arm, his face so near that his chill-inducing breath showered her neck. Madeleine forced herself not to recoil, even when his fingers touched her chin and traveled down her neck.

"You always knew how to flatter a man," he said, his fingers anchoring around her throat. "You're quite the expert on using your charms to get what you want, aren't you?" When she said nothing, he brushed his thumb down her gullet before withdrawing his hand. "To think, you tried to offer yourself to one of my sailors in exchange for hiding you."

Madeleine rolled her eyes skyward. "That is not what happened."

"Oh no?" He tilted his head as if genuinely curious. "What did happen, pray tell?"

Drawing in a breath, she snapped her gaze to the corner, where the edge of his tent flapped in the breeze. "I never offered myself to anyone," she said quietly. She knew with a bitter twinge that she couldn't tell the real story without endangering the fool's life. Better for Stefano's crew to suppose her still a prostitute than for another man to die.

"He says otherwise, and I'm inclined to believe him." Stefano ogled her again in an open manner meant to unnerve her. "After all, I once fell victim to your deceptive ways myself. Great power can be gleaned from a man's desires, and you know just how to wield your *skills* to harness it."

Her eyes flashed as her gaze latched with his, meeting his challenge. "You were never a victim. You saw what you wanted and you took it. You're as predatory as I ever was when I sought to betray you."

His mouth wrinkled wryly. "Perhaps. And now you're here with me once more, defenseless. I can indulge whatever *desires* still linger when I look at you."

Madeleine swallowed, her pulse picking up speed. She knew from experience what kind of twisted fancies Stefano had. He wouldn't be tempted as his subordinates were. He'd had her in the flesh and always wanted more. That grotesque excitement mingled with hatred overtook his stony features as he reached for something behind the chair.

"You present an interesting proposition," he said, the harsh scrape of steel stiffening her. "It might even work if I wanted a resolution without bloodshed or suffering. But I have better ways of getting you to talk, and I'll have a lot more fun performing them."

Icy panic rolled over Madeleine in waves as a sharpened blade rose into view. Against her will, she flinched, its glimmering surface launching her heart into uncontrollable palpitations. *Just a few more minutes,* her mind screamed. *It can't be but a few more min-*

227

utes. Yet as the smell of steel passed beneath her nose, she doubted she had that long.

"If you kill me, you'll never find the treasure," she managed. "I promise, it's so far buried that you can't find it without me."

Stefano laughed, the grating sound ringing in her ears. "This blade can do a lot more than kill." His dark gaze descended it lovingly, wringing Madeleine's gut.

"Christophe will never work with you if you hurt me. He'll turn on you." His knifepoint was trained on her now, nearer to her face with every breath.

"Roux is a fool," he said, pressing the blade gently to her throat as if trying it on for size. "He still believes he might win you over, woo you into telling him the island's secrets. Everyone but him can see he's pining after a woman who will never love him. His crew will turn on him at the first sign of trouble."

The breath rasped from Madeleine's throat as each touch of his blade blasted shivers through her body. He posed it expertly, just hard enough to bring her a hint of pain without piercing her skin. Higher the knife prodded, moving up her neck until it rested just below her ear.

Stefano drew close, his hot breath swirling on her skin, the scent of his vanilla-tinged clothes swimming about her head. "There were so many things I wanted to do when you lay in my bed. Even as you slept, I'd dream of it, knowing you would leave if I ever tried."

Nausea stirred in her middle. Madeleine's chest surged at a rapid pace, the feel of his blade pushing into her cheek leaking cold sweat over her brow. She'd seen that same delirious luster in his eyes the day he'd cut her as they fenced in his practice room. The idea of hurting her excited him in a perverse way she'd never quite grasp. As she was falling in love with him, dreaming of the life they might share, he was picturing his knife at her throat.

The knife's tip finally nicked her on the tender skin below her jaw. Madeleine cried out, instinctively shielding the injured spot with her shoulder. Stefano stared breathlessly at the small trickle of blood oozing out, the urge to hurt her again building to a crescendo on his frenzied face. Madeleine realized with dwindling hope that she must fight, or the tiny cut swelling with pain on her neck would be the first of many more serious wounds.

Yet what could she do now? Her fingers writhed fruitlessly behind her back, unable to unravel the knots he'd looped around them. She had not a weapon to defend herself, only an arsenal of fighting skills and charm that were no use to her now. The blade swiped her skin again, a deeper cut stinging below the first. Madeleine inhaled a shaky breath, determined to withstand whatever malicious act he could conjure if it meant her husband's survival.

Stefano's nostrils flared, his lips snarling in pleasure as he aimed the blade on her again, toward her undulating collarbone. She sucked in a breath, preparing for an assault and then another. How many could she survive before she fainted and fell prey to even darker schemes?

"Cavaretta!" a voice penetrated the terrible buzz in her head.

Her attacker paused, his knife a mere hair from her chest.

"Cavaretta!" the voice came again from outside the tent, more insistent this time. "Cavaretta, I know she's in there. This isn't part of our agreement. You bring her out before I come in there and kill you with my bare hands."

Irritation shone in Stefano's gaze as he dropped his knife into the dirt, his frenetic breath slowing. He looked at her for a long moment, indecision twisting his lips. Then with a growl, he stood and whirled toward his row of chests, yanking out a silver-handled sword. With one strong flick of his wrist, he threw back the tent flap and emerged into the morning light to confront Christophe Roux.

Twenty Three

Madeleine couldn't stop her nerves from hammering no matter how hard she tried. She closed her eyes, nearly forgetting she still sat with arms tethered behind her in Stefano Cavaretta's tent. The canvas walls and furnishings floated into a haze. Breath still flew from her mouth in desperate waves, her heart thumping against her ribcage. Blood trickled down her neck, trailing along her chest and into her bodice. Stefano's knife lay discarded on the dirt floor, a reminder of the sinister slices it had impressed in her skin only moments before.

The rumble of angry men's voices snapped her attention back to the argument ensuing outside. Madeleine employed every bit of strength within her to lift off the ground and toddle to the door Stefano had just departed. The disturbed flap left a small gap just large enough for her to spy through. Squinting, she made out Christophe's imposing form standing tall in the clearing with most of his men not far behind. Closer to the tent, Stefano had planted himself in the dirt with equal fortitude.

Knowing she had little time, Madeleine tried again at the knots around her hands, but they defied her best efforts. If she knelt, she could certainly retrieve the knife from the floor, but how could she possibly maneuver it in a way to break through her bonds? Weary from battling her own fear, she sank begrudgingly back in the chair and peered through the gap again.

"You and I agreed that she would stay under *my* protection," Christophe said through clenched teeth, his neck muscles ruddy and taut.

"She walked in here of her own accord, Roux," Stefano said. "Ask any of my men here. She wasn't captured or forced into my camp. She sought me out."

"And now I'm here to take her back to mine, as we agreed."

Stefano's condescending laughter echoed from tree to tree. "Do you really think I'm so daft to let her go once more so you can lose her as you did the last time?" His head shook. "No, my friend. Our arrangement ended the moment you let her slip into the forest, forcing my men to waste their time looking for her and delaying discovery of the treasure we came for."

Sword drawn, Christophe took two sizable steps forward. "If our arrangement has ended, then we are at war. I ask you to consider your next steps wisely, Monsieur Cavaretta. We are a trained group of warriors. We fight each day as a profession. It won't take much for my men to subdue and defeat yours."

Stefano's dark gaze wandered over the throng at Christophe's back, a smirk creeping across his lips. "Do you not think I employed just as skilled a crew as yours to seek out a treasure worth fighting for?" His arm swept the men sprinkled through camp, each looking poised and eager to engage their intruders. "You must ask yourself a question, Captain. Are your men ready to fight and die to save one woman just because you love her?"

The query sparked a scattering of whispers and gestures among Christophe's crew. The brawny captain tightened his grip on his sword, arm muscles bulging in the morning sun. "My men know the truth behind the fight ahead of us. It is not only for a woman, but for the knowledge she possesses. Men have lived and died for decades in this place, unable to find the Moon King's bounty. She is the only person here who can reveal his secret and make us richer than we ever dreamed possible."

Confidence emboldened his sailors now, many nodding, others standing taller and grasping the hilts of their swords. Aboard ship, Madeleine had often witnessed Christophe's uncanny ability to fortify and unite them, even when dissension stirred among their ranks.

Stefano raised an irritated brow. "The woman herself has said over and again that she's unwilling to divulge the treasure's location to anyone, least of all you or me." He pinned his gaze briefly on his tent, causing Madeleine to gasp and retreat out of sight. "If I am the only one willing to truly press her for the information, then so be it. At least we'll have it at long last."

Christophe lifted his sword, nostrils flaring. "What did you do to her?" Fury rammed through his every stiffened muscle, ire flaming from his sky-like eyes toward Stefano.

His opponent calmly simpered back. "Not much of anything, *yet*. Though I do very much like the look of her as she is in my tent at this very moment." Perverse laughter lit across his men, their expressions and lewd gestures leaving no doubt as to what they imagined. If only they knew she sat still fully clothed and bleeding, that their leader took pleasure in much darker shades of expression.

The captain's jaw clenched, his rage nearly uncontainable. "You will make her presentable and hand her over to me now or I will have your head. No more of your games."

"And what will you do if I refuse?" Stefano broadened the shoulders beneath his fine linen shirt and embroidered waistcoat. "Are you prepared to fight for her? My methods will produce the treasure we both are after, I assure you. If you want me to stop, you're going to have to face us all."

Madeleine's heartbeat thumped wildly as she watched the indecision warring over Christophe's face. Of course he didn't want to endanger his crew if he didn't have to. How many among them shared Stefano's desire to force the information out of her? He risked splitting apart his crew and causing not only a battle with Stefano, but a civil war within his own ranks. Yet as his chin rose and his face took on the strength of steel, she knew he would never let her be harmed without throwing himself on the fire to protect her.

"There is no need for my men to fight today," he said with resolution, inciting more whispers from the *Sirene's* crew. Christophe's boots propelled him forward, stomping clouds of dust into the air before coming to rest in the clearing's center. "I challenge *you*, Stefano Cavaretta, and you alone. Fight me. Brandish your sword with mine, and the better of us will take her as prize."

Straining against her bonds, Madeleine felt her head begin to spin. *No, no. Don't do this.* Surely as a seasoned pirate, Christophe knew how to fight, but not like Stefano. The crazed man spent hours every day dedicating himself to the art. He'd mastered technique. He knew how to spot an opponent's weakness from a single glance and exploit their every move against them. He would prevail, and Christophe would die for nothing.

Cavaretta grinned, his wicked gaze tumbling to his own weapon as it rose into the glimmering sunlight. "I like this idea," he said, his every languid movement mocking the one who'd challenged him. "I accept." Two words alone stabbed fear so deep into Madeleine's gut, she could barely breathe as both groups of men faded into the trees and their leaders began to circle each other with predatory gazes latched.

Their boots pounded the dusty clearing. Wind bearing the smell of ocean and sand tousled their hair. Christophe's forearms tensed beneath his rolled-up shirt sleeves, his broad chest pumping as his blue eyes expertly surveyed his foe. Stefano's countenance housed only amusement, as if he stood face to face with a child barely old enough to hold a sword in hand.

Christophe struck first, blade aimed at the other man's side. Easily avoiding the blow, Stefano responded with a jab that narrowly missed the captain's neck. On and on they went, swords clanging and scraping, grunting, gasping for breath. Fixed to the edge of her seat, Madeleine watched with growing certainty that Christophe possessed more skill than she had recognized. Indeed, the two made an even match.

Teeth gritted, Christophe thrust his sword at Stefano's middle. Stefano spun away, aiming his weapon at his opponent's back. The blade nicked his shirt, but Christophe managed to whirl the other way in time to avoid being cut. Their swords crossed in the dancing shadows cast by billowing treetops. Steel bashed with steel again and again, resounding through the forest and disturbing the squawking birds.

Both men were out of breath, sweat seeping from their glistening hair. With each motion that compelled them, their movements came slower, more lethargic. Someone would tire and the other would seize the advantage, surely. *God, let it be Christophe,* Madeleine's lips silently pleaded. Already, both sets of sailors appeared ready to jump in and defend their leader if necessary. A war stood on the brink of eruption, and she could do nothing but watch from within the confines of her tangled ropes.

Just when both men had tired enough to stand back, simply glaring at each other through narrowed eyes with chests pumping furiously, a voice came whizzing through the leaves. At first, only an indistinct holler touched their ears. Then, the words sharpened as their messenger neared. "Fire! Fire!"

Every eye in camp rolled toward the source of the tumult, where a breathless sailor emerged from the brush moments later. "Signore, someone has set fire to our ship. The inferno is too large. She'll be eaten by flames before the day is over." The distant scent of burning wood coasted from the sea, planting a triumphant smile on Madeleine's face.

Stefano spun back to Christophe, fury raging on the features he'd kept so cool before. "How dare you?" he shouted, veins popping along his neck. "You speak endlessly of our agreement, then you pull an insidious stunt like this? Whatever promises we exchanged before we set sail are void now. It's each man for himself."

Genuine shock had frozen the captain's face in horror. Now he glared at his accuser. "You really think I would do this? What purpose would it serve me? I can't have my ship weighted down with the lot of you."

"You wanted us to be weakened! To live only at your mercy!" Stefano charged Christophe with sword extended. "You destroyed our food and supplies. You knew we would starve without those provisions."

Lifting his weapon, Christophe blocked the enraged man's attacks as they fell one after the other. "We're dependent on those supplies, too!" he tried to reason. "We'll all starve without them." But Stefano couldn't be reached. He kept flying at Christophe, blind with wrath, casting aside his practiced grace. All around them, his men followed suit, crashing into one another or smashing their swords together. Madeleine gripped her chair, fear and victory mingling. *It worked, Gabriel. It worked.* Yet still their lives were in just as much danger as this morning.

The smoke intensified, drifting through the trees and blanketing them in an acrid mist. Through the haze, Madeleine spied the two men still locked in combat, teeth exposed and muscles raging. Gone were the swift and elegant moves that had once propelled their fight. Now they swung at each other with brute force, shrouded in the desperate need of soldiers fighting for their lives.

Stefano had Christophe cornered near a tree, Christophe's back shifting over the bark as he defended himself. The breath hitched in Madeleine's throat. She sensed the Italian's advantage. Christophe had nowhere to run, so little maneuverability from his position. He could only block or duck the onslaught of blows bearing down on him.

With a guttural roar, Stefano plunged his blade toward the captain's middle. Madeleine held her breath. This hard of a hit would surely kill him, no matter where it landed. With polished quickness, Christophe sidestepped the advance, letting Stefano's sword dive into the wood where he'd once stood. Panic flitted over Stefano's brow, his arm frantically trying to yank his blade out in time. But Christophe took no time delivering the final blow. He'd planned it this way, baited his opponent into an ill-fated trap.

Madeleine winced as Stefano stumbled backward, Christophe's sword still deep in his stomach. The captain pulled his weapon back, blood drenching the blade and spilling over Stefano's torso. A quiet moment lingered where the melee around them seemed to vanish into a rumble before Stefano blinked, hands rising to his middle. His mouth opened in disbelief. So many hours he'd spent dedicating himself to this very moment, and still it had conquered him. He collapsed to his knees and slumped sideways into the dirt, as every man who'd fallen before him without celebration.

In seconds, Christophe had darted through the battle raging throughout camp and thrown Stefano's tent flap back. His tense body visibly relaxed when he beheld her sitting there, still alive despite the cuts now clotting on her neck.

"Are you all right?" His breath came hard as he shoved his sword, still slick with Stefano's blood, back into its sheath. Dropping to his knees, he examined her wounds with brows gathered. "You're bleeding. What did he do to you?" The fire in his eyes said he'd kill Stefano again if given the chance.

Madeleine trembled with the shock of what she'd just witnessed. "I'm fine. I'm just—shaken."

Seeming to understand, Christophe nodded and moved around her. "Here, let me get you out of that chair." His fingers deftly worked to untie the knots Stefano had cinched around her wrists.

When the cords fell away, her skin both sang with relief and stung with deep indentations.

"You need to tell me where that treasure is," Christophe said as he bundled the rope and flung it toward Stefano's tidy bed. "That's the only way I can see to save more of my men from dying out there." His worried gaze drifted to the tent wall, through which the rasping screams of war hadn't stopped.

Madeleine sighed as she rubbed her injured wrists. "I don't know where it is, Christophe. I promise I would tell you if I did."

His eyes flashed. "What do you mean, you don't know where it is? You saw Henri Clement's map, didn't you?"

"Yes, I saw it, but his map clearly indicated that the treasure lay behind the waterfall." Her head shook in response to his hopeful expression. "It isn't there. I checked twice, in every space around and behind it. The treasure's gone. Either someone took it already or it was never there to begin with."

Shooting to his feet, Christophe seized a handful of his messy blond hair. His thoughtful gaze ricocheted around the tent, searching for a miserably elusive answer. "It can't be. It just can't. Every person who has lived on this island has been marooned here by force. If they found the treasure, they would have bargained for their lives with it—not dumped it into the ocean like some fool. There has to be some trace of it *somewhere.*"

Her shoulders lifted. "I'm sorry. I know it isn't what you wanted and it doesn't make sense, but it's the truth."

Christophe released a frustrated growl. "And now my men are dying in a battle I can't stop."

Pulse surging, Madeleine debated how much she should tell him. Hadn't she started this war on purpose, so that Christophe and Stefano's men would turn their vengeance on each other rather than her and Gabriel?

"It doesn't matter now," Christophe said, stooping to snatch Stefano's knife off the ground. "Here, take this. Run to my camp.

It's empty now; it will be the safest place to wait until a resolution comes of this battle. I must stay here and fight."

Finding Stefano's sheath, she thrust the knife inside and wagged her head. "No, I must go check on my husband. He could be in grave danger out there."

Christophe stopped an arm's length from the door and swiveled back to her. "Your husband is in Rome. Have you taken complete leave of your senses?"

Pushing past him, she emerged into the chaotic battle with one goal in mind. "Gabriel is here. He followed me." She glanced back at the stunned pair of eyes tracking her. "Who else do you think set fire to Cavaretta's ship?"

Twenty Four

Smoke burned her nostrils, filthy air tunneling down her throat and irritating her lungs. Madeleine raced through the foliage, her chest pumping and legs aching. Rocks and jagged tree limbs jabbed mercilessly at her bare feet, but she kept on. The clamor of fighting raged at her back, men's shouts lighting the air before her. She burst from the forest to the sight of an orange and black sky, Stefano's ship a mere ball of fire bobbing atop the waves beyond the lagoon.

Shielding her eyes from the sun with one hand, Madeleine squinted through the haze. Men still jumped from the blazing vessel, most of its remaining crew scattered over the water, swimming to shore. Scanning every face, every body moving toward her like a bunch of drowned ants, she stepped into the icy tides and let them wash over her feet. Her heart thundered wildly. She didn't see Gabriel among them.

How certain he'd been as they lay tangled together in that cave. If they did nothing, they both faced certain peril, but if they shifted the status quo, perhaps they could obtain the upper hand. Neither of their rivals could afford to stay on the island long with their food and supplies burned. If such destruction did not spur them to fight, as Gabriel suspected it would, at least they would leave this place long enough for him and Madeleine to escape.

Oh, but at what cost had their plan unfolded? Stefano lay on the brink of death, if not dead already. Countless others had joined him, unsuspecting victims of the island's insidious curse. It did not welcome lives; it took them. The thought made her shiver as Madeleine stared after the blazing ship, praying she'd see her husband leap from it at any moment. Yet the longer she waited, the more that hope trickled thin.

Unable to contain herself any longer, she thrust Stefano's sheathed knife beneath her bodice and charged into the ocean, her feet splashing the wild waves until she stood thigh-high within it. With a giant breath, Madeleine dove beneath the ocean's surface. The clear water immersed her in its freezing grips, drenching her from head to foot. She thought of nothing but Gabriel's safety as her arms and legs propelled her over the sea, against the tide of men escaping the blaze.

The closer she came to Stefano's ship, the more her lungs worked, begging for clean air. Peering through the black smoke billowing over the water, Madeleine found a rope ladder barely clinging to the bulwark. Her limbs protested and her chest smarted as she pulled herself from the water, but she kept climbing. She would walk through the flames themselves if it meant keeping Gabriel from harm.

When she reached the railing, terror gripped her. The deck of Stefano's ship shone red with reflected light, flames burning on every side. Above her, the mast swayed and threatened to give way. Madeleine covered her mouth and nose with her arm, the smoke stinging her eyelids and forcing a sputtering cough from her burning throat.

Careful not to catch her dress on fire, she crawled over the bulwark and stumbled across the deck. If Gabriel had been able to perform their plan as discussed, he'd snuck aboard and climbed below decks to avoid detection. Any fire he could start on deck would be quickly noticed and extinguished. Madeleine had advised him to find their sleeping quarters where torches were kept and light the blaze from within the ship. That way, he'd have time to escape before anyone noticed his presence or the fire.

Fruitlessly searching the parts of the deck not already consumed by fire, Madeleine's hopes began to diminish. Her feet pummeled the floorboards, scorching beneath her defenseless skin. She ducked under blazing sails, now drooping and being eaten away. Soon, she would have no way of escape herself.

Madeleine had nearly given up hope when she spied a crumpled form lying behind a wall of fire. "Gabriel." The word barely squeezed from her weary lungs. He looked unconscious, a large gash reddening his temple. Her pulse hammered in violent frenzy as she rushed toward him, wondering how she would circumvent the flames between them.

Just then, a form blocked her path. Madeleine jerked, looking up into a face she recognized. Had not the same man nearly trapped her as she drank water from the river? Yes, as his beady eyes surveyed her, she had no doubt. She'd kissed this man in order to survive, the repugnant taste of it forming anew on her tongue the longer he examined her exhausted form.

Irritation seized her. She didn't have time for these games. "Why haven't you fled the ship yet, you fool?" she asked. "You're sure to die along with it if you wait any longer."

The man glanced up at the rigging as another rope snapped and a sail tumbled to the deck, instantly catching ablaze. Madeleine had only to look at his bulging pockets to answer her own question. Even in the face of peril, greed had subdued any reason. He would risk his life to plunder his own ship.

His gaze darted to the man lying unconscious behind her. "That's him. The one who set fire to the ship." Understanding dawned on his face as he glanced back and forth between them. "That's your man. You came here to save him."

Blood pulsed furiously through Madeleine's veins. She couldn't waste any more time. "Just go. We can only have minutes before that entire mast comes down on us." One finger speared toward the structure dangling precariously over their heads.

A sick smile meandered over his lips. His dark head shook almost playfully. "I let you escape once. Don't think I'll do it again." Lunging for her, he seized her wrist before Madeleine could think to retreat.

She huffed. "Cavaretta is dead. There is no one to take me to any longer."

He laughed, his breath smelling of cheap liquor as it swept her cheek. "You're a clever liar, but I will not be deceived by you again. Now, come on. Get moving before we both catch fire." His fingers tensed on her wrist, yanking her back the way she'd come.

Madeleine glanced at Gabriel, still lying broken and vulnerable, mere seconds from the fire's rage devouring him, too. Teeth clenching, she dipped her free hand below her neckline and extracted the knife Stefano had nearly killed her with. Bringing the tip to the man's jaw, she summoned her most menacing expression. "I am going to save my husband. You can either go down with your ship or flee *now.*"

Despite her threat, amusement still lit the imbecile's eyes. They ran down her blade to her rigid arm before he released her and displayed both palms in the air. He appeared as if he might concede until he reached for his belt and whipped out his own knife. His witless laughter buzzed around them as the fire spread higher.

"I can't let you rescue the man who destroyed my employer's ship." His head cocked, eyebrows quirking apologetically. "I do hope you will understand." Quick on his feet, the man jabbed his blade at her, narrowly missing her stomach.

242

Madeleine jumped backward, painfully close to the flames sizzling behind her. Teeth exposed, she charged back at her opponent, her knife nearly slicing his arm. He appeared to possess some skill as he quickly recovered, circling her with eyes narrowed. Had Stefano taught him personally as he had taught her? Perhaps he made his men practice for just such an occasion.

Her feet felt numb and her shoulders spasmed as she forced them into the dance she'd learned so long ago at the hands of Stefano. She ducked and lunged. She swung when she had the advantage and leaned away from the whooshing blade when she must. It felt like a dream to her now, a shadow of her former life. She had taken on the skill out of love for Stefano. Now it felt hollow, empty, a tool she must employ but wanted no part of.

The man was surprised at her ability. She could see it in the way he held his knife uncertainly, the sloppy swings that stabbed through the air at nothing. Madeleine grabbed hold of this advantage, attacking him ruthlessly until his chest rose in uncontrollable waves.

In one motion, she slammed her foot on one of his and stroked downward with her knife toward his hand. As expected, the startled man opened his hand, the weapon clattering to the deck and skittering over it. His frightened eyes briefly flashed toward the knife, gleaming with reflections of flame, before he spun on his heel. "You can die with him," he threw back, disappearing over the ship's edge in seconds, the sound of his splash punctuating his departure.

"Gabriel." She said his name as if coming out of a trance. Stuffing Stefano's knife back in her dress, Madeleine whirled toward the sleeping body now precariously close to the flames. Through the choking clouds, she saw that his chest still rose and fell, but for how long? She had to find a way to get past the blaze tauntingly dividing them.

Desperate, Madeleine looked this way and that. Her gaze caught hold of a bundled sail not yet consumed by fire. With every bit of strength she had left, she hugged her arms around it and hauled it away from the ship's edge. Working as quickly as her trembling hands would move, she unfurled the sail and spread it over the flames, forcefully enough to devour them, but careful not to fan them toward her unconscious husband.

Heart thrashing against her ribs, Madeleine scampered over the scorched sail and knelt next to him. "Gabriel." At first, he moved not a muscle when she planted her palms over his cheeks and tried to rouse him. Her fear heightened. "Gabriel, you must wake up. I can't swim back to the beach with you on my back." Her hands lovingly moved down his neck to his shoulders, where she grabbed hold and shook him like a limp rag doll.

Languidly his eyelids eased open. The blue eyes beneath fluttering lashes shone out in confusion before they expanded. He glanced rapidly around them, chest ballooning. Then he peered back into her eyes and his panic seemed to dissolve into affection.

"I almost got away with it," Gabriel said, wincing as he touched the injured spot on his temple. "I was steps away from diving back into the sea when they caught me and hit me over the head with something." His shoulders fell. "I'm sorry, I really tried."

Smiling, Madeleine took his dark head in her hands. "You did more than try. You did what you set out to. The island is in sheer chaos because of you."

His lips lifted sadly. "Yes, but you had to jump into the fire for me. You always rescue me."

Her heart lifted as she leaned close and pressed her forehead to his. "We always rescue *each other.*" Despite the murky air and the danger looming near, her lips found his in sweet union. What a precious gift to know they each valued the other's life above their own—that they would come for each other whenever the need arose.

The mast over their heads creaked, reminding Madeleine of their perilous position. She ripped her mouth from his, rotating up to see the flaming mast cracking in the middle. The top half appeared about to plummet to the deck at any moment.

"We don't have much time." Seizing Gabriel's hand, she stood and yanked him up beside her. His protective arms sheltered her as they sprinted toward a spot of bulwark not yet aflame, dodging bits of fire and falling sails along the way. The mast splintered just as they'd clamored atop the side, its crash resounding in her ears a moment before she hit the water.

Madeleine's world turned to black—a jumble of garbled sounds and reflected light piercing the gulf. Pumping her arms and legs, she struggled through the cold, perplexing mass of bubbles and saline until her head emerged into open air. All around her, burning pieces of the ship floated on the ocean's surface. Her stomach flipped a moment before Gabriel popped up near her, gasping for breath.

The pair cautiously avoided the ship's debris, swimming side by side toward the beach she'd never imagined so precious. Though it was midday, the heavy clouds of smoke trundling over the pristine sky lent it the appearance of dusk. Madeleine propelled herself steadily through the water, trying to ignore the angry red monster still raging behind her. They'd barely crossed into safe waters when Stefano's ship groaned and collapsed on her side with a massive splash.

Waves from the ear-splitting crash carried them to shore. Out of breath and dizzy with exhaustion, Madeleine clung to the jagged rocks of the lagoon so the sea couldn't sweep her out again. Only moments before, she'd been surrounded with soot and fire. Now clean, clear water rushed over her. Her toes sank into snowy white sand, the shivering palm fronds overhead welcoming her back. She could almost laugh if aching fatigue hadn't absorbed her entire body.

A gentle hand anchored around her shoulders, and Madeleine looked over to find Gabriel regarding her with pride. He swept her to him, cradling her head at his chest, kissing her drenched hair. She relaxed into his sturdy form, her worries washing out with the rolling tides. In spite of every obstacle stacked against them, they had prevailed. They had survived an impossible plan together. Tilting her chin up, she basked in the warmth of his lips as they moved over hers, the safety of his arms transporting her to a place of perfect peace where no harm could befall them.

Someone up the beach cleared their throat, snatching the entranced couple's attention. Madeleine looked up to see Christophe and a band of his men, standing there watching the private exchange. A disenchanted look teemed from the captain's narrowed gaze as Madeleine scrambled up with Gabriel close behind.

Christophe's penetrating stare wandered her face sadly before it pinned distrustfully on Gabriel. The two had always disliked each other, but something deeper stirred in the depths of that look. Even with all of Christophe's power and skill, Gabriel possessed the one thing he never would—the ability to make her fall in love. Envy dripped from the captain's every seething feature as Gabriel pulled her protectively against him.

"You set fire to that ship," Christophe said to the man at her back. "You started a war between my men and Cavaretta's."

Gabriel stood taller. "The two of you started that war a long time ago when you began squabbling over my wife." His solid arm hooked her waist. "I only did you a favor."

A hard look passed over Christophe's flattened mouth before his slitted gaze coasted to the jungle. "Yes, well that *favor* has resulted in the death of half my men. Cavaretta is dead, and those who remain of his crew are wandering around the island no doubt dreaming up ways to kill the rest of us. There *is* only one ship left, after all."

The burly man at Christophe's side stepped forward, drawing his cutlass. "I say we kill 'em, Captain. They're traitors—the both of 'em."

Amusement tickled Christophe's mouth, his angered expression saying he seriously considered the suggestion, at least in Gabriel's case. Then his hand moved slowly out to restrain the incensed sailor. "No need for that, Blanc. They might be useful to us yet."

With purposeful languor, he stepped over the rocks toward them, his boots crunching the uneven ground. Madeleine's heart pattered faster the closer he came. He truly had the power to extinguish Gabriel's life in an instant, but would he do it knowing she'd despise him forever if he did? Surely they'd survived too much together now for such cruelty to exist between them.

Christophe's gaze languidly ascended from Gabriel's arm shielding her body to her face. His vulnerable heart poured out to her for a moment, then he expertly slipped an icy shell over his emotions. He swallowed before he uttered a single word, like the very thought took effort.

"In spite of our obvious grievances, we still have a job to do," Christophe said, loud enough for his comrades to hear.

"Surely you don't mean the treasure," one of his men said. "They'll kill us if we venture into those woods. Better to get back on board our ship and leave the cowards here to fend for themselves." Murmurs rumbled through the gathered assembly, some nodding their agreement, others looking doubtful.

Irritation crumpled Christophe's brow as he pivoted toward his men. "They may be cowards, but we are not, gentlemen. We will not be scared away from what we came here for by a group of untrained Italians." He looked back at Madeleine and Gabriel. "Besides, we are not barbarians, either. I will not maroon anybody here by force. If Cavaretta's men wish to join our ranks, we will welcome them."

This sparked a string of heated whispers among the men. Madeleine blinked, staring into Christophe's impassioned gaze, understanding his meaning. He had already devised a plan for them. He wouldn't let them be killed or abandoned unless forced by his crew.

"We are mere hours from sinking our hands into riches beyond compare," he said, no doubt sensing their division and knowing how to unite them. "In exchange for rescuing her from Cavaretta's clutches, Baroness Clement here revealed to me the location of Clement's treasure."

His statement sent her blood pumping madly, but Madeleine managed to keep a collected expression. Whatever his plan, she and Gabriel had no other option. At least they stood a chance with Christophe.

"She told you where the treasure is?" The man called Blanc stumbled a few steps over the sand, cutlass still gripped in white knuckles. "Where?"

Gaze flitting to the tops of the cliffs, Christophe jabbed his index finger their way. "There. At the top of the summit, in a crevice yet to be found." Feigned triumph moved over his face, bright with reflections from the stirring water. "We've had enough excitement for today. We're tired and we need to rest. We'll set out tomorrow morning and claim our prize, Cavaretta's men be hanged. They'll be begging to join us once they see what awaits us."

Though a few dissenters remained, most of Christophe's remaining crew shouted as if already holding their victory in hand. How aptly he steered them out of troubled waters and converted their doubts to praises. No wonder he'd been able to usurp Jacques Chapelle's power.

"Where are we supposed to sleep tonight?" Blanc asked above the clamor. "Cavaretta's men will gut us if we remain in camp together. They'll attack us when we're at our most vulnerable."

Christophe put his hands on his hips confidently. "We'll spread out through the island, as they have done. We'll whistle the signal if one of us comes upon them."

"And those two?" Blanc tipped his head toward Madeleine and Gabriel. "What do we do with them?"

The captain's hawk-like gaze clamped back on Madeleine, the pieces of his plan already clicking into place. "These two are coming with me."

Twenty Five

Madeleine and her companions barely spoke, their quiet footfalls the only sound between them as they stealthily traversed the wild landscape. Danger lurked on every side—armed men sprinkled about the bushes and rocks, their hope of survival resting in how many of Christophe's men they could kill. With a shiver, Madeleine wondered if they would wait for the treasure to be found, or if they would spring an attack that night. Either way, she would have to confront them soon. The Clement family had been right all along—no treasure existed.

Dissatisfied with the explanation provided, Christophe insisted they journey to the waterfall so he could have a look himself. Madeleine thought of snatching Gabriel's hand and running when the ship captain disappeared beneath the falls, but instead she reached for the canteen slung over her back. Her body was too weary to run after such a harrowing day, and they needed each other if they hoped to prevail over Stefano's men.

Perching on a rock, Madeleine stooped down and collected the flowing water with the mouth of her canteen. The late afternoon sun was barely dribbling through the trees, the river higher and easier to access at this time of day. She capped her canteen and reached a hand to Gabriel, smiling lovingly at him as he plopped his canteen into her hand. No matter what came of this day, at least they had each other.

Some twenty minutes later, Christophe's head bobbed up from beneath the waterfall. A grim look captured his handsome features as he paddled to shore, arriving before the married couple with his long hair plastered to the sides of his face and his linen shirt clinging to his muscular torso. He took a moment to wring out the ends of it before releasing a defeated sigh.

"There is nothing behind there," he said, climbing up the river-bank. "I searched everywhere I could think to look, but I found nothing."

Madeleine quirked one brow. "I believe we told you the same already."

With a disgruntled glare, Christophe glanced between her and Gabriel. "Are you sure you saw an 'x' on the map indicating the waterfall? This wouldn't be another one of your tricks, is it? Trust me, it's not the time for games."

Gabriel rolled his eyes. "Why would we lie about this, Roux? Madeleine and I both saw it with our own eyes. Henri clearly painted a map of this island and put a significant 'x' behind that waterfall." His finger aimed at the flinging spray behind them. "So unless there is an identical island somewhere, this is where he hid his treasure."

Christophe's brows cinched, his fingertip tapping his chin where whiskers had begun to sprout. "No, the letter had specific coordinates that led us here. It can't be anywhere else." His square shoulders fell as he gazed longingly back at the crashing waterfall. "Could someone have found it already? Perhaps one of the sailors marooned here discovered it and hid it elsewhere on the island."

"Or another ship simply found it and carried it away," Madeleine said. "I came here first with a Captain Blondeau. You're not the only crew who knows about this island. The Guardians knew exactly where to look."

Christophe nodded. "Chapelle worked in coalition with a small group of pirate captains who knew the treasure's location. They all agreed to send their errant sailors here and split the reward if the booty was ever found."

"A likely scenario," Gabriel said with a laugh. "Honest pirate captains upholding an agreement with countless riches on the line."

The other man's eyes flashed. "How much do you know about pirate captains, Baron? Have you met enough of us to know we do not hold true to our vows?"

"I only need to know one to have assumed as much." Gabriel's eyes narrowed, his steely gaze drilling through Christophe.

Madeleine stepped between the two fuming men, one palm raised at both. "Enough of this. We don't have room for discord between us with Stefano's men already lying in wait to bring us harm. Let's put the past away, shall we? After all, we need each other."

Both men visibly relaxed, though silent arrows still shot from their glaring eyes at one another. Christophe knotted his thick arms over his chest. "I still haven't received a proper explanation on how you arrived here," he said to Gabriel. "How did you so quickly find a ship willing to follow me?"

The baron tilted his chin up, meeting Christophe's distrustful frown. "I bribed a merchant ship en route to the Bahamas." His jaw flexed with his lie. "They took me just beyond the reef over there and gave me a boat to row ashore with, then left."

"Yet another crew to contend with knowing of this place," Christophe said, lip snarling. He regarded Gabriel a contemplative moment, as if trying to read how much truth his story contained, before he grunted and bent to retrieve his pack off the ground. "We need to find a place to camp soon. It's coming on dusk, and we don't want to be out in the open like this when night falls."

Madeleine glanced at Gabriel as they fell in step behind the captain. Should she tell him about their secret cave in the cliffs? They would be safer there, but did she want to surrender the last secret they still held from him? The idea of bringing Christophe to the sacred place she and Gabriel had reunited in marriage launched a chill through her that convinced her mouth to stay closed.

After a short trek through the jungle, the trio came to a spot bordered in a huddle of trees. Christophe shrugged, looking at the pair in question, receiving a silent nod from them both. How lovely a fire would be now, but Madeleine realized as she watched the two men spread blankets over the earth that the flames would attract too much attention out in the open like this.

Their supper ambled by in dismal silence, only the sound of her chewing filling her ears. Scooting up to Gabriel, Madeleine leaned into him and relished the rather stale bread and salted fish churning between her teeth. His strong hand hooked her waist, attracting Christophe's gaze to linger there a moment before fluttering off to the gathering darkness.

Sighing, Christophe collapsed on his back and stared up at the feathery treetops. A thousand different emotions flooded his face, his jaw working furiously. As angry as she'd been over his deceptions, Madeleine couldn't help mourning for him now. How disheartening this day must have felt, to have something he'd sought with his entire soul for so long come within arm's reach and then slip away again. It couldn't help to have her and Gabriel's love for one another flaunted in front of him.

"What will you tell them in the morning?" Madeleine asked, prompting Christophe to look her way. "When your crew awakes, they'll be eager to go after the treasure."

"No doubt some of them are up on the summit at this very moment." He looked at her thoughtfully before his gaze swung back to the trees overhead. "I must keep hope alive, for all of us. Some of these men sailed with Chapelle before we were even born.

They've dedicated their entire lives to the quest for it. If I tell them it isn't here, some of them will just as soon stay here and die."

The thought stirred a sad ache within Madeleine. She laced her fingers in her lap, drinking in the hibiscus and coconut floating on the breeze. Darkness had begun its gradual descent over them, the warm glow of dusk melting into black shadows. So many men had bled and died for this treasure. It didn't seem fair that it could simply not be where Henri had promised it would. What a cruel joke to play on the world.

"If one of those poor souls on the beach did find it," Christophe said, "you can be certain I'll leave no stone unturned to locate the place they put it. I'll rip this island apart if I have to."

Gabriel reached for his pack and set it on the blanket. "It would make sense for them to do so. I know if I were stranded here and found it, I would hide it elsewhere to gain the upper hand. That way, I'd be the only person in position to negotiate with whomever put me here, even if the map was found." He lowered himself to the ground, stuffing the pack beneath his head.

"Precisely." Christophe exhaled from his nose, the sound radiating through the darkness. "It's still here. I can feel it in my gut. No matter what that map said, the Moon King's treasure is real and it's in this place. Every rock and tree reverberates with its glory."

The beauty of Christophe's devotion warmed Madeleine's soul as she stretched out beside her husband and felt his arm drape over her. From what she knew, Jacques Chapelle had simply been motivated by greed. If he had to kill a thousand men to reach Henri Clement's money, then so be it. Like his fondness for the sea, Christophe had a love affair with the idea of finding the elusive treasure whispered to him in his youth. His obsession went so much deeper than gaining great wealth. He wanted to prove himself the captain that none of the men before him could.

Somewhere within the haze of her wandering thoughts, Madeleine drifted to sleep. Against the chill of salty wind sweeping the island, Gabriel's comforting warmth seeped in. Her dreams produced visions of home, of Paris's streets and that little bakery tucked among the ancient buildings where love had enfolded her. The ever-present danger of Cavaretta's men, the shock of seeing a man she'd once loved gutted through, the disappointment of the hollow cave beyond the waterfall—they all seemed to dissolve as she floated amidst happy images of the cottage of her earliest days.

The rustle of leaves and fronds woke her at some point in the night. Madeleine lifted her head and glanced around, at first fearful that someone had crept upon them. Then, as another cool gust of ocean air rocked the circling trees, she relaxed into Gabriel's embrace. His heartbeat pounded steadily at her back, much like the even chirp of cicadas whirling up from the ivy-strewn earth.

Madeleine peered through the trees, where a smattering of stars twinkled from an endless ebony canvas. What must Henri have thought as he camped under a similar sky, dreaming up how he would direct his family to the fortune he'd acquired throughout his lifetime? Had he lay beneath this awe-inducing production of nature, picturing the night sky he'd paint across his ceiling? The words he'd tucked into the library book tolled over and again in her mind—*let evening stars be your guide.* How beautifully poetic a message he'd left for his descendants, even if they never found the pot of gold supposedly waiting at the end of the rainbow.

Struck, Madeleine bolted upright from the blanket. Gabriel groaned, but simply threw an arm over his face in his slumber. *Let evening stars be your guide.* Her heart picked up speed as she pictured herself bent over the river, filling her canteen in the rising waters before dusk. Why hadn't she thought of this before? She'd seen the nocturnal tides push the river higher, but she'd never imagined how that might alter the pool behind the falls.

Twisting back, she nudged the slumbering man beneath her. "Gabriel," she hissed through the chilly air. "Gabriel." Her hand gently rustled his chest until his eyes lethargically drifted open.

After floating around the night, his confused expression finally landed on her face. Madeleine put one finger over her lips and waved him up with her other hand. No use waking Christophe if her idea came to nothing.

Gabriel followed her through the thicket of trees and into the forest beyond. Excitedly, Madeleine seized his hand and guided him, taking no heed to the rough ground beneath her feet. The waterfall's thunderous laughter already reached them, coaxing her heart to hammer faster as she tugged Gabriel along.

"What are we doing out here?" He yawned, rubbing his sleepy eyes with the back of his free hand. "I was rather enjoying my sleep."

Madeleine laughed softly. "You can sleep when we're back at home, safe in our bed. This is too important not to wake you for."

As they passed through the trees and the river came into sight, Madeleine squeezed his hand. A glowing ribbon in the moonlight, the water tripped over rocks and gushed to the open sea in a winding display of beauty. The waterfall's spray littered her arms and face as they approached, thrilling the already anxious soul within her.

"What is it?" Gabriel asked, brow wrinkling under the soft moon. "What made you come out here in the dead of night?"

Eyes aglow, she turned back to him. "It just dawned on me as I lay there sleepless beside you—the river ebbs and flows. It changes with the ocean's tide."

Gabriel nodded. "Oui, some rivers do."

"Look." Her finger pointed toward the riverbank, where the water lapped significantly higher than the hours before dusk when Christophe had swum beneath the falls. "See how much deeper the river is now? I had to bend over to get water this afternoon. Now those rocks are nearly submerged. The pool behind the waterfall can't possibly look the same this time of night."

The long-buried passion for seeking Henri's treasure stirred again in his bright eyes. "You may be onto something. Henri knew the patterns of this island. He had to if he chose this place to house such a prize."

The wind swept her loose hair back, rushing over her skin. "Let evening stars be your guide," she said into the gleaming strands of water plummeting from the ledge high above their heads.

"Beyond the water, endless treasures hide." Gabriel gripped her hand, the electricity between them growing. After all this time, could the unrivaled fortune rumored about the Clement name really lay just beyond their feet? The very idea infused excitement in her bones.

"You weren't planning to go looking without me, were you?" An unexpected voice made Madeleine start. She reeled around to find Christophe standing not a meter back with hands on his hips. His trained footsteps hadn't made a discernable sound if he'd followed them all this way.

"I most certainly was," Madeleine said, guilt prickling her at the hurt on his face. "We would have told you if we found something. There's no use hiding it. I didn't want all three of us drenched to the bone if this quest is as fruitless as the others have been."

Christophe's untrusting grimace shifted to Gabriel. "You certainly managed to inform *him,*" he said, not attempting to conceal the bitterness in his voice. "Either way, I'm coming with you. I don't care if it's fruitless. I have to see for myself." Already shouldering past them, he advanced toward the river before crouching low to remove his boots.

With a shrug and a roll of his eyes, Gabriel followed suit. The pair would never get along, but perhaps they could unite with her for a common goal. If the Moon King's riches really did hide in the place she thought, they'd need their combined strength to keep both it and themselves safe.

By day, the river had chilled her. By night, it sank so far into her core that Madeleine couldn't help shivering. Her teeth rattled as she ventured farther into its depths, careful not to trip on the loose rocks beneath her toes. When the riverbed dropped out from under her, she forced her arms through the glacial water, her worn gown fluttering behind her kicking legs.

Beneath the hammering falls they passed, one after the other. When Madeleine did not immediately breach the surface beyond, panic rammed through her veins at the thought of being lost in the dark, rushing waters. She propelled her limbs harder, swimming up until she finally emerged from the river's frigid gulf. Gasping, she looked back through the crystal falls reflecting the moonlight and realized she'd nearly reached the top.

So little could be discerned in the cavern's darkness. The ceiling, once high above their heads, now rested just beyond arm's length. The ledge they had used to explore the cave was nowhere in sight, presumably submerged beneath the water. With growing awareness, Madeleine realized that when the river rose with the tides, it nearly filled the hollow space hidden beyond the falls.

The two men beside her glanced around the grotto in a similar fashion, their arms gently lapping the water's surface. Gabriel paddled to the wall they'd explored only a day before, his narrowed gaze fixed above. Reaching out of the water, he probed the rocky surface with both hands, stretching until they clamped around an unseen edge. "I think I found something," he said, breath coming hard.

Madeleine and Christophe trailed him, watching in silence as he lugged himself from the water with a grunt. A ledge like the one they'd found below must have existed here, because his form disappeared in the muddled shadows a moment before emerging again to help them.

"I can't see anything back here, either," he said, extending his hand to Madeleine.

Latching her palm with his, she climbed out of the water as Christophe clamored up beside her on his own. Gabriel was right—nothing but darkness met their arrival. With flailing hands, Madeleine managed to detect the opening of a smaller cave, but how could they hope to explore it without proper lighting?

"Why would Clement pick a spot where a lantern is impossible to bring?" Christophe voiced the question plaguing her mind.

"It doesn't make any sense," she said. "He wanted us to come here at night. Everything points to it, from the poem he left in the library to his star map. Night is the only time this cave is accessible, yet it makes finding anything here absurd."

"If only it was like the room we found in the château," Gabriel said through the dark, "with torches lining the walls. You don't suppose there's another entrance where he might have brought such supplies?"

Yet as the trio stared into the empty black well beyond, only the wind creaking the trees answered back. If they truly wanted to delve beneath the layers the Moon King had so masterfully constructed, they would have to throw all caution to the sea.

Rising on her hands and knees, Madeleine began crawling under the arch she'd felt above her. The first ledge they'd found had been just a platform, but here, a narrow mouth tunneled into the rock. Gulping back the fear threatening to cripple her, she kept on despite the jagged floor cutting into her knees.

"What are you doing?" Christophe asked at the sound of her body scraping the rocks.

"I'm going to find the Moon King's treasure." Madeleine grunted, teeth gritting as the rocks pierced her open palms. "We've come all this way. I'm not about to stop now."

Christophe exhaled, then scrambled after her. "You're going to get yourself killed, and the two of us along with you."

Gabriel simply chuckled as his boots crunched after them. He knew by now once a goal captured Madeleine's mind, she wouldn't stop until it reached fruition—especially not if it involved the survival of those she loved.

The passageway she'd discovered constricted even tighter as she journeyed into it. Blood pulsed along Madeleine's burning skin, hastening when she imagined being trapped in this dark tunnel. She pictured the tide washing higher, the water pushing upward and blasting over them. The fresh, invigorating scent of the waterfall faded into a dank odor the farther they went. How long had this passage existed with not a person to explore its secrets?

Before long, they reached a point where the tunnel widened. Madeleine paused with her hands above her head, discerning the spot where two distinct tunnels forked off from one another. "There are two tunnels here." Her breath rose in exhausted pants.

"Perhaps we should each take one," Christophe suggested.

"We shouldn't split up," Gabriel said from the darkness behind him.

"Wait." As Madeleine's fingertips swept the cave's floor, its natural bumps gave way to a smoother portion, clearly manipulated by someone. "There are etchings here." Her fingers brushed the indentations, a laugh escaping her throat. "A rose, a circle, and a cross—the symbols from the key. He meant for us to go this way."

Heart in her throat, Madeleine led them to the right, where the tunnel gradually began to spill open. Peering through the muddled dark, she made out a strange glow emanating from around a bend. The roof here sloped upward, allowing her to clamor to her feet with her companions close behind.

Madeleine reached for the wall to her left, where a bluish tint grew stronger. Holding tight, she came around the bend and stopped dead in her tracks. The two masculine forms behind her bumped into her back, the sound of their scuffling boots cut short. All three could do nothing but stare, the sight before them more than Madeleine had ever imagined possible.

Twenty Six

"What is this place?" The words pressed from Madeleine's breathless lungs, echoing into the spectacular chasm beyond. Forcing her immobile legs to work, she stumbled down a rocky embankment to the luminescent pools beneath it.

Everywhere she looked, a magnificent glow shone with blue light. The roof of the cave expanded high over them, the light revealing thousands of stalactites dripping down like frosty icicles. Shallow pools dotted the floor, their rocky surfaces covered in some type of plant that produced the mysterious glow, radiating around them in breathtaking rays.

"Why do these plants glow?" Madeleine asked, falling to her knees to inspect the curious phenomenon. "How do they even grow in a place like this?" As far as she could tell, no sunlight could breach the walls to accommodate them.

"I don't believe these are plants." Gabriel knelt beside her and reached below the water's surface to run his fingertips over the peculiar shapes clinging to the rocks. "They appear to be organisms that thrive in such damp conditions. I've read about these. They're called animalcules. They produce a radiant glow so that predators won't eat them."

Madeleine's mind buzzed with the unfamiliar words passing through it. She could simply sit back and marvel at their existence. "They're incredible." How could such beauty have been tucked away all this time with no one to admire it? How many secrets did the world possess, unknown to human minds?

"Look." Christophe's command seized her attention. Madeleine's gaze lifted from the glowing orbs below the water to the sea captain, who stood frozen by the far wall. His pointed finger indicated a shadowed portion of the cave, where the vague outline of shapes huddled in the corner.

After bolting to a stand, Madeleine raced over to him. The craggy cave floor barely touched her bare feet as she sprinted past him. Though bathed in shadows, the mysterious shapes assumed more definition the closer she came. "They're treasure chests," she shouted behind her, breathless. "So many I can't count them all."

Quickly joined by Christophe and Gabriel, Madeleine began twisting the locks and tossing back the lids to what must have been dozens of ancient chests. The ethereal glow from the pools barely touched this far, but she distinctly saw the glimmer of gold and jewels, rising forth for the first time in hundreds of years. Behind her, Christophe let out an unbridled whoop. They'd really found it—the unattainable treasure sought by so many. The idea felt impossible, dribbling through her like warm, dizzying drops of rain.

"How did they manage to get all of this up here?" Gabriel wondered, glancing around himself gleefully like a child in a candy shop. "These chests must weigh a hundred pounds. They couldn't possibly have swum up carrying them."

Christophe sat before a particularly large chest, pawing through an assortment of rubies and pearl strands. "My guess is very slowly. They must have brought them up a few bags at a time. Imagine how long that must have taken. Henri was certainly serious about keeping his treasure hidden."

Madeleine's gaze swept the glimmering chests while she wiped her sweaty hands on her skirts. "And the Martine family kept his secret all that time. I wonder how he managed to convince them not to come back and take all this for themselves."

"By paying them handsomely, I'd imagine," Christophe said. He hooked one brow. "I'm sure threats played into the equation. No one wanted to be the first of the skeletons littering the beach."

A rattling sound diverted Madeleine's attention to Gabriel, who knelt before a box smaller than all the others. Brows gathered, he shook it again, his fingertips attempting to pry it open. "This one appears to be locked. Why would he lock this one tiny box among all these riches?"

"Perhaps it's the most valuable one." Madeleine leaned over him, eyes wide. Just when she thought the thrill of unearthing Henri Clement's treasure had reached its zenith, a new piece of the puzzle snagged her in its grips.

"It's a shame we don't have that key," Gabriel said, turning the box over in his hands. "Perhaps it had more than one use. It doesn't sound like there's much inside, but he must have locked it for a reason."

Christophe cleared his throat, compelling both Clements to look at him. In his raised fingers rested the glimmering key he'd stolen from Madeleine, the attached chain still dangling from it.

Eyes ablaze, Gabriel strutted forward and snatched the item from Christophe's hand. The two shot unspoken arrows at one another before Gabriel whipped around and lifted the box off the floor. With precision, he thrust the key into the lock and twisted. An excited smile tweaked his lips as the spring popped back with a gentle click. Both of his companions gathered close with bated breath, eager to see what lay inside.

With one thumb, Gabriel pushed back the box's lid. Madeleine clenched her fists, expecting to find a rare item inside—perhaps a royal gem from a far-off land or the key to an even bigger fortune.

When the bluish light only revealed a stack of folded pages, her shoulders fell. Why would Henri Clement protect this box above all others?

Mesmerized, her husband took the yellowing pages carefully into his hand and tossed the box aside. With gaze fixed reverently on them as if they truly were the greatest possession from among the dazzling collection, he ambled toward the glowing pools and sat cross-legged before them. Madeleine followed, sinking down beside him and laying her cheek on Gabriel's upper arm. How beautiful a moment to witness—the man she loved connecting with his ancestor of old as he unfurled the pages and scanned the fanciful script inside.

"My dearest family," he read, his voice resounding through the small space. "While I pen these words, I find myself wishing I could foresee the future. I know not whether this fortune I leave behind will be found soon after I'm gone, many years in the future, or perhaps never at all. It could be lost to this wild place forever and become a part of its hidden beauty. Yet I must leave it here, praying it does not fall into the wrong hands and hoping it finds you at the right time.

"This island is a very special place to me. My father was an adventurer intent on sailing about the earth, looking for something that hadn't yet been found—I was never sure what. He often took me along with him, despite the loud protestations of my mother." Gabriel laughed, putting a smile on Madeleine's lips. "Some of the best times of my life were spent aboard ship, sailing into uncharted waters, the threat of danger and the thrill of adventure calling to my adolescent soul."

Christophe's boots scuffed the cave floor as he approached and settled down across the glowing pool from them. He bent near with his chin posed on his hand, an enraptured look overtaking his striking features.

"I was about eleven or twelve when we first discovered this island," Gabriel read. "I'll never forget the way I felt when we landed here that day—the warm white sand under my feet, the palm trees fluttering in the breeze and flowers of every color greeting our arrival. My father had imagined he might expand Louis XIII's exploration efforts and befriend a native tribe. Instead, he found an uninhabited paradise with fresh flowing waters and birds we'd never seen before. Neither of us could be disappointed as we explored this island together."

Warmth trickled through Madeleine to imagine the young boy venturing beneath the trees with his father, climbing the cliffs and swimming in the river. What a gift it would have been to bring her own parents here. Her heart ached for them anew as Gabriel continued on.

"My father decided to camp here for a week. He ordered his men ashore and set up a makeshift shelter near the cliffs to block the wind. We spent every day collecting what we could for King Louis, trying to find something that might warrant his praise. We never found much of anything. It's impossible to bottle the emotion that courses through you when you first see the island. You can put sand in a jar and pluck leaves that will wither in days, but my father knew Louis would have no interest in this place. It would be special to us alone, and I liked it that way."

Gabriel flipped to the next page, the papers rustling in his fingers. "On our last night, I couldn't sleep. The island called to me, speaking of something mysterious that I had yet to uncover. I thought of waking my father, but a voice inside told me to go alone. So I set out across the jungle with only the moon to guide me, and I came to the true gem of this island—its glorious waterfall. I long stood in awe of its beauty, bathed in moonlight, before I stripped off my shirt and dove into the river.

"My father and I had swum beneath the waterfall before, so I was surprised when I struggled to reach the surface behind it. The falls produced enough strength to hold the pool at bay and propel me to this magical place. I couldn't believe my eyes. I pinched myself, wondering if I walked through a dream. I dubbed this place *Grotte des Merveilles*, and vowed never to tell anyone of its existence. It became my private oasis the many times my father and I returned to this magnificent patch of land over the years."

Lips curling, Gabriel lowered the page. "He called this place the Cave of Wonders and his home the House of Dreams. What a whimsical man he must have been." His curly head shook, love for his ancestor gleaming from his eyes before he lifted the next page and kept reading.

"When Louis XIII died, the kingdom fell to a child. The people of Paris were already starving, already up in arms about the injustices they faced. With so much uncertainty and unrest rocking our beloved nation, I knew I must go to the palace and offer my services to the young king and his advisors, to keep peace among my people until Louis reached the age of maturity.

"I was there when a group of citizens broke into the palace and stormed up to the child's very chamber, demanding to know what he planned to do about their suffering. Louis was understandably terrified—a small child who had never seen anything but wealth waking to an angered mob standing over his bed. I rushed to his chamber, spoke with the intruders and convinced them to leave. After that, my relationship with Louis would never be the same. He trusted me, and I grew to love him as my own son."

Madeleine's brow wrinkled as she thought on his words. Hadn't Henri Clement used King Louis' power for his own gain? That was the story as she'd always heard it from his descendants.

"Louis is a smart man," her husband read, "one of the smartest I've ever had the privilege to know. He sees the infirmities plaguing his people and where that uproar will eventually lead. His instincts have allowed him to gaze into the future, where he anticipates a great calamity befalling our nation. Because of this, he has entrusted me with a secret I now pass to your shoulders."

Each of them stiffened, instinctively leaning forward. "In my lifetime, I have endured much ridicule and scorn. Louis's other advisors simply do not understand the bond we have formed and have sought to undermine me at every turn. They hate that Louis has shared such a heavy burden with me while excluding them. They have stirred slander and invented lies against me. Yet it is a load I gladly bear in service and love for my king."

Gabriel's eyes rounded, fervently scanning the scrawled lines. "It has been no small feat to transport this large of a fortune to the middle of the Atlantic. People have taken notice, seen what they should not have, assumed the very worst. Many have falsely accused me of abusing my position as general and stealing from my beloved monarch. They call me the Moon King from the depths of their envious hearts only to mock me.

"The truth is, my dear family, that everything you see here *does* belong to the mighty House of Bourbon. They are treasured keepsakes, spoils of war, the greatest of Louis's spectacular collection at Versailles. But I, the humble servant of my king, had no part in stealing them. King Louis XIV of France entrusted these precious items to me, charging me to find a place for them where no man will touch them until the time comes when they are needed.

"Dark times are ahead, the king says," Gabriel kept on. Madeleine hugged her legs close to her chest, suddenly chilly. How right he'd been. "Louis believes there will come a time when these riches are not safe in his home, or indeed, any of the royal treasuries at his disposal. So he has asked me to find a temporary shelter for them, where his family can trust them to be returned at their darkest hour.

"I charge you, reader of this letter, not knowing who you are or how many years in the future you will find your way to my secret hideaway." Gabriel sucked in a breath, his fingers gripping the page trembling. "This treasure does not belong to you because you have found it. Everything you see here rightfully belongs to the House of Bourbon and its descendants thereafter. Save this family from destruction. Return their fortune to them in their hour of need, and all will be well."

Head wagging, Gabriel finished the letter with tearful eyes. "Despite the stories perhaps woven so eloquently to you, this treasure was never meant for your possession. The adventure in finding it—well that is an entirely separate matter. My gift to you is my home—the château, the land, the barony as it stands today—a loving manifestation of my efforts to make it a place truly worth living in and striving to keep alive. There is no wall I haven't worked on, no field I haven't helped to plow, no space in that entire estate that will not echo back my love for the generations who come after me if you truly listen. Carry on my legacy. Fill it with children. Love it as I have loved it, and it will never steer you astray.

"Now, my cherished family, I must end this, my final letter to you, trusting that you will cast any selfish desires aside and don the mantle of integrity. Make the Clement name proud. Protect the House of Bourbon. Live your lives with honor and respect until you join me in the hereafter. With my utmost esteem, your *grand-père,* Henri Clement."

With a weighty sigh, Gabriel let the pages waft to the cave's floor. His batting lashes blinked back the tears sprouting beneath them as he reached for Madeleine's hand and clasped it tightly. "I never thought of him as Grand-père before." He let out a sad chuckle. "I always believed he was a power-chasing fool who cared more for money than he did his own family. All that time, he was only trying to protect Louis. He endured so much ridicule to be faithful to his king, and here I was, chief among his scoffers." His head hung low, one hand shielding his face.

"You didn't know." Madeleine squeezed his fingers. "You can't blame yourself for believing what you were told. Henri made the decision to accept Louis's challenge, knowing his name would be slandered for years to come."

Gabriel kicked a smattering of pebbles into the luminescent pool. "Little good it did, since his family turned their backs on his memory. Think how differently the Revolution might have transpired had my ancestors found this treasure and given it to the king. Louis XVI—he might have used his grandfather's hidden wealth to aid the people of France and prevent a war from brewing."

From across the pool, Christophe snickered. "Louis had no sense or skill with money. He would have spent it on himself and that wanton wife of his and lost both of their heads even faster."

"You don't know that," Gabriel said, glaring back.

"No, but I can safely conjecture how that might have gone." Christophe tossed a pebble into the pool, watching as it plopped below the surface and formed rippling rings around it. "Anyway, it didn't happen. There's no sense in trying to erase a war that erupted when we were only children. None of us could have prevented it."

Moved by Christophe's doleful eyes, Madeleine brushed her hand over Gabriel's arm. "He's right; we can't change the past. We have only the here and now." How desperately she wished her words were a lie as the pain of her and Christophe's shared orphanage filled the quiet space.

Gabriel inhaled another deep breath. "We can't go back, I know. But what do we do with this fortune now, with the monarchy dissolved and a new leader in power?"

Silence fell over them as they all gazed at the treasure chests sitting lonely in the shadows, their opulent contents winking. Henri had gone through so much trouble to get Louis's riches here so his future generations might thrive, but could they have mended a broken nation? Did they matter now to his forgotten descendants, who had no idea the treasure even existed?

"Marie-Thérèse is still alive," Gabriel said. "She seems like the rightful heir to all of this."

Christophe's brows lifted. "The rest of the royal family might disagree with you, as they're all descendants of the Sun King, too." He shook his head. "You're bound to start another war if you give all this to the Bourbons, anyway. They're living in exile. Napoleon would surely construe it as an act of treason and aggression toward his rule."

"We would be executed if he found out," Madeleine said, remembering the threats she'd endured from the ruler himself the night she'd spared his life. Napoleon did not take kindly to those who might encroach on his power.

A muscle in Gabriel's jaw tensed, his gaze narrowed on Christophe. "The alternate being to keep it for yourself, I suppose. I should expect nothing less from a man who makes his living stealing and killing."

Christophe compressed his lips, but said nothing. The sizzling air between the two men carried enough animosity to silence the ocean's distant roar. Madeleine realized with growing concern that they might have more problems now that they had uncovered the treasure than before when they so badly needed an advantage.

"Let's not think about what we'll do with it just yet," she said, rubbing her husband's forearm. "Let's just enjoy this moment. How many years have you dreamed about finding your ancestor's hidden fortune? Surely this is a joyous occasion."

Gabriel's intense stare battled Christophe's a few seconds longer before he found her face in the glowing light. Despite his warring emotions, the slightest of smiles pinched his lips. He drew her to him, planting a kiss on her forehead and sighing against her.

"It's been a long night, and I fear an even longer day stands ahead of us," Gabriel said. "We should go before the sun comes up and Cavaretta's men start to prowl. If they find this place, we might have more trouble than we can handle."

The waters of the cave behind the falls had already begun to recede when the three explorers crawled from its mouth. When they'd first discovered the cave, the water's surface had been close enough to climb from. Now, it sloshed a good distance below, seeming to be sucked out as if funneling through a sinkhole.

"We should jump out that way," Madeleine said, pointing toward the falls. "We don't want to hit the ledge down there and break a bone."

Nodding, Gabriel laced his fingers with hers. With a quick breath, they leaped together into the ebbing pool. The cold rush of water enveloped Madeleine as she plunged below the water. Her hand unlatched from Gabriel's with the force of their collision, the river's current tugging her beneath the wall of water hurtling from above.

Madeleine watched with delight as Gabriel and then Christophe emerged from beneath the falls behind her, tired but exhilarated. No matter what stood ahead of them, they had found the Moon King's bounty. They had conquered a foe so many before them had faced and failed to tame.

How glorious a feeling encapsulated her as she scampered up the riverbank and took Gabriel in her arms. He laughed against her sodden hair, his breath tickling her neck. Merriment danced in his light eyes. The moment they'd wanted for so long had finally come, and nothing could sever the joy she felt.

"I can't believe it," she said, taking his face in her palms. "We actually found it." His hands pressed her lower back, her unhampered joy mirrored on his dripping face.

"Found what?" a new voice stabbed through her perfect moment.

Both of their heads swiveled toward the source of the sound, the sight before them shooting icy pangs up Madeleine's spine. For there, in the soft light of early morning, stood a band of Stefano's men, each with a sword or a pistol aimed in their direction.

Twenty Seven

The breath hitched in Madeleine's throat as she stared into the angered throng of Italian sailors, their weapons pointing her way. She saw among them the man she'd outwitted near this very spot and prevailed against aboard Stefano's burning ship. Several of Stefano's associates she recognized from Venice stood at their helm, their normally ironed waistcoats and snow-white shirtsleeves nothing but soiled, tattered rags hanging loosely from their bodies.

A man named Diego Vivianno stepped from the mass, his chest pumping and his pistol trained on her head. "I warned him about you, Antoinette," he said, his teeth gritting. "I told him a woman like you wouldn't just leave her profession to live in a foreign country with a man too busy to pay her any attention. He wouldn't listen. He was too enamored with you with those rouged lips and low-cut gowns you always wore."

Madeleine's hands slipped from Gabriel's face, rising defensively as she turned toward her challenger. He stood as tall and broad as Stefano, his square jaw and thick brows so much like the man she'd once fallen in love with. Only a sprinkling of white hair amongst his dark locks betrayed his age. Stefano would never admit it to her, but she'd often wondered if the two were brothers.

"If only he had listened," Vivianno said, tears sprouting in his ebony eyes. "If only he had taken my advice and never let you into his life."

Her heart mourned at the grief spilling unchecked from his face. "Diego, I'm sorry."

"He is *dead!*" The hand gripping his pistol shook. "His life has been cut short, as yours should be now. You killed him the minute you walked through his doors."

Gabriel gripped her arm protectively. "She didn't force Cavaretta to come here, nor was it her blade that pierced him. If he hadn't chased a foolish vendetta against my wife, he would still be alive and well."

Vivianno's cruel gaze slipped to Gabriel, then to the sea captain standing nearby. "A strong man doesn't let a deed against him go unpunished. Stefano wouldn't, and neither will I." His finger hooked around the gun's trigger, its barrel still menacingly aimed at Madeleine.

The water drenching her mingled with cold sweat. Madeleine flinched as a piercing whistle lit the air behind her. She'd half expected Vivianno's gun to fire on her that very second, but she quickly realized Christophe had signaled his men with his teeth.

The gun shifted to Christophe, who broadened in the face of imminent death. "They'll never get here in time to save you," Vivianno said. "One blast is all it will take to put down the man who took Stefano's life."

"And what will you do once I'm dead?" Christophe's fists clenched at his sides, his eyes narrowing in challenge. "The men I have left outnumber yours, and there are more aboard my ship. They're better fighters than you. They proved that yesterday when they obliterated your forces. You don't have a leg left to stand on if you kill me. They'll attack you out of revenge alone."

Vivianno considered his words, glancing briefly at the small group of Christophe's men already gathering across the river at his signal. The morning sun had just begun to drip through the treetops, highlighting the Italian's pronounced cheekbones and stern chin. He readjusted his booted feet, his confidence waning. He had trained with Stefano as often as she, but Christophe had the numbers. As soon as Vivianno's bullet took one of them out, they would face a fatal charge.

"We will not cower," he said with conviction, though his Adam's apple bobbed. "We will fight you until every last one of us falls—for Stefano."

Christophe splashed through the shallows, standing tall at the river's edge. "You needn't fight us. I'd rather you joined us." At Vivianno's disbelieving scowl, the captain spread his hands in supplication. "I don't want to lose any more of my men today. There has been enough blood spilled upon this dirt. Join our ranks and help us load the treasure aboard the *Sirene*. You will take your share of the booty, just like each of my crew."

A slice of sunlight moved over Vivianno's face as he threw back his dark head in a humorless laugh. "Thank you for your offer, Captain. How generous of you to use our strength to your advantage, then shoot us all or leave us here to die."

"I give you my word that will not transpire," Christophe said. "We will grant you safe passage back to Italy with your portion of the spoils."

Vivianno's gaze scanned the growing group at their backs. "Even if you could promise such a thing, your men would never allow it. I see the hatred on their faces. We killed their comrades today as they killed ours. There can be no reconciliation between us."

A grunt issued from Christophe's throat. "They are *my* men. I will make them see reason."

His mournful eyes converting to stone, Vivianno held his gun higher. "You promised Stefano a generous share of the treasure, too. Then you thrust him through with your sword for the sake of a woman." His accusing stare slid to Madeleine. "I will never trust any of you."

In spite of the fear raging in Madeleine's veins, she lifted her chin. "Then what will you do, Diego? You have one bullet to shoot before Christophe's men devour yours. Will you take your revenge on the woman who scorned Stefano or the man who killed him?" Something deep down prayed it would be her. At least Christophe would have another chance to make a better life for himself.

Vivianno's nostrils flared, his fate falling to a simple choice. He shook his head, accepting neither. "*I* will take your ship and the men on board its decks. *You* will come with me."

Terror gripped Madeleine at the faces of Stefano's men. They looked like a pack of dogs eyeing a piece of meat with drool on their lips. She knew what would happen to her the minute she passed into their hands. The dreadful image froze her in place, ice prickling her entire body.

"You will take her nowhere." Gabriel stepped in front of her. "If you want a hostage, take me. You will not lay a hand on my wife."

Vivianno laughed, his teeth sparkling in the dawning sunlight. "That's admirable of you, Baron, but your life means nothing to these men. They would shoot us the moment we turned our backs. This one, on the other hand—" His pistol swung back to Madeleine. "I know the lengths Captain Roux will travel to keep her safe. He will let us board his ship to save her life. Won't you, Captain?"

Christophe's jaw flexed, telling emotions shifting over his face. Of course he would, but would his crew ever allow it? Madeleine shuddered to think of what leaving her life intact even meant. An hour in their company would make her wish for death, surely.

"There is another way," Christophe said, silencing her rampant imagination. "I'll go."

"Captain, don't," said Monsieur Simon, Christophe's quartermaster.

The captain turned, his blue eyes flickering over his faithful quartermaster, before they landed squarely back on Vivianno. "I risked the lives of my men when I brought them to this place. It is my duty to see this through. I vow they will not fire upon you with me in your ranks. They will let you safely board my ship."

Whispers rumbled over Christophe's crew as Vivianno nodded and yanked the captain to his side. Dissention clearly divided them, arguments erupting through the group as two men stepped forward to clamp giant hands around each of Christophe's arms. Madeleine could only stare at the sorrowful man, his full attention fixed on her. Yes, he had used deception to bring her here, but he had also saved her. The dissonance of his crew lodged an ominous ache in her belly.

Steeling herself against the river's icy chill, Madeleine waded through the water and scrambled up the other bank. "We can't let them take him," she said, out of breath. "Surely they'll kill him once they're aboard the ship. We can't allow him to sacrifice himself."

When she received only a mingling of distrusting stares and down-turned eyes, she huffed and turned toward the quartermaster. "Monsieur Simon, won't you go after him? You two have always been loyal to one another."

"Aye, we have." The quartermaster's eyes took on a laden sadness as he watched them haul his captain away. "He knows we won't let them take the *Sirene*. It would mean the death of us all. He expects to die."

Nausea funneled down her throat and into her stomach. "So you're just going to let him? How can you so easily give up on the man who has led you through so much?"

The one called Blanc stepped forward, fire in his ruddy cheeks. "The captain is giving up his life for *you, petite fille*. You've turned a once great man into a fool. We cannot follow a fool and hope to survive. It's only a shame he let a woman steal the moment he finally found the Moon King's treasure. It's all he wanted for years until you came along."

Madeleine blinked, looking from face to face, desperate for one of them to step forward for their own dignity. When she only met blank or angered faces, sickening reality dawned within her. "You're going to leave him here. You're planning to go after the treasure and leave Christophe to these monsters, knowing what they'll do to him. You planned this even before this morning, didn't you?"

Monsieur Simon shook his head vehemently. "No."

"Yes," Blanc growled, snapping Monsieur Simon's gaze his way. "Some of us did, and I'll stand by that decision. The captain has grown weak and inefficient. It's time we chose a new leader—one who commands respect."

Tears squeezed into Madeleine's eyes as she examined Christophe's men. Some of them looked shamefully down at their boots. Others glanced around in bemusement, as if hearing this news for the first time. A select few met her gaze with ugly glares, confident in their desire to overthrow their captain.

Madeleine glanced back at the group of men hauling Christophe through the trees toward their camp. If she did nothing, he would die. Her mind drifted back to the day they'd met on the beach—how he had rescued her from this place. Even in his deception, he'd respected and defended her at every turn. He'd risked his very life when Stefano had her in his treacherous claws. He did the same today. Swiping an arm over her perspiring brow, Madeleine knew she couldn't live with herself if she let him die for her.

Fire blasted through her arms. In a lightning-fast motion, Madeleine twisted back and yanked Blanc's sword from its hilt. The man gasped, leaping back with eyes round as if he expected her to gut him. Madeleine gazed back hotly a long moment before she whirled around and marched back toward the river.

"What are you doing?" Blanc asked from behind her. "You're going to get yourself killed!"

"Better to die with dignity than to live a coward." Madeleine tilted her chin up, ignoring Gabriel's concerned expression as she passed him in the river.

"Madeleine, please don't do this." He caught her arm, his fingertips gently constricting around her wrist. "I know you want to save everybody, but Christophe Roux made his bed a long time ago. If this doesn't kill him, something else will. It's his way of life."

Madeleine met his imploring eyes, her resolution unwavering. "Yesterday morning, he saved my life. Stefano would have killed me in the most gruesome way possible had he not intervened." She paused, chin quivering at the emotion spilling from his eyes. "I would not be the woman you fell in love with if I just stood by and did nothing to repay that debt."

With anguish threatening to crumble her, Madeleine tugged her arm out of his hold and climbed up the river bank. Stefano's men had nearly vanished between the trees now, a few heads still visibly bobbing through the underbrush. Madeleine drank in a breath of courage, channeling sheer determination, before she launched herself after them. No matter what came of her actions, at least she would make her father's memory proud.

The group had just breached the clearing that emptied into Stefano's camp when Madeleine caught up with them. Through the shivering leaves, she made out dozens of men lying dead across the ground, their blood staining the dirt. Gulping back her terror, Madeleine glanced over her shoulder at the second band of men trailing her with Gabriel at their head. She had no desire to start another battle between them.

Recalling the strength Christophe had summoned to strut into this very camp and demand her release, Madeleine straightened her back and silenced her hammering nerves. Vivianno had nearly reached Stefano's tent. It was now or never.

"Diego," she called, her voice cutting through the dewy air like glass. Every head in camp swiveled her way, the one she sought revolving slowly, his eyes cold when they fell on her. "His men refuse to fight, but I *will*. Unhand Captain Roux at once or face my blade."

Twenty Eight

S tunned silence blanketed Stefano's camp, only the flit of birds' wings in the trees overhead lacing the morning air. Strange power coursed through Madeleine's blood as she inhaled the scents of jasmine and plumeria sprinkled around camp, covering the grizzly odors that so much death had left behind. Stepping around the bodies strewn over the ground, Madeleine walked until she stood at the center of camp with Blanc's sword posed regally.

"Madeleine, don't," Christophe said from between his two guards, his muscular frame straining toward her.

An irritated look flashed in Vivianno's dark gaze as it swung from her to the *Sirene's* crew now flanking the forest. "We made a deal. I will retain Captain Roux until my men are safely aboard ship. Unless you're so sick with love for this man that you must join in his captivity." His joke produced a scattering of snickers at her expense.

Madeleine squared her jaw, her nostrils flaring. "I refuse to accept your deal. The captain has offered to let you join his crew for the journey home, even promised you a portion of the treasure in exchange for your help. There is no need for division amongst us."

Vivianno's face hardened. "Look around you. Men lie dead at your feet and you suggest we unite for a common cause?" His head shook ruefully. "We are at war. One of us will triumph and the other will meet their demise. There is no compromise when two sides have already slaughtered one another. There is only victory or death."

Victory or death. Hadn't she adopted a similar life motto when she'd chosen to cast aside her moral virtue in order to fill her empty belly? Nothing had mattered but her own survival. Now, so many faces paraded across her mind's eye—people who had hurt her one moment only to turn around and save her, a brother she loved yet despised, Christophe himself, who had nurtured her with one hand while stabbing her with the other. Life could never be so black and white—not with the conflicting nature of humanity.

She saw it vividly in the man she faced. His sturdy form bespoke confidence, while his gaze shifted warily to the sword in her hand. Cruelty teemed from his stern face, yet from deep within, a wounded child peered out on the world. He had just lost the person dearest to him. While her heart ached to consider it, Madeleine knew she must seize this weakness if she wanted to beat him.

Her gaze moved to the trail of blood swiped unnaturally over the dirt. It began where Stefano had fallen and led to his tent. They must have dragged his body inside, perhaps hoping he would survive. The thought twisted her gut.

"I loved him too, Diego," she said, her gaze entwining with his. "In the time I lived with him in Venice—I really did love him. He was the first man I cared for in such a way."

Vivianno's lip curled. "You loved him so much you betrayed him. You stabbed him in the belly and left him for dead. Some concept of love you have. It's disgusting."

"I had no choice when he fought me. I could have defended myself or died." Her free hand covered her surging ribcage. "I still bear his scars as he bears mine. Our union was of fire and blood, always. We are bound together by our transgressions, even against each other."

Her opponent strode toward her, fists balling at his sides. His neck muscles had taken on a scarlet hue, taut beneath purple veins bursting to the surface. "You were deceiving him every moment you were together. You have nothing but the memory of a lie."

Madeleine stood firm as he stomped to rest before her, every muscle in his body quaking. Just like her, Vivianno had trained under expert tutelage. He would attack with precision and strength, yet the angrier she could get him, the weaker he would become. Perhaps if she could goad him into fighting her, she might create just enough chaos to allow Christophe's escape. She could see him from the corner of her eye, primed to spring to action the moment danger befell her.

"I loved him," she said again, ignoring the frantic expression Gabriel sent her from the trees. "I wanted to build a life with him. If he hadn't turned on me, we might have had a chance at it. We might have had something real. But Stefano could never have any genuine human contact, could he?"

Vivianno loomed near, eyes wild and teeth clenched. "Say his name again and I'll stab you through, you filthy harlot."

Courage rammed through her body despite the legs beneath her soiled dress threatening to give way. "I had moved on with my life, married and found true happiness. But he could never—not with his obsessions and twisted fetishes. I loved the man I saw, but underneath it he was nothing but a perverse soul, lost in the dark of his own making. He was a demon dressed in fancy clothes."

With a guttural grunt, Vivianno drew his sword. The swift scratch of steel lit the air, prompting Madeleine to step back and lift Blanc's sword. Energy pumped from her hands up the lengths of her arms, her hands tightening around her weapon's hilt. Another battle wouldn't ignite this way, she knew. Christophe's men would never defend her as they had him. If only she could distract his captors enough to allow his escape, the tables would turn in their favor. The *Sirene's* crew would again have the advantage in every way with their captain safe to command them.

Mere seconds passed before Vivianno charged at her with his sword extended outward. Madeleine easily sidestepped his advance, turning to counter his next attack. Her heart thrashed against her ribs, the practiced moves coming one after the other, her sword slicing the air and glimmering beneath the risen sun. Sweat seeped into her loose hair and below the arms of her dress. Heat blazed up her working arm. With determination driving her every action, she kept on, praying to attract enough attention for Christophe to escape.

Their swords tangled in the crystal air, their movements like a dance. How many hours had they both spent, learning from the man who now lay dead in his tent, dreaming up ways they might best him? As Madeleine ducked and swung, lunged and leaped backward, she felt as if standing within that practice room in Venice again, trying desperately to please a man who could never truly love her. Vivianno's eyes flashed in the same way, his brows gathered in concentration. The resemblance he bore to Stefano stung in a way she hadn't foreseen.

His silver blade swung at Madeleine, compelling hers to clash in meeting. She blocked another blow before returning her own, a hit that narrowly missed his torso. Nose snarling angrily, Vivianno charged at her recklessly, his sword driving through the air when she spun to the side. The move left him undefended. Before she could think, Madeleine turned and thrust her weapon into her rival's shoulder, cringing at the snap her action produced.

Reeling backward, Vivianno screamed. Her sword withdrew, leaving a stream of blood to stain his silk shirt. Stunned, he took only a moment to touch the spot she'd injured before he turned glowing eyes to her. Madeleine breathed, knowing she'd angered a beast beyond the brink now, preparing for his attack. A nauseous ache bloomed within at the crimson staining his shirt and dripping to the earth, but she must keep on if she hoped to survive.

His blows came harder this time. Madeleine braced herself with every one, the power behind them nearly buckling her. She could match his skills, but never his strength. Fear began to grab hold as Vivianno's strikes bore down on her, their frenzied speed increasing. His blade swished through the air, ruffling her hair and gusting her ear. He wouldn't give her the chance to attack. She could only guard against each cruel swing, her strength waning.

With sickening horror, Madeleine realized he'd backed her into a thicket of trees. She had nowhere to run, his blows assaulting her one after the other until her arm ached for reprieve. Leaves fluttered against her skin, her hair entangling with the branches. The thick scent of body odor engulfed her every sense. Out of breath, she hardly managed to block his final strike before the sword clattered from her hand and Vivianno tugged her against him.

A shout of victory rambled over Stefano's men. Madeleine's bleary vision took them in—Christophe still firmly in the grips of his captors, a host of others gleefully eyeing her like an animal snagged in their trap. The crew of the *Sirene* stood motionless and quiet, Gabriel's horrified face emerging from them with skin whiter than a winter snow. She'd tried and she'd failed. Now, she would have to face a consequence she'd hoped he'd never have to witness.

Vivianno laughed—a hollow, wicked sound that rang in her ears. Madeleine stiffened within his hold, his chest heaving at her back, his stale breath whispering over her skin. His blade pressed to her throat, where her pulse thundered wildly. And then, she knew, the end had come.

Twenty Nine

Madeleine's blood surged, the rush of thundering above her heart all she could hear. A mild breeze, laden with brine and exotic flowers, brushed her blistering skin. She barely breathed, aware that even the slightest of movements could dig Vivianno's sword into her gullet. It already rested at the base of her throat, its sharpened edge taunting her.

Her vision growing hazy, she slammed her eyes shut and tried to accept her fate. She couldn't stare another moment into Gabriel's afflicted face. Like never before, vivid scenes of her life danced across her mind's canvas. She saw nothing of brothels and war, only glossy visions of her father seated before the glowing hearth, tickling her below the ribs. Of her mother with arms outstretched, twirling through the high grasses and laughing. Warmth began to thaw her core as she remembered each day she'd fallen deeper in love with Gabriel and their reunion on this very island. She had lived a good life. Death could not erase that.

The solid arm around her tautened, throwing Madeleine's eyes open. She blinked to find Gabriel closer now, his chest pumping fervently. "Please," he said, tears springing to his eyes. "I'll give you anything. *Anything.*"

With overwhelming sadness, Madeleine realized nothing could grant his plea. Vivianno already had his leverage in Christophe. She was nothing but fodder—a convenient way to see revenge exacted on Stefano's foes.

"I sympathize with your pain," Vivianno's voice hummed in her ear. "It can't be easy to watch your wife suffer." His chest pitched harder against her back, his passion growing. "So you shouldn't have married a harlot."

Ignoring the scattered laughs and howls around him, Gabriel took several more steps. His mouth clamped into a firm line, his hand reaching for the knife Madeleine had secured in his belt. He would defend her to the bitter end, even at the cost of his own life.

"You will stop where you are." Vivianno's command halted Gabriel, arm frozen in midair. The blade at her throat pushed expertly against her skin, piercing it just enough to release a thin trickle of blood. Madeleine tried to suppress the gasp that hissed from her throat, but the sudden surge of pain prevented it. Her skin throbbed where his blade had sliced, warm blood oozing from her wound.

Gabriel stood helpless, his curly head tilting, his eyes desperate to save her. *You can't, my love. You can't.* Forcing her lips to lift at the corners, she tried to reassure him in any way she could. They would be separated here, but the world to come held adventures beyond their most cherished dreams. She would walk with him on the sea of glass, their fingers interwoven, their hearts united forever.

Even from this distance, she felt her heartbeat mirroring his. The seconds dwindled, Vivianno's blade straining harder, his cut deepening. A thousand promises poured unspoken to Gabriel from her eyes—to love him always, to wait for him in the hereafter, to smile with contentment down on the life he lived without her. Tears streamed unchecked down his cheeks, his fingers rising as if to caress her face. Though distance kept them apart, Madeleine felt his touch like he stood before her.

The memories flowed faster now—a perfect ribbon of hope absent of sorrow. Peace blanketed her soul, even as Vivianno's caustic scent enveloped her, as his sword gouged her skin. She focused only on Gabriel and the eternal love they shared. Her fear dissolved, replaced with gratefulness for a life brimming with love, from her first moments to her last.

Even from within her trance, Madeleine couldn't miss the shift in the crowd looking on. Many of Stefano's men stood straighter, their gazes moving beyond her to Madeleine's right. She wanted desperately to look, but with Vivianno's weapon still positioned at her neck, she dared not move. Hope leaped on Gabriel's face, a dangerous hope that spurred her own.

"Let her go," a familiar voice ordered, quickening Madeleine's heart.

Vivianno pivoted them both far enough to find Auguste standing but meters away, a pistol aimed at her captor's head. A band of men larger than Christophe and Stefano's remaining crews combined stood at his back. He looked stronger than when last she'd seen him, definition rippling the muscles of his clenched arm. His determined face shone with health rather than the dark circles that too much drinking had once etched below them.

Jaw hardening, Auguste clicked the hammer of his pistol back. "I told you to let her go, and I won't say it again. If you fail to obey my command, my bullet will be the last thing you see."

Reluctantly, Vivianno's arms released her. Madeleine stumbled forward with a hand to her bleeding throat, hardly aware of the swarm of men descending on Vivianno and his company. Gabriel's face materialized quickly before her, his hand already whipping a handkerchief from his waistcoat to quell her bleeding.

"It's all right—just a scratch," she said, her voice hoarse. Yet still, he fussed over her and dabbed at her wound until the cut began to clot.

"Oh, Madeleine." Gabriel pulled her against his chest, his warmth like shelter after a treacherous downpour. Nestling her head beneath his chin, she drank in the musky cologne still clinging to his clothes, mingled with the wild scents of the island.

After several beautiful moments, he pulled away, cupping her face in both hands. His adoring gaze poured over her, taking all of her in as if she might vanish from his hold. His thumb swept her cheekbone, his fingertips skimming her jaw. With a yelp of unhindered delight, he covered her lips with his own, his kiss an abiding vow never to let her go again. Madeleine returned his affection, her love for him unbound and all-consuming.

"Well, isn't this a sight?" a new voice penetrated her blissful moment. Madeleine spun around to find Cecile and Désirée trailing the group of sailors now binding Stefano's men with ropes.

Gabriel sighed. "I thought I told you two to stay aboard Auguste's ship unless it was absolutely necessary to come ashore."

With a dismissive puff of her lips, Désirée waved him off. "As if we could watch Cavaretta's ship burning in the lagoon and not come with the crew to save the two of you."

Cecile wrenched Madeleine from Gabriel's grips, her emerald eyes bright as they examined her. "Dear Maddy." Her arms came around Madeleine, a tight embrace bespeaking the love and fear she'd harbored for her friend.

"I can't believe you all came for me," Madeleine managed, her ribs squashed against the slender maid.

"Are you jesting? I've had the time of my life." A mischievous light glinted in Cecile's eye as she pulled away, the luminescent strands of sun flaming in her copper hair.

Désirée shook her head knowingly, capturing Madeleine in her arms. "We'll have to share all about our adventures. We were so worried." She drew back enough to look at the wounds checkering Madeleine's neck. "Oh Maddy, what have they done to you?"

Madeleine's head wagged, her hand rising to cover the stinging sores. "I'm all right, I promise you. They look much worse than they are." Joy claimed her heart as she hooked a finger to summon Désirée and drew her mouth to her ear. "It's real," she whispered through her golden hair. "The treasure—we found it. It's here on this island."

Eyes lighting, Désirée looked back with mouth agape. How fiercely she'd clung to the dream of finding Henri's treasure. Now, pure bliss captured her pretty face as she covered her mouth in one hand and shared a giggle with Madeleine.

Something shimmering on Désirée's hand caught Madeleine's attention. She reached up, covering the woman's fingers in hers, pulling them down to find a thin gold circle banding one finger, a magnificent ruby affixed to the top.

Désirée blushed, her gaze flitting up to Jean-Paul, who had just approached from the band of Auguste's men securing their enemies. "I couldn't wait to tell you. It happened aboard ship on the way here."

"But I haven't even been gone a month," Madeleine said, breathless.

Jean-Paul stepped forward, his loving gaze enfolding Désirée. "I finally worked up the courage to tell her how I felt. I couldn't wait to ask her, not for another second."

Overwhelmed, Madeleine released a delighted laugh and squeezed Désirée's fingers. "Sisters twice over," she said through the joyful tears blooming beneath her lashes.

Her baby brother's enormous arms wrapped around her, lifting her off the ground. "Don't you ever run off like that again," he said into her hair. "I've never been so frightened."

Madeleine relished the boom of his deep voice, his clean scent and powerful warmth. Her bare feet touched the soil again, her head shaking as she pulled away. "Never." She felt it deep in the recesses of a soul newly restored. She had no reason to leave again—not with the pure love and acceptance that surrounded her now.

An uneasy twinge bit at her middle as the group around her parted and one person was left to face beyond them. Broader now, Auguste wore the billowing linen shirt and buckskin trousers of a ship captain, a belt with weapons attached sheathing his slim waist. His brown hair, normally cropped close to his head, now fell in shaggy waves past his ears. The eyes that had condemned her with blazing madness when last they'd met now held sorrow and regret.

She stumbled a few steps forward, unsure what to say or do in his presence. He'd nearly killed her on their last meeting, the feel of his body propelling her over the château's railing still fresh in her aching bones. How desperately she'd tried to please him for so long, and still their bond as siblings had crashed to a miserable end with her life barely intact.

August opened his mouth but said nothing, the vulnerability in his face ripping her heart open. He looked just like that little boy from her beautiful collection of childhood memories—the boy who had played with her in the fields, caught bullfrogs in the pond, giggled with her under the table as they orchestrated a trick on their unsuspecting mother. Gone was the drunken rage that had converted him into a stranger. This was her brother—the true brother she loved with every fragment of her being.

"I know you have no reason to trust me after what I did," he said, raking a hand through his long hair.

Without giving him a chance to say further, Madeleine rushed into his arms, planting her head on his chest. Auguste gave a surprised chuckle before returning her embrace. The two stood pressed together for several glorious moments, the wounds of their past alleviating more with every second their hearts beat against the other.

"You saved me," Madeleine said. "I love you, brother."

Auguste's fingers closed on her dirtied gown at the back. "I love you, my beautiful sister."

The island assumed a new face to Madeleine as the day passed, and the sun journeyed from one side to the other. The fear she'd harbored as she awoke in this mysterious place had melted to a keen sense of appreciation. Under the shivering tree tops, she could look up at the sky and feel peace wash away the terror. So many had died on these shores, but she would leave here free and renewed. The island's curse vanished beneath the warm sands as the sky swam into evening. Perhaps it was no curse at all, but a diviner of the good or malice in one's heart.

Once Stefano's men had been restrained, Auguste's crew led them back to Christophe's camp, where a large group guarded them at all times. Though once enemies, Christophe and Auguste cast aside their differences and planned their evacuation of Henri's treasure. They'd both assured her they wouldn't fight over the hoard, but Madeleine still watched them carefully. They had agreed to lay the treasure's fate on Gabriel as its rightful heir, yet who could trust a band of pirates with riches at stake?

Evening came on with a sweep of sea air and pinks blending with purples across the endless horizon. Once a desolate, isolating place, the island boomed with voices and merriment. The two crews mingled together as one, joining in gaiety as they prepared to unearth Henri's prize. The rocks around the waterfall glowed with unearthly light as more and more lanterns dotted their surface, casting a radiant shimmer across the water.

Madeleine laughed to watch an eager bundle of men dive into the blasting falls with a ladder suspended between them. Gabriel had suggested they might wait again for the tide to rise, but the sailors would not hear it. A jaunty tune lifted from their lips as they passed the enormous chests from the cave's mouth and under the falls. Soon, the river glittered with diamonds and emeralds as wayward gems escaped their confines.

A celebration commenced at the river's edge, groups clustered everywhere she looked. Near the falls, Désirée stood in Jean-Paul's arms, watching with fascination as each new chest was dragged up the riverbed and dumped on the shore. Cecile had an entire group of sailors hanging on her every word, her hands flapping gracefully through the air as she spoke. Laughter echoed from tree to tree, the men who weren't working clutching jugs of rum and chugging the beverage to their hearts' content.

Only one face was missing among the revelry—someone Madeleine had expected to be issuing commands and enjoying himself the most. Her gaze darted about the assembly in vain until she noticed a shadowed figure winding through the woods. Gabriel was busy helping to lug chests to shore, so Madeleine pushed off the rock and found a shallow place to ford the river.

Her chest surged and blood had heated by the time she jogged through the ferns and emerged from the trees. Beneath the canopy of leaves, it was nearly dark, but here on the beach, the bright colors of dusk shone through patches of gold-rimmed clouds. Madeleine's feet padded the grainy sand, carrying her toward the lone man now sitting cross-legged near the gentle tide, watching the sun melt into the horizon.

She uttered not a word when she slipped down beside him—only gazed at the magnificent sky rolling like boiling water, its golden glimmers easing into the dusky purple beyond. Wind laden with salt and hibiscus brushed her skin, tossing her long hair from her face.

Madeleine looked down at the soiled dress clinging to her body. How self-conscious she'd been when she'd first made his acquaintance on this very sand. How his square jaw and solid form had caused her heart to flutter. The thought almost made her giggle despite the sadness that touched her as he stared longingly at the sunset.

"You won't join in on the fun?" she asked tentatively. "It's your victory as much as anyone else's. You deserve to take part in the celebration."

The hint of a smile lifted one side of Christophe's mouth as he reached for the jug between his legs. "I have all the celebration I need right here." He brought the jug to his lips and swallowed, his loose blond hair fluttering in the wind.

Understanding, Madeleine smiled. He *had* always enjoyed the comfort of his solitude—a lone wolf at the head of his pack. A chill skittered up her arms to imagine him alone forever, heartbroken because of their complicated friendship. How often she'd considered him romantically, but the truth encompassed her every time Gabriel was near. She could love only him, as much as it hurt her to imagine Christophe's pain.

"It was good of you to leave the treasure's fate up to Gabriel," she said, flattening her forearms across her knees. "I know how long you've dedicated your existence to its discovery. It can't be easy to put it in someone else's hands to do with as they please."

Christophe squinted toward the thickening sky, his jaw working. "I suppose it no longer holds the same allure, now that we found it." He sighed. "It was never about acquiring riches for me. It was all in the adventure, the thirst to discover it. I don't care if a single one of those gold doubloons passes through my fingers."

A frown creased her forehead. "Surely your men will care. They expect payment for following you on these wild exploits, don't they?"

"Oui, I'll give them enough to appease them, but not enough to lose my crew entirely." His head shook. "Most of them will waste it on booze and"—he caught himself, eyeing her sheepishly—"ladies of ill repute."

Madeleine laughed with him, the pure sound dispersing into the sparkling air. Days ago, the idea that she had once shared ranks with such women had sickened her. Now she felt free to be someone new, perhaps to help those still thrust into similar fates.

"And you?" she asked, watching the way the waning sunlight illuminated his eyes. "There isn't anything you want to change about your life, anything that could be worth spending your hard-earned riches on?"

He considered her question a long moment, staring at the *Sirene* as it bobbed among the shallows beyond the lagoon. Sadness overtook his gaze—a hollow longing she felt deep within as he let his gaze wander into hers. "I've dreamed of that treasure since I first stepped aboard Jacques Chapelle's ship as a youth. Now everything I've ever wanted or loved will sail from this island in the morning."

His unmistakable meaning cut through her. The dream he'd so long cherished of finding Henri's treasure had ended in victory, but the hope he harbored for their love never would. Instead, he would watch her sail away, safe in the arms of another man.

"You will find something else to dream about," she said into the wind, "someone else to love." Brushing back the wayward strands of hair whipping into her eyes, she offered him a hopeful smile.

Christophe let his gaze meander her face, over her forehead and high cheekbones, down to her chin as if memorizing her. When his eyes came back to hers, sad resolution had dawned in them. "I still have my ship and the sea. She's all I need."

As darkness gently cloaked the shore, Madeleine found his hand and squeezed it. In spite of their tumultuous moments, love for this friend had burgeoned in ways she'd never expected. Her wayward heart was finally content. She could only pray he would find such peace as he ventured again into the Atlantic's waters, the world stretched before him.

The island's festivities hadn't weakened when Madeleine and Christophe made their way back to the waterfall. Someone had fetched a fiddle from camp, a jolly melody singing over the gathering as the man plucked at his strings. Drunken dancing had commenced, sailors chortling as their boots splashed through the river. Many linked arms over each other's shoulders, bellowing a bawdy tune as they swung their legs to and fro.

Madeleine found Gabriel near the falls, his eyes bright and chest pumping as he dragged another haul to shore and stood back to admire it. The child in him beamed from his face—the same child who had once hung on his aunt's provocative tales, hoping despite what his father said that such glorious treasure really did exist beyond the sea.

Out of breath, he set his arms akimbo when he noticed her approach. "That's nearly all of them," he said between gasps for air. His proud gaze swept the host of treasure chests piled on the dirt, strands of sparkling gems spilling out. Patches of dirt checkered his face and forearms below his rolled-up sleeves, water dowsing his trousers. How different he looked from the man she'd first met in the parlor, fixated on the letter in his hand and unattuned to the world around him.

Gabriel bent to snatch a string of pearls bunched on the ground. With tender affection curling his lips, he lifted it over her head and secured it around her neck. "A bit of adornment for my queen," he said, pulling her into a quick kiss. "Though you alone dazzle far more than these riches ever could."

Secure in the arms wound around her waist, Madeleine gazed at the spectacle unraveling around them. Désirée and Jean-Paul looked so very in love as they stood together at the water's edge. Men frolicked like children engaged in summer play. Atop the rocks, Christophe raised his jug proudly, shouting, "To the Moon King!" A host of whoops and hollers lit around him, rippling laughter up Madeleine's chest.

She turned to her husband, his face so alive with the glorious unfolding of his dreams. "Have you decided what you'll do with all of this? It's almost unfathomable how much Henri hid within these rocks."

His brows lifted as he surveyed the impressive collection. "It's more than I ever imagined possible." His gaze latched with hers, filled with the utmost love. "Henri was right, though. We have far more than we could possibly need in the barony alone. What he left for us will carry on through the generations, sustaining our children and theirs. We don't need one piece of this treasure to make us happy. Besides"—the arm hooking her waist dragged her closer—"I already have the greatest gift of all." His thumb brushed the divot in her chin, his warmth and affection seeping into the depths of her soul.

An idea had dawned in her mind, but she hadn't yet found the words to voice it. Looking at him now, with the night breeze unsettling his curly hair and lamplight dancing in his eyes, assurance seized her.

"I thought about what Henri said in his letter," she said, the ancient words still echoing in her ears. "His greatest wish was for this treasure to sustain a monarchy that is already dead." She swallowed, her heart lifting at the rampant possibilities. "What if we gave it back to her people, the citizens of France who need it the most, the children being reared in orphanages without their parents, as Christophe and I were? Think of all the good we can do."

Gabriel's eyes filled, his thumb sweeping her cheek. "What do I think?" His enchanted expression poured over her, taking her in. "I think I love you more in this moment than I ever have before." Quick as the ocean's tide, his lips crashed against hers. Joyous laughter hummed between them, the salty taste of his tears mingling with hers. Holding him tight, Madeleine kissed him with the beautiful knowledge that they would live side by side, fighting the same fight, defending one another.

The last lingering rays of sunlight sank behind the distant horizon, a banner of stars replacing its radiant glow. The treetops rustled, the cadence of crickets striking up their nocturnal rhythm beyond the raucous party still bustling beneath the falls. Under the rising moon, the island seemed to release a long-held sigh. For at last, the reign of darkness and death had ended, and the earth could live at peace again.

Books by Laurie Sanford

The Winds of Freedom

November Rain
Moon Over Blazing Star Field
Midnight Road to Heaven

The Memory Chase

The Guardians' Plot
The Moon King's Bounty
Traitor Isle
To Capture a Unicorn

For exclusive scenes you can't get anywhere else, head to
www.lauriesanford.com/signup.

Acknowledgments

My sincerest thanks to anyone involved in the production of this book. It was quite the journey releasing another trilogy so many years after my first, and I owe much gratitude to so many people who have rallied around me and motivated me.

To my #1 cheerleader Shauna Alarcon, thank you for reading my books and getting excited about the characters like I do. It makes writing them even more fun. To my editor Jacelyn Schley, thank you for your thoughtful critiques and encouragement. Sometimes those words are what get me from one book to the next. To Evelyne Labelle, thank you for another beautiful cover.

To anyone who has read this far into the series, thank you for coming with me on this journey. Madeleine inspired me with her bravery and kindness, and so I'm glad I found the words to share her story with you. I hope you will carry her triumphs with you as you go about your lives, and may you be truly blessed.

About the Author

Laurie Sanford is a writer of historical Christian adventure and romance. Her first series, the *Winds of Freedom* trilogy, tells the story of a young woman whose experiences on an antebellum cotton plantation lead her on a journey of self-discovery and ultimate freedom. Her new series, entitled *The Memory Chase,* is an adventure through Napoleonic France and beyond, through the eyes of a woman devoid of memory.

Laurie attended Pacific Union College in Napa Valley, where she earned her Bachelor's Degree. She studied to become a teacher, but wound up as a dispatcher, a job she loves and finds fulfillment doing. Laurie is happily married with two small children.

When she's not at work or wrangling little ones, Laurie enjoys writing (her first love that now comes in fourth in line), reading or watching anything historical, traveling (32 states and counting), exploring nature, playing guitar, and studying genealogy. Having a family is the greatest blessing she has ever been bestowed, and everything she has she owes to Jesus Christ.

Made in the USA
Columbia, SC
13 February 2023

11810854R00183